As Paris devolves into chaos amidst the French Revolution, three lives intertwine.

Xavier, a devout priest, struggles to hold on to his trust in humanity only to find his own faith threatened with the longing he finds for a mysterious American visitor. Thomas fights against the Catholic Church to win Xavier's heart, but hiding his undead nature will threaten the love he longs to find with this abbé. Xavier's sister, Catherine, works with Thomas to bring them together while protecting the family fortune but falls prey herself to evil forces.

The death, peril, and catastrophes of a revolution collide with a world of magic, vampires, and personal demons as Xavier, Thomas, and Catherine fight to find peace and love amidst the destruction.

A NineStar Press Publication

Published by NineStar Press
P.O. Box 91792,
Albuquerque, New Mexico, 87199 USA.
www.ninestarpress.com

The Vampire's Angel

Printed in the USA
First Edition
March, 2018
Print ISBN: 978-1-948608-29-9

Also available in eBook, ISBN: 978-1-948608-23-7

Warning: This book contains sexually explicit content, which may only be suitable for mature readers, graphic violence, and mentions of off-page rape.

THE VAMPIRE'S ANGEL

ANGEL

The Realm of the Vampire

Council, Book One

Damian Serbu

To Paul: My Life, My Love, My F

Part I: The Dawn of Revolution

One: Angel Sighting

14 MAY 1789

The night at last darkened as Thomas wandered the Parisian streets, feeling the people's anger. Though the current French environment shunned the wealthy, Thomas's commanding presence allowed him to walk about with little resistance. Besides, if his personality failed to assuage someone, his American citizenship placated them soon enough. Coming from a land that had already tossed out a king provided him a certain reverence.

The evening proved calm, however, with no one shouting or rioting. Perhaps later, Thomas might venture to the salons for conversation, but for the moment, he watched the common people as he headed from his flat along the Seine toward the Bastille. He sought the poor that evening, not the stuffy rich who bored him even in their nastiness.

Thomas dodged a puddle of mud and almost ran into a wealthy woman.

She grunted but then smiled when she looked up at him. "Pardon me."

"It was my fault." Thomas bowed. "I should apologize to you."

She giggled and walked away, but not before turning around to glance at him one more time.

His reflection in a nearby window reminded him why so many women and men stopped to admire him. His muscular frame, his long black hair tied in a bow at the base of his neck, and his all-black attire, which defied the contemporary fashion of men wearing bright colors, combined to create an allure. Thomas knew he possessed a sex appeal. He captivated them so much they seldom commented with their usual prejudice on his darker complexion.

He turned onto Rue St. Louis and headed north. The houses there were dingier, the streets narrower, and the people dirtier. He traveled well into a residential area and found a secluded corner, the perfect place to watch for that night's prey.

A few workers stumbled by, already drunk and searching for their homes, then some children frolicked along with a group of women. Still, nothing tempted him. Next, a soldier patrolled the streets and stared at him with suspicion, a prey that proved more to Thomas's liking. Unfortunately, he saw goodness in the soldier's face. He would not tempt fate with that one. The young man brushed a lock of blond hair out of his eye and passed as Thomas watched and marveled at his beautiful tight backside when he faded into the night.

Thomas nearly lost his breath when he turned and looked the other way. An angel?

The man had short brown hair, piercing hazel eyes, and soft skin. He carried the slight tone in his muscles, which so attracted Thomas, with a hint of nervousness. Not too masculine, but neither too feminine.

As the gentleman passed, Thomas fell in behind to study him further.

Only after Thomas almost drooled over the beauty in front of him did the clothing hit him. A priest. Thomas shook his head. How on earth did a godlike creature end up serving that vile Catholic Church?

He followed, anyway, hiding among the buildings and trailing so quietly that the priest never suspected a man behind him scrutinized every angle of his body beneath the black robe.

As they passed a narrow street, the priest turned and peered toward the cramped passage, then dashed down it. Thomas rushed to follow and hid in a doorway nearby.

"Can I help you?" the priest asked. "What is it?" He knelt before a young girl, perhaps no more than four, and placed his hand on her shoulder. She sobbed and slumped against the priest, who wrapped his arms around her. "Talk to me. You're safe. What can I do?"

Her breathing finally slowed. "I'm lost."

"What's your name, dear?"

"Delphine," she whispered.

"Well, Delphine, we'll find your home. Can you give me some clues?"

Thomas listened as the priest quizzed her. She relaxed as the conversation continued and giggled as the priest joked and moved down the long alley with her, talking to her until he stooped down and picked her up while continuing to chat.

"Do you think we're close?" he asked.

"I think so." She looked around, clinging to him.

"Ah! Delphine!" A woman ran toward them, so the priest put the girl on the ground and stood aside as she sprinted to collapse in the woman's arms.

"Mama," she shouted.

"I've looked everywhere for you," her mother replied. "What did I tell you about wandering away? We have just moved, after all. You'll get lost in this big city." Then she crossed herself. "Abbé, God intervened yet again to save my daughter."

"Merely one of his servants, Madame." The sound of his resonant voice sent waves of passion through Thomas.

"How can I repay you?" she asked.

"You owe me nothing," the priest said as he turned to Delphine. "And you, little one, you must be careful in Paris. You can get lost easily, so stay close to your mother."

She giggled as he tickled her stomach. "I will, Abbé."

After they left, the priest turned and his eyes widened when he saw Thomas. He paused.

"Monsieur, pardon me. I didn't see you."

"I didn't mean to startle you, Father. Good evening." They gazed at each other for a long moment.

"No harm. Good evening, sir." The priest nodded and walked away.

Too good to be true. Thomas stalked the priest as he turned the corner and entered the gate of a small church. There, Thomas leaned against a building, breathing heavily from the passion that erupted inside him, a longing he must satisfy. He wanted to stand outside the church and wait for the priest, or even knock on the door and talk to him again, but he was too unsettled. He remembered an establishment nearby that would serve his purpose well, so he raced to it, slammed through the doors, and sat before he fell, when a young man of about eighteen years approached him.

"Monsieur, you look unwell. Can I assist you?"

The youngster wasted little time. He needed a bath, but otherwise presented an adorable face and solid little body.

"What are you offering?" Thomas smirked.

"Come, I'll show you." He grabbed Thomas's hand and pulled him up a stairway and into a dimly lit room. "I assume you know this'll cost you, and that I don't play the passive role."

"Quite the entrepreneur. I can pay what you charge." Thomas closed the door and embraced the youth as he kissed him. With great speed, he threw the youngster onto the bed and tore off both of their clothes.

"Slow down," the young man pleaded.

Thomas did so and kissed the boy's neck. His fangs descended, and he softly pricked the dirty skin to taste the blood before he took their interaction further.

"Do you enjoy biting?" the boy asked.

"Only momentarily," Thomas replied before he plunged his fangs into the vein for a deeper taste.

As the hot liquid flowed across his lips, images of the boy's life saturated Thomas's mind. The vision confirmed what Thomas already ascertained. The young man prostituted himself part-time and was a useless degenerate who attacked and robbed innocent people. He assaulted children, including his brother, for sport. Ah, yes. And, of course, he murdered without remorse.

He grabbed the young man's hair and kissed him, then rolled him over against his will. He struggled for the first time, but Thomas held him tightly.

"I told you," he said, "I don't—"

Thomas clamped his hand over the victim's mouth. "Relax." He stopped squirming and Thomas let him go. "What if I double the price? Or triple it, even?"

The lad contemplated for a moment. "Triple? Just to bugger me?"

Thomas petted his hair. "Yes."

"Fine. But I won't like it." Yet he ground his ass into Thomas's crotch.

Thomas thrust inside of him and pounded. The young man wriggled and bit his lower lip, but he never tried to stop Thomas until the vampire finished, his tension released as he exploded inside the nice bubble ass.

Sated, he released the lad, who pushed him off, cursing. "I told you, and I warned you, you ass." He scrambled off the bed and snatched a knife from under the mattress, and in his nakedness came toward Thomas.

When the youth tried to stab him, Thomas grabbed his wrist and squeezed hard until the blade dropped to the floor. He pulled the young man toward him and stared into his eyes, his expression terrified.

"I thought we had an agreement? Besides, you can't win. You won't haunt this city anymore. Go peacefully."

Thomas bent the boy's head to the side and plunged his fangs back into the flesh, sucking the delicious blood until the youth's heart stopped.

Thomas kissed the puncture wounds to heal them and flung the corpse to the floor before dressing, loving that a large city meant no one questioned yet another death. Sexually satisfied and fed, he brushed his clothing off before hurrying down the stairs and out the door without anyone noticing.

Two: Background Politics

15 MAY 1789

Nothing excited Catherine in her thirty-one years like the political events swirling around her over the previous few months. She hated the famine and unrest that accompanied the changes in Paris, but still relished the intrigue. Despite being alone, she rolled her eyes as her middle brother's voice echoed through her mind.

"Catherine, you're of noble birth. It's not proper for you to engage in these political discussions," Michel repeated so often it nauseated her. Of course, he only repeated what too many men of his class blabbered about in order to keep women subservient to them. He always followed that comment with his trope about how "your fierce independence and refusal to marry embarrasses the family."

Liberty, equality, and égalité. That excited her! Not proper decorum and floating about the house as a mindless idiot.

"Abbé," she exclaimed, jumping out of her chair at the sound of footsteps coming down the hall. "You're late, and it's already dark. But come here, I've a lot to tell you."

Xavier smiled as he walked into the room. She saw her brother almost every day, but never stopped marveling at his angelic face, his dark hair, and his hazel eyes that sparkled. Even his clerical garb added a forbidden allure. Her friends lamented his entering the priesthood, and thus terminating his eligibility, but Catherine suspected Father Saint-Laurent desired something else.

"Would you please just call me Xavier? I can't be your abbé. I know too much about your sins." Xavier held his cross to his chest as he leaned over to kiss her cheek. Then he sat opposite her and smiled again. "I assume that all of this unrest excites you?"

"This is the dawn of a new era! Women may be able to vote. Did you see the riot this morning?"

"I heard about it. People protest the famine. They won't starve without a protest."

Dear Xavier, he always worried first about how it affected others. She sighed. He fretted too much, consumed with anxiety and seldom able to relax or enjoy himself.

"You worry too much."

Xavier ignored her comment. "Perhaps we'll see something new since the Estates General is meeting at Versailles after all these years, especially since Louis doubled the Third Estate to include more of the masses."

"These bread riots can't continue forever." Catherine smoothed her dress over her abdomen. "The king and church better pay attention. Can you forgive my denunciation of your precious church?"

"Ah, the lovely church in Rome," he said. "I love that it ignores the poor and supports the elite. God didn't give Louis some ordained right to reign. I've always found the sentiment preposterous."

"Still defiant after all that training."

"Stop teasing me. The church owns too much land. It makes too much money at the expense of commoners. And even the common curé suffers in poverty while the church hierarchy lives in luxury. But this turbulence alarms me. The king already sent troops to quell the riot at Faubourg St. Antoine when the workers rebelled in April. How will the violence end?"

"How else will change occur?" Catherine arched an eyebrow. "On the bright side, Louis must listen to everyone now. Can you imagine what Michel must think?"

"I'm sure he abhors it."

She shrugged. "I hope that this broadens his horizons. Since Father died, he takes such responsibility in caring for us, in acting like the patriarch. He should restrict his ordering people about to the military."

"But he does have charge over us. It's custom. What can he do?"

"He can *pretend* to lead us and do his responsibility without pushing." Her voice rose as she spoke. "Who ensures the family investments? Who meets with the financiers and managers? Who pays the bills? I do. So, what gives *him* the right to appear three or four times a year and pretend that he rules the house?"

Xavier nodded without a word.

"I've thought about opening the doors of this house to anyone who would like to discuss the current political situation. What do you think Michel would have to say about a Saint-Laurent Salon?"

"I'm sure he'd relish the idea," Xavier said sarcastically.

"And he still frets about your choice to serve in that god-awful parish."

"That god-awful parish deserves God's guidance as much as those who parade off in the finest clothes once a week to pretend to follow His word while they exploit people the rest of the week," Xavier snapped.

Catherine scurried over to him and gave him a hug, then pecked him on the cheek. "Got you. I knew that some passion hid in that black finery somewhere. Come, let's go to the terrace." She turned without waiting and walked toward the wall of windows and doors that led to a large veranda overlooking Rue St. Denis. The Saint-Laurent compound—the largest on the street—housed only Catherine and servants now that Michel served in the military and Xavier slept in his rectory.

Catherine spun around and hugged Xavier again as he walked through the door. "Forgive me for teasing you."

"Only God can forgive your transgressions," he said with a sigh, though a smile hovered on his lips.

"Don't you sound like a Huguenot. I thought the pope bestowed the power of God upon Catholic priests."

"Blasphemy!"

"Oh, and did you hear what else is happening?"

"I can't keep up with your mind."

Catherine grinned. "The city formed a new government. I heard rumors in the salons for weeks about it, and when I went to Madame de Tesse's salon yesterday—and spare me the admonitions of being careful about where I go—they said that the riots prompted a reorganization to a bourgeois militia because of the looting. How exciting! Now, let's go. Walk me to the church so I may light an indulgence for Father and Mother."

"Of course. To Notre Dame." Xavier headed for the door.

"No, I want to see *your* church."

"I hardly think you need to venture into that neighborhood."

"Stop sheltering me. You sound like Michel. Besides, you hate seeing the elders who run that big old church, and the river stinks this time of year."

Catherine pulled him into the street and they headed east, toward his small parish.

THE SAINT-LAURENTS

"Stay for dinner," Catherine commanded Xavier when they returned to the house after visiting his church. "You don't eat enough, and that parish can't feed you."

He laughed. "I'll stay." Xavier watched Catherine rushed around the house, telling the servants to prepare dinner. His sister possessed more energy than all of the horses in the king's army.

Xavier made his way into the dining room, followed soon by Catherine, who raced in and smiled as she fell into a chair.

"What?" she asked, petulant. "Why are you looking at me?"

"I'm in awe of your interest in the revolution. You weren't the least bit scared today."

"That's not remarkable."

"Do you think the violence will persist? I hate it. I have to shelter people in the sanctuary while everyone runs around the streets fighting like lunatics. If the bishop found out how I assisted with this mess—"

Catherine barked a laugh to interrupt him. "How on earth can the bishop claim you're involved in the riots by harboring innocent people?"

"The sanctuary is a holy place and reserved for appropriate worship of our Father in Heaven."

"Please. Maybe we should ransack Notre Dame to give them a taste of reality."

Xavier laughed. He tolerated church politics because the Parisian elders seldom ventured into his impoverished parish so near the Bastille.

"Did you hear Madame Bregat when we passed her?" Catherine asked, polishing her silverware with her napkin.

"Yes, she was so terrified that her voice quivered."

Catherine rolled her eyes. "Typical aristocracy. All of this has them in a complete tizzy. Don't they see the chance for profound change?"

"Did you ever think that most of them despise the thought? They're not accustomed to the bourgeoisie running about demanding governing rights, let alone peasants rioting on country estates."

"Well," Catherine stated flatly, "I'm not afraid."

But instead of launching into another polemic, Catherine grew quiet and stared past Xavier.

"Your silence unnerves me more than the rioting." He reached across the table and squeezed her hand. "What is it?"

"You know what today is, don't you?"

"I try to forget. This entire month brings sad memories." Xavier fought the pain that had weighed on his mind all day.

"I wish I could forget. It hurts. What would he think about the turmoil?"

Xavier rubbed his forehead, remembering how his father had tried to mediate between the monarchy, the bourgeoisie, and all the lower sorts. He died the previous year of "natural causes," though it seemed unnatural at the time because of his age. The doctor had said his health failed. Xavier missed him. His father, more so than anyone else in his family, understood his choice to enter the priesthood and even accepted his decision to avoid Catholic politics in so doing. His eyes welled with tears.

"Oh, dear. I didn't mean—" Catherine took Xavier's hand and squeezed, as if to pinch the pain out of him.

"I'm fine," he muttered, brushing at his eyes. "Don't worry. I think about him anyway. Talking about him feels good."

"How can this be good?"

"Because it honors him, reminds me of what he taught, and keeps me focused on helping people."

"It's peculiar. Until I went abroad to tour, I never realized our privileged position," Catherine said. "Not because he sheltered us, but because he didn't. He wanted us to see all classes of people and consider ourselves members of mankind without concern for wealth. It surprises me that he instilled this so well in all three of us."

Xavier patted her hand. "I have the strangest conversations with fellow clergy because of him. They either come from the aristocracy and spurn the common people or from the lower ends of society and sneer at the rich. I see both points of view, and they think me insane, on both sides. Only Father could create a theology that allowed me to enter the rigid Catholic Church, with all of its emphasis on power and privilege, and not forget to honor everyone."

"I miss him, too," Catherine said. "He'd be so proud of you."

"Speaking of the unrest," Xavier mused aloud, "how would Father handle this? He insisted we obey the king and act as middlemen between the monarchy and the people."

"But what happens when everyone wants to overthrow the king?"

"No one wants to overthrow the king. You always take things to the extreme."

She snorted. "If Americans threw King George out, perhaps the French will dismiss Louis. Father envisioned stability so long as everyone respected each other, but with starvation and poverty and high taxes, things have to change. See why we need a salon here?" She stopped when a servant entered the room. "Oh, look, dinner."

"How can dinner possibly surprise you when you ordered it?"

"Don't patronize me."

He rolled his eyes. "I wonder what Michel thinks."

"Our brother probably ignores it."

"Stop it. Try to consider his point of view. Michel must be having a hard time reconciling his loyalty oath to the crown and what Father taught us."

"Father made one big mistake." Catherine gripped her fork. "He allowed Michel to enter the military too soon. The army shaped him too much. Michel got lost in that disciplined world."

"It was a noble calling, Catherine. Michel wanted to please Father by following in his footsteps."

"I know that. But Michel doesn't have Father's independence. For example, look at your name. Everyone expected Papa to name you after some member of the monarchy, but he refused because he had served with a Basque general. To honor their friendship, he named you after that man's favorite saint. So you walk around with a Basque name in the middle of Paris because of Father's friendship and respect for someone who helped him." She said her monologue in one breath, paused, took a drink of wine, and continued. "The difference being that Michel would obediently name you Louis and be done with it." She set her glass back down. "That's all I'm saying."

"Thanks for the history lesson. Are you finished?" His stomach clenched, knotting like it always did when he and Catherine argued.

"No. One more thing. Michel already cautioned me about the riots, remember? He can't decide what to do. That proves my point," she exclaimed.

"No one put you on trial. I agree, Michel's afraid. I remember sitting with Father while Michel asked over and over again about the paradox of obeying the king and helping the people. He explained that the monarchy, by its very nature, rules because we need an established order. But the king's privileged position prohibits him from understanding the bourgeoisie and the poor. So the nobility exists to explain to each group how to behave."

"You listened to Father's lessons. I forgot half of what he said. I liked to look out the window. Michel must have stared at the ceiling too much too." She smirked.

He set his fork down. "Can we forget about Michel before you start arguing with him, even when he's not here?"

"You're too good. You need a little more spite in your blood to spice up your life."

"That's why I have you."

She giggled. "It *is* hard to live up to our name and change with the times."

The name. Xavier heard a million times growing up about the importance of the name. Saint-Laurent. A noble clan. How many times did he hear about his great-great uncle who tutored Philippe D'Orleans? Or others who served kings or rose to prominence in the army and church?

"Since you almost empathized with Michel," Xavier announced as he pushed back from the table, "I'm leaving on that peaceful note."

"Please stay."

"I have to return to the church."

"Why? Do you have to wax a crucifix?"

"Catherine, please."

"I'm sorry. Seriously, stay."

"I really have to leave."

Too late. She had figured it out.

"The garden!" She laughed as Xavier turned red with embarrassment. "You still try to grow edible food in that garden?" She escorted him to the door.

"Perhaps."

"Well, I do have some business to review. So I'll let you go off to your futile enterprise."

Xavier shook his head, still marveling that she managed all family affairs. Thank heaven their father recognized Catherine as the most intelligent of his children and thus defied convention by tutoring her to run the family, not one of his sons. Xavier kissed her on the cheek and headed down the front steps with a backward wave before walking away.

GARDEN MEETING

Back at his church, Xavier worked in his small garden even after darkness fell and the nearby lantern barely illuminated the street around it, let alone his humble plants.

"Abbé?"

Startled, he whipped around.

"I'm sorry to startle you again."

Xavier cleared his throat, nervous. It was the man from earlier in the day, with the long black hair, piercing brown eyes, and American accent. "I didn't hear you approach." Xavier wiped his hands on his robe.

They stared at each other until the stranger broke the silence. "Perhaps I should introduce myself. Thomas, Father. Thomas Lord."

Xavier cocked his head, quizzical. "You're not from Paris."

"What gave me away?"

"Your accent. And complexion."

"I'm here on business."

"Welcome to Paris. Let me know if I can be of any assistance." Xavier wanted to say more, to keep the man near him, but he was at a loss for words. How strange.

"I—I wondered if... Can I go to confession? With you."

Xavier smiled. "You're not Catholic, either."

"No," Thomas said. "I'm not. I'm not Catholic, nor of any religion. And I'm not in Paris on business. I'm here by myself and felt lonely. I saw you protect that little girl earlier this evening and thought perhaps you could show me around Paris. I'm from America and wanted to see the rioting." He stopped. "Sorry to babble."

Xavier studied Thomas, noting his musculature, even in the dark. It prompted the most sinful of thoughts. "I doubt you'll find Paris too welcoming these days, but I'd be happy to show you around." He paused, considering. "You needn't lie anymore. Just ask if you want my company."

"Can you forgive me, Abbé? I was confused about your being a priest and what etiquette to use," Thomas said, watching for Xavier's response.

"You weren't sure if I had the time for a heathen?" Xavier smiled. "Or did you fear some divine judgment? Well, don't. As I said, I'd be delighted to show you Paris."

"You don't mind that I'm not Catholic?"

"Not all of us are so narrow-minded as to demand a certain brand of faith from everyone we meet. All of us are God's children, after all."

"What am I supposed to call you, then?" Thomas asked, picking at the sleeve of his coat. "Abbé? Father?"

"Since you don't seek spiritual counseling, and so long as you promise not to enter my confessional, how about Xavier?"

Thomas grinned and a strange little spark danced down Xavier's spine. "Agreed," he said. "What would you think of starting my tour of Paris at the Seine? I love the breeze and view of Paris from there."

"I'd be delighted." Xavier nodded and smiled in return.

They sauntered toward the river, engaged in easy conversation. Xavier told Thomas about the riots, about the king, and about his view of the revolution. They chatted about mundane matters with no particular destination or motive. Xavier hated that the night ended when they returned to his church and bid adieu. He hoped, with butterflies in his stomach, to see Thomas again, but his fear of rejection kept him from saying anything further.

Three: He Returns

16 May 1789

It was too dark. Xavier felt like a fool in the garden as he weeded at a time of night when most people went to bed. He came out after dinner with Catherine, hoping that Thomas might return. But it was too late to count on a visit.

What had Xavier expected, anyway? His weakness angered him. Why did he hope for a forbidden dream and delude himself?

All day, he went over their conversations again and again. They talked about so much, the American revolution, monarchies, French politics, even religion. Thomas at first resisted revealing his atheism, but Xavier guessed and pulled it out of him, then had the hardest time convincing him that it didn't matter. Xavier divulged little of his own opinions, however, because he still struggled to share personal feelings.

Most of all, Thomas's bold presence intoxicated Xavier. He ordered himself to stop those thoughts, however, because of his duty to God. He must repress these unnatural yearnings.

Xavier picked himself off the ground and smelled the flowers in the soft breeze that blew through Paris, overpowering the other less attractive smells in the air. He collected himself and started toward the church. For the second night, his neighborhood was quiet except for the sounds of a few children and revelers, typical for a spring evening, and not indicative of a riot.

He sauntered toward the church and admired its simple, small beauty. The diocese tried to close it a number of times, but the political clout Catherine exerted with their family name kept it open. She thought she'd kept her protection of her youngest brother from Xavier, but the bishop had told him about it, rather bitterly. Regardless, Xavier loved serving there, amidst the common people, helping them through their daily struggles.

The sound of footsteps broke his contemplation.

"Abbé, I hoped to find you here. I'm sorry about the late hour. I was doing business."

Xavier's heart pounded at the long black hair, broad smile, and Thomas Lord's confident voice.

"I thought you didn't come to Paris on business?"

"I didn't," Thomas answered and looked away. "But I still have matters to attend to. I promised not to lie to you anymore. I've kept my word."

"I'm sorry. I didn't mean to imply anything."

"No offense taken." Thomas smiled again.

"What can I do for you?" Xavier struggled for words, but, too nervous, instead sounded like the authoritative priests he despised.

Thomas's smile turned to a frown. "I didn't come here to be insulted."

"No, no. I'm sorry. I didn't mean it that way," Xavier backpedaled. "I enjoy your company. I just had some things on my mind. Please—"

"Perhaps we need to stop being so nervous with one another. Can we be friends? Pardon my forward behavior, but last night, I felt an attraction to you and wanted your company. I confess my ignorance of French custom, so I don't know if I'm crossing some boundary. But can we become friends without all of the pretense and nervousness?"

Xavier listened, exhilarated and terrified all at once.

"Excuse my boldness," Thomas continued, "but I want companionship beyond the casual acquaintances I've met thus far. I love spending time with you. My friends say that my biggest fault is telling people how I feel, but now you know."

They stared at each other before Xavier glanced at the ground. Thomas's proposition came with innuendo. The mere idea of a personal friendship made Xavier nervous, but was Thomas suggesting something else? He was lost. His entire life he'd fought his sexual attraction to men. He had entered seminary, hoping for a magical cure within the priesthood's celibate world but instead found only more admonitions to control oneself and no solutions.

Xavier's heart almost pounded out of his chest. "I'm sorry. I don't know how to respond."

"For one thing, you have to stop apologizing. Every other sentence out of your mouth requests forgiveness. The Catholic Church's teaching on guilt means too much to you."

"I'm sorry, I only mean—"

"See? There you go again," Thomas said. The gentleness in his tone caused Xavier's breath to catch in his throat.

Xavier smiled when he almost apologized yet again.

"Is something funny?" Thomas asked.

"If you want this friendship, then *I* have a confession, one I think you already know. I don't have friends." He raised his hand to ward off any response from Thomas just yet. "I know. It sounds preposterous, but I have colleagues and parishioners, and I have an intimate relationship with my family. But no other personal relationships."

"I guessed as much. But you should revel in life from time to time. You'll find that I take things to the opposite extreme. I'll teach you all you wish and more. May we sit?"

"Of course."

Xavier ushered him toward a bench, with only a faint lantern for illumination. Thomas sat next to him and looked into his eyes. The proximity aroused Xavier, sending panic through his body as his stimulation increased. Before either of them said anything, Thomas laughed.

"Abbé, you astound me. Why are you petrified? Your face is bright red."

"Please, it's Xavier." He never said that to anyone outside his family. The church forbade such intimacy, and Xavier was not close to any of his colleagues except one nun.

"Xavier it is, then. Do you always look so distressed?"

"No, really—not usually. I just don't know what to do with this...friendship." He drew out the word, savoring it, uncertain what it meant.

"Well, what can I do to help?"

"I'm not sure. What *do* we do?"

"I see I have my work cut out for me," Thomas said dryly. "We just do what we did last night. We talk and learn from each other. And there will be times we need to help each other. I'll never need a priest, but I may need companionship." Thomas patted Xavier on the back, sending that thrill down Xavier's spine that he both loved and feared. "It's difficult to explain how friendship works. Make this agreement with me. We'll just enjoy the company, and when you need clarification or feel the urge to apologize, tell me and we'll address those concerns as they come."

"I'll do my best, but tell me when I fail."

"You'll never have to guess about my feelings. In fact, I already have a concern."

"What?"

"I hear a lot of anticlerical sentiment in Paris. What keeps you safe?"

Xavier shrugged. "They lash out at the establishment. My parish never threatens me. Worship attendance has suffered, but I don't fear the people."

"Will the militia assist you?"

"There's no need for extreme measures. They attack that which threatens them, and this small church in no way endangers anyone."

Thomas seemed assuaged, and for the next hour, they chatted as they had the night before, about the riots, government, and Paris. The more they talked, the more Xavier relaxed. But his initial hesitance embarrassed him. He found Thomas's familiarity liberating and fun, with no inhibitions or threat of condemnation. Perhaps friendship was simple, and as they talked behind the church, Xavier lost track of time. He was jolted out of their leisure when he heard steps echoing up the catacomb's entrance behind the church.

How could he forget Maria? All this talk of friendship and he forgot his one friend in the Catholic Church. Maria and he arranged a visit in the late evening to ensure the secrecy of their plans without the watchful eye of church authorities, but in his infatuation with Thomas, he forgot.

Xavier jumped off the bench and away from Thomas too late. Thomas looked befuddled and then saw the approaching figure. The plump nun, dressed in black, stood off by herself.

"Is this a bad time, Abbé?"

"Sister, good evening. No, not at all. Please come," Xavier said. As he floundered around, Thomas rose and headed toward the gate. He nodded and smiled, as if to say he understood, though Xavier worried that he had offended him.

"Good night, Abbé. Thank you for your counsel. It brought me comfort." Thomas walked away into the night and Xavier stared after him, then caught himself and turned to Maria.

"Did you forget our plans?"

"Of course not. The gentleman sought comfort about a...a business and personal matter."

"Is there anything wrong?"

Xavier wiped his brow with his shaking hand. "No."

Maria raised her eyebrow, but he ushered her into the sanctuary and closed the door. She walked forward in silence. Did she suspect? Did she somehow know?

BLOOD PASSION

Thomas left Xavier with the nun, glancing back only to show that all was fine between them. Xavier's sudden jump from the bench and startled expression shocked Thomas until he saw the nun appear from the catacombs. Too bad she had appeared, because he wanted to ravage that priest's body.

Thomas walked through Paris, never bored with watching humanity during the night. Other vampires longed for the sun and questioned the goodness of their souls while they pronounced themselves evil. Not Thomas. He never wondered about such divine nonsense. Instead, he reveled in eternal life and his power.

When Anthony had made him, he taught Thomas to only feed on criminals and to never touch the innocent. Anthony had commanded him to obey the ethic, that no other lesson meant more. Thomas had obeyed the code more than anything because Anthony said the Vampire Council would otherwise kill him.

He walked toward his favorite bars in Paris, craving people. A man's blood. Thomas licked his lips. Xavier, that innocent, angelic priest, brought out the worst in him. He grinned at the irony and set to work hunting to quell his rising hunger.

It never took long in these modern cities to find fitting victims. One only had to look into another's eyes to view evil. Indeed, a candidate for the night's amusement stood before Thomas, and moments later, he left the degenerate soul dead in the alley. Thomas wiped the blood off his mouth, avoiding another taste of it so as not to see a repeat of the man's murderous existence. The one curse that came with his vampirism was the fact that, in tasting the blood, he saw the victim's life pass before his eyes.

Fed, Thomas felt better and so dashed through the darkened, damp streets to his flat, where he reveled in the serenity of his home and removed his clothing. He loved being naked.

Without meaning to and within minutes, he had pleasured himself while sitting on his favorite silk chair. The young man from the night before had barely satisfied him. He wanted something deeper. And so it served his purposes more to satisfy the urges alone, to envision Xavier underneath him, clinging in love.

Ah, Xavier. You haunt me. Thomas frowned, thinking about him. Was he already thus smitten? Besides, could the priest ever accept his own sexual longings? Thomas saw fear on Xavier's face when they sat near one another or when Thomas brushed his hand against Xavier's. Sighing, Thomas stood and began pacing throughout his apartment. What to do? He ached for Xavier, but the mere thought irritated him. He wanted him as a mate, even when he scolded himself that they had just met.

The one thing he longed for, the one area of his life that remained unfulfilled and empty, was the absence of a partner, an emptiness that made him bitter and angry at times. Perhaps, if Xavier could accept the love of another man, it would destroy his faith in that damnable Catholic Church and allow Thomas to tell him everything.

Thomas stood at the window and gazed into the night. How to proceed? Anthony had made the lessons simple for him, about how easy it seemed to navigate through eternity. But he'd failed to explain that emotion persisted in the darkness, that desire for love and companionship intensified the longer Thomas remained alone. True, Anthony had mentioned the need for a mate and had hoped for such companionship from Thomas, but both proved too strong-willed to stay with each other as lovers.

Thomas wrapped a silk robe around himself and went onto the balcony. The still darkness of the street surrounded him with peace. But loneliness plagued his mind. He knew it now more than ever and realized he wanted a lifemate. He wanted Xavier.

Four: Catherine – Betrothal

24 MAY 1789

Catherine wondered what Xavier was hiding. For the past few days, he'd left earlier each night. They spent almost every evening together, having dinner, reading, and talking until they were too tired to continue. But recently he'd left even before sunset, mentioning some nonsense about obligations and work. Or his ridiculous garden. Catherine suspected something else.

Catherine listened until curiosity got the better of her. "Where do you go when you leave here?"

"Go?"

"At night, when you leave here." Catherine poured more tea and took a sip. "You're doing something." She looked at him. "You leave before dusk now. Why?"

"I return to the church," he hedged.

"To do what?"

"What do you want to know?" Xavier's face turned red.

Comprehension dawned. "You've met someone! Who is it?"

Xavier looked at the floor and fumbled with the cross dangling from his neck.

"You're seeing someone. I knew it." She sat back, surprised but delighted. "Tell me everything."

"Catherine, please." Xavier looked around the room. "I took a vow of celibacy. There's no woman in my life."

"I never said that." She wanted to blurt out that she knew Xavier fancied men over women but thought better of it.

"Fine. I have a new friend from America. There's nothing else. He isn't Catholic." Xavier leaned forward with a huge grin. "I've never had anyone from outside the church to talk to. So that's my secret. Rather anti-climactic."

"Well, thank you for sharing. Besides, we just got through the anniversary of Father's death and now today arrives. How are you?"

"I know this day affects you and Michel. It certainly hurt Father. But I can't recall it."

Catherine strained to remember their mother, strained to remember that fateful day. The Saint-Laurent household had buzzed with excitement because the promised baby was soon to arrive. She and Michel had heard over and over about their responsibility in helping their mother after the birth. Catherine and Michel waited in the room adjacent to their mother's quarters when the nurse raced out and shouted for the butler to get a doctor. Soon thereafter, their father ran through the room without looking at them. When he got into the bedroom, he roared with grief. It was the first sound from behind the door, their father wailing and beating his fists against the wall.

The nurses pushed him out of the room, where he fell into a chair, broken, his hands limp at his sides.

Then the baby cried. She recalled the vivid memory that had burned into her young mind. A baby was crying.

The nurse brought the small bundle into the room. "Monsieur, he needs you," she said to their father. "Take him." She thrust the child into his arms and retreated to the birthing room.

Tears streamed down his face as he clutched the babe in his arms. Michel sat at attention in the corner, bewildered. Not Catherine. She'd had enough and slid off the sofa, going toward her father. She crept up to him and glanced at the baby.

"Papa? Who is it?"

Her father, despondent, gathered his senses and looked at her. He smiled through his tears and held her hand. "This is Xavier, darling. Michel, come here and meet your brother." Michel plodded across the room and gazed at the baby. With one arm holding the baby, their father embraced his other two children in a hug and resumed crying. And then he told them that their mother died in childbirth.

Catherine's eyes misted as she thought about the soft-spoken woman who'd raised her with love and devotion. She still missed her. But, if God had taken her away, He had left a perfect replacement in Xavier. Michel, her father, and she had embraced the new baby as the reincarnation of their mother and vowed to raise him as she would have, with patience, love, and reverence.

Catherine wiped at her tears.

"I'm sorry." Xavier hugged her and the warmth of his embrace eased her pain.

"It's a pity that your birthday is also *that* day. We tried to give you all of the attention, but—"

"And you did a marvelous job. I didn't know the meaning of this day for a long time, not until I could comprehend it. I didn't mean to be flippant before. I just never knew her."

"Oh, this is silly," Catherine said. "I know that, and you needn't worry. Let's talk about something else. I'll revel in the misery later, when you go see your friend."

Xavier smiled, as if he wanted to speak further on the subject, but a heavy footstep across the hall startled them. Catherine recognized the cadence and leapt to her feet as a man appeared in the doorway.

"Michel!" She ran across the room into his arms, his frame solid like a rock against her. "Don't you cut a dashing figure in the king's uniform?"

"I've missed you," Michel said with a laugh. He turned, and his expression lightened even more. "And Xavier. What a pleasant surprise." They embraced and kissed each other on the cheek.

"Are you in Paris because of the revolts?" Xavier asked.

"No, I came on other business. But I see the rioting persists in our fair city." Michel clapped his brother on the shoulder and motioned for them all to sit down. Catherine waited for them to sit, then stood before them to ensure her brother knew he could not command her to sit like a dog.

"Well, they're starving," Catherine intoned. "What do you expect them to do? The king and that Mademoiselle Antoinette spend extravagantly while the people can't feed their own children."

"I think you best watch yourself," Michel said in a tone reminiscent of their father. "Louis won't sit around as the masses ruin his country."

"Well, Louis better not wait too long, or there'll be more blood on his hands," she retorted.

"That's treason, Catherine."

"Oh, I swear." Catherine rolled her eyes. "Can't you see that things are changing? They have to."

"Are you sanctioning this rebellion? Certainly you don't participate, do you?" Michel barked his questions.

"Of course, I watch. It happens right outside my door. What do you expect? I won't crawl into some hole while the world destroys itself. What if I can do something to help?"

"Help?" He scoffed. "Help the riffraff that threatens your country? Help the peasants who vow to overthrow their king? Listen to yourself. You sound insane."

"That's enough," Xavier shouted. "The two of you never agree, so can we stop it?"

Catherine turned her attention from Michel and saw the pained expression on Xavier's face. He so hated it when Michel and she bickered, which they did more and more since their father died. For Xavier's sake, she stopped herself before she launched into another tirade against Michel's reverence for the monarchy.

"I apologize," Michel said through gritted teeth.

"As do I." Catherine hoped she at least sounded sincere. "So. Michel," Catherine continued, "what brought you here?"

"You did." He waggled his finger at Catherine. "I have wonderful news."

Something in his tone unnerved her and she sat down, twitching her leg as Xavier placed his hand on her knee to calm her. "Well?"

"I've betrothed you," Michel announced, a hint of triumph in his tone.

Catherine's face burned red. "You did *what*? You've no power over me." She stood, rage swelling in her throat. Xavier and Michel both jumped up in response. "You wander around Europe with that damn army while I maintain everything important to this family. Then you come parading back with an announcement about my future? How dare you?"

"Catherine, listen to me," he said, trying to placate her, but she stormed out of the room, cursing as she left.

"No man—brother or husband—will command me."

DEFIANCE

Xavier stood dumbfounded. Had Michel not learned anything after all these years with Catherine? Betrothed? Without her knowledge? And where did she go? Catherine was too headstrong, and Michel too lost in his role as family patriarch.

"Did you see that?" Michel asked, pointing at the ghost of their sister.

"What did you expect?"

"I knew she'd resist. But she didn't hear me out. She didn't listen." He turned back to Xavier.

"You'll never command Catherine like one of your soldiers. She makes her own decisions."

"How can I allow the defamation of the Saint-Laurent name because she refuses to marry? Father entrusted me with upholding our legacy."

"No, Michel, society gave you that responsibility. Father taught you to obey when it served the right purposes and to disregard tradition when necessary. Perhaps this is a time—"

"What about her safety?" Michel yelled his interruption. "She rants about maintaining the family wealth. Yet if something happened to both of us, the only males in this family, what do you think the government would do to her? Do you think they'd look the other way and allow a woman to control such a vast economic empire? *Men* control the world, and Catherine needs to remember that." He stood, hands on his hips, as if daring Xavier to argue with him.

Xavier remained calm. He had heard Michel's argument a million times, but Catherine loved her life and managed her affairs quite well. "Regardless of your worry, it won't help to defy her. I know you want the best for her. But you drive her away."

"It's more complicated this time."

"How so?" Xavier prodded.

Michel stopped and looked at him again. "The man. This will hurt him terribly."

"Who is it?"

"Jérémie Metcalfe."

Xavier gasped. "How could you put such an old family friend in such a position? He's like a brother. I had no idea he had feelings for Catherine."

"Nor does she."

Xavier rubbed his temples. "How did this come about?"

"He passed through a port where I was stationed a month ago. We had dinner, and we asked about our respective families. I told him how I worried about Catherine. Before I said much, he blurted out a confession that he wanted to marry her. I was ecstatic. I thought she loved him as well. Lord knows she'll never see it my way, but I did it for her. He asked permission to marry her and I granted it. We planned to meet here today to tell her." Michel sighed, forlorn. "I thought she guessed. Jérémie told me he visits often." He looked at Xavier then. "I must swear you to secrecy. I promised Jérémie not to tell a soul until she responded. He didn't want to face public humiliation if she rejected him."

"But she did no such thing," Xavier corrected. "She rejected *you*."

"I know, but Jérémie won't see it that way. Swear to me, Xavier. He'll be here soon."

"You invited him *here*? What were you thinking?"

"Damn it, there's no time for this. Swear to me."

Xavier stared at him, torn between his siblings. "Of course," he answered as a servant announced Jérémie. With his heart pounding, Xavier greeted their old friend.

"Jérémie," Michel greeted him. "Come in. We need to talk."

Xavier nodded politely, noting that Jérémie was indeed a handsome fellow with his soft white skin, height, and green eyes. He greeted Xavier and followed Michel out of the room.

Xavier stayed behind, bewildered. The footsteps in the hall startled him. He turned to see his sister, always beautiful in her flowing dresses and blonde hair even when scowling as she stormed down the hall.

"Is he still here?" she spat.

"Yes. Jérémie as well."

Catherine's eyes narrowed. "Come with me." She pulled him into the library and ushered him to a seat, then leaned against the desk piled with letters and papers.

"Can you believe him? Help me."

Xavier dreaded involvement in the fight but hated to see Catherine so distressed.

"You have every right to feel angry. But listen to him. Give him a chance."

"I won't tolerate a monarch in this house. France prepares to throw out the king, and yet I suffer one here."

"But you told me that you want to marry someday. At least listen to him."

"*I* want to choose my partner."

Someone knocked on the door. "Catherine? Xavier?" Jérémie timidly entered. "Michel left."

"Good," Catherine said.

Jérémie came in, smiled at Xavier, but never looked at Catherine.

"I missed you today," Catherine said to him. She sighed. "At least you don't have a brother telling you what to do. Can you believe him?"

Xavier cleared his throat. "I'm sure Jérémie doesn't want to hear about it."

"I don't mind." Jérémie offered a smile. "It must be difficult."

Catherine pushed herself away from the desk and rushed to Jérémie and pecked him on the cheek. "Why can't you be my eldest brother? You're the most charming man. You understand me. I can't tie myself to someone who dictates my life. Especially a brother who runs around in the army fighting people away from home. He probably picked some authoritarian general to push me around."

"I'm sure the gentleman meant well," Jérémie whispered.

"If someone wants to marry me, he better tell me about it, not my brother."

"Perhaps the gentleman was concerned with decorum," Xavier said. "I'm sure he meant the best."

Jérémie flashed Xavier a surprised glance. To Catherine, he said, "I have to leave. I'm expected elsewhere." He bowed and left.

"Jérémie was odd." Catherine frowned. "He came yesterday on the pretense of business but chatted for a while, like the typical Jérémie. He seemed morose today."

"Just be patient," Xavier hinted.

"You're strange. Aren't you here a little late today? You usually bolt away to see your new friend."

Xavier blushed. Catherine perceived too much.

THE WOULD-BE BISHOP

Xavier hastened through the streets, only greeting the people with whom he usually stopped to converse with a quick nod. Michel's return, the news about Jérémie, and Catherine's reaction kept him at the house longer than he'd anticipated.

"You look distressed."

Xavier jumped at Thomas's voice. "You scared me."

"Your brow is creased with worry. Should I go?"

"No. Please, stay." Xavier wanted nothing more than to lose himself with Thomas. Without prompting, he launched into the entire tale as Thomas listened. Instead of continuing toward the church, they walked around Paris, passing a few angry people discussing the Estates General, but most went about their business.

"You feel too much responsibility for them." Thomas put his hand on Xavier's back. The masculine touch sent chills through Xavier.

"Can we talk about something else?" Xavier had had enough of the Saint-Laurents. "I need to forget about it for a while."

Thomas turned Xavier down a quiet, abandoned street, his hand still on Xavier's back.

"This is the first time you've said much about your family history," Thomas said. "I take it you come from a great deal of money?"

"Yes," Xavier said with a trace of irritation. He hated talking about their wealth.

"It's nothing to be ashamed of. It makes you more intriguing."

"How?"

"I assumed you were poor, with your small parish in a rather nasty part of Paris. I don't think many people from the nobility receive such assignments. How wealthy are you?"

"I've no idea. Catherine handles all that. It's extensive."

Thomas stopped and held Xavier's shoulders. His eyes burned into Xavier's soul. "You're beautiful."

Xavier squirmed. He looked away from Thomas's piercing brown eyes, but Thomas grabbed his head and forced them to look at each other. "Why do you serve in this filth? Your family must have connections in the church."

Xavier turned his head and looked at the ground as he pulled away to remove himself from the sexual tension. He resumed their walk.

"It's not about power," Xavier said. "My family has served the monarchy for generations. Becoming a bishop would be easy for me, but I prefer my small church. I could send Michel a letter tomorrow and move to a new location overnight, but I can't imagine serving the wealthy and listening to them pretend to practice their faith, while in reality. They disregard human need."

"Doesn't the poor condition of your church bother you? Why do you grow vegetables when other clergy eat four-course meals every day?"

"I don't do it as some form of penance. I eat with Catherine most nights anyway. I know it sounds preposterous. Michel says so all the time."

Thomas stopped when they reached the Bastille's edges, the dark structure that housed so many of Paris's criminals casting more blackness over the night. Xavier glanced at it, wondering how many people truly belonged in its confines. It loomed over them as Thomas stared at Xavier. Passionate feelings of lust, infatuation, and fear flooded through Xavier.

"Your moral standards astound me," Thomas said.

Xavier wanted to get away from the Bastille's wicked eye so he headed north, toward his parish. "I'm sorry."

Thomas smiled. "There you go, apologizing. Doesn't Catherine support you?"

"Yes, of course, but she relates it to her independence. Mine isn't about myself. I feel an obligation to humanity." They reached Xavier's church and leaned against a small fence. "When I work here, I touch people. For a moment, for a day, however long, I ease the pain."

"Do you accept Catholic theology?"

Xavier thought for a long moment. "Is this just between us?"

"I'd never betray you." Thomas grabbed Xavier's hand.

"I don't believe all of it. Some higher being exists, which we can't understand. It's impossible to believe this happened by accident. Mankind seeks to answer this question, and for many, those answers come through the church." He stared at their clasped hands with a thrill. "I serve the church because I was raised in it. It's how I come into contact with the spiritual world. It also allows me to help people. Really, this sounds ridiculous."

"Not at all." Thomas squeezed his hand and let go. "It makes sense. The first day we met, I saw you help that little girl find her mother. You never hesitated or got angry. You just acted. That's a profound love that few feel. I wish I shared such zeal."

"You make me a saint prematurely." Xavier managed a wan smile. "I get angry with the world and fail to live by my own standards. I almost never succeed with my brother."

Thomas moved them to a bench and sat opposite him. Xavier struggled to control his urge to sink into the shelter of Thomas's powerful arms.

"What about your brother? I thought you cared so much for him."

"Oh, I do, I do. I cherish my brother and sister. Remember what I told you about Catherine, about how Michel has taken his responsibility to lead this family too far?"

Thomas nodded.

"He does the same to me. It enrages Michel that I refuse to accept a higher position in the church. He claims that it degrades the Saint-Laurent name. He sees religion differently, as more of a duty, another cog in the government. I try to listen, but I get so angry. Then yell at him."

"Forgive my bluntness," Thomas said. "Your biggest weakness is that you're too hard on yourself. You expect perfection of yourself, but you're fallible. Let yourself be."

Thomas spoke the truth, yet Xavier thought of all the people who *did* expect perfection of him. The Catholic Church elevated priests to a false pedestal, and Michel and Catherine doted over him all the time. His eyes filled with tears.

Thomas patted Xavier on the shoulder. Without a word, he moved closer and hugged him as he whispered into his ear. "I understand, Abbé, I understand." They sat that way for a long moment before Xavier sat up, collected himself, and smiled.

"Thank you. I'm sorry."

"You apologized again," Thomas teased.

Xavier struggled to stay awake and allow the moment to continue, but the evening had worn him out. His head bobbed once, and then he heard Thomas laugh.

"Are you exhausted?"

"I'm tired. I get up early to read and then work through the early afternoon so I can visit Catherine in the evenings."

"Should I let you rest tomorrow?"

"No, please, come back."

Thomas stood and accompanied Xavier toward the church. He held the door open for Xavier, who walked in and turned around.

"Good night." Xavier smiled.

"Abbé." Thomas smiled in return and turned. He paused at the gate, looked back, waved, then disappeared into the night.

Xavier hated that his stomach ached when Thomas disappeared.

He had fought these longings his entire life and scolded himself for them. Many of his colleagues ignored their vows of celibacy, and more than a few "friendships" developed in seminary. Even bishops knew about these arrangements and entered into them. Yet Xavier could not bring himself to defy the church so openly. For every accepting curé or official, another might expose his blasphemy and ruin his chosen path.

Anguish. Bitter, aching anguish engulfed Xavier. Why did he struggle with these feelings for Thomas? He groaned. Those dreams of lying with another man and feeling his strength overpower him with its protection overcame Xavier. He longed to run his hand over tight muscles and feel coarse whiskers against his cheek. It was too easy to fantasize in the dark.

Five: Marcel André

26 MAY 1789

Xavier looked twice from his rectory window to see who approached, then squinted against the sun to confirm that Catherine walked up the path. He closed his Bible and raced down the stairs.

He flung the door open and hurried over to her. "What's wrong?"

"Did Satan chase you out here? You look terrified." She grinned.

"Why did you come to my church?"

"Can't I visit? Come with me. I have exciting news."

"Where are we going?"

Catherine pulled him into the muddy streets. "I'll explain on our way."

"This isn't about converting our home into a salon, is it?"

"No." Catherine shook her head. "Not yet. It's something different."

Xavier pulled back and waited.

Catherine whipped around with a frown. "I need you, now more than ever. Come on." She tugged at his arm, but he refused to budge. "I'll tell you everything if you'll at least walk." She yanked at him until he followed.

"I need a man," she announced. "I know, it sounds dreadful. Not that I include you in that category, but decorum requires a man to accompany me. Not just any man, someone from the family. Michel thinks he has the right to perform these functions, but his attitude bothers me. So I came to you instead." She glanced at him. "Let's see..." Catherine looked around before continuing down another road. "Oh, look, all these people. Probably protesting King Louis again. Where was I? Oh, you, of course. I need your sanction."

He stared at her, perplexed. "What on earth is going on?"

"All right." Catherine threw her arms up. "I need you to approve my marriage."

"What? Are you mad? To whom?"

"To the most delightful man I've ever met. We're going to meet him now."

"Two days ago, you flew into a rage at the thought of some man controlling your life, and now, without any warning, you pull me through Paris to some man I've never met with the intention of having me sanction a marriage? Have you lost your mind?"

Catherine stomped her foot and stopped in the middle of the road, a cart barely missing her. "If I wanted Michel's attitude, I would've gone to him. Go back to your damned church and leave me alone."

Xavier took a deep breath. "Can't we just discuss this?"

"I'm sorry. Please meet him, and we can talk afterward. Please?"

Xavier motioned her ahead and followed without answering as she charged through the mud. They arrived outside the shop of a merchant who advertised imports. The items in the window were expensive— many of them from Asia or the Americas. Catherine opened the door and entered with Xavier in tow. Despite the pleasant appearance and vast array of foreign goods, Xavier noticed a damp, moldy smell. Catherine walked behind the counter and into the back without saying a word while Xavier waited in the entrance, afraid.

She returned, grinning, in a few seconds. "He'll be out in a minute. You won't believe it. I found the man of my dreams, the man I'll marry. We're engaged, and I need you to approve. I need to know that you'll allow me to make this decision without Michel lording over me. He's everything I could ever want. He even makes me tea! Imagine, no servants yet he makes the tea without expecting me to do it because I'm a woman."

Xavier wanted to believe her, but she sounded like a lunatic. He had never heard her dote over someone other than himself.

"He's the most handsome man—"

"You embarrass me in front of your brother," said a baritone voice with a slight edge.

Xavier was startled to see an older gentleman, probably in his late fifties, behind the counter. He tilted his head downward, to examine Xavier as if looking over the top of a pair of glasses. An odd little chill settled in Xavier's stomach.

"How could I embarrass you? Xavier, I want you to meet my fiancé, Marcel André."

The man bowed his head even farther. "Abbé, I've heard all about you."

Xavier mustered his courage. "It's a pleasure," he lied.

"Marcel owns this business. He imports things from all over the world. We met on business. I needed some furniture and came by his shop one day. I bought two chairs, and before you knew it, we were doing business. Then he proposed to me and I agreed!"

Catherine prattled on while Xavier almost fainted. She was insane and taking her defiance too far, clearly doing it to attack Michel. A bell rang in the back, thankfully, and stopped her as Marcel excused himself.

Xavier stared at her. "Are you really marrying him?"

"Don't talk to me that way."

"What are you not telling me?"

"I told you everything. I chose Marcel. He's charming. Our merged empires will be extraordinary."

Xavier breathed air deep into his lungs and put his arm around her. "What's going on?"

She glanced at the floor and smiled as her eyes welled with tears. "I told you the truth. I find him enchanting."

"But?"

"But, well, you know. I don't love him. Not yet, anyway."

"Listen to me. This isn't the time to make a case for your independence. I know you want to spite Michel, but you can't ruin the rest of your life to make a point."

"I want to give this a try."

"A 'try'? You can't just end a marriage if your mood changes."

Catherine took Xavier's face in her hands. "You're my most treasured possession. I don't expect you to understand. But I intend to do this, with or without your approval. Or Michel's."

Xavier's stomach ached. "Even though you just met him?"

"Yes. I can't explain the instant passion. Have I embarrassed you? He attracts me in a way I can't explain. If I must marry, why not embrace this lust?"

"Catherine, could you come here?" Marcel called from the back.

She took leave, but Xavier followed her. He hid in a doorway and saw them in a small room full of bottles, dead animals, and other peculiar artifacts. The room frightened Xavier more than the front space.

Marcel, glancing about, handed Catherine a glass of some strange blue liquid. "Here, my dear, drink."

Catherine gulped the substance down, then staggered backward, almost falling. She steadied herself and then reached up and pinched Marcel on the cheek.

"Abbé, come in," Marcel said. Marcel peered in his direction, making Xavier's skin crawl.

Xavier walked toward them but with a great deal of hesitation. Marcel glared at the priest, but Xavier ignored him, taking stock of more odd things. A dried bat, the feet of chickens, herbs, powder, and skulls. The room chilled Xavier unlike anything in his life. In seminary, he had learned about evil places that repelled religiously devout people but brushed it aside as superstition; now he wondered about its truth. Perhaps his friend Anne from the New World could explain it to him.

"I see you like my room," Marcel said to Xavier.

"Intriguing."

"I suppose it shocks you. It's voodoo. I learned it in the New World. Nothing to worry about, just a little magic to protect those I love and help my business."

Voodoo. That's what Anne called her religion.

Catherine finally noticed Xavier. "Marcel doesn't believe in that old Catholic theology." She giggled and giggled.

"Catherine, will you wait for us outside?" Marcel asked.

"Certainly." For the first time Xavier could remember, Catherine obeyed an order.

Marcel's comportment changed as Xavier walked backward and clutched his cross. He said a silent prayer as they stared at each other.

"Stay out of this. This is no place for a priest. Don't mind that little drink, either. She likes it." Marcel grinned at Xavier. "Father, may I make a confession? I offered her a small potion that gives her the power to love. You see, she told me about how much tradition constrains her. I took that to mean she wanted my help. The drink frees her mind. Just a Haitian remedy I learned on my travels."

Xavier bumped into the wall and his whole body shook as he turned and ran from the room. Marcel had manipulated Xavier's vow to keep him from doing anything. He'd asked for a confession because it bound Xavier to silence. Xavier sweated profusely as he reached the street, damning his loyalty to an oath that so many failed to follow. Catherine, who stood with her typical confidence, looked at him with surprise, the glassy gaze gone.

"Xavier, what on earth?"

"I have to go."

Catherine muttered a protest, but Xavier raced down the street without her. His heart pounded. Nothing had scared him more in his entire life. Evil. He had encountered pure evil. And it wanted to marry his sister. Xavier tore off his collar and rushed to the church where he collapsed on his bed. His two worlds, family and church, collided with a violent force as he buried his head in a pillow and wept.

JÉRÉMIE'S PAIN

Xavier cried himself to sleep after running away from Catherine and Marcel. Marcel had trapped him into silence, and now a thousand questions ran through Xavier's head. What was that liquid? Was Catherine under a spell? It sounded absurd. But Catherine had acted so differently after she drank it.

After his nap, his nerves calmed, Xavier headed toward the Saint-Laurent home, deciding to wait to talk to Thomas before doing anything about Marcel. Xavier drew all the courage he could muster as he climbed the stairs and entered the house. To his surprise, he found Catherine sitting with Jérémie in the parlor.

"Xavier! Have you recovered? Are you sick?" Catherine asked.

"I'm well," Xavier lied as he knelt and kissed her on the cheek, then nodded toward Jérémie.

"Your timing is exquisite," Catherine said. "We were discussing my engagement. Jérémie had no idea. Can you imagine?" Jérémie glanced miserably at Xavier as Xavier took his seat and prepared for an evening of torture. "I told him all about Marcel, and the money—did I tell you about his holdings?"

"Yes," Jérémie whispered.

"Did you tell Jérémie that you don't love Marcel?" Xavier tried to coax some sense into her.

"A minor detail." Catherine rolled her eyes. "My brother dislikes the arrangement. He believes in marrying for love and devotion. I'll never be able to love in a situation where someone dictates my life. So I chose based on financial interests and pure attraction. Look at you two," she added. "You're acting forlorn."

Xavier rubbed his temples. How could she be so blind? "Is it an attraction to him or to spite Michel?"

"Don't patronize me. *I'll* choose my husband. Spiting Michel is just an added bonus."

"It sounds as if you've decided," Jérémie whispered. "I don't understand the haste. As for Michel, I'm sure his suitor will leave you alone so you can take your time."

"You're so sweet. I won't rush into anything. Besides, Marcel leaves soon for a voyage. Part of his business, which suits me well."

"What are you talking about?" Xavier asked.

"His business takes him all over the world for months at a time to collect the goods that he sells."

"And this is good?" Jérémie asked with a frown.

"Of course, it's good. It means he'll leave me alone to govern my own life."

"It makes little sense." Jérémie sighed.

Catherine put her hand on Jérémie's knee and implored with her eyes for him to agree with her. "You can't understand the plight of a woman. I'm cursed with the necessity of marriage. What chance do I have for love? It's an absurd fantasy, and I can't lead my life with the notion I may find it by accident. I have to act. So, I chose a man who only takes a limited amount of my freedom, who travels a lot, which preserves my autonomy." She sat back, satisfied.

Xavier shook his head. She told the truth. She articulated her philosophy to him a hundred times, and it always made sense; he just never envisioned the vile Marcel.

Jérémie spoke as he rose from his chair. "Catherine, do what you wish. You're too good a person to bow to others. Yet you sell yourself short. With such a good soul, a passion for life, and all the beauty in the world, there are men who would love and care for you without taking away the independence that makes you such a wonderful woman." He paused and drew in a deep breath. "Love exists in this world. I wish you'd give it a chance." He bowed and took his leave.

"He's so sweet," Catherine said. "We're lucky to have him as a friend."

"Indeed," Xavier responded, throat dry.

"If you're going to be morose, you can leave, too."

He stood to do so.

"Wait. Come back." Catherine pulled at his arm. "I didn't mean it."

He disengaged her arm. "I respect your independence, you know that. I'll honor your decision, you know that, too. But you can't coerce me into agreeing with it."

"Fine. But come back." She pushed Xavier into a chair. "I need my freedom."

"I pray for your happiness every day. I see the same world as you, with all of its faults and unrealistic expectations. Maybe I'll understand over time." But he knew he never would. Xavier grabbed her hand as she kissed him on the cheek and put her head on his shoulder.

Six: The Announcement

27 MAY 1789

Thomas listened to Xavier tell about Catherine's engagement as he followed him toward the Saint-Laurent household for the first time. He'd fed earlier than usual in order to devote his full energy to Xavier that night. Xavier accepted too much responsibility for his sister, who did what she pleased, yet Thomas cherished Xavier's concern for those he loved.

The increased looting and riots in Xavier's neighborhood also concerned Thomas, as Parisians grew angrier by the day. He especially worried that some blamed the Catholic Church for not providing relief while it never paid taxes and received financial support from Louis's government, but Xavier insisted that nothing threatened him. If only Thomas felt so certain.

That night, Thomas had panicked when he first saw Xavier's church because an angry mob surrounded it, shouting expletives. He'd raced over to find Xavier in the middle of it, listening to them rail against the government and Catholic hierarchy. Thomas had stood outside until Xavier convinced those gathered to return to their homes. He'd also invited those without food to dine at the church, where Xavier found enough to feed the few who remained. Afterward, Thomas had pledged a large sum of money to Xavier to assist with his cause. Xavier had resisted, saying that Catherine gave him plenty, but Thomas had insisted.

"Thomas? Did you hear me?" Xavier asked as they continued toward the Saint-Laurent home.

"Of course. I'm just worried."

"About the mob?"

"A little."

"Don't worry about them. They just need to voice their grievances." He pointed up the street. "We're almost there. Are you ready? Do you have any other questions about my family?"

"I already know too much."

Xavier smiled. "Here we are." He paused, then trembled and played with his cross.

"After you." Thomas ushered Xavier forward and followed him into the enormous house, further confirmation of the Saint-Laurent wealth that Xavier so desperately tried to conceal. Catherine decorated it in the latest fashion, although it retained an older charm. They stood in a vast entryway, illuminated by what looked like a thousand candles. Xavier walked toward a hallway when someone approached from the other direction.

"Xavier? Is that you?" A uniformed man came down the hall. Quite handsome, Thomas thought, though without the baby-like innocence of his brother. Michel's features were harsher, perhaps from his time in the military.

"Michel, allow me to introduce Thomas Lord."

"My pleasure," Michel bowed.

"I'm happy to put a face with your name, Lieutenant. I've heard much about you and your family."

"Then I suppose you heard about the latest problems." Michel turned to Xavier. "She gathered us to make an important announcement and thinks I've no idea. But Jérémie told me about her little scheme. Can you imagine that she invited him as well? This beast is sitting in that room with her."

"Beast?" Xavier repeated while Michel shrugged and hurried them down the hall and toward a side parlor.

Xavier leaned into Michel and whispered enough that only Thomas's vampiric senses overheard him. "Be kind. You can't do anything if you anger her."

Another room, more opulence, and plenty of tension. Xavier introduced Thomas to Jérémie, who sat by himself.

"I thought Catherine was with you?" Michel asked.

"Still spying on me?" Catherine said from behind.

"I only meant—" Michel started.

Catherine pushed past him without acknowledgement. "You must be Thomas. I'm so glad that you're here. Xavier talks about you all the time." She put her hand out, and Thomas kissed it. "He used to spend more time with his lonely sister, but now runs off every night to see you. I was anxious to meet the person who can hold my brother's attention even more than that little parish of his."

Thomas smiled politely. She was as charming as Xavier described, though the abbé stood red with embarrassment. "I assure you, mademoiselle, that the pleasure is mine. Your brother has offered a most fitting introduction to Paris."

Catherine laughed. "That's typical Xavier, a martyr for any cause. But I dare say, monsieur, that you hardly fit the part." Her eyes twinkled as she winked at Thomas. With that, Catherine bustled past them into the room. Everyone followed as if she were a monarch and they her servants. Even Jérémie stood and greeted Catherine without a hint of the despair Xavier had mentioned.

The gathering eased into various conversations, and Thomas found himself near the bar, away from the others and with Catherine.

"I'm glad you've befriended my brother," she said. "He needs strong men in his life. Though you seem like more than the usual man running about Paris."

"What do you mean?" he asked.

"I'm not sure." Catherine turned and strode to the middle of the room. "Well, I suppose, as usual, you're waiting for me. You all know why I called you here. Jérémie and Xavier already know, and I suspect one of them told Michel." Catherine stood defiantly, controlling a group of men as if they were children. Thomas admired her spunk when she looked at him. "Don't tell me. Xavier can't keep a secret from you. He dotes over you all the time—"

"Catherine, really," Xavier said.

"Enough chatter," Michel broke in. "What do you want to tell us?"

"Very well," she said with a dismissing shrug. "I want you to meet my fiancé, Marcel André. I'm having dinner served and it will be friendly and civil. There's nothing to discuss. Understood? I'm sure that Thomas doesn't wish to hear us griping."

As she spoke, Marcel entered the room, and Thomas disliked him at first sight, even more so when he noticed Xavier step back, shaking. Thomas walked to his side and patted his back, and Xavier relaxed and leaned into Thomas's arm. In some animalistic way, Marcel alarmed him. He remembered how Xavier described a feeling of evil when he entered the shop to meet Marcel, a fitting description.

"Come here," Catherine cooed. She, too, changed when Marcel entered. "Marcel, I want you to meet Jérémie. You already know Xavier. This is his friend Thomas, and this is my brother Michel. And, now, dinner is ready."

Again they followed Catherine like ducklings, avoiding her wrath with their obedience. Xavier had told Thomas that no one agreed with her course of action, but no one moved to challenge her. Thomas, too, hid his discomfort. However, halfway through the first course, Xavier stared at him from across the table. Without a word, Thomas tilted his head and grinned. Xavier glanced away, his face turning red.

Thomas stopped listening to the mundane conversation and wondered if a chance existed for the romance he sought with the adorable priest? They acted like a couple on more than one occasion, with a look, a glance, or a casual touch.

Thomas spent most of dinner gazing at Xavier. He noticed the grace with which Xavier kept his brother and sister from bickering, how he comforted Jérémie without giving away that he knew anything, and how he avoided Marcel without anyone realizing it. Xavier's laughter sent chills through Thomas. He was so beautiful. A couple more times Xavier discovered his stare and looked away. Such a sheepish love.

Never did anyone acknowledge the family problems. It was a bizarre display, but it afforded Thomas the opportunity to learn about the family what he needed to know to protect Xavier. Catherine lived in her own world but would never hurt Xavier on purpose. They loved each other and understood one another on a profound level. Michel, however, stood outside their circle, trying to control and act like the patriarch society expected, but impotent around their self-assurance. Jérémie was a lost puppy longing for a home now that Catherine had crushed his dreams, though she seemed oblivious to it.

Marcel was another matter. The others Thomas could leave alone, but Marcel surreptitiously glared at Xavier. He sensed sinister forces around that man. And from Marcel's snarling at him, he deduced that Marcel knew about his vampirism, too.

Thomas was almost disappointed when dinner ended and everyone retired to the parlor.

THE VAMPIRE AND THE WARLOCK

Unlike a typical household, where women and men separated after dinner, Catherine's hold on the Saint-Laurents kept the sexes together. How odd, Thomas finally noticed, that no other women joined them that evening. They all followed her to the parlor for their après dinner conversation.

Michel served the drinks and Xavier took his glass and gulped half of it down in one motion. Thomas almost teased him when he saw the abbé's eyes widen and so glanced to see Marcel put something into Catherine's wine, which fizzled for a moment, added a blue tint, and then turned the liquid to a dull gray.

"Jérémie, you seem sad." Catherine took the drink from Marcel.

He grimaced. "I just have a lot on my mind."

"You've never fretted over things before."

"Maybe we should move to the porch. It's nice outside," Xavier interrupted to save his friend.

"Good idea," Catherine agreed. "Thomas, you need another drink."

He inclined his head. "I'll get it myself. You may escort your entourage and I'll join you in a moment."

Jérémie, Michel, and Xavier followed her, with Xavier smiling at Thomas's reference to an entourage. Marcel, however, stayed behind.

"I need more wine, too," he said, and he poured himself a robust red wine, staring daggers at Thomas. Thomas killed more powerful and sophisticated men than Marcel, and potion or not, he could break Marcel's back in one motion.

Yet Thomas's intimacy with the entire family gave him pause because murdering Marcel threatened to disrupt more of the delicate ethic Anthony had articulated after Thomas's transformation. He could hear the litany of laws Anthony recited the very first night: we must never interfere with the course of human history except on a limited basis. Doing so could bring discovery. Mundane interactions escape human attention, and even killings can be concealed to look natural. But once we become intimate, Anthony had emphasized, the danger of exposure by interfering in their lives increased tenfold and must be avoided at all cost.

Thomas returned Marcel's gaze. His human feelings and longings for Xavier, his passion to protect, made it difficult to maintain the ethic. How could Thomas balance the perfect caution that concealed vampires for thousands of years with his longing for a mate?

Marcel studied Thomas. "Do you hold some enmity toward me?"

Thomas raised an eyebrow. "You mistreat people," he stated flatly.

"You know nothing of me."

"I know that you poison Catherine." Thomas watched him.

"She knows what I give her," Marcel defended himself. "Just not when. And besides, it's a matter between my fiancée and me."

"She's a prize to you, isn't she? A beautiful animal to cage and control as a pet."

"What does it matter to you? Between men, she's quite a beauty. To have her in my bed will add countless hours of pleasure. It's none of your business."

"Disgusting." Thomas sneered and realized too late that his fangs had started to descend. Marcel backed away and trembled, his masculine bravado gone. But he regained his arrogant posture and stalked toward Thomas.

"Not human," he said. "I knew it. The old voodoo priestesses warned me that such animals haunt the earth. So, you threaten me? What if I expose you? Your little Xavier wouldn't like this little secret." Even as he spoke, his hands trembled.

Thomas gritted his teeth and spoke with a clenched jaw. "Don't you ever go near him. I'll hunt you down and torture you if any harm befalls him. Do you understand?"

Marcel laughed. "Sodomites. Protective sodomites. I never expected to confront such disgusting behavior around Catherine."

"Powerful words coming from a quaking fool."

"If my lessons were correct, there's not much you can do in the daylight to protect your priest-come-mistress."

With a swift motion, Thomas grabbed the idiot by the neck and lifted him off the ground. He held him high above, glared into his eyes, and allowed his fangs to show. Marcel turned purple and wet himself from terror.

Thomas dropped him on the floor, where he gasped for air. "You're a monster, an unnatural beast." Marcel coughed between words.

"I'm a monster who will do more than make you piss your pants if you ever utter another unkind word about Xavier."

"Just stay away from me and I won't touch him. I want the girl. And I won't harm her either. I just want to make sure she's mine. But you think I can't come up with something to counter you? Maybe I'll expose his sick sexual urges to the world. What would be worse for him?"

"How can I trust you to abide by an agreement? If you do anything to him through the day, I'll hunt you down. I'll torture you for a long, painful death."

"Listen to me," Marcel said, gaining his feet but keeping a distance. "I'd never touch him. Not because of Catherine, not even because of your lame threats. The potion, the charms I use, they come from an ancient religion I learned in the New World from slaves. They warned me never to attack a priest because it alters the order of things. Sodomite or not, that one holds power. Otherwise, he'd already be dead for interfering. I think we can agree to leave each other's little exploits alone, no?"

Thomas actually believed the groveling idiot. Besides, his proposition solved the ethical dilemma to ensure his abbé's safety while allowing the natural order of things to continue with Catherine and Marcel.

"Fine. But you won't utter a word about me to Catherine, Xavier, or anyone else."

"That wasn't part of the bargain—"

"You're in no position to barter. Agree or I'll kill you. Don't go near him and say nothing of me."

"Then you agree to the same."

Thomas nodded once. "Now, get out of here. You reek of piss."

BROTHERLY LOVE

Catherine felt triumphant after dinner. Despite the discomfort, she forced her brothers, Michel in particular, to understand that she would control her own destiny. If society demanded a husband, then Marcel was perfect. A little old, but with money and attractive in an odd way. Most of all, she chose him to protect her freedom because he spent less time in Paris every year than he did on a boat or in other ports around the world.

She also enjoyed meeting Thomas and watching Xavier act so uncharacteristically giddy. Yet something was different about that one, more than just the obvious infatuation he had for her brother, but she failed to pinpoint what worried her.

The cool Paris night soothed some of her anxiety as she stood with the men in her life, whom she loved with her whole heart. Michel, Xavier, and Jérémie. Tension or not, fighting or not, she loved them.

Michel clenched his jaw and sighed, ending Catherine's moment of revelry. "This is insane. We don't know anything about him and he's old enough to be your father."

"If anyone has explaining to do, it's you."

"What do you mean?" Michel's face turned bright red.

"Marcel told me that you threatened him. That you'd get rid of him one way or another."

"I threatened him?" Michel pounded his fists on a table. "*He* threatened *me*! He told me that I'd better not stand in the way or he would get rid of *me*."

"You can leave if you can't accept it," she retorted with an icy glare. "I don't believe you."

"And you can't throw me out of my own home. I have an obligation to protect you, as I promised Father."

"You play on battlefields and only saunter into Paris once or twice a year. How can you know what I need?"

"I don't need to be here to know that this is ridiculous."

"Shut up, Michel. You make me—"

"Stop it." Xavier stepped between them. "Both of you, just stop it. I can't deal with this fighting anymore."

Catherine hated when Xavier commanded them to stop because it hurt him. The tears in his eyes yanked at her heart. Worse, it gave Michel the upper hand. Michel would use the peace to lower his voice and reiterate his perceptions. She would refuse to counterattack because it led to more shouting that hurt Xavier further.

"I'm just worried," Michel said. "With mobs all over Paris, who will protect you, Catherine? A husband who ventures around the globe can't guard you. Paris has never been so volatile."

"I've protected myself for all of these years. I'm safe. I don't need some man to watch over me every hour of the day."

Silence. Xavier put a hand on each of their shoulders, and glanced at Michel, then Catherine.

"Please, just love each other." He sounded desperate, and she nodded slowly, but only after Michel acquiesced. Jérémie stayed in the shadows the entire time.

Thomas's voice at the door halted the awkward scene. Although she'd noticed his handsome face and powerful body when they met, his striking figure astonished her again. With the candlelight and darkness enveloping him, he became the most beguiling creature.

"Marcel asked me to give his regrets," he explained. "He had to leave. I'm afraid that I must go too."

Thomas glanced at Xavier, another silent communication between lovers, regardless of whether or not Xavier admitted it to her.

"I'll walk with you," Xavier said on cue.

Thomas made his goodbyes to Jérémie and Michel, then grabbed Catherine's hand to kiss it.

"I do hope you'll bring my brother around more often," she said.

"Madame." He bowed and turned to leave with a grin.

Xavier and Michel made some plan to meet in the morning, and then Xavier came to her. He hugged her and whispered, "I'll help, just don't argue with him."

She held him and whispered back, "Your friend is a handsome one."

Xavier blushed and followed Thomas without another word. Catherine sighed and strolled to the edge of the porch to look onto the street below. The air had grown chilly, so she wrapped her arms around herself for warmth. Xavier and Thomas looked so comfortable together as they walked along the street, with Thomas's hand placed on the curé's back. Were they in love? Catherine hoped so. Xavier deserved more than he got from that parish. She wanted Xavier to run away, out of Paris and away from the church. She wanted him to find the love that he sought for other people. If he sought love with a man, she would never stand between them as people stood between her and her ambitions.

She jumped when she noticed a figure behind her, but it was only Jérémie placing his jacket around her shoulders.

Seven: Michel and Xavier

28 May 1789

Xavier tapped his foot on the Saint-Laurent porch as he sipped his tea and glanced across the table at Michel. The quiet tension unnerved him, and he flinched when Michel finally spoke.

"I assume that you summoned me to scold me again."

"I never mean to reprimand you," Xavier almost whispered. "You know that."

Michel sighed. "I do. But you and Catherine never understand the strain of *my* position. I hold the burden of leading this family now. Catherine has no respect for that. Do you know she's thinking about opening a salon? I won't allow it. And I went to her with the proposal from Jérémie to make her happy, but she never even listened. Then, while I decided to let things calm down and encouraged Jérémie to talk to her, she went off, in just a day, and decided to marry that man, whatever his name is—"

"Marcel," Xavier said, distaste on his tongue.

"Marcel, who's old enough to be our father. Without asking anyone's permission," Michel growled the last sentence.

Xavier both agreed and disagreed with his brother. "It's the insinuation of her needing your permission that makes her do these things."

"I'm trying to help her." He slammed his open palm on to the table.

"She has dreams that don't conform to your vision. You have to let her pursue them, even if it means this engagement. I don't like Marcel any better than you do. If she thinks you're dictating something, she'll defy you, even if she knows you're right."

"Normally, I get it. But this is too risky, even for her. Don't you think that she loves Jérémie? He'd allow her all the freedom in the world."

"I can't think of a better husband," Xavier concurred. "But that's not the issue. If you try to demand she marry Jérémie, it'll fail like an attempt to tame a lion."

Michel clenched his jaw. "How can we get her to make the right decision?"

"By leaving her alone. Maybe if Jérémie went to her and explained things... Have you asked him?"

Michel snorted his answer. "Of course. But after last night, he won't even talk about it. He was in turmoil even before that. He wanted to approach her, but, because of our friendship, didn't want to offend me by not consulting with the head of the household first. I told him to talk to her, forget about me. He was too afraid, and then last night happened, and you know how he can retreat into a shell. Should I just forbid her marriage?"

"Are you insane?"

Michel didn't answer, and they drank their tea in silence, both at a loss for answers.

"How is your parish?" Michel asked after a while.

Not that attack again. "Fine." Xavier resisted the urge to roll his eyes.

"Have you considered my suggestion?"

A million times. He stared into his tea. "I'm not ready for you to ask the bishop to promote me."

"You act like Catherine sometimes. What about honoring the Saint-Laurent name?"

"I can't abandon my parish."

"Let someone from their own ranks help them," Michel said dismissively.

"I know you worry about me, but I'm safe. Nothing makes me happier than helping them."

"You sound like a Huguenot, with your castigation of the church hierarchy. Or Catherine. Heaven forbid that either of you listen to me."

"Michel, I'm just answering my call."

"Your *call* is to your country and family. It's a disgrace to the Saint-Laurent name that you suffer in such a damnable place full of filth and squalor. Rioting." He stood without another word, without hugging or so much as a glance at Xavier, and stormed out.

SEDUCTION

Xavier hurried out to his church garden, earlier than usual and too anxious to accomplish anything of substance as he waited for Thomas, his heart pounding inside his chest.

Of course, he struggled against his urges and vow of celibacy. But they only ever talked. So long as he kept it at that... Yet he dreamed about doing more as he lay in bed, wishing that Thomas cuddled next to him, over and over again praying for forgiveness against even such innocuous fantasies that he had no control over when they stormed into his head.

And every night left less and less doubt as to whether Thomas had the same feelings. He touched Xavier more often, he leaned a little closer, and he gazed into his eyes the entire time without looking away. Xavier, too, occasionally stumbled closer to Thomas in order to feel him nearby. Every time, Thomas maintained their proximity or moved to catch Xavier, fondling his arms or chest. Xavier admitted a great deal of naiveté, but regarding Thomas, he knew the truth.

Xavier swooned at the sight of those familiar, broad shoulders, almost racing into the grasp of Thomas's arms every time. And the calves, those glorious, well-defined calves, close to bursting out of the black tights. Regardless of current fashion that put men in colorful costume, Thomas always wore black.

"Thomas," Xavier greeted him, a childish grin spreading across his face.

"Xavier." Thomas gripped his shoulders, and they kissed on the cheek. When Thomas pecked Xavier's left cheek, however, he held the priest close to him, his lips lingering longer than they should. It was maddening.

"I'm glad you came," Xavier said, pulling away.

"I thought we agreed not to doubt that anymore," Thomas said as Xavier waited for him to sit on one end of the bench before sitting on the other. Thomas slid over to the middle.

"You look troubled," Thomas said.

The abrupt comment startled Xavier. "It's my family," he mumbled. "I worry about them. Constantly. Michel won't listen to me, regarding Catherine. I calmed him enough for now, though."

"How did he treat you?"

"Nothing unusual. Just the same complaint about my serving this parish. Our parting was bitter, again."

"Forget about your brother. You make a wonderful priest right here."

"Thank you." Xavier relaxed in the solid comfort he derived from Thomas.

"Is that all?" Thomas asked.

"Really, yes. Well, I can't stop thinking about them, I mean—"

Thomas reached up and placed two fingers on Xavier's lips. "Stop. Just tell me."

"I wish *you'd* tell me more, though. We always dwell on me."

"I told you I lead a dull life. But I'll bargain with you. You confess what plagues you, tell me the honest truth, and I'll divulge the one thing that haunts me."

"Agreed," Xavier said, surprised and intrigued. Still, he paused a moment before continuing. "I always feel guilty. I worry about Michel and Catherine, but I don't think about them as often as I should. They've always bickered. Always. When I'm around them, I try to stop it, but when I leave, I put them behind me. I should do more. I shouldn't be able to forget their quarrels with so little thought."

"It sounds natural to me," Thomas answered. "Maybe I don't understand guilt, but you can't fret about it every waking moment. That won't help anybody."

"But I become selfish, just thinking about things that I want. Even when I'm serving my congregants, I have a hard time getting away from my private desires and hopes."

"Do you believe that you worry about yourself more than anybody else?" Thomas stared at him in disbelief. "You never seem to give yourself time. You should spend *more* time on yourself. You talk about Catherine and Michel a lot but never share your desires."

"It's my curse, I suppose. It's your turn now. You promised. What's bothering you?"

Thomas leaned closer, mere inches from Xavier's face, and whispered. "May I confess?"

Xavier's heart pounded. "Please, tell me."

Thomas strained closer, their lips nearly touching. "I want you," he whispered. "I want to feel your lips, your entire body."

Xavier jumped off the bench as if struck by lightning. He looked around to see if anyone else might have seen as he battled the excitement welling within. He turned to see that Thomas stood, calm as ever.

"Did I offend you?"

"No. I mean—I only—" It was useless. Xavier fought with every ounce of strength not to go to Thomas and finish what he'd started, to feel those masculine lips smash against his, to explore that enticing mouth with his tongue. Instead, he turned his head to the ground and struggled just to whisper. "I can't."

Thomas again stood behind him. "I understand." He placed his hand on Xavier's back. "It's your vows. Your dedication to the church is impressive."

"I do it for them." Xavier motioned toward his parish. "They count on me to uphold what the church teaches. Those who remain need to see the truth of what I teach. If I can't obey the laws, how can I expect them to?"

"Why should the laws imprison you?"

"Somehow you knew from the beginning about these tragic longings within me. You test them more than ever."

"So, you *do* feel the same way?"

"You know I do."

"Listen to me. Stop shaking. I won't hurt you."

Xavier believed Thomas and moved closer. They sat again on the bench, still in intimate proximity. "I understand how you feel, even if I don't agree," Thomas continued. "I don't live with a fear of some unknown force that dictates arbitrary rules. Just promise me this, that you'll keep your mind open. I'm not going anywhere. I love you. I long for you. And if you ever change your mind, if ever this church casts you aside, I'll catch you."

Xavier lost himself in Thomas's seduction, but could never abandon those he served. They reached an impasse and fell into a comfortable silence. Xavier was about to mumble an apology when he saw a shadow move in the bushes, causing him to tense up.

Xavier almost spoke when the figure started toward them with a knife. Before the attacker reached the bench, however, Thomas dashed across the yard and knocked the vagrant to the ground. Xavier rubbed his eyes in disbelief. Impossible. Thomas could not have covered that distance so fast. Xavier rose to his feet, confused.

A few feet away, the man screamed in agony as Thomas hovered over him. Thomas had ripped the knife out of his hand and grabbed the man's throat, and now he clenched his jaw and scowled. Xavier stood paralyzed and speechless.

"You'd attack a priest? You're sick. I should kill you."

The man cowered beneath Thomas.

"Thomas, please." Xavier came to his senses and hurried forward to place his hand on Thomas's shoulder.

The intruder's arm hung loosely at his side and at a strange angle, broken, perhaps by Thomas. Thomas's demeanor softened and he seemed embarrassed, so he released the man, took a step backward, and then glanced away from Xavier.

Xavier knelt next to the man, who breathed heavily, in obvious pain.

"If you need food or money, just knock on the door," Xavier said.

The man relaxed a little but crawled away from the priest. "Father, forgive me. Oh, please let me live. Oh, please." He scrambled to his feet and stumbled away.

"You need a doctor. Wait!" Xavier tried to get him to stay, but he ran down the street. On the next block, he screamed with fear, clutched his arm, and raced around a corner.

Thomas stood without making a sound a few feet away. "He would have killed us."

"I don't think he meant to murder." He turned to Thomas. "What did you do to him? Would you have killed him?"

"If he threatened me, yes. If he came after you, absolutely. He's of no use to the humanity you love. He's a murderer, a fiend who attacks without provocation."

"Maybe compassion could change him," Xavier said. "Did you break his arm?"

"Yes," Thomas said, unnerving Xavier with his calm. "His arm snapped. He wasn't going to whimper away until I controlled the knife and him."

Xavier sighed and walked toward the church, his mind in total chaos. "I need to lie down."

"Is that it, then? Or may I return tomorrow?"

Xavier nodded, but walked inside and closed the door.

Part II: The Vampire

Eight: Vampiric Love

5 JUNE 1789

Thomas had to test the ethic, even though he tried to uphold it. Even after less than a month, his love for Xavier threatened to consume him. He needed to act. Anthony had warned him that his impatience would put him into dangerous and unethical situations. Thomas agreed, but with Xavier, it had become too difficult.

So that night, he determined to test the limits of the rules. Since first meeting her a week earlier, Thomas had spent a couple of evenings in Catherine's company with Xavier. He preferred having Xavier all to himself, but Xavier could never abandon his sister, so they compromised with a couple of visits per week. Thomas liked going to the house, especially since Michel seldom appeared to quarrel with his siblings, and he found Catherine charming, much like himself in her zest for life and obsessive protection of Xavier.

Alone, Thomas walked up the steps of the enormous Saint-Laurent house.

"Thomas," came Catherine's voice from above.

He looked up, eschewing a knock.

"Come in," she implored. "Don't wait for the slow servants."

Thomas entered and walked through the halls and onto the gigantic stone porch that overlooked Rue St. Denis. The Seine's cool breeze felt better and better as the summer's heat crept upon them. After joining Catherine on the balcony, Thomas kissed her and smiled.

"Where's Xavier? You mean you two aren't attached at the hip?"

"Don't worry. I'm meeting him later," Thomas said.

"I just heard the most interesting news," Catherine announced. "The dauphin has died." Thomas cared nothing about the news, but she continued, "The king's son, Thomas. He just died. It has sent Louis into such a depression he can't function. If he refuses to do anything, everyone fears the riots will increase, and then, who knows? Maybe we'll move toward democracy after all." Her eyes sparkled with excitement.

"You and Xavier might be the only French aristocrats I know who don't entirely support the monarchy," Thomas said.

Catherine laughed and patted him on the chest. "You have strong muscles." She let her hand linger on him. "Speaking of Xavier, why on earth did you come alone?" As she asked, her demeanor changed to cautious. She yanked her hand off his chest before backing away with a recognition. Catherine looked around, her eyes growing wider. "What are you?" she whispered. "What do you want from us?"

"Catherine, I'll never harm you." Thomas held up his hands in surrender. "I would never hurt you. You don't understand. Let me explain."

"What are you?" She backed farther away until she clutched the balcony railing and tensed. "You're not alive. And you're pale. Your heart—it doesn't beat? I couldn't feel it beating."

Thomas bowed his head. "Yes. Most would call me a vampire."

Catherine gasped and touched her throat reflexively.

"Please listen to me. I'll never hurt you. I've meant everything you've ever heard me say."

"You won't hurt me?" Her shoulders sagged a bit, though she still clung to the stone railing.

"Never." He walked closer.

"Oh, my God. It's Xavier," she said in hushed tones. "You want to take Xavier, don't you? Why him? Why—"

"No, you don't understand. Let me explain, please. I'd never hurt Xavier, either."

"Then why are you here?"

Thomas paused. "I love him. Desperately. In fact, that's why I came to see you alone tonight."

Catherine measured him with a harsh glare.

"Catherine, listen. I'd risk a thousand deaths for him. I'd relinquish immortality to lie with him for even one night."

"I believe you," Catherine said but continued her icy stare. "You seem like a good person, or whatever you call yourself. And I've known since I met you about your feelings for my brother. I even wanted you two to stay together. I wanted Xavier to flee the church and go with you. He deserves it.

"When Xavier was just coming of age, before society taught him to check himself, he told me about his dreams of spending his life with a man. One day, he just stopped, as if the dream disappeared. And now it just haunts him. He entered the priesthood to escape it. When I saw you two together, I thought he could realize his dream." As she talked, her shoulders relaxed, her posture lost its tension. "I don't know what to feel right now. I need to know more. Tell me what you are."

VAMPIRE NATURE

Catherine's mind buzzed between fascination, shock, and yet predictability. The minute Thomas had arrived alone, she knew he came to discuss his relationship with Xavier. But she had never anticipated discovering something inhuman.

It had terrified her at first, leading her to inch over to the ledge and contemplate leaping off the balcony. Gradually, she came to accept his pleas for understanding, especially as she relaxed and thought about his obvious love for Xavier.

Still, her mind raced between apprehension and acceptance; between dread and desire to learn everything possible about such a creature.

"So," she said, "may I ask you some questions? Are you a vampire?"

"Yes. I subsist on human blood. That's the brutal reality."

"But you won't hurt him?" She glared at him.

"Legend portrays all vampires as sinister beings who lurk in shadows, killing innocents because we're condemned by God for drinking some vile blood. I don't fit that category, nor does my maker. I kill only to sustain myself, and never arbitrarily. I kill degenerates. I hunt those whom the world no longer needs."

Catherine could not stifle a giggle, in part because he humored her and also to relieve the tension.

"Something funny?" he asked with a raised brow.

"I never believed that vampires existed. Then, when you told me, I acted like a silly zealot, assuming that you came from hell to hurt me." Her anxiety diminished. She laughed more forcefully, which made Thomas grin. "Now, I just want to learn more."

"Such as?" he asked.

"Can you die? Stakes? Cutting off your head?"

"Of course." Thomas laughed. "But not with a stake. Something may stun us for a moment, but vampires heal fast to their former strength, so a stake becomes a minor annoyance. And I don't like to contemplate someone chopping off my head. It'd take more energy, but our body would heal this, too."

"What about garlic?"

"It gives me bad breath."

"Crucifixes? Holy Water? Religious relics?" she asked.

"Did you forget? Who have I spent the last month with?"

That was funnier than anything. She walked to a bench and sat down, holding her side from laughter. He walked everywhere with Xavier, and her brother always wore his cross. Thankfully, Thomas laughed, too.

"If it weren't Xavier, I'd laugh even harder that you picked a priest, of all people."

"I suppose it's ironic, but I think religion trifling. It brainwashes the masses and makes them pawns to the existing powers."

"Oh, I agree. But you don't think such awful things of Xavier, do you?"

"He defies the norms."

"Are you a bat?"

Thomas let out a loud laugh. "No. I can't change into any animals."

"You must be very strong," Catherine said.

"Upon death, the vampire body is chiseled into its finest form. My hair is this length forever."

"Are you a savage?" Catherine lowered her eyes, embarrassed. "I'm sorry."

"I've heard much worse. I do have Indian blood."

"Sex?"

Thomas reddened. "I'm fully capable of sexual interactions."

She giggled. Thomas remained the man she'd originally met: endearing, protective, charming, and funny. Still, the killing worried her. "Tell me about the blood."

"I drink it to nourish myself. I need it, though not every night. As the blood passes through my mouth, I see the history of that person in my mind."

"Yet you're so human."

"I *was* human once. And I still have every emotion that plagued me before death. I'm essentially the same man as before the transformation."

"I suppose that brings us to Xavier," Catherine said. "Is that what you want? I don't want you to hurt him."

"I've heard of vampire couples that have been together for hundreds of years. That's what I want."

Catherine was unsure how to respond. She liked Thomas, but could she relinquish Xavier to him? Then again, was it her choice?

"I've never lied about my feelings for Xavier," Thomas continued.

"I believe you. But you have to understand that I raised him. He was always innocent, as pure as he is now." Then Catherine laughed. "It is ironic that you fell in love with a priest. And one who abides by all of the church's ridiculous rules. But he doesn't always agree with them, and that's your chance."

Thomas sighed. "That's why I came to you. I want to tell him the truth, but he can't even acknowledge his attraction to me. So if he learned about my true nature..."

Catherine frowned. "I wanted Xavier to run off with you, but that very thought scares him to death. And that's without your being a vampire. What is your goal, here? What's your scheme with Xavier?"

Thomas blanched, her words sounded so much more cold and calculating than anything in his heart. "Vampires mate for life, forever if possible, just like humans. Even those of us who prefer the same sex. And the process of transforming a human to vampire takes a lot of time and care, not to mention approval." Thomas grew silent, choosing his words with care as he applied them to Xavier. "I'm not sure what I'm asking him. Certainly nothing beyond his own will. What do you want me to say? I came to you for help. I'm not sure how to handle his blend of strict Catholicism, the priesthood, and some pagan, individualistic ideas. I think I know him well, but he won't release his emotions." *He's locked tight. And I want the key.*

"Thomas, he loves you. He hides behind the church, and guilt controls him, but his actions betray him. He longs to be with you." She paused. "However, he's sensitive. The church confuses him because it offers absolutes that conflict with his instincts to trust the goodness within people. He channels his passion for helping others through Catholicism but recognizes when the church harms people, yet he can't turn that intellect on himself. He thinks he has to abide by every rule."

"He does that all the time," Thomas agreed. "He disregards papal teaching when he thinks that it leaves out the poor. He even called the pope ludicrous. But when it comes to him, he won't use the same standard."

"He's believed that for many years, even before he entered the monastery. I don't mean to be melodramatic, but you bring to him a battle between good and evil and want him to apply it to himself, something he's always resisted. He didn't become a priest because of his faith. He entered the priesthood to hide from himself."

Thomas frowned and his shoulders slumped toward the ground. "So there's no hope?"

"I didn't mean to imply that," she said gently. "I've always feared that it might destroy him when something forces him to see reality. Maybe you can save him, but he won't be able to cope with his sexuality and vampires at the same time."

Thomas sighed. "But he may hate me even more if I lead him away from the church and then he can't accept—" Thomas stopped, too frightened to finish.

"Move with deliberate speed. It looks like a big enough task to get him into bed." She winked.

"Catherine!" Thomas laughed, thankful that she lightened the mood.

"Do you think that just because women hide behind some constructed gentility that such thoughts never enter our minds?"

"Do I have your permission, then?" he asked.

"It's not mine to give. You need Xavier's permission. I do have one more request."

"Please."

"Keep me informed."

"Of course." Thomas stood to leave and then hesitated. "Thank you, Catherine."

Nine: The Sexuality Dance

6 JUNE 1789

Darkness enveloped Paris as Thomas hurried along, afraid his conversation with Catherine took too long and kept him from his beloved curé. Although lamps illuminated many of the streets, the fog rolled off the river and reduced the lights to glowing embers. And the narrower passages between older residential dwellings and rows of salons had no light posts. Thomas saw well with his undead eyes, but the darkness added to Paris's mystery.

He passed by one street and then halted when he spied a vagrant hovering in the corner. Feeding. When hungry, he could smell the blood running through a human's veins from afar. Thomas walked toward the individual to ascertain whether or not he was fair game.

The man, in his thirties, lay sound asleep on the sidewalk against a wall. He was filthy, and the bottle next to him indicated, drunk. Thomas leaned toward the man, who made no move as he slept. A prime target.

Without more thought, Thomas ripped the man's shirt off, gripped him by the neck, lifted him an inch off the ground, and sank his teeth into the man's bicep, happy to find at least one patch of semi-clean skin where the shirt covered his arm. As the blood flowed down his throat, though, Thomas almost dropped the man. Nothing. No sign of evil. No harm done to anyone.

But Thomas brought death, anyway, as a mercy killing. He never contemplated such an act before, but seeing the man's history in the blood propelled him to do it. He suffered from extreme poverty and from diseases that pained him. He drank to forget. His family had cast him out, society shunned him. He begged people for death. He often ventured into dangerous areas and picked fights with the hope of a swift execution or harbored thoughts of jumping off bridges but could never bring himself to a suicide. The deed done, and with the blood reviving him, Thomas ran the rest of the way to the church, where Xavier sat writing at an upstairs table. Ah, his beautiful priest, and just like that, memories of the man he killed faded into the past.

Xavier noticed Thomas after he'd entered the garden, jumped from his chair, and ran downstairs. He came outside and greeted Thomas here he waited.

"I thought you wouldn't come this evening."

"I had other pressing matters. I'd have left you to sleep, but I saw Catherine and she indicated that you often stay up late Saturday night."

"I was afraid I angered you the other night and chased you away."

"Stop it. I told you I won't just disappear. May I enter?"

"Of course." Xavier stepped aside and ushered Thomas into the church. "Why did you go to Catherine?"

Thomas paused, regretting that he went to Catherine in his desperation. What if she told Xavier? Too late. He had once again violated the ethic and risked everything in his quest for Xavier.

"I needed advice about matters she can help me with here in Paris."

"Business? She knows more than you'd expect."

They snuck through the back of the sanctuary and up the stairs to Xavier's quarters, because when they met later, Xavier took Thomas to his rooms to avoid being seen by unwelcoming eyes. Xavier fell onto his bed and, as usual, waited for Thomas to begin. He looked adorable as he propped his head in his hands and smiled like a damsel in love.

Thomas sat down next to him. "Why are you still awake?"

"It takes me a long time to prepare for Sunday mass. Sometimes, like today, I finish early. I still stay up, though, and read. And what brings you at this late hour?"

"I never need a reason—" He moved closer. "—but I do have something to tell you."

"What?" Xavier's hand trembled as he sat upright and tucked his knees beneath his chin. He wore a pair of pants and white shirt, nothing else, and his thin frame and slight but enticing musculature showed through.

"You already know. The other night, I tried to kiss you. We pretended that it never happened. We discuss everything else constantly, but this we ignore. You don't need to say anything, but I have to say this: I love you, Abbé. It's unlike anything I've ever felt. I love every minute with you and swoon when I look into your eyes. You believe the church's teaching about sodomy. I don't. I'm not forcing anything on you. I just wanted you to know where I stood."

Total silence. Thomas held his breath, wondering if perhaps he had gone too far.

"Thomas, you know—at least I think you know—oh..." Xavier fumbled with his toes. He whispered, Thomas realized in prayer, and then blurted, "You know I feel the same. I love you, too. But I can't defy God. I can't serve my parish if I can't abide by the faith I proclaim. Please understand. It's not you. And it would help, if, well, if we couldn't mention it again."

"I understand. Forget it. Let's change the subject," Thomas said. "Your understanding of Catholicism fascinates me. You adhere to all of its laws and precepts to the letter in your life, yet you defy the rules as they pertain to your parish. Why is there a difference?"

"I vowed to obey the Lord. Don't misunderstand me; I sin all the time. But I must work to remain true to my vows. People will sin, and priests need to help them or even help other priests when we fail. If I fall too far from a true path, how can I expect to lead them back to it?"

Amazing innocence, but it hid a sadness. They drifted through more theological topics, and then Xavier told Thomas about his sermon. Thomas basked in yet another night with the man of his dreams and recognized the battle ahead of him, but would risk everything if even a small chance existed for them, and Xavier's proclamation of love offered hope.

MARIA'S CONFESSION

Xavier smiled as Maria and he walked down the narrow street, connecting with the people of the parish but also able to spend time together on a Sunday afternoon.

"You brought your basket again." Xavier pointed to it. "I thought I convinced you that you needed a bigger one to feed all these people."

"I've had this basket forever." Maria's plump cheeks reddened as she grinned back.

"It's too small. Remember the day I met you, when bread fell all over the ground? I had to help you before the birds got more than the people."

"See? Without this small basket, we may not have met and continued this tradition."

Maria and Xavier continued on their way, enjoying the conversation and gossiping about church politics. They stopped only long enough to greet someone.

At last, on a deserted street, Maria focused her clear gaze on him. "Abbé, something's bothering you."

He sighed. "I have a problem that defies the church."

"Why don't you go to confession? That's what you suggest to us."

"This can never enter the confessional. We keep things from our colleagues for good reason."

"What is it?" she pressed.

Xavier hesitated. "It might defrock me. But it won't go away."

"I'll never betray you."

"I have impure thoughts," Xavier admitted in a rush.

"Sex?" She looked at him, eyes wide. "This is about sex?"

"Well, yes."

"Just say it. I think I already know, anyway."

"I love him. The man you found me with that night in the garden. I've the most sinful longings for him. I pray every day for strength and mercy, but the passion only increases."

Maria chuckled and sat on a bench. She was sweating profusely and breathing heavily from walking so fast. "Is that it? Stop fretting so much. Do you think that you're the only one in the church struggling with this? You'd be surprised what goes on in this church."

"What?" Xavier's heart pounded.

"Do you think the nuns around you are blind? I know about your fellow priests who took a vow of chastity that doesn't seem to apply to them."

"And do you feel this way?"

"Toward men? Heaven's no." Maria winked at him. "But, yes. You've entered a very secretive world, that's all, one that's kept hidden. I know that it goes against our beliefs. But I also know that we all sin, and that this, which is about love, is a smaller sin."

"Do you have a particular lover?"

"More than one."

He gaped at her.

"Not many, but more than one and I consider all of them my girls."

More than one? His mind reeled. "I don't think I could have more than one. I love Thomas. For me, it's about my passion for *him*."

"Promise never to tell him or anyone else about this. This is a private matter, within the church."

"But you have multiple lovers."

"Within the church," Maria stressed each syllable for emphasis before she stopped and looked at a family coming toward them. "Good Lord. We forgot the Gustavs—we'll talk later. But you must keep this in the church. Put this Thomas out of your mind." With that, Maria transformed into her professional self.

Xavier, on the other hand, had a difficult time hiding his confusion. Her little fiefdom of nuns and priests, running around in the dark, held no allure. True, he had seen that behavior in seminary a hundred times and heard the rumors about priests still engaged in it. Xavier had resisted such temptation, but Thomas changed his heart.

Thankfully, the Gustavs distracted him. He and Maria had to administer a baptism that the rest of the church refused because the mother became pregnant prior to marriage. They joked that they had a hidden church within the Catholic Church. Xavier could immerse himself in becoming a bridge between the church and his people in order to forget his own anguished love.

Ten: Marcel and Catherine

8 JUNE 1789

Michel's note that morning sent Catherine into a flurry of preparations when he announced his imminent arrival and required a room. He also hinted that things had escalated between the Estates General and king, which prompted the army's mobilization, and thus required that she protect the family legacy by hiding heirlooms in secret rooms, passages, and cellars, as well as to move their financial assets out of France.

As she raced around a corner, she almost ran into the head butler. "You frightened me."

"Sorry, Madame," he answered.

"What is it?" she asked, seeing his expression.

"Mr. André is here to see you."

"Blast. I forgot." She smoothed her hair as she walked down the stairs into the entry hall. "Marcel, I forgot our appointment. Please come in." She pulled him into the parlor and pushed him into a chair.

"Catherine, slow down," he ordered. "What are you busy with?"

"Michel's coming home soon."

"Oh, joy," Marcel drawled. "I can't wait to see him again."

She ignored his comment. "Would you like something to drink?"

"I'd love a glass of wine, but I refuse to drink alone. Join me."

She poured wine and handed him a glass.

"I see that you've moved a few things," he said and pointed across the room.

She looked but saw nothing unusual, so turned back to him. "No, nothing in here." She took a sip of wine and noticed that it bubbled in an abnormal way but tasted delightful. Her head swam. "So, what brought you today?" she asked, feeling giddy and aroused.

"Nothing in particular. I had business in the area." Marcel stood, came toward her, and hovered, creating an indescribable thrill.

She leaned closer to him. "I love your visits. But you seem agitated."

"A customer refused to pay for goods. It was the second time. I'm stuck with these items in my shop. They're dreadful. No one else will ever buy them, and so he saddles me with their uselessness. I warned him that this time I wouldn't take kindly to his dumping stuffed bats and the like on me. So I cursed—"

"Dead bats? How odd. And what did you mean by cursed?"

Marcel smiled too sweetly. "Nothing to worry about. If you must know, I have certain connections in the Americas. They traffic in a religion particular to that area. Voodoo. Things like bats and snakes play a part in their rituals, but they also become a novelty among Frenchmen."

"That's repulsive," Catherine said, wrinkling her nose and imagining a stuffed bat in the parlor.

"Well, they're not very charming to hang about the house, I agree."

"But you haven't answered my question. What did you mean by curse?" A spike of warning pierced through the little fog in her brain. "Do you practice this magic?"

He waved to dismiss the idea. "I dabble in it."

"And the curse?"

"It was just an expression. I went to collect my money."

"Well, do me one favor. Don't tell Xavier about this hobby."

"If I never had to see either of your meddling brothers again, that'd be fine."

She frowned, irritated. "You could try harder to get along with them, Xavier most of all. He means a lot to me."

Marcel paced the room as if plagued.

"Michel is a nuisance," he finally said.

"Did you threaten him? He says that you did."

"He lies just to try to drive a wedge between us."

"Let me handle him."

"Fine, but you'd best watch the little abbé too. You trust him too easily."

"Marcel, are you jealous? You're wrong about Xavier."

"If he were so good, he wouldn't bring that vile Thomas into your home. They're both disgusting."

"Enough. That's enough of your ranting."

She escorted him to the door and he followed slowly, but she regretted her tone the second she closed the door. She raced through the house and onto the balcony. He had only reached the bottom of the steps when she called to him.

"Marcel, Marcel! Wait. Forgive me?"

He looked up at her, smiling, but the gesture almost chilled her. "Of course. I feel churlish today. I'll come by when I feel better again."

Eleven: Love's Anguish

12 JUNE 1789

As always, by the end of their nights together, the darkness surrounded Thomas and Xavier. Xavier had taken Thomas to dine with Catherine, after which the two walked the bustling streets, talking about a thousand unimportant things.

Thomas avoided mention of their relationship, though he often wanted to throw Xavier against the wall and kiss him until he submitted. Instead, their conversation turned to religion.

"Sometimes our theological conversations make me uncomfortable," Thomas said.

"Why?"

"You talk about helping other people, but what about helping *you*?" He glanced at Xavier.

"Nothing fulfills me more than seeing them happy. I'm called to serve them."

"Abbé, you never even give yourself so much as a glance. You can't always be a martyr and sacrifice your whole life for others. What about your desires?"

Xavier slowed his pace and Thomas saw his tears. His heart broke, so he wrapped his arm around the curé and cursed himself for pressing him.

"I upset you," Xavier whispered.

"Relax."

"I can't worry about myself. I don't know how to change. I try to make you happy. I thought that spending my time with you *was* self-indulging."

"Xavier, listen to me." Thomas gave him a light squeeze. "It *is* a way, and of course you're trying. Just keep thinking about it." Thomas then held Xavier, who allowed the embrace. "Forgive me for causing you anguish. I'm just concerned about you. I'm afraid that your lofty view of humanity will some day break your heart."

"But it's true," Xavier said.

"That's what concerns me. There are people who will harm others for no reason, who will take advantage of your good will for their gain. The other night, did you think that man intended to steal food? That you could bring him into the church and change him after he drew a knife on us?"

"*Yes.*"

Thomas sighed in frustration. "But he wanted to kill us."

"Why does that make him evil?" Xavier retorted, stubborn.

Thomas rolled his eyes. "Of course, you're right, why would murder be evil? This is what I mean. You place humanity on an impossible pedestal."

Xavier wept again, saying nothing.

"Enough for tonight," Thomas relented. He led them silently back to the church and stopped outside the door, still angry. "I'll see you tomorrow." With that, Thomas motioned Xavier through the door and left, refusing to even turn and look at the priest as he fought to control his temper.

He headed to the river and watched the rats and people. Across the way, an army general payed for sex. Fascinating. With his power and wealth, that man could have sex with almost anyone he chose and in virtually any location. Yet he hovered under a dirty bridge with an average maiden, exposing himself to the world. Amusing.

Around a bend, Thomas came upon a troop of boys in the shadows. One of them, a teenager, solicited him when he came close, with a false earnestness about his cherubic little face and bright blue eyes. He wore tattered clothes but was bathed to please his patrons.

"I'm not interested," Thomas said, brushing him off. But the boy persisted.

His beauty enchanted Thomas, but he was not game for a kill, or at least he gave off no evil vibe. Still, they slid behind a building and the young one nuzzled up to Thomas. His lips on Thomas's neck felt divine as Thomas reached and rubbed his tight ass.

But when Xavier popped into his head, he shoved the boy from him and flung a pile of money his way. "Here. It's not you."

The youth looked hurt and alarmed, so Thomas took out more money and handed it to him.

He clutched him by the shoulders and looked into his eyes. "Use this for a new life. Get away from this." Without looking back, Thomas raced to his flat.

Had that encounter been treason against their love? Xavier and he had never discussed the matter and Xavier's refusal seemed to grant permission, but regret gnawed at Thomas.

Thomas marched into his flat and ripped off his clothes. They suffocated him, especially the undergarments since Xavier sent his passion into overdrive. He opened his desk, grabbed a quill, and wrote at a furious speed.

My dearest Anthony,

I write in utter dismay.

I have fallen in love. As you feared, as you warned me, I am not one to wander the earth alone for centuries upon centuries. I need a companion. You wanted me to wait, to learn about myself and my powers, and I intended to follow your advice, but then he crossed my path. Fate has interfered with your carefully laid plans.

I worry about him daily and want him to follow me as I once followed you. Don't worry. We are more compatible as a couple than you and I ever were. But he confounds me because he is a priest and will not give in to physical passion. I need to hear your thoughts. What would you do?

Anthony, no scolding. No more rules. I am in love, but things have reached an impasse.

Yours forever in the blissful darkness, Thomas Lord

Thomas sealed the letter and put it outside his room for delivery to London. Though early, Thomas remained in the flat the entire night. He read and organized financial matters, wrote a series of letters to his men in New York, then walked around his rooms and wondered what it would be like to share them with Xavier, his thoughts suffused with sadness and turmoil.

Twelve: The Dawn of Revolution

15 JUNE 1789

The noon sun shone brightly, so Catherine had lunch served on the patio in part because of the warmth and also because the light's brilliance helped her ignore Michel, who sat across from her and next to Xavier.

Catherine bristled when Michel got right to the point. "I came with news from the king."

"What is it?" she asked, tense.

Michel, as always with state secrets, looked around to see who listened, while Xavier sat in his typical silent contemplation.

"I've returned to Paris with a very small advance party of soldiers from the royal army," Michel said. "We're blending into the crowds undetected because the rioting has increased and they're printing treasonous libel against the king. We've come to assess the climate in preparation for a vast troop movement into the city. The monarchy has spies everywhere. More than anything, I want you to be safe."

"Fascinating," Catherine said.

Michel glared at her. "I'm not sure I would use those words. It's terrifying. This could lead to the crumbling of France. Louis may fall."

"But you won't follow him if it injures the people with questioning it?" Catherine pushed.

"I protect everyone's interests, but if their instability threatens the government, it risks everyone in the kingdom, not just Louis. It even threatens the very people who rebel."

Catherine rolled her eyes. "For God's sake, Michel, do you think the citizens are that stupid? Maybe Louis is the stupid one."

"This talk, if anyone heard—"

Xavier cut his brother off. "Perhaps both of you have good points."

Michel nodded but clenched his jaw. "If Catherine keeps running about Paris, talking about women voting and democracy, it could endanger both of you."

Catherine's temper boiled and Xavier jumped out of his chair. He stormed out of the room and down the hall. Since the patio overlooked the front street, she went over and saw him running down the front steps.

"Michel, you're blinded. You suffer from your obedience to everything that Louis or the military demands of you. You follow orders without thinking. Father instructed us to serve the king, and I do the best I can. But he also urged us to think, especially about the people." She measured her tone. "Perhaps it's time to take a stand. Instead of obeying Louis's orders, you should ponder why the rioting began in the first place."

He scowled. "Listen to your rambling—is this about your wanting to open a salon? And did you ever try to see my position? I'm commissioned in His Majesty's Army."

"This goes well beyond orders and laws. This is about your attitude since Father died, your distorted sense of obligation. For one, you've exaggerated your responsibility to Xavier and me. Did you talk to Xavier again about leaving his church?"

Michel shrugged and stood. "Yes."

"How could you?" Catherine jumped out of her chair to level her gaze on his. "We should praise him. Instead, you badger him and make him feel guilty. It makes me sick. I can handle the nonsense that you engage in with me, but how do you justify making Xavier feel guilty?"

Michel backed away. "I know we agreed to leave Xavier alone. I know how it hurts him. I worry about your safety too much—yours and Xavier's. It's not easy. I love you both."

"Then try harder to think about how your words and actions affect us."

"I think about it all the time," he said to defend himself. "I love you. I always have loved you and Xavier. I forget to compliment you on handling our affairs with such determination and grace. You've done even better than our father."

"And all of that from a woman."

"I never said that."

"But you implied it."

"Give me time, please. I'm just worried for your safety. Things are more heated."

She walked to the patio's edge and looked down at the quiet street and people going about their business, which hardly betrayed the undercurrent of unrest that fomented. Then Jérémie approached, perhaps for one of the frequent visits she so enjoyed. As she watched him ascend the steps and the servants invite him in, she returned to Michel.

"Xavier and I love you too. But you allowed Father's death to change you too much. Relax and be the Michel we knew growing up."

"Reprimanding your brother again?" Jérémie asked as he entered.

"Hello, Jérémie." Catherine swept across the porch, her arms outstretched for a hug. "I was giving Michel further instructions, though he doesn't listen."

"I *do* listen," Michel countered.

"You're too hard on your brother," Jérémie said, as he wrapped his arms around her. "He tries his best."

"I'll be nicer, so long as he doesn't bring up marriage again," Catherine said as a final peace offering. Michel withdrew and said nothing. Jérémie, too, retreated and lapsed into silence. Catherine shook her head. Strange, these two men, with their secrets and inhibitions.

JÉRÉMIE AND MICHEL

Xavier returned later that day for afternoon tea, after fleeing for a bit to let the heated exchange between Catherine and Michel fade away. Thankfully, Jérémie had joined them, because his presence softened some of his sibling's arguments. Tea went well, with good conversation and no outbursts, leaving him at peace until Michel pulled him aside to talk alone.

"I need your help," his brother whispered. "Jérémie is suffering."

"What can I do?"

"If I speak with him, will you conceal yourself to listen to how he reacts?"

Xavier blanched. "Spying?"

"He forbids me to tell anyone about his feelings for Catherine. He's embarrassed. But I need your guidance."

"Jérémie could speak with her and heal all these wounds."

"He won't. Please, Xavier, for me?" Michel implored.

Xavier nodded with reluctance as Michel explained where to hide.

Immediately after Catherine whisked away, Xavier pretended to follow, but instead retired to the parlor window just inside the balcony and sat on a fainting couch.

"Is there anything that I can do?" Michel asked Jérémie.

"I've dreamed of making Catherine happy my entire life," Jérémie answered. "Then in one moment, my world collapsed. There's nothing anyone can do." He sounded hopeless.

"But you still come to see her," Michel pointed out.

"She relies on our friendship."

"You misunderstood her reaction. Catherine's quarrel is with me, not you. You can't allow my mistake to ruin the rest of your life."

"Whatever chance existed for a solution vanished when she announced her engagement. And I don't blame you. It's my fault."

Xavier heard Jérémie choke back tears and his heart went out to him.

"I think it's worth one more try," Michel coaxed. "She gets angry at me, but listens to you and Xavier, even when she disagrees."

"I won't subject myself to that humiliation."

"She'd never do that to you."

"Don't you see?" Jérémie half-yelled. "I can't."

That ended the conversation. To save Jérémie's pride, Xavier made a commotion about returning to the porch. Both men smiled and Jérémie changed the subject, pretending to discuss Paris.

"Do you really think that it requires troops?" Jérémie asked Michel.

"Nothing has stopped the rioting so far. I meant to tell you and Xavier, by the way, to be careful. Remember that the king has spies everywhere."

Jérémie and Xavier nodded and smiled. Neither had ever inclined toward political involvement, and Michel finally got the inside joke between them. As the three men relaxed, Michel's next suggestion caught Xavier off guard.

"I've one other request, Jérémie," Michel said. "Would you be willing to move into the house with Catherine in a guardian's capacity? For her safety?"

Xavier glared at his brother. Michel had manipulated Jérémie into a situation where the poor man could not bow out without revealing the truth to Xavier that he worked so hard to hide.

"Michel, I—let me think about it. Perhaps her fiancé will want the duty of protecting her. I think it best if I stay away unless she requests my services. Speaking of which, I must return to my family." He made a show of glancing at the sky, as if gauging how late it was.

Xavier stood and embraced Jérémie, perhaps trying too hard. He and Michel escorted Jérémie to the door, and after his departure, Xavier whipped around and stared at his brother.

"How could you do that to him?"

"I only want to help them. Maybe I should get rid of Marcel instead."

"Michel!" Xavier threw up his hands. "You need to back away. Leave them alone. You know that I'd love to see them marry as much as you, but no good will come from our continued interference."

"Is that you two? Still?" Catherine called out as she marched into the room. "I'm having dinner served on the porch."

Xavier smiled and nodded. "Shall we?" He motioned them to proceed and he followed behind, contemplating Michel's behavior.

Thirteen: Dear Anthony

18 JUNE 1789

Thomas stood alone in his flat. He used to love that time of night, when all the world slept and he returned to his quarters to think about what he had seen and done that evening. It relaxed him. He forgot about being a vampire, forgot about his strength, his problems, and reflected on another day gone.

Since his argument with Xavier, however, he detested these quiet hours and instead brooded. Thomas continued to visit his abbé every night, and their conversations resumed as usual. Indeed, neither had the bravery to bring up the argument. So they pretended that nothing had happened, yet the tension floated thickly in the air.

But Thomas wanted to talk about it and come to some settlement. Dancing around their intimacy became harder for him because, even with the strain, he grew fonder and fonder of the priest. It took every ounce of patience to keep from grabbing Xavier in his arms and not letting go until the abbé admitted and accepted their love.

Thomas paced back and forth in front of the window as moonlight glistened off the Seine, a time when anger welled in him beyond control. True, he regretted his actions of two nights before, when he'd flown out the window and ruthlessly murdered the first two criminals that crossed his path. Afterward, he had promised to cage himself in his flat after he left Xavier to avoid such occurrences.

Still, he wanted to blast through the window and rip off the head of the next human who dared so much as glance at him, guilty or not of any crime. He gripped his own head to gain control of his emotions.

Anthony. The thought of his mentor made him even angrier. He had written the letter days prior and still no response. How could his one friend abandon him? Thomas slammed down the desktop, ripped out a parchment, and grabbed the feather. When he reached for the ink, he gripped it so hard that it exploded all over the room. He took a deep breath and snatched another bottle from the drawer without bothering to clean up the mess.

Dear Anthony,

Still no answer?

Perhaps you do not realize the gravity of the situation. I am at a loss and need advice.

Spare me your smug admonitions for patience. Time, my friend, is a plague. I hear the clock chime every hour and it sends daggers through my heart.

I have killed more in the last weeks than in the previous year altogether. Don't worry, I hold to your precious ethic. But the longer I wait, the longer things remain unchanged, the more I want to throw it away and rule the earth as I know I could with my strength and cunning.

I know you think I overreact. I know you think me too quick to judge. But I am alone with this trauma, and with every day, those two things, overreaction and impatience, come more and more to bear on my actions.

Stay away if you will. Refuse to answer my pleas for help. But do not fly into Paris on some shroud of holiness and condemn my sins after I doom myself and others, for your reticence is as much at fault as my temper.

Yours in darkness, Thomas

He broke a couple more things before he finished, but he felt better upon doing so. Thomas sealed the envelope, set it outside the door, and returned to the window to feel the first rays of sun peer over the horizon.

Fourteen: Versailles

19 JUNE 1789

Xavier glanced at Maria and smiled. They'd donned their finest clerical garments and headed out of Paris with masses of people early in the morning. The week before, when Xavier first heard rumors about what might occur, he had a difficult time believing them. On that day, it became a reality, so Xavier and Maria traveled in a Saint-Laurent carriage to the Palace of Versailles to witness the historic event. Other clergy and hundreds of citizens joined them on the trek to the countryside.

True, Xavier had never cared to hear much about the Three Estates. They seldom did anything that helped anyone, but that moment signaled the dawn of a new era. Some of Xavier's colleagues who governed the Catholic Church agreed to join the Third Estate, a momentous occasion. If a number of clergy bolted from their separate Estate and joined in solidarity with the commoners in the Third, Louis would have to consider their political demands.

Xavier was the first in his party to see the palace. Its grandeur still struck him after all of these years, and unlike many Parisians, he had been inside its walls on more than one occasion when his father had met with the king. The immense palace showcased immaculate decorations and struck awe in every visitor with its opulence and finely trimmed yard. However, it also created the indemnity that Louis now fought. If people watched loved ones starve to death and then came to either Louis's residence in Paris or ventured out to Versailles, they of course lashed out.

Although a number of people were amassed outside the palace, the guards kept everything in order and no one threatened a riot. Maria and Xavier wandered around the premises and talked with people they recognized, especially church representatives to the official government.

Xavier was not surprised to see a few merchants profiting from the events. They sold mostly food and beverages.

Inside the gate gathered a predictable allotment of the wealthy, military, and other powerful denizens of France. To Xavier's surprise, however, he met the eyes of Marcel André. Xavier recognized his devious smile and narrow eyes at once and his blood ran cold at the sight of his sister's poisoner.

"Good day," Xavier said through the fence, maintaining decorum.

"Abbé, I'm surprised that you ventured from your church."

Xavier ignored the jibe. "And what brings you here? Profit?"

"I came upon the king's business."

"Really?"

"His Majesty purchases various wares from me. I'll get away from this rabble as soon as possible. I can't believe anyone questions the sanctity of the king's ordained authority."

"You mean you profit from his wealth and power and don't want to lose this lucrative revenue."

"Harsh words for your future brother-in-law," Marcel said, eyes narrowing. "What would Catherine think?" He didn't wait for an answer and walked away.

Xavier watched Marcel walk right up to a soldier and blow powder in his face. The soldier failed to react, instead giving way and allowing Marcel further entry into the palace grounds. How had no one seen his crime?

"Is that he?" Maria asked. Xavier jumped, not having seen her catch up with him.

"Unfortunately. And it's upset my stomach. I know we came to observe, but perhaps I've seen enough."

Maria nodded in understanding. "Of course."

"Then let's return to Paris." They withdrew from the crowd and walked back toward the carriage. Though Xavier enjoyed seeing the palace and feeling the changes in the air, he wanted to get back to Paris to ensure his parish remained serene and to regain his composure. They got into the carriage, rode silently into town, and then walked back to the church. Their conversation drifted to a variety of topics until Maria giggled.

"I almost found a man for you," she said.

"Maria!" Xavier looked at her with distress and embarrassment.

"No one's listening. I met with some of the nuns and asked them if they knew anything about the 'priestly side of things.' A couple of them gave me some clues and I went to approach the particular priest about it, but they transferred him out of Paris a few weeks ago."

"I appreciate your efforts," he said, "but I wish you'd discuss things with me beforehand."

"But that's how we do it, Xavier. I met quite a few of the ladies before I settled down with my favorite ones."

"I don't want to hear this," Xavier said.

Maria laughed. "Are you afraid to hear about lovemaking inside the sacred convent walls?" She stopped because she started laughing so hard that she had to hold her stomach as her face turned bright red, which even made Xavier laugh. "I'll spare you the details, if you'll spare me your religious condemnations," she managed to say.

"It's not the morality that concerns me. For me, it's personal. I need to love someone before I can think about anything else. It doesn't work for me to dream of romping from priest to priest. I came to you because of how I felt about Thomas."

"I know. And not everyone in the church has multiple partners. I'm not sure how the priests handle it. But don't do anything with this Thomas. It's crucial to keep this within the church. We can't risk others finding out what happens. Can you imagine the scandal? This talk of revolution already has people spewing venom against the Catholic Church."

"I love Thomas. You must understand that, for me, this is about my heart, not some man who walks through the door with whom to have sex."

"You'll change your mind," she said with certainty. "Just let me know when you're ready."

They arrived at the convent, and Xavier gladly watched the sun disappear. It was time to meet Thomas. He grabbed Maria's arm and wished her well.

ANGER

Thomas awakened feeling better after his rage-induced tantrums from the night before and looked around his room, embarrassed at the mess he'd created. Ink stains covered everything. He wrote orders for his servants to have the soiled furniture replaced by tomorrow and set the instructions in the basket outside his door with a generous tip.

Thomas hurried around his flat and dressed, also cleaning as much as possible, then set out for the night. He raced across town so fast that no human saw his passage. He arrived at the church in seconds to find it empty. No Xavier. So, he plopped himself outside the cathedral windows and whistled while he waited. His heart leapt when he saw a priest's robe approaching and Xavier walked up, smiling.

"Have you been waiting long?"

"Not at all."

Xavier smiled broadly, cast his eyes down, and shuffled back and forth. "I hurried back. I was afraid you'd leave."

"My little abbé, you're always fretting about something. I'd wait an eternity for you." Xavier blushed. He then launched into his usual discussion, going from topic to topic with no direction or purpose. Thomas loved to listen without saying a word. He cherished the sound of Xavier's voice, liked his enthusiasm, and always remembered their first meetings when the priest hesitated to say a thing.

In these moments, Thomas reveled in his total love and lost all appetite for random sexual contact. He only wanted Xavier now.

Xavier still gabbed about his day, but Thomas half-listened and concentrated more on the cadence of his voice as Xavier played with the cross at his neck.

The world, however, angered him. He had never understood its laws and morality, especially when it regulated people's love. Was anyone hurt because two men went to bed together? Thomas never believed in faith, that some divine presence revealed truth to certain men so they could proclaim it to humanity. Faith was a power game negotiated through religion, yet it was a stalwart force.

After Xavier explained that the priests joined the Third Estate and the National Assembly became bolder, Xavier became repetitive.

Thomas stopped him. "Abbé, what is it?"

Xavier looked at the ground. "Never mind. I'm not ready."

"Did anything else happen at the palace?"

"Not really. It was peaceful."

"I'm surprised guards didn't try to arrest or intimidate anyone," Thomas mused.

Xavier shot Thomas an exasperated glance. "I forgot. A poor woman, not even part of the protest, almost died. The king's guards came racing from Paris and blundered right through the crowd. I barely had time to push her out of the way. The guards didn't even glance back to see about her safety."

"*You* pushed her out of the way?"

"Yes."

Thomas grabbed Xavier and pressed his lips into his hair. "Be careful," he said in a soft voice.

Xavier blushed. "I'm careful," he said. "Here, let me show you this." Xavier revealed a letter with the bishop of Paris's official seal. Thomas read it, which provoked anew his anger at the church. How could anyone write such things about Xavier? The bishop warned Xavier to stop administering the sacraments to those outside his parish. He threatened defrocking.

"What does this mean?" Thomas handed the letter back before he tore it to shreds.

"I commune anyone who requests it, which is strictly forbidden. They want everything done in the sanctuary under controlled circumstances. But if people need these things, why should I keep it from them if they have to work on Sunday or if their husband forbids their going to church? I never adhere to these edicts anyway."

"Don't they come after you?" Thomas was aghast.

"I hate admitting it, but I rely on my name. The Saint-Laurent legacy protects me and the bishop knows it, so he sends the letters hoping that I'll comply but knowing he can't act."

"I don't understand. Why is he against you?"

"I'm not sure. Maybe wealth. He disliked me from the moment they assigned me to this parish. The order came from above him."

Despite the topic, Xavier smiled, glanced to the ground, and then refused to say anything.

"What is it?" Thomas asked with a slight smile.

"I've *never* told anyone about this, except Catherine. This is a secret."

Thomas leaned forward, interest and hope piqued.

"You swear that you won't utter a word?"

"Xavier, you already know the answer."

"I have—well, I want you to—" Xavier struggled for words. "There's someone that I'd like you to meet."

ANNE HÉBERT

"You want me to meet someone?" Thomas stared at Xavier, puzzled.

Xavier had decided a few days ago to tell Thomas how much he cared about him, and introducing Thomas to his clandestine liaison—his private friend—might show Xavier's true feelings. No one else except Catherine knew about his friendship. Thomas moved close enough that their legs touched.

"Yes. I want to introduce you to a secret friend."

"It means much to you, that you want to share this person." Despite his words, Thomas appeared confused, or at least curious and apprehensive.

Xavier jumped from the bench, grabbed Thomas's hand, and pulled him toward the street. He paused for a second, surprised at how comfortable it felt to touch Thomas. It excited him, too, the strong, rough, hand in his.

The masses slept in their beds and most deserted the silent streets as the two men headed into even quieter neighborhoods. The houses there were more dilapidated, the air stronger with wretched smells, the mud deeper, and little light guided their way. The parish lay beyond Xavier's and no priest wanted to serve the district of the crime and poverty. Xavier came into these parts at the behest of people he knew or to help the destitute.

His meetings with his friend broke several taboos. She was female, a poor laundress, black, and practiced pagan religions from the New World. Certainly not someone a respectable Catholic priest should spend time with. But he loved her because she grounded his soul.

The street was dark except for the glow emanating from her window, where she always burned a fire and stayed up late. Xavier knocked on her door.

"Come in, Abbé!" She always knew it was him without looking.

She was laughing heartily when they entered. "And you brought a friend this time, I see." Her dialect, a combination of broken French with a slave cadence, always put Xavier at ease. But when she saw Thomas, her smile dissipated and she backed away, looking at him through squinted eyes. Xavier suspected some hidden communication between them as she relaxed soon thereafter. It unnerved him and then made him jealous before he forced himself to ignore it.

"It's good to see you," Xavier said to Anne.

"What brings you to these awful parts, Abbé? You're always coming down into the muck to see me. People will talk." She laughed again before turning to Thomas. "And who have we here?"

"Thomas Lord." Thomas bowed. "It's a pleasure to meet you, mademoiselle. Any friend of Xavier's is safe in my presence."

"Well, I'm certainly glad to hear that," she said in a strange tone.

"What are you two talking about?" Xavier asked.

She chortled even harder. "You mean he doesn't know?"

Thomas stared at her, expression hardening on his face, but she paid it no mind.

"Oh, my precious priest, was there ever born a more innocent soul?"

"What do you mean?"

"Never mind, Xavier," Thomas said through clenched teeth. "It's nothing."

Xavier stammered, just to say something. "This is Anne Hébert."

"Yes, that's the name. And if you ever call me mademoiselle again, bad things will come to you." She smiled broadly, sweating from the heat of the fire. Her skin was light brown, her mixed blood giving her a lighter complexion. She was short, well built, not petite nor hefty, and carried herself in a masculine manner.

"I hope you'll forgive me for bringing Thomas."

"You mentioned him last time." Anne chuckled and turned to Thomas. "He walks in, all sulky, and tells me about a problem. I'm thinking the church burned down or he had a visit from Jesus, he's so serious. But what is it? He tells me he made a friend. Did I get a chuckle outta that one. Still makes me laugh. I said to him, 'What am I?' and he giggles and admits that we're friends. So, we calmed him down and I told him it was just fine to have a friend. So long as you assure me you don't mean any funny business, you can stay with me because I trust Xavier's judgment." She plunged into a chair, motioning for them to follow.

"You've nothing to worry about, mademoiselle."

"It's Anne. Don't make me feel like one of them silly ladies all dressed up in the frills." Then she looked at Xavier. "At least he isn't someone from the church." And she winked.

"Of course not." Xavier glanced at Thomas. "Anne and I talk a lot about religion. Much of it pure heresy."

"Only to you," Anne said.

"You two agree on theology?" Thomas raised an eyebrow.

"Oh, never," they answered together.

Xavier burst into laughter. "We disagree quite often."

They talked about how Xavier and Anne met on one of Xavier's wanderings and began debating at once. Xavier still remembered their first conversation as the most engaging theological discussion ever. She had been articulate, intelligent, and knew more about faith than all of the monks and priests combined. She'd supported him in his defiance of traditional Catholicism, and he'd listened to her concerns about being a pagan in a very Catholic world.

"So you're from America, too?" Thomas asked her.

"Yes, but not in the same way as you. Born in Haiti, a slave. Then I fled the violence with my master and his family to New Orleans, and after, right here to France."

"Did you escape?" Thomas moved a pile of her laundry and sat closer to her.

"No, heavens, no. I'm not that bold. They got tired of me and started losing money here. So they just left me. So I turned to doing the rich folks' laundry as a free woman."

Xavier still marveled at Anne's good nature, despite all she had experienced.

"Well, Thomas, I'm glad Xavier brought you here tonight." Anne, as was her custom, ended the evening without warning. "He's said a lot about you, and it's nice to have a face with the name. But if you two gentlemen will excuse me, I need my beauty rest, or I won't be able to seduce all of those gentlemen customers into allowing me to wash their undergarments."

They took their leave, and outside, Thomas and Xavier said nothing, embracing the quiet night. The air was still, temperate, and even the common smells were masked for the moment. As thoughts of wanting to stay with Thomas forever drifted through Xavier's mind, Thomas grabbed his hand. They kept walking with their intimate contact. It scared him, but it was wonderful, Thomas's warm, powerful grasp leading Xavier through the night.

Thomas stepped in front of him before he closed the church door. "Thank you for tonight."

"It was nothing."

"No, it was profound, and I know it."

"Thomas, you know, I mean—" He could not release the emotions flooding through him because there would be no return. Better to hide in the misery and denial than banish himself from the world he knew. Oh, that he could run into those strong arms and feel the wetness of those lips. If only he could relinquish control of his body to the one he loved with all his heart.

"Good night, Thomas. I'll see you tomorrow?"

Thomas smiled and brushed Xavier's cheek with his hand. "Of course."

Fifteen: Voodoo

20 JUNE 1789

Xavier's beautiful hazel eyes, those sparkling gems Thomas often dreamed about as he drifted to sleep, flooded with tears. Thomas had wanted to say so much more when Xavier asked if he would see him the next evening but bit his tongue. He understood the magnitude of Xavier taking him to Anne and holding Thomas's hand spoke volumes.

But the warped Catholic Church's religion scared Thomas more than ever. He might ultimately overpower Xavier's sexual fears, but how would he explain the vampirism?

After he left Xavier at the church, the night still young for a vampire, Thomas retraced their steps and went right back to Anne, another outsider in Paris, another outcast from society.

The light from the fire flooded out of her rooms even brighter. He heard her scurrying around and then knocked.

"Come in, you fool," she said with impatience. "And how did I know you were headed back here? You gentlemen and your hearts." She shrugged, as if such things were self-evident. "Sit down and relax for a minute. I can see that you're always in a fuss, always hurrying things along. But the whole world's asleep, so we can take our time. I told you to sit."

Thomas reluctantly followed her orders.

"I know about your other secret, too. What do you call yourselves these days?"

"I assume you mean vampires," Thomas said with caution.

She howled. "That's it, that's it. Undead. Demons. I've heard it all. I heard lots of people talking about your kind, but I never met one before. Can't say that I ever wanted to."

"I won't harm you."

"I already know that, or you wouldn't be sitting here. I know where to go to get away. You never signaled a threat. I figured as much when the two of you first came in. Then I realized that poor Xavier has no idea, so I kept my mouth shut. You're indebted to me because I don't like keeping secrets from a friend."

Thomas stared at her for a moment, assessing. "Thank you, I suppose."

"I've seen all sorts of things in life, good and bad, evil and holy. I know enough not to judge." She grew silent and waited for him to begin.

Thomas slumped. "I love him. Desperately. I know he wants the same. In a million ways, he tells me so. But he's afraid, and the Catholic Church has poisoned his mind. He's too trusting, too pure, too worried about helping others and what the rest of the world thinks. I know you can make a spell to lure him to me."

She laughed.

"Please, help me." He wondered if he sounded as insane as he felt. As he had when he went to Catherine, he violated the ethic and went too far in his quest to win Xavier.

"I care about Xavier a lot myself. Not like you, but I care a lot about him. I wish I could help. But I don't know any such magic."

Anger and frustration roiled in Thomas's gut. "You're lying."

She shook her head. "Even saying that, I knew something like that could get me killed. I can't go around doing those things. Don't you know what they'd do to some poor black woman who went around practicing evil? And maybe you haven't seen this revolution heating up, and the people saying things in public about the church. What do you think it'd do to me in this climate? I'd become an easy target. Besides, I don't know what you're talking about. Spells, potions, love. Nonsense." She waved her hand in the air, as if dismissing him.

He leaned forward, trying not to allow his anger to cloud his judgment. "You *do* practice a faith or religion, whatever you call it. You were doing it when I arrived tonight. And if your powers of perception were so great, then you'd know that I could not care less about the Catholic Church. No one from that vile institution would ever find out what you did. As for the revolution, it fascinates me and little else."

She pursed her lips and sat back, studying him. "I imagine you don't care about any gods, either?"

He rolled his eyes.

"Well, then, neither do I."

He glanced around the room and sensed a life form behind a pile of clothes. Not human, he would have known that in an instant, but important to her. He stood and peered behind the mound, and she burst into hysterics. While she laughed, he grabbed the enormous snake.

"Do all laundresses house snakes for their protection?"

"You put him down. He has no quarrel with you."

He didn't. "I need your help. Please stop playing games."

"All right, then. Listen to me. No more playing with the vampire, no more hiding. Just put my snake down."

Thomas set it on the floor and returned to the fire.

"I never imagined in the wildest visions a vampire, eternal life and all that power, but he's groveling at my feet in love." Then she became serious. "I can't do a spell or give you magic or a potion for this. Magic is dangerous, and you don't just throw it around with no care. These powers that you want to dabble in can do great good and tremendous harm.

"You listen here to a woman and forget those spells. You already have his heart. Can't you see how smitten he is with you? He may claim to worship Jesus Christ, but his eyes worship you. If you're so confident that you want to spend eternity with him, what's a few more months or even years waiting for him to come around? Xavier's too worldly to hide in that church forever. Mixing magic into this can do no good."

She stood, walked to Thomas, and then grasped him by the neck and stared into his eyes. "Nah, the old tales about your kind aren't true, are they? Just like us, good and bad, and this one here's a good one. Though I sense an anger in you. I won't tolerate it. Especially if you aim it at him." She patted his shoulder. "Give him time. He loves you. And watch that temper. Now, get outta here. You can come back another time if you want, but there's only so much darkness left and I have to finish something. Your damn dead essence is going to chase away my spirits." And with that, she bustled him out the door.

His head spun in a million directions. Relief that she offered advice. Dread that she knew about his anger and more so that she was right about it. And concern that he once again violated the ethic and became too intertwined with humans. Anthony would be furious.

KILLER

Thomas walked back to Paris after Anne pushed him out the door. Of course, she was right. If he planned on eternity with Xavier, waiting for even a couple of years meant little. The only risk was Xavier's mortal safety, but Thomas could protect him.

Still, he hated that Xavier fought his true nature, and despite the peace within him, his passion against the church intensified. Against his better judgment, with Anthony's voice scolding him inside his head, he headed for the Seine and the glorious Notre Dame Cathedral. It took no effort to locate the bishop. He scaled a wall, opened a window, and seated himself on the end of a bed. The figure at its head slept soundly so Thomas wiggled the mattress.

The man woke and screamed in terror. With superhuman haste, Thomas covered his mouth and ordered him to stop. "I won't kill you if you obey," he said. He let go of the bishop, who cowered under his sheet.

"We need to chat." Thomas got up and walked around, taking in the room's opulence: the expensive furniture, the ornate china left from dinner, the silk vestments, all the finery that one would find in the homes of Paris's elite. He compared it to the sparse conditions of Xavier's room: the blank walls and broken desk. Thomas ran his hand along the crucifix, mocking its inability to protect the allegedly holy man. After a grand pause, he turned back to the bishop.

"I know I woke you and it's late, but I didn't think that you'd accept my request for a visit."

"What do you want? Take anything." The bishop's voice shook.

"Do I look like a common thief?" Thomas waved his hand at his own expensive clothing. "You and I have other business." He took a seat on the bed next to the quivering man and ran his fingers along the wrinkled cheek, delighting in the bishop's terror.

"It's about a mutual friend. But I warn you, our friend has no idea I'm doing this. If you utter one word to him, I'll break your neck. The same will happen if you speak of this to any other soul or seek retribution. Agreed?"

The man nodded, hands trembling on the sheet.

"I need you to write a letter of retraction regarding the things you've said about Abbé Saint-Laurent. You must admit you were incorrect and commend him for his fine work."

"He defies the laws of the church."

"That's not why you harass him," Thomas said, leaning forward, tone dangerous. "I couldn't understand it before I saw you. Why would someone insult a priest who serves a parish few others would even enter? You tried to seduce Xavier and he rebuked you."

The bishop's pallor faded even more at Thomas's words. "I don't know what—"

Thomas nestled up to the man, put his face nearby, and massaged his leg. Though Thomas glared, the bishop refused to look at him. Thomas blew into his ear and then grabbed his genitals.

After a second, he released them and jumped off the bed. "Still want to deny it, Father?"

By now, the bishop was weeping as he shivered. Thomas marched to a desk, snatched a parchment, and thrust it at him. The bishop obeyed every command. He wrote three letters: one for his official files, one to the Vatican, and one to Xavier, apologizing for his mistaken condemnations and instead praising the young priest for exemplary service. Thomas took them when he had finished, sealed them with the bishop's emblem, and slid them into his coat pocket.

"You have what you want. Leave me," the bishop said.

"Do you understand what I mean to do if this isn't the end of it?"

"Go away. You've won."

Unconvinced that the bishop grasped the severity of his threat, Thomas grabbed the foot of the bed and broke it from its hinges. The mattress crashed to the floor and the bishop rolled to Thomas's feet. He cried and quaked anew. Thomas reached with a swift motion and broke the man's little finger. As the man howled in pain, Thomas smashed through the window and jumped two stories to the ground.

Now, to celebrate. Time for a kill.

As usual, people crowded the bars and drank, gambled, had public sex, and railed against Louis. The tawdry scene would produce a worthy victim or two. Thomas entered an establishment and took a seat. Nothing unusual caught his eye. No one longed for his fangs to end an unseemly life, until he heard a familiar voice. He turned, slowly, and saw Marcel seated nearby and talking to the likes of whom Thomas never wanted to even touch. They stank of men hired for dirty, illicit, and violent tasks.

There was a group of worthy victims. He could kill all of them, including Marcel, and rid himself of a major problem. Then Thomas remembered those damn ethical guidelines Anthony pronounced: never meddle in human affairs. Killing Marcel, even in a vial setting, violated that principle. And he had already gone too far in violating the ethic with his visit to Notre Dame. But that logic seemed faulty, until he recalled his conversation with Marcel. What if the demon placed some spell on Xavier to protect himself if Thomas came after him? Was such a thing possible? Thomas had no idea what to do.

Frustrated, Thomas listened.

"You're fine gentlemen, as always," Marcel was saying. "I hardly believe you dispatched that customer so fast and without a mess. I appreciate your efforts on my behalf—"

"Enough talk, old man, get to the point," one of the men said. His breath hit Thomas from two tables away, stinking of tobacco, rum, and a gross assortment of decay.

"Don't take that tone with me. I have a spying assignment, to watch two men. I need to know their patterns, their friends, and their beliefs. Discover any weaknesses, any material for blackmail, anything they conceal. Try to find out where they keep their money and when they sleep. I must know anything and everything about both of them. Monitor the two Saint-Laurents. One of you watch Michel, the other take Xavier."

"How long do you want us to do this? It'll cost you," the other added.

"I'm well aware of your prices, and believe me, this is worth the cost. I'll expect a weekly report. One more thing. Never go near their sister. When they visit her, walk away."

Marcel described Michel and told them where to find him and Thomas pictured the route to Xavier's church as Marcel gave it to the other man, depicting him, as well.

Thomas let Marcel leave, against his better judgment, as the rules haunted him and his magic concerned him. He followed the other two, however. He sensed enough to know that killing them would not violate the ethic, at least not as much as if he had gone after Marcel. These two had never met anyone from the family, so Thomas decided they stood outside the ethic's prohibitions. They walked a few blocks, singing drunken songs, proud of Marcel's coins and then entered a salon with rooms for rent. Thomas stayed close behind when they entered their room. He waited a few seconds and then burst in as they counted their money.

In a complete fury, he first grabbed the one intended to spy on Xavier. He almost failed to notice the terror on his face as he crushed the man's skull between his hands. He paused as the cranium crunched like a seashell and gore exploded all over the room. He dropped the corpse and swore under his breath. He'd waited too long. The second man had escaped the room, and his screaming brought other patrons into the hall to see about the commotion. Thomas kicked the dead body before he swiftly went into the hall and vacated the building. He could not risk going after the remaining man as he stood among all these onlookers. Instead, he went to feed, once again hungry for blood after several nights of depriving himself.

Part III: Intensification

Sixteen: Mounting Unrest

26 JUNE 1789

Xavier admired the fine furnishings of the Saint-Laurent home, especially the latest items Catherine had added, as he waited for his family. Louis's troops had arrived outside Paris, signaling the chance for profound change. Michel's authoritative steps could soon be heard before he marched into the room.

He hugged Xavier tightly. "Are you safe? Things are unstable. I worry about you and Catherine."

Their sister swept into the room before Xavier could say a word. "Can you believe all the military surrounding our city like an occupational force?" she asked as she kissed each of them.

"Where's Jérémie?" Michel asked, ignoring his sister's question. The interaction reminded Xavier of his brother's latest attempt to force a marriage by moving Jérémie into the Saint-Laurent home. Catherine had balked at the arranged protection, but relented after speaking with Jérémie and because of their friendship. She still had no idea he was the mysterious suitor.

"A revolution is inevitable." Michel grimaced. "You must protect yourselves. I see that you hid the valuables, Catherine, an excellent decision. Stay near the house or church. And, Xavier, stop ministering at the prisons, especially the Bastille."

Xavier sighed at Michel's latest dictates. "The prisoners need my services."

"That place is a symbol to the angry citizens of what Louis does to his people." Thankfully, Michel then turned to Catherine. "You're sure Jérémie came to the house?"

"Why on earth would I lie?"

"Is there other news?" Xavier asked.

"What else do I need to tell you?" Michel went rigid again. "I just said there's going to be a revolution. Louis is paralyzed. People riot every day. France is in chaos."

Xavier was chilled by the words. "I swear I'll be careful."

"And you, Catherine?" Michel asked. "Will you stop being foolhardy?"

Xavier practically felt the rumbling before she erupted. "Do I need an army of men to protect me? I know the danger. When my friends criticize Louis in public, I withhold my opinion, but I won't become a prisoner in this house." Silent anger filled the room as Catherine paced the floor and turned again to her elder brother. "How dare you think I'll change."

As Catherine ranted, Xavier listened with dismay until Michel shot out of his chair and stormed out. He and Catherine stared after him.

"I suppose I'm too hard on him," Catherine said, already calm.

Xavier could not help but chuckle. It was meek, bold, defiant, and humble all at once. Classic Catherine.

"He always wants his men to watch over me." As these words escaped her mouth, Jérémie entered the room.

"Jérémie, Michel thinks I need armed guards, but you're staying here pacified him. You're like a brother to me. Thank you."

"I'm not sure that I want to be a brother if I receive the same wrath," Jérémie said.

"You're like Xavier," she corrected. "Kind, gentle, and loving, not like the ogre who just left."

"How about more wine?" Xavier asked. He went to the bar and began uncorking a bottle to distract his sister from her tirade. To Xavier's relief, Jérémie changed the subject back to the revolution and thus ended the latest sibling quarrel.

Seventeen: Xavier and the Revolution

27 JUNE 1789

Xavier enjoyed the fresh air as he waited for Michel and wondered about his brother's mood after storming out of the house the previous night. A light breeze blew as Xavier smelled the flowers and looked at his finely kept garden.

The minute he noticed Michel riding through the mud on his horse and the dark expression on his face, Xavier knew that Michel's mood was much worse than before. Michel dismounted, tied his horse to the fence, and marched toward Xavier as if he were a general over Catholic priests.

"Good morning," Xavier said, hoping to defuse Michel's temper.

"May we go inside?" Michel asked.

Without responding, Xavier led them into the sanctuary and beyond, to parts of the church that even he seldom visited. They passed a couple of elderly women who cleaned the church, nodded, and went on their way. Even in the daylight, these back rooms had little light.

"I come upon the king's business," Michel said.

Xavier slumped into a chair.

Michel sat erect, still the officer. His medals and uniform insignias spoke of his success and the reverence he held for his duty.

"Louis has ordered all clergy to join the Third Estate. Even the nobility. He's trying to appease the masses."

"Will this stop the revolution?" Xavier asked, numb.

"Will you obey?"

"Do I have a choice? I'll do so if it helps the people."

"Your allegiance should be to the king," Michel said.

"You know what I meant. I'm loyal to him too."

"I'm glad that you listened to me," Michel said. "I've heard, and I can't divulge my sources, that you and a nun do secret ceremonies. Stop it. Do you understand?"

"I'm not a child, Michel." Xavier shot Michel an angry stare. "Keep your secret informants, hire spies to follow me, but I'll continue ministering to these people. Do you ever consider your arrogance? You risk your life every day in the army. But that won't stop you, even if Catherine and I pleaded for you to protect yourself. Why is my occupation different?"

Michel jumped up. "Don't you care about your security?"

"What does that have to do with serving these people?"

"What about the other things that you do? One of my soldiers is from your parish. His mother glows with admiration for you. But he recently told me something more disturbing. About your lover."

Xavier sat, dumbfounded. Lover? Did he mean Thomas?

"Don't look at me like an idiot," Michel said. "How could you let others see you?"

"I don't know what you're talking about," Xavier lied.

Michel leaned in front of Xavier and put his hands on his brother's knees. His face was no longer red, though the priest fumed. Michel ruffled Xavier's hair and pulled their foreheads together.

Then he spoke low. "I don't care about your affairs. But you have to be careful. I'll never forgive myself if anything happens to you."

"I don't know what you mean," Xavier again lied as tears flowed.

"I have to go," Michel said. "I'm ordering you to stop the private rites and never go out in public with this man." Michel strode out of the room with those words.

Xavier was embarrassed, angry, confused, sad, and humiliated. He resolved to change nothing. It was none of Michel's business.

He was still weeping when a soft knock sounded at the door. A woman's voice said from the other side, "Abbé, there's a man here for confession."

Xavier wiped his eyes and thanked her as he raced to the confessional. He slid into the booth, opened the screen, and addressed the individual.

"Forgive me, Father, for I have sinned." Without waiting for an answer, Jérémie launched into a tale. "I'm afraid that you know me too well. But I need help and had nowhere else to turn. My confession, my secret longing, is for your sister. I love her. It's torture to keep all this locked away in my mind and hide. Forgive me."

"I see no sin in your love," Xavier said.

"Thank you, Father." Jérémie bolted out of the confessional.

Xavier hurried from his, too, wanting to embrace Jérémie, but by the time he did so, it was too late. Jérémie was gone.

Xavier returned to his duties around the church, absorbed in work to forget about Michel and Jérémie and Thomas and all the misery these times wrought. As the world swirled into activity around him, within his family, his personal life, and the political future of France, Xavier hid in the reality of helping one person.

Eighteen: Tricolors

9 JULY 1789

Catherine worked in her study when the butler announced that Xavier and Jérémie waited in the parlor for her. She hurried to greet them, and after the usual pleasantries, Xavier and Catherine stared at Jérémie, who fidgeted with a coat button and glanced about as if looking for something he lost.

"The Third Estate is acting," he announced. "This is open revolt. The Third Estate declared itself a National Assembly today. The bourgeoisie is in complete control."

"Did the king move against them?" Catherine asked.

"Not yet."

"Was there violence?" Xavier asked.

"The peasants are rioting throughout France. They're starving, after all."

"Jérémie, what on earth is that scarf you're wearing?" It struck Catherine that, in addition to his usual suit and stoic clothing, he wore a tricolored scarf of blue, white, and red.

"The symbol of freedom," he said. "Parisians adopted these colors to support the National Assembly. They call themselves patriots."

"Where can I get one?" Catherine tugged idly on the ends of Jérémie's, wanting to feel part of the movement.

"I brought you one." He pulled out another tricolored scarf from his pocket and waved it in front of Catherine, who squealed with delight. She tied it around her neck and marveled at the fact that colors, nothing more, could inspire the passions of hundreds of Frenchmen.

"What on earth are you doing? Have you lost your minds?" They all jumped at the sound of Michel's thundering voice. "My house is full of traitors!"

"Everyone is wearing these colors in Paris," Jérémie said. "If we walk around Paris, we're safer from the people if we wear these scarves."

"See, Michel, you're not always right, so leave us alone," Catherine said petulantly. "The Saint-Laurent household must transform itself into a safe center for discussing ideas and change. This family has guided France through a multitude of transformations, and it must once again be at the forefront."

She had already planned for her salon and for the possibility of violence, so intended to hire guards.

"Good Lord, you've lost your mind," Michel said.

"I think it's a wonderful idea," Jérémie exclaimed.

"What does your darling fiancé think?" Michel asked sarcastically.

"That's my affair. Jérémie is with me. What about you two?"

"I'll not listen to this." Michel slumped into a chair, but Xavier's silence bothered Catherine more than Michel's bombast.

"Let's retire to dinner," she announced. "I want everyone's opinion. Except yours." She looked at Michel and shoved them toward the dining room. As Michel and Jérémie went ahead, Catherine walked with a slow pace beside Xavier.

"Are you angry?"

Xavier smiled. "No. You know that I don't like to provoke Michel."

"So you approve?"

"I trust your judgment."

"Then what is bothering you? Tell me."

"I'm scared. It all portends some impending violence."

"Have you talked to Thomas?"

"He finds it fascinating and isn't bothered."

She squeezed his arm in support. "Perhaps we'll discuss that later." She pulled him gently with her. "This has become the first official meeting of the Saint-Laurent salon," Catherine pronounced as she entered the dining room. "All opinions are welcome. I suppose even yours, Michel, so long as you're open to everyone else's ideas."

"I'm open to discussing this plan, especially its danger."

"Please sit. Xavier speaks first." She did not mean to put Xavier on the spot, but she had heard enough from Michel and her wish would keep him quiet. She was ablaze, giddy, with the mere potential for converting the house. She had the financing, the location, and now, supporters.

CHICKEN BONES

Thomas raced toward Xavier's church, but even his speed seemed slow as he worried about the abbé. He awoke earlier to a commotion in the street and discovered from a passerby that the city had erupted into rioting and people were attacking symbols of power, especially those within the church. Thomas found the church empty so went to the Saint-Laurent home. He went up the front stairs and heard voices through a window—his abbé's soothing laugh relieved him. Thomas wanted to run and hug him but thought better of it, so he turned around and walked at a slow pace back to the church to wait.

Thomas burst into the chapel without knocking and headed for the priest's private quarters. Since they talked there for privacy, he often let himself in. Thomas wished that he could take Xavier to his flat but feared that Xavier would ask too many questions or see something that Thomas wanted to hide. Within the small room, Thomas looked out the window and at the things Xavier collected. He had very little for someone of his wealth. Clothes, all clerical garments, quills, parchment, and books—everywhere books, all intellectual and sterile, nothing to betray the deep emotion within the man, nothing personal.

Thomas stretched out on the bed, loving the smell of Xavier upon the sheets. He sat up and looked around one more time, always surprised that one crucifix hung over a dresser, with nothing else on the walls. He glanced at the sparse setting, everything in its place, but there was not much there and nothing out of order. Xavier even alphabetized his books. Thomas was shocked, however, to see a discarded bone on the floor near the dresser. He stooped over to pick it up and saw even more underneath the dresser. His blood ran cold. The one set of bones looked like a chicken wing.

He struggled to control himself as he suspected that more was afoot than a thrown away pile of bones. Thomas decided to handle the situation himself, so penned a note and left.

Thomas moved with inhuman speed and, as predicted, Anne sat in front of her fire despite the July night's blistering heat.

"If it isn't my favorite creature of the night. And no, I'm not about to do any potion."

"This is serious. I don't want to put you at risk, but I need confirmation of something. In your religion, do chicken bones signal evil intent?"

"Not talking about love tonight, I see. Instead, you bring disturbed spirits into this place. If I were you, I wouldn't want to know about those bones."

Thomas pulled the bones out of his pocket. "It's too late."

Her eyes narrowed. "Voodoo, maybe. Perhaps hoodoo. Depends on the source what it means. This is grave. Chicken bones have the ability to call up evil spirits if ordained with the right words. If you know who did it—"

Before she finished, Thomas uttered a sincere thank you and rushed from the room. She confirmed his suspicion that the barbarian planted those bones in Xavier's room to inflict ill upon him and that their first confrontation had failed to quash Marcel's plans.

Thomas wanted to snap someone in half and kill the devil who haunted Xavier. Without thinking, Thomas slammed his fist into the wall of a small bakery, regretting it as the wall swayed and a hole opened where his fist hit, and then, almost in slow motion, the wall crumbled. Thomas rushed from the scene as people ran out to see what happened.

He discovered Marcel milling about the bars and profiting as usual as he bartered tricolor scarves to patrons who gobbled them up. Thomas rushed forward and whispered to Marcel that they needed to talk. To emphasize his point, he took a fingernail and slashed Marcel's wrist with a slight gash.

Alone in an alley, Marcel drew a knife and glared at Thomas. Thomas grabbed Marcel's arm and forced the knife from his hand.

"I thought we had an agreement," Thomas said, enunciating each word.

"I haven't harmed the priest."

"No games. I know about the spy and I found the bones." He had Marcel by the neck and pushed him against the wall. "I should snap your spine in half."

"I wouldn't risk killing me until you know what those bones are about."

Anthony haunted Thomas. Marcel's presence was about Catherine, not Xavier. Marcel knew too much, and now so did Catherine. Thomas had to be careful.

"I thought that voodoo taught you not to harm or threaten a priest?"

"I'm just trying to keep him from interfering with my engagement. I thought our deal allowed that."

Thomas slapped him. "You're to have *no* contact with him unless by chance, with Catherine in the room. No spies. No bones." Thomas leaned his face one inch from the man. "Stay away. This is the last time I'll warn you about Xavier."

He threw Marcel against the wall. His head cracked against the wood, and he fell to the ground, dazed as blood ran down his neck. Yet he still smirked at Thomas, glaring at him with a dangerous menace.

It took all of Thomas's willpower to leave him alive. To control himself, Thomas fled to the church, where the sight of Xavier talking in the street relieved him immediately. Xavier smiled and beckoned for Thomas. He was talking to a huge man with a gruff appearance and musculature that indicated regular labor.

"Thomas," Xavier said, "I'd like you to meet Denys Girard."

Thomas bowed.

"If you'll excuse me," Denys said, "I have to go. I was on security patrol and we're worried about our abbé's safety. We took it upon ourselves to initiate a guard."

Thomas bowed again as the man departed. "Not many priests have a personal guard."

"Denys came a couple of nights ago and insisted. I think it unnecessary."

"I've been worried about you too. I wondered what would protect you from the idiots who indiscriminately attack anything that represents that which they hate."

"I'm safe in this parish."

They drifted through their night time ritual of talking, first about the revolution and then about more and more intimate topics. That night, Thomas held Xavier's hand as they sat in his room and nestled against each other. Xavier stayed close to him, yet indicated he would go no further. Thomas even hinted at same-sex love and the church's teaching. Not surprisingly, Xavier saw nothing wrong with it between two of his parishioners, but would not even broach the subject about himself.

VAMPIRE DEUX

After Xavier went to bed, Thomas wandered around Paris because he hated being alone with his desperate feelings toward the priest. Thomas walked along when he sensed a presence, something he had not felt in Paris until now. A vampire.

The softer footfall, the quick pace, the almost inaudible breath that only his vampire ears could hear. Urban landscapes offered vampires havens because of their anonymity. During his first weeks in Paris, Thomas looked for signs of the immortal and was shocked that none materialized. He became so comfortable he forgot about other immortals.

But the distinct sounds of a vampire followed him.

And the strange approach alarmed him. Vampires greeted openly to avoid hostility. The vampire near him hid instead. Thomas readied for combat by staying close to the lamps, having used fire to fight off past attacks. He slowed and waited for the next move, turning a couple of times to confirm that a vampire shadowed him. He also moved away from people, toward a quiet, residential street.

Thomas went down a new street, stopped, and spun around. Without hesitating, he flung himself back three lampposts and prepared to attack when he heard a familiar laugh.

At the sound, Thomas relaxed. "Were you trying to get killed?"

The laughter continued, and then Thomas saw the hunched figure two houses away. Someone shouted from their window to shut up, but the noise continued. Thomas rushed over to the figure.

"Thomas, really, you're always ready to fight. I appreciate that you remembered the tactics I taught, and you even obeyed the ethic, for the most part. I'm quite surprised." Anthony stood and embraced him. "Don't be angry. You can't blame me for assessing your demeanor first."

Thomas managed a smile, torn between anger that he hadn't heard from Anthony in so long and relief that he was at last there. He looked him over, appraising. Anthony cut a striking figure. He stood about Thomas's height, an unusual six feet three inches, but his hair was long and sandy blond. He appeared Nordic with those locks and his piercing blue eyes. His muscles bulged out of his clothing. Anthony's hair fell in his face as he smiled, and his seductive eyes enchanted him. If only one of them had been willing to take the passive role. They complemented one another well, Anthony with his quiet restraint and Thomas with his brash defiance. Unfortunately, both had to dominate and so the relationship floundered.

"You're lucky I didn't flame these beautiful locks." Thomas grabbed Anthony's hair.

"No, you're the lucky one. Can we go to your flat? I hope you've room for a wayward traveler. My rooms at the hotel won't be ready until tomorrow."

Thomas smiled. "Follow me."

"It took you forever to detect me," Anthony said.

"It shocked me. There are no other vampires in Paris."

"That doesn't surprise me," Anthony said.

"Why? A gorgeous city with a lot to offer— I think it's even more anonymous than London. I expected to find legions of undead."

"Did the revolution escape your attention?" Anthony asked, tone wry.

"Why would human problems influence vampires?"

"Revolutions are unpredictable. There's more threat of a fire, and someone could burn a building in defiance."

"I've taken precautions. And other vampires' fears have given me a city to myself."

"Your letters didn't portray such a cavalier attitude."

"I'm a little unsettled, no thanks to friends who abandoned me."

"You know that's not true," Anthony said. "I made you wait because I needed to know you could handle the adversity by yourself. And you did, remarkably well, until the last letter. Then I knew you needed me and I came at once. I'm here now."

"It could've been too late. I killed an innocent, you know."

"Your letter explained as much, but you also said you stopped when you realized it, until you figured out that he wanted to die and it became a mercy killing, which is permitted. Would you like to brood some more, or can we go out?"

"All right. We'll talk later. Follow me. You'll love my favorite hunting ground."

Nineteen: Mercy Killings

10 JULY 1789

The vampires headed to Thomas's favorite brothel. He did not come here often in order to avoid suspicion, and male whores held no allure since he'd met Xavier. But Anthony's arrival called for the best location, and such an establishment offered both companionship and worthy victims. They sat at a back table in the shadows, away from prying eyes. Thomas looked at the dirty floors, drunken old men, and vicious harlots, then as casually as possible asked Anthony about the revolution.

"If vampires are afraid of revolution, aren't *you*?"

"Not really. I enjoy the atmosphere as much as you, though I loathe the French."

Thomas started to answer when Anthony launched himself from the table toward the door. Thomas alone saw him at that speed and followed just as fast across the street and up a flight of stairs, into someone's flat. By the time Thomas arrived, Anthony fed on a rather hideous large man.

"Hungry?" Thomas asked.

"He was beating a woman. I pretended to burst in to save her, and when she left, I drank his blood."

"You just violated the ethic," Thomas said with a grin.

"I'm not part of their lives. I went in and now I'm leaving. Unlike you, who goes in and befriends an entire gaggle of people, tells them you're a vampire, and then can't figure out how that puts us all in danger. Instead of the brothel, let's just return to your flat."

Anthony put his arm around Thomas as they walked away from the carnage.

A few blocks from his place, Anthony broke the silence. "I came the minute I sensed the desperation in your letters. I know you well enough not to try to change your mind, and you know me well enough to realize I don't approve of all you've done."

Thomas took a deep breath before he answered, "I knew you wouldn't like how much I was pursuing him. But since we agreed our relationship would never work, after trying hard and wandering all over America, we also accepted our disagreement about how soon I should look for a permanent mate. I'm not as patient as you."

They entered Thomas's apartment, and Thomas settled on a couch, though his legs twitched.

Anthony walked to the window, then paced about and looked at the many priceless artifacts. Thomas had seen him act that way a million times, whenever he offered a lesson about vampirism or reprimanded Thomas. His posture dominated, his expression became stern.

"Don't take my warnings lightly. I want to protect you, but this situation is more serious than anything you've confronted before and your impatience frightens me."

Anthony made Thomas feel like a small boy. He remembered his mother teaching him, his father scolding him, other members of his community instructing. Thomas regressed to the young man from the American frontier who had just become a vampire and looked with awe upon Anthony.

"You've been angry since I first met you," Anthony said. "Charming and flirtatious? Yes. Loyal to a fault? Of course. But you grew up with an anger, and it's haunting you now."

"I control it."

"Are you lying to me again, or are you that blind about yourself?"

Thomas rolled his eyes, hurt that Anthony again referenced how Thomas seduced him to become a vampire. "I never meant to hurt you. I wanted you to be happy, and I didn't mind taking the passive role with you."

"You did so in order to become a vampire, against your nature. I shouldn't have trusted you."

"Speaking of that," Thomas said, "how did you not figure that out when you drank my blood to make me? You should have seen it there."

Anthony nodded. "Perhaps. But I was blind with love, and it wasn't one of the details I focused on. I just wanted to bring you over to me as fast as possible. And nice attempt to deflect from our conversation. Because now you've turned your wiles to someone else. You've not told him anything yet, and when you do, it will cause unbelievable pain, as it did with us."

"You know I love you. I thought we had gotten over this."

"We have," Anthony spat through clenched teeth. "I couldn't be your friend if I still had the same emotions for you. This isn't about us."

"What is it, then?" But Thomas knew. He just didn't want to say it. His anger.

"Have you ever admitted, even to yourself, why you're so angry all the time?"

"Don't make me rehash this. I hate it."

"A young half-blood, mocked and isolated on the frontier. You portray it as a happy childhood, with loving parents and a carefree existence of wandering around Massachusetts. Except for the insults and for your parents wanting you to behave perfectly to protect yourself. Except for the white men who beat you, and the Indians who despised your impure blood. When I met you in 1755 and brought you over, I saved you from that torment. I thought the protection of vampirism would heal the anger from the discrimination and pain. I was wrong."

His words cut too deep into his soul. The past prejudice created the anger, true. But loneliness continued to fuel it. An abiding fear that he would never find someone. Every time his anger got the best of him, he knew it was because something evoked those feelings of seclusion.

"Maybe I don't want to be alone like you are."

"I taught you a lot, Thomas. But I'm afraid my teachings on coupling fell short." Anthony's authoritative voice soothed Thomas, despite knowing he would disagree with him. "I told you vampires couple for eternity. Some relationships falter over time, some vampires decide they like being alone, but this is the general rule. I failed to explain its profound meaning, though, because I was hurt by our failure together. It doesn't happen through magic."

"That's what happened, though! Xavier's an angel, not something I sought. He fell from the sky at my feet."

"You still have a lot to learn, and you can't bring a mate into your life when you can't answer all of the questions yourself. It takes decades to evolve."

"Why don't you just say it?" Thomas spat.

"You're too young. It's too soon. How could you know what it means to be a vampire, to live from generation to generation, through all of the extreme changes of history?"

"You'd understand if you met Xavier," he retorted.

"Why hurry? Your damn impatience, it's the one thing that concerned me even before I crossed you over. You begged for it every night. You didn't want to wait, to learn, to understand the full extent of what it meant. You wanted to experience it at once and educate yourself by trial and error. Slow down, Thomas. Slow down."

"But if this is right, why wait? If this is my soul mate, why risk his human death?"

Anthony's expression softened, and he crossed the room, then passed his fingers along Thomas's cheek and stared at him with those beautiful blue eyes.

"This longing for a mate, it contradicts everything else you stand for. You despise convention. Yet you want to immediately conform to this custom. Why not revel in sexual escapades? Why are you conforming?"

Thomas grabbed Anthony's hand. "I'm not conforming. I told you I always wanted this. Why do I need a grand reason? Who cares if it goes against the other things I do?"

"But why the urgency?"

"Humanity is the urgency. I could wait for years if I knew he'd be protected throughout the day and nothing would happen to him while I can't be there. Instead, not only do natural dangers threaten, but this damnable revolution might take anyone with it."

Anthony kissed Thomas on the cheek and then moved to another chair. He ran his fingers through his hair, troubled but not angry. "Do you remember that I made you say goodbye to your parents and all humans? That wasn't easy, yet you did it quickly so I'd cross you over. That rule was created for a very good reason: to protect our kind. Despite our power and cunning, we're threatened. All of these regulations are designed to keep us safe. We can't overpopulate the earth.

"This relationship with Xavier has led you very close to disobeying these laws. We can't interfere with human affairs, but you engaged with his circle in intimate ways."

"You did the same with me," Thomas tried to point out.

"No, I didn't. I got to know you, but I never met anyone else in your circle. I could have abandoned you at any time in the process without threat of discovery, and during it, you were the only human who knew anything."

"So I see them," he said with a wave of his hand. "I can leave, too, and no one would follow me. Other than Xavier's sister, they don't even know I'm a vampire."

"Good Lord, Thomas, you told her?"

"No, she figured it out." And Thomas realized, then, how that would seem to Anthony.

"This must stop," Anthony said in a quite tone. "No more contact."

"Why? I don't threaten anyone but myself. I maintain the ethic. And I'm careful."

"You do threaten people with your temper. You've violated the ethic constantly, often by your own admission. Quit deluding yourself. I won't even comment on your being careful."

"Where is my sin against vampires? Who do I endanger?"

"Yourself! And Xavier, if you can't get it under control. Vampires follow these rules, though some have challenged them. They've threatened us with discovery, and so they were executed. When a group of older vampires come together there's little that can stop our force. It's the oldest vampires who enforce these laws, and we watch to ensure no one disobeys."

Thomas had long held conflicted feelings about the Vampire Council, and Anthony's role on it. More than anything, its secrecy and Anthony's refusal to talk about it annoyed him. "So you watch me for them, because you made me?"

"Thomas, I don't want to antagonize you. You're not in peril. And I'd defend you to the bitter end. I'd even murder Xavier if I had to in order to protect you."

An icy admission, one that Thomas dared not think about because he would defend Xavier to the death, even if it meant his own or Anthony's.

"You need better balance. If you want to explore things with Xavier, go ahead. But you're immersed in his entire life and all of the people around him. Why go so far?"

"Because it's important to him. Besides, I *am* careful. I haven't touched the vile man who's engaged to Catherine. I told you about that."

"You've done well in that, but you still threatened him. And he also knows you're a vampire, so that makes two of them, not just Catherine. If you're correct and he has a spell on her, what will keep the two of them from hunting you down or exposing you to Xavier?"

"I understand," Thomas admitted through gritted teeth.

"Are there more?" Anthony leaned forward, expression hardening.

"Just one, a friend of Xavier's. She's a voodoo priestess, but she doesn't know any of the other Saint-Laurents."

"This is what I've been warning you about. All of these people know about you. That's why I want you to slow down. I'm not naïve enough to believe that you'd stop seeing Xavier, but at least take more precautions. You're young. You have plenty of time to find a lifemate."

"It's been thirty-five years." How much longer would he have to wait?

"That's nothing. You're immortal, after all."

"I love him," Thomas continued in his stubborn defense. "You like to live alone without a partner, so how can you know what I feel?"

Anthony got out of his chair and turned his back to Thomas, silent. "I never told you this," Anthony said softly. "For hundreds of years, I've failed to deaden the pain. I had a lover. I remained alone for my first hundred years until I found one that I cherished as you treasure Xavier. We were lifemates. For decades, we traveled the world together. But there was a flurry of violent activity, a war between the elders and a rogue vampire who tried to kill us all. Many died fighting him, including a number of elders. I was added to their circle afterward because so many died. I survived. I was part of the final assault. Unfortunately, this one manipulated us by going after those we loved who were defenseless. My mate was burned to death in an inferno of evil. So I feel your longing. It's mine too."

Anthony turned around, his face stained with bloody tears.

"Anthony, I never—"

"No, there's no need for that. But now you know I understand what you feel and want with Xavier. Will you listen to me? For your own good and Xavier's?"

"I promise I'll try."

"It's dangerous to move too fast. Look how I erred with you. Not that I regret it. I'd transform you all over again, but move with more caution. I'll stay in this miserable city with you and enjoy watching the French destroy each other if you assure me that you'll listen to my advice."

"Agreed," Thomas said.

"You'll consult me before you act?"

"Yes. Did I not send you letters asking your advice?"

Anthony cocked an eyebrow. "True. So you'll act with care when you do?"

"Yes." And he said it with as much conviction as he could muster.

"Then I'll stay. Which means tomorrow I have to find my own flat. I love you, but I hate your taste in décor."

Thomas laughed, relieved. "You always did."

"And since I'm staying, I'll need to meet Xavier."

"Let's go now."

Anthony rolled his eyes and sighed. "Slow down. I'll tell you when it's time."

RIOTING

Catherine marveled at how things changed every day. Paris erupted overnight. One day, peace reigned as the National Assembly challenged Louis, then constant riots and shouting ruled as people took to the streets with weapons, more and more wearing the tricolors. Catherine touched the scarf at her neck that Jérémie had given her.

More exciting, the plans to transform the Saint-Laurent household into a revolutionary salon proceeded. Various gatherings became more frequent, more people participated, and Catherine learned much about politics, economics, and the potential revolution.

That afternoon, Catherine worked with Jérémie, which always enlivened her because he was funny and his passion equaled hers. At the moment, she sat with Jérémie talking about current events and sharing a bottle of wine when someone knocked on her office door. Catherine opened it and blushed as the passion flooded her body when she saw Marcel.

"The servants should have announced you."

"I told them I knew the way," he said. "I came with your latest supply of medicine. I trust you have been taking it?"

"Of course."

His smile disappeared, though, when he saw Jérémie. He tipped his hat to him but addressed only Catherine. "If I've come at a bad time, I'll leave."

"I won't have your jealousy," she said, poking him in the stomach before entwining her arm with his. "Would you like something to drink?"

"I'd love some wine. Jérémie and I can chat while you get it."

Marcel came into the room and sat near Jérémie. In getting Marcel's wine, she snuck out of the room to a bar that her father had installed before his death so he could take leave of associates but still listen to them. It sat on the opposite side of one office wall, with gaps in certain boards so that one could overhear everything.

"Jérémie, you need to stay away from Catherine."

"My affairs with the Saint-Laurents are pure."

"What must others think of my fiancée living with a single man?"

"Catherine handles her reputation well, and there's nothing between us to impugn it."

And so they squabbled, neither yielding. Jérémie's willingness to confront Marcel surprised Catherine because he usually shrank from such. He charmed her with his defense of her right to live with whom she chose. Marcel, on the other hand, irritated her.

Annoyed and bored at the same time, Catherine poured herself a glass of wine, took a huge gulp, then grabbed another bottle and raced back into the room before their quarrel escalated.

"Marcel, that's enough," she demanded. "The same with you, Jérémie. If you could give us a moment?"

"Of course." With a final dark look at Marcel, Jérémie retreated from the room.

Catherine handed Marcel the bottle and took another big swig from her glass. She smiled a too sweet grin and sat near him. "I know you're jealous, but you can't chase Jérémie away."

"Catherine," Marcel said, "would you like some medicine?"

"Yes. These headaches only go away with it," she answered and handed him her glass. He plopped in a small blue substance from a bag of medicine and the wine fizzled. Marcel had explained that lots of women in the Americas took such drugs, and Catherine loved such exotic things. She smiled as it flooded her body with warmth. Soon after, the wine took over and she wanted Marcel, even more than ever.

Catherine approached Marcel and kissed him on the cheek, then moved to his lips and grabbed his body. He let her lead as she guided his hand onto her breasts.

As she yielded, lost in his magnificent manhood, authoritative steps in the hall signaled Michel's approach. She gathered her senses, pushed away from Marcel, and ran behind the desk. As she straightened her dress, Michel marched into the room, always the commanding general.

"At your service," she said.

"I'm delighted to see you, too, Catherine."

She assessed him. "Michel, what is it?"

"Rioting."

"That's not all. Enough with the secrets."

"I came to see that you were safe," Michel said and stiffened his posture. "So shout at me again. Scream about your independence. There's a mob one street over breaking into homes and stealing food. My regiment is combating them, and I was worried about your safety. Good day."

Catherine felt awful and began to apologize when she had another interruption. In the midst of it, Michel stormed out.

"Catherine, forgive my intrusion, but is Xavier here?" Thomas asked.

"No, Xavier sent word this afternoon that you're to meet him at the river, whatever that means."

Thomas laughed. He came across the room more gracefully that any man she knew and took her hand. "Was ever there such beauty combined with cunning and humor?"

"Perhaps Cleopatra," she said.

Thomas almost responded but instead turned toward Marcel. Catherine felt an increased tension the minute they made eye contact. Thomas took leave, smiling at her but glaring at Marcel.

"The other men in my life have a strange reaction to you," Catherine said.

Marcel grabbed her close to his body and said nothing in response.

SPELLS ON CATHERINE

Thomas rushed to Anne Hébert's door and whispered to the air, asking the spirits not to flee so she would chat. He knocked.

"You again! Get in here, before someone sees your undead self at my door. Are you here to undo my magic again? Last time after you left, things were in a flurry, everything unsettled and angry. I gave up for the night and went to the graveyards, collecting supplies."

Thomas waited for her to finish complaining. "Only you can help me in another matter."

Anne stoked the fire and turned back to Thomas. "I thought I told you I wasn't making any love potion. You think coming 'round here every night will make me obey you, but it won't. Bring him over on his time, not yours."

"I've developed an infinite amount of patience. I love Xavier but am willing to wait 'til the end of time for him to come to me. It's not about Xavier—at least not directly—but it's serious," Thomas said.

"What? If not about him, what other common interest could we have?"

"Xavier's sister, Catherine. She's in trouble that you alone can solve." Thomas kept his arms crossed, prepared to argue his case.

"You're doing it again, trying to put me in the middle. Maybe I want to stay *out* of trouble, when it comes to rich folks in particular. They don't like my kind."

"Xavier's sake."

She pondered and then smiled. "For him, not for you." She sat in a pile of clothes and gazed into the fire. "Well, I'm waiting. I may die before you tell me."

Thomas sighed. "Catherine's under a spell and unaware of it. She's engaged to an insufferable man, who'll stop at nothing to get what he wants. He's even sent men after Michel and Xavier, and I saw him putting something in her drink. She changes around him and becomes giddy and almost blind to reality. I don't know anything else, but that the wine fizzes from the medicine and soon after, she swoons."

"I see." Anne stroked her chin. "And the night you came storming in here and shoved the chicken bones in my face, those came from him too?"

"Yes. What do you know about this?"

"Voodoo, or some deranged form of it. New World. You don't see much of that around here. Oh, yes, he's in tune with it all right, but sounds manipulative, using evil."

Thomas waited, but she said nothing further. "Is that it?"

"What do you want me to say? This is no good, nothing positive comes from his kind and interfering is dangerous. The quicker he's gone, the better. So I'd recommend you get rid of him."

"I can't."

She looked at him with a skeptical stare. "Can't or won't?"

"Do I look like I have trouble killing parasites?"

"So what's different about this time?"

"There's a vampiric ethic I must follow, a protocol that protects us. I can pursue Xavier, but I promised to stay away from his family, at least insofar as it concerns their daily lives."

Anne laughed again, a deep, guttural cackle. If only Thomas found it funny. "Now, this is too much. I expect you to storm around the earth, taking what you want, when and where you want it. Instead, you have some code of ethics. Who would have guessed such a thing? First, you're in love with a priest, but can't bring him over. Now, we've a fiend on our hands, yet you can't do anything about it. There's a humor in that, you know."

Thomas ignored the last comment. "There's more. Marcel may have a spell on Xavier and others that would endanger them if I killed him."

What would you have *me* do?"

"Anything to protect her. And more than that, it's Xavier. It would crush him if anything happened to her."

"I refuse to get into black magic. There's enough evil in this world that I'll not contribute to more pernicious forces haunting us. I never use my knowledge for wicked purposes. I won't."

"But you can do *something*?" Thomas pressed.

She was quiet before responding. "Maybe." She avoided his gaze.

"For Xavier."

Another long silence. "I'll look in on her. But give me some time and don't show up tomorrow night expecting results."

"Oh, thank you." Thomas kissed her on the cheek.

"I hope you never ask anything more personal of me, or I fear the consequences." Another hearty chuckle. "You got what you want, now be gone." She shooed him out the door.

The breeze whipped at his coat as he headed back to the Seine and away from the area's stench. Euphoria swept over him when he saw Xavier standing alone, watching the waves hit the shore. People shouted nearby but out of sight. He grabbed Xavier from behind without warning and spun him in the air. The priest's soft hair whisked across his face.

Xavier shouted in astonishment before Thomas put him down but maintained his hold.

"Thomas, you scared me to death. What are you doing? What if someone sees us?"

"Abbé, what if I refuse to let go? What if I decided to steal you away under my arm?"

Xavier's muscles relaxed. Thomas almost picked him up and fled.

Thomas brushed his lips along Xavier's neckline and let go.

Xavier hugged himself and turned back to the river. "Isn't it beautiful?"

.

Part IV: Storming the Bastille

Twenty: Loving Men

12 JULY 1789

They had established a routine, and neither wondered whether the other would show up. Thomas and Xavier spent every evening together, talking at the Saint-Laurent Salon as they did that night on the grand porch, or meandering through Paris, as they had the previous day. As an observer of human society, the revolution around them intrigued Thomas, but as a lover, it terrified him. He awoke all the time to news about more rioting or attacks against the clergy, only finding comfort after he saw Xavier alive and well.

But that night, Thomas feared something different: exposure. Xavier had asked him once again as they walked along the Seine the previous night to visit him during the day. Thomas became quiet when Xavier posed the question again, which unnerved Xavier.

"Never mind," Xavier said and clamped his lips together.

"Tell me why you ask that of me."

"Maria, the nun? She thinks it's strange that you come only at night. None of that concerned me, but it did make me wonder if you were telling me everything."

"What do you want me to say?" Thomas asked tersely.

"Nothing. I'm sorry. Never mind."

Thomas, angry at himself, paused, clenched his fists, and took a deep breath. He walked to the priest and put one hand on each of Xavier's shoulders. "I come whenever I can. I'll explain everything, soon."

Xavier blushed. "I'm just jealous."

Thomas grinned and cupped Xavier's chin in his hand. "You've nothing to worry about."

"What about your clothing?" Xavier asked, making Thomas wonder if he had missed a segue. "You wear black. You need to wear the tricolors? Parisians are coming to expect it."

Thomas laughed, despite himself. The revolution did not frightened him. Besides, these Parisians dressed like bad American flags, with blue, white, and red draped across their bodies.

"I'm an American. I embody everything they want."

"I didn't think of that," Xavier answered, his shoulders slumping.

"Do you like how I look in black?" Thomas asked to change the subject.

"Yes," Xavier said and smiled.

"You're cute when you blush. That's the second time tonight."

"Someone might overhear."

"Is it okay if two men kiss?" Thomas pressed.

"Stop."

"Is sodomy permissible?"

Xavier fidgeted with his cross and looked around. "I think that all sorts of sexual practices take place, and so long as they don't harm anyone, it's not a problem. I can't imagine castigating one of my parishioners because they did something with someone of the same sex, if that's what you mean."

Thomas sighed. Of course, Xavier thought of his flock first. Here, again, was Xavier's odd dualism. For others, he demanded respect and love. All moral precepts came after and were based on specific situations. But none of it applied to him.

"What about yourself?" Thomas asked.

"You know we're celibate," Xavier said. He scrambled into the house and backed away from Thomas.

"Relax," Thomas said once in Xavier's private room. "I'm sorry. You're safe with me."

Xavier flinched when Thomas put his hand on his shoulder. Thomas felt the tension in his muscles through the black robe. He squeezed the tight muscles with a gentle grip as Xavier slumped into a sofa, then leaned over and kissed the top of Xavier's head.

"I love you," Xavier whispered. "But I made an oath to the church. It can't be as you wish." Xavier was crying. "Forgive me for leading you to this. But I do love you."

Xavier collapsed into Thomas's arms and buried his hands in his black coat. He clutched at Thomas, drawing him near. Thomas held him tightly without saying a word with tears of blood running down his cheeks. When Xavier went limp, Thomas wiped at his face, then looked into Xavier's eyes. He held Xavier's face and leaned forward as Xavier trembled in his arms, closing his eyes as Thomas's face came closer and closer. Thomas kissed Xavier's eyelids, the right and then the left. He moved his mouth across Xavier's nose, pecked the tip of it, and brushed their lips together, not a full, passionate kiss, but enough to make his point. Then he let go with his heart in complete turmoil.

Xavier swayed back and forth. "Good night, Thomas."

"Good night, my abbé."

As he reached the door, Thomas turned and saw Xavier leaning over in agony where he sat on the couch, watching him heave like a distressed lover. Yet, even in the saddest of moments, Thomas swooned at Xavier's beauty, perhaps even more evident in his sorrow.

"I love you too," Thomas said.

ANTHONY THE SPY

Thomas closed the bedroom door, raced outside the salon after telling Xavier he loved him, and leaned against the stone wall, unable to support himself or think with a clear head. His head drooped to his chest and he grabbed at his hair. So love could sting. The pounding people described in their hearts at last came to Thomas.

Anyone else, in any other situation, would have garnered Thomas's scorn, especially if the other man's expectations differed so much from his. With Xavier, it only revealed the passion for humanity that so endeared him to Thomas. Blood flowed anew from Thomas's eyes, onto his shirt and all over his hands as he wept.

In his mourning, he didn't see the person who approached. By the time he reacted, Anthony's fragrance engulfed him, and when his friend pulled him away from the wall and into his arms, Thomas yielded to the embrace.

They walked in silence back to Thomas's flat. The tears stopped, and Thomas felt stronger, more himself, though confused. He was not angry, yet a pit in his stomach ached with dread even as his determination to overcome the obstacles increased. Then why the tears?

Thomas remembered when he twirled Xavier in the air near the Seine, when he wanted to capture the priest and run. The abbé's beautiful smile burned into his mind. Then he flashed back to Xavier earlier that night, his eyes closed and his body yielding.

As he reveled in the anguish, he realized that Anthony had watched somehow. It irritated Thomas.

"You spied on me," Thomas accused him, voice rising in anger.

"Was I to assume that you told me everything? Was I to trust your emotions? You still lose control. I wanted to see Xavier with you, and you with him."

"So you spied." Thomas lowered his gaze, sullen.

"Yes. I concealed myself in the salon. I couldn't predict that intimacy."

"You should've warned me."

"I apologize. But I can't help you if I don't know. Now, can we forget this?"

"Only if you'll tell me what you think now."

"You've described the situation to me in accurate detail. I feared that you were blinded by your passion for Xavier. It's obvious he loves you. I was also surprised, and again shocked, that you didn't try to force the issue. You're patient with him."

"But?" Thomas asked testily.

"But you think that these things guarantee success, and they don't."

Thomas fought to control himself. Since the day he met Xavier, he had worked to acknowledge reality and stay patient, waiting for Xavier. He launched out of the chair and paced in front of the window. Paris at night, such a perfect setting for complete wretchedness. It was damp and misty. Darkness consumed everything. Even the lanterns were lost in fog. Yet underneath lay an indescribable beauty. He loved cities, with their density of buildings and masses of humanity, the constant energy and persistent bustle of activity.

He rapped his hand against the window, his torment mounting. At the bursting point, he smashed his fist into a table. The top broke into a million fragments that flew across the room, its lamp burst into pieces and the oil leaked everywhere. More maddening, Anthony sat motionless and ever more composed.

"Everything you tell me, everything that these damned rules dictate, relates to controlling me," Thomas bellowed. "It's all about the collective good of vampires and humans. What about *me*?" Thomas pounded his chest. "What about *my* suffering?" He glared at Anthony. "Fuck society. You and your rules can go to hell. Look at what the constraints have done to Xavier. He's the most delicate man I've ever known, but he suffers because the things he feels inside are forbidden. And why? For nothing. Yet all these men who seek power refuse to act in a rational manner and instead proclaim inspiration from God, that somehow they know more about faith and truth than everyone else. And what advice do I get? Be patient, be calm, wait for things to change."

His fist went through more wood, next a shelf along the wall, spilling its contents.

"And you—" He pointed at Anthony. "You taught that vampires were no different from everyone else except that their blood gave them eternal life. You promised that none of the ancient teachings against us were true, that only evil vampires fit the myths. Well, let me tell you something about our commonness: I despise it. I wish we came from Satan. I could wander the earth as a pernicious demon forever, wreaking havoc, frightening people, ripping off their heads. If only the church had it right," he said with a bitter taste in his mouth. "I could be a perfect devil. Instead, I'm damned to feel like a human. And it's worse, because vampire ethics, irritating invented rules, condemn me. So spare me your comments. I've heard enough."

Thomas clutched the back of his couch, ripping the fabric with his nails. And there sat Anthony, like a Greek statue.

"Finished?" he asked in a calm voice.

Thomas did not know whether to say yes or punch him in the face.

"This is exactly why I commanded you to listen," Anthony began. He got up and stood inches from Thomas. "I listened to you, now you do the same. You're correct. This isn't about society or the ethic. This is about your temper and impatience. I know, you'll insist that I dwell on them too much. And I know you work on it. But you haven't conquered them." Anthony motioned around the room, pointing out the evidence. "Will you please sit down and hear me? For God's sake, if you don't realize by now that I love you and am on your side, then you're hopeless."

Thomas forced himself to sit. Anthony sat next to him and grabbed his hand.

"Your temper is the only thing that can derail this. What if Xavier sees this? He'd shrink away from you forever. He trusts you but this would poison your love."

Thomas nodded. Dear God, what if Xavier had witnessed his display?

"Do you see that it's worse when you're in love?"

"I know. I know. But what can I do?"

"*Slow down.* Allow me to help you. Give it time." Anthony paused. He got up and walked back to his chair. He started to sit but instead crossed his arms. "Xavier loves you. And you're patient with him. Before your tirade, I tried to warn you about the one threat to everything. You must accept the possibility that Xavier may never change. He's committed to his religion to depths even I don't understand, and you want him to not only accept his sexuality but also understand vampires. There's a good possibility that you'll fail."

All along, Thomas *had* known the truth in his heart but was too frightened to say it. Speaking it might make it real. He sought promises of victory in a climate that assured nothing but love.

"That terrifies me," Thomas said.

"Try to see things from Xavier's perspective. Think what he thinks, not what you want him to think. And, when those conclusions go someplace you don't want them to, don't force him to change. When it becomes too much and overwhelms you, come to me. Don't try to do it alone. Allow yourself to be vulnerable."

Anthony ended the night by hugging him, a simple but wonderful gesture that gave Thomas the strength to face another night.

Twenty-One: Devotion

13 JULY 1789

Riots. Bread riots. Political riots. Military riots. All riots. All violence. What had become of the revolution, Xavier wondered, to elicit such savagery? He tried to cope by focusing on daily activities but could not escape the fact that a peaceful solution failed France.

He tried to forget other things, too, though with even less success. Just the other day, he witnessed Marcel drugging Catherine again. Anne's words haunted him, too. "Those markings you discovered etched under Catherine's desk aren't good. Get rid of them," she instructed Xavier the other night. "Black magic." But she refused to say more.

And, of course, he wanted to forget about his longings for Thomas. The night before, when Thomas kissed him, Xavier almost fell into Thomas's arms forever. He almost pleaded for Thomas to sweep him away to America or some exotic locale. But the people needed him, and he could only fulfill his mission if he refused to act on these sinful emotions.

That evening, he and Maria completed a mundane task, which helped him forget a little bit. While they preferred interacting with people, tonight they spent hours cleaning the sanctuary.

Maria glanced sideways at him. "Abbé, do you think my girls and I are doomed to hell?"

"Of course not," Xavier said.

"Even if we lay naked together, our fingers in unseemly places?"

"I don't want that image in my head," he responded, rubbing at a spot on a pew.

"You wanted to think that the convent housed virtuous women who sat around all day worshipping God. We do, but there's plenty of worshipping each other too." She giggled.

"Maria, stop. I know you and the other nuns love each other in a variety of ways."

Maria laughed and Xavier knew his cheeks were flaming red. "Speaking of forbidden love, I'd best get going before your evening visitor arrives," she said and gave him a sideways glance.

"I don't want to hear this."

Maria threw her hands in the air. "Only speaking the truth. I won't say a word. Anyway, before I go, help me load these things. They're the hocus pocus we need for tomorrow."

"The sacraments?" He cocked an eyebrow at her.

"Oh, enough. God hasn't struck me down yet."

Maria headed out, box in tow. The minute she stepped around the corner, Xavier whirled around and raced to the other end of the sanctuary. He had seen Thomas enter as he said goodbye, and his arrival sent a thrill through him.

"Thomas," he said, tone colored with urgency, "I worried—"

"You don't have to talk about it." Thomas reached over and ruffled Xavier's hair and smiled. He must have read his mind before Xavier even got his words out.

And so they slighted their love at Xavier's request. Yet his best efforts did little to force his mind to forget it. The turmoil hung in the air. Thomas always yielded at the beginning of the evening, but as the time to separate came closer, Thomas became bolder. Xavier anticipated such a scene tonight, Thomas hinting, Xavier encouraging it, and then, at the breaking point, Xavier would run to the shelter of his religion.

Xavier brushed past Thomas and led him into the garden, where they had to be discreet. Xavier launched into a comment about the revolution and explained what he and Maria intended to do the following day.

"It's harder and harder to do our secret services," he finished.

"Then maybe you need to stop," Thomas said.

"But they need me," he muttered.

Thomas's protectiveness in wanting him to stop made Xavier feel loved. Yet he could never follow through with his request, no matter how much comfort Thomas gave to him.

"Haven't you heard what's happening to other priests? I'm not talking about curés in distant regions of France. I'm talking about your colleagues right in this city, some of them mere blocks from your church. They're attacked by their own parishioners. People hate the church. Louis and his armies no longer protect you."

Thomas dropped his voice, becoming even more serious. "Today, another priest went into his neighborhood and the people attacked him. They stripped him, raided the church, and left him for dead. Does that sound like rational behavior?"

Xavier had heard about that incident when Denys Girard and others ran to find him right after. Of course, two men already protected him when the rest arrived. People lashed out at priests as a symbol of oppression, but none of the people around Xavier's church felt like that. None of those curés had organized patrols of parishioners who followed them.

"I'm careful, Thomas."

"Can't you stop until things settle down?"

"No."

"Your devotion to these people baffles me. With your family and wealth, you could do anything that you want. What *drives* this?"

Xavier sighed, wondering if he wanted to risk explaining such personal matters to the man he knew he loved.

Xavier's Theology

Thomas relaxed as Xavier sat back in the bench outside the church. He was frustrated but remembering to be patient. Even his concern about Xavier's safety led to a dead end. Thankfully, Xavier hit upon something that interested Thomas: Xavier's theology.

Xavier leaned forward. "First, Rome has nothing to do with it. I'm Catholic because I was raised Catholic. I entered the priesthood because it offered the best opportunity to serve people. I believe that God exists and sent His son to die for us. It's such a profound notion of love and sacrifice. The priesthood is the vehicle that allows me to act upon the way I think people should treat each other."

"Most of your colleagues do it for power," Thomas said.

"I think people are better than that." Xavier smiled in an innocent way. "I comfort those in need. When hurt by others or saddened by the reality that surrounds them, their faith offers solace and guides them. They want the church's authority, and if I weren't here, someone else would do this and not care as much."

If anyone else had made these grand proclamations, Thomas would have laughed out loud. But Xavier believed the sentiment deep in his bones.

"I see what you believe, but you didn't expect me to convert?"

Xavier laughed. "No."

"Doesn't this revolution make you question all of your beliefs?"

"Yes," Xavier answered without hesitation.

"I don't understand why you don't protect yourself and give up on people."

Xavier grinned, so sweetly and still with utter naiveté. "I'm not trying to save the entire world. I just want to help as many people as possible while I'm here. If I can help one person, then maybe they'll help someone else and, in the midst of this misery and sorrow, make their small part of the world better."

Thomas smiled but arched a brow, his cynicism taking over.

"I have a thousand examples," Xavier answered his expression. "A servant girl came to confession. I shouldn't be telling you. Her name is Melisent; she's pretty. Her mother works in a textile shop and her father is a blacksmith. They have a lot of children. Melisent always smiles when she sees me and walks around whistling, even at work. She's a domestic servant for one of Paris's wealthy families and my father knew them well.

"But she came to confession in tears. She cried. Then, almost so that I could not hear, she asked if it were a sin to kill yourself. I assumed that she knew someone who committed suicide and tried to comfort her by saying that I didn't believe God would forsake them. Then I realized that she wasn't talking about someone else." Xavier's eyes teared. "Against all rules, I got out of the booth, pulled her out of hers, and took her into the back. She collapsed into my arms, a sobbing mess, trembling with fear. 'Who is it?' I asked.

"'Abbé, I'm pregnant. I've sinned. If I disappear, if I can make it look like an accident in a riot—' She stopped and wept as if her heart would break.

"'Don't do anything drastic,' I said. 'But, Abbé, God says it's my fault for not controlling myself. I sinned, I'm not married or even betrothed. No one will listen.'

"Then I asked about the father, which made it worse. She confessed that it was the master of the household. The thug"—Xavier's voice had an unusual edge to it—"raped her and threatened her if she said anything. He did it all the time, though she stopped resisting because he beat her and it ended faster if she gave in. She hadn't told him about the pregnancy because he'd beat her even more. Of course she thought of suicide. As she continued to cry, I did too." Tears flowed down his cheeks.

"That's why I serve. No one else would help her. It doesn't have anything to do with the church, sin, or salvation. It's simply that I was in the right place and could assist her."

"What did you do?" Thomas asked, feeling Xavier's pain.

"I fetched Maria. We belong to a clandestine network of clergy and nuns throughout France, who trade in the destitute. We relocate them and give them new identities. So Maria and I spirited Melisent out of Paris, to a rural village. To everyone there, the priest introduced her as an orphan and widow, her family and husband having been murdered in the Paris the riots."

Thomas walked over to Xavier. He loved him more now than ever. Unfortunately, his heart reminded him that they were a perfect couple with an ideal balance between Thomas's cynicism and Xavier's compassion.

Then he moved away, afraid that he would grab Xavier and force a kiss upon him. He had to talk about it. He motioned for them to retire inside, away from others. Reluctantly, but as always, Xavier obeyed.

THOMAS'S LOVE

As he prodded Xavier into the church's seclusion and up to his room, distraught with love, Thomas fretted. "Xavier, this story about Melisent, that's what attracts me to you."

Thomas paced across the room, his black clothes blending into the shadows in such a way that his white skin seemed to glow. He controlled himself by staying away from Xavier. Xavier curled up on the bed in a ball, his knees tucked under his chin, his foot bobbing up and down with nervousness as he stared at the floor.

"Your faith in humanity makes me love you," Thomas said in a soft voice. "But we have to end this, for better or worse, because I can't pretend that our love doesn't exist. I love you, Xavier. Not platonically, not as friends, but as a lover. I'm devoted to you. I yearn for you. I want to kiss your lips and feel your heart pound close to mine."

"What do you expect me to say?"

Thomas moved across the room, daring to sit on the end of the bed. "The truth that you give everyone else but me."

Without hesitating but with tears streaming down his face, Xavier let out a flood of emotion. "I love you, too, in all the same ways. I dream of lying in your arms. I want you to take me and have your will with me in every possible way. In those moments when I'm alone in this room, I close my eyes and dream of falling asleep in your arms. But it can't happen. What would others say? What would I tell Michel and Catherine? The church—my God, we preach against lust." He wept then, shaking, his head buried in his hands.

Thomas grabbed him, and Xavier allowed the embrace. The love that Xavier condemned on behalf of his church, felt more genuine and pure than anything Thomas had ever experienced. Yet he, too, was frightened. Not of religion or of Xavier's refusal to leave the church. Something even more frightening stalked him. If mere physical contact threw Xavier into so much turmoil, how would he ever deal with vampirism?

As they sat motionless, neither making the next move, Thomas smelled Xavier's hair and noticed the it body beneath the robe. The thought again came to steal away with him and offer no choice. What was left but hopelessness?

Xavier stopped crying after a bit and ceased clutching Thomas. He stayed close but relaxed, adjusting his head on Thomas's chest, so he might look at him. His eyes betrayed uneasiness.

Thomas ran his fingers through Xavier's hair and smiled. "I'll never force you."

"I know. Can you accept why I can't do anything?"

"Give it time. Think about it, think about your life, think about what's happening in Paris, and think about us. Nothing will change our friendship and my devotion to you. But do me the favor of allowing yourself to reflect on our circumstances before you cast it away."

"I will," Xavier said.

Xavier's reply was more than Thomas had hoped to hear. He expected an instant dismissal and another explanation about how the church condemned their love. "Perhaps I should leave. You need to rest."

"If you don't mind," Xavier said and wiped away the teardrops as he collected himself with a weak smile.

They parted with a platonic hug, though passion still welled in Thomas.

In the hot night air of Paris, Thomas was ready for action.

The damnable Catholic Church. Always admonishing people and condemning, always judging as if the church leaders were God. He hated the institution. He despised the church. He went over the multitude of reasons, all of them coming back to power and controlling people. Hypocrites, who preyed on the minds of those within and without their ranks.

It was time to hunt, and Thomas knew the perfect game.

He moved as fast as possible through Paris until he saw it. What a beautiful church, Notre Dame Cathedral, full of opulent décor, built of the finest stone, with sculptures of saints, intricate stained glass, the Virgin Mary all around, and Christ, the sacrificing, crucified martyr, stared at Thomas. So different from Xavier's simple sanctuary. The wood was glorious in the seat of Catholic power. Only the lustful, egotistical priests worked here, only they wanted a gothic setting where the rich gathered to pretend they led holy lives.

Thomas slipped into a back pew, waiting. He watched for his victim, careful to assess the priests who passed. He dismissed the first as too young. His haughty attitude would someday fit in quite well there, but Thomas doubted he had done anything dastardly yet. He was amused that the priest looked at the vampire with suspicion.

A few minutes later, no doubt sent by the first priest, a middle-aged official walked up to Thomas. He had the air of superiority that Thomas sought.

"You can't be here."

"My apologies, Father. I thought the church was open to all of God's children when in need," Thomas said, amusing himself.

"I'm afraid no one can help you at this hour."

"May I at least provide a humble offering to the church?" Thomas asked as he pulled out a bundle of gold coins from his coat pocket.

The greedy fool's demeanor changed at once. "Perhaps we could make an exception."

"That's most kind, but you'll have to accept double the amount in that case."

"Oh, you're too generous. What might I do for you?"

"May we speak in private?" Thomas asked, trying to appear as if something troubled him.

"Yes, this way." The priest nodded and gestured toward a side alcove.

Once alone, Thomas wasted no time. With his back to the priest, his fangs dropped and he adopted a horrific expression. When the priest turned around, Thomas received the hoped-for reaction. The priest backed against the wall, his eyes wide, and clutched the crucifix around his neck. He mumbled some garbled Latin and Thomas smiled. In seconds, he latched onto the priest's neck and sucked the life from him.

The blood haunted him with the victim's memories. A boy, innocent and trusting, bleeding and crying as the priest thrust in and out of him; an elderly woman, running from the village church in agony because her grandson could not be baptized; a curé, pleading at the feet of the man because he was throwing him out of the clergy for spilling consecrated wine; a man's life in ruins because the priest spread false rumors that he fornicated because the priest did not like him. On and on the images went, of countless people's lives destroyed by the sanctimonious man.

Once drained, he dropped the priest into a chair and positioned him to look as if he died without cause. Instead of leaving things in such an innocent scene, though, Thomas added a religious touch. He retrieved the gold coins that he had given to the priest and replaced them with thirty silver coins from his pocket.

These he threw on the table, saying, "Good night, Judas. Rest in peace."

ANNE AND JÉRÉMIE

Xavier tried to forget what had happened by trying to sleep soon after Thomas left, but his head spun. What did Thomas want? What did Xavier want? One minute, he wanted to run to Thomas, but the next, it frightened him too much. Trying to sleep was useless.

Instead, Xavier dressed and headed for the Saint-Laurent home. It buzzed with activity at all hours since Catherine had converted it to a salon. Xavier greeted a few people and smiled to himself when strangers looked at him with suspicion because of his clerical garb. Nothing enticed him, so Xavier strolled around until he ran into Jérémie, sitting alone doing paperwork.

"How are you?" Xavier greeted him.

"Fine," Jérémie said as he put the pen down. "Aside from trying to keep up with the finances. Catherine and I never expected such a positive response. We need more help." He rubbed his forehead. "What brings you here at this hour?"

"It's hard to sleep these days," Xavier answered without explaining the vague statement.

Jérémie poured them some wine without asking, reminding Xavier of carefree youthful days, when Jérémie and he would sneak into the house and get drunk while they discussed everything imaginable. Xavier smiled, remembering their first encounter with drunken philosophy at the age of eight. They attended dinner that evening, barely able to stand up, and spent the meal giggling. The adults, thinking them too pure and innocent, assumed childhood nonsense possessed them and suspected nothing else.

"Thank you," Xavier said and took the glass.

They fell into easy conversation about nothing in particular, but soon a familiar laugh echoed down the hall. Jérémie squinted in puzzlement, but Xavier rushed to the hallway as Jérémie followed.

"Anne?" he said, both puzzled and worried.

His friend howled with delight.

"I came to see Catherine, at the request of a friend. It's none of your business, but it's good to see you." She smiled. "They say she's retired or out." She shrugged. She pushed past Xavier into the room, got herself a glass without asking, and poured it full of wine before drinking. Then she turned around, still smiling, and pointed for Jérémie and Xavier to sit. "You can help me, young man," she said to Jérémie. "Maybe we can do something about that broken heart of yours."

Jérémie's eyes widened, stunned.

"Oh, get those ridiculous looks off your faces. I know you didn't tell me about him, Xavier. And I know we've never met, Jérémie, but we don't have time to get into all of that." Though a thousand questions raced through Xavier's head, and no doubt Jérémie's, they followed her command. "Catherine needs protecting. I might be able to do something about it. I might not. This is a dangerous thing that we discuss." Anne took another gulp of wine. "Catherine is engaged to a fiend, and I've seen plenty of evidence that he dabbles in the black magic."

"What?" Jérémie stared at her, confused.

"This is evil we're dealing with and almost impossible to counter. I suspect in this case that the victim won't help us. So the three of us must do what we can. The less we do, the better. We don't want to be messing about with this religion any more than necessary. It's *evil*." Anne shook and rubbed her shoulders as if chilled by the thought, and then she howled with delight at the expressions on Jérémie's and Xavier's faces.

She never ceased to awe Xavier with her pagan religious tricks.

"Whenever you do something," Anne continued, "you must be extra careful because it'd be a disaster if she found out. Especially for you, young man, who loves her so much." She regarded Jérémie with a measured stare. "She would turn on you first, and your dreams of being with her would forever be destroyed. And if Marcel discovered anything, he'd put spells on the both of you and we'd have a terrible time doing anything about that. We first need to figure out what he's doing, and I've no idea right now. Gather information for me, about what he says, what he does, and how she acts around him. Watch him like a hawk when you see her with him and think of what has changed about her of late."

"Anne," Xavier said, "I'm not sure that this will do anything. And I'm worried about Michel. Marcel threatened him. How will this help, if all we're doing is watching?"

Anne became serious and patted each man on the knee. "She can't know, because she'd tell him and then he'd come after us. I'm hoping, though, that you can provide me with some hints of something we might do. Perhaps we can save her in time. I'm afraid, for better or worse, that this is all we can do."

"Did Thomas send you?" Xavier asked, suspicion creeping into his thoughts.

Anne smiled, then another laugh erupted from her gut. "Abbé, you make me laugh. You weren't thinking about him, were you?" More laughter, a fierce cackling. "I'm sorry." Anne grabbed his arm with both hands. "Yes, Thomas asked me to look into this."

"Xavier, is that true?" Jérémie asked. "That you never told this woman anything?"

"I didn't."

"Then how did you know? Anne?"

Anne grinned at the corner of her mouth.

"If someone betrayed me, I need to know it," Jérémie said.

Anne shrieked with laughter. She bent over, then hugged Jérémie, who sat erect in his seat. "No one betrayed you. Rest assured that this abbé would never do such a thing. I don't know who else knows your little secret. Let's just say I have ways of knowing things."

"You read my mind?" Jérémie's eyes narrowed.

"I suppose you could call it that. You conceal it well. Hardly a handful of people could guess. But right now, I need you to focus on making her better."

Jérémie nodded, yet Xavier saw his anguish. Catherine's voice interrupted the conversation. From the sound of it, she was charging down the hallway in typical Catherine fashion. Xavier looked over at Anne, imploring her to leave.

Anne jumped to a back door, turned, and smiled. She hurried away as Catherine entered.

"What on earth are you two sitting here for? You look as if you're in the middle of a funeral," she scolded. Catherine glanced at the bottle of wine on the table. "Perhaps the wine made you lethargic. Come, I need some help. I'm thinking of reconfiguring a room."

With that, Catherine sent them on a frantic journey through the house. She acted like her usual, distracted, frenzied self as she talked fast and changed subjects without warning. Xavier did her bidding, glad to have a familiar Catherine to deal with.

Twenty-Two: Reconciliation

14 JULY 1789

Xavier sat drowsily in the hot Saint-Laurent home. Catherine, Jérémie, Michel, and he simmered in the library's heat, suffocating after Michel shuttered the windows and closed the doors.

Michel spoke with wisdom when he told them the breaking point had arrived. It meant more violence, worse than before, and increased danger for the military and aristocracy.

"Would all of you consider fleeing Paris? Most of the aristocrats have already left."

"We can't leave," Catherine said and frowned to emphasize her point.

Michel clenched his hands. "Do you understand what I said about increased violence?"

"But what about the hospital?" She looked at him, imploring. "Jérémie and I converted the second floor into an emergency hospital. It's needed even more now."

Michel sighed. "At least promise me you'll fortify the house."

"I agreed to that," Catherine answered.

"I've one more thing to ask you." Michel dropped his voice to a whisper.

"What?" Catherine asked.

"Where's Marcel?" Michel asked. "Why isn't he protecting you?"

Xavier wondered the same thing, but expected Catherine to erupt and so said nothing.

Instead, she sat quiet, unusual for her, with a strange glassy look to her eyes. "He had to leave Paris."

"He left you alone in Paris?" Michel gaped at her.

"He asked me to come along, but—well, I think that—he's frightened of the violence, positively frightened for his life. He insisted they'd target him, such a wealthy merchant, and so he had to leave the city. He begged me to go, but I won't leave."

Xavier noted how Catherine handled herself. She stayed calm without lashing out at Michel, yet the minute they mentioned Marcel her face became red and she scratched at her neck. Michel nodded at her.

Xavier exhaled in relief. They'd avoided an argument.

After Michel hugged Catherine and Jérémie, he asked Xavier to walk him to the city's edge. "One of my men will escort you home."

Xavier agreed apprehensively. "The men from my parish will follow to protect me." With that, the two men headed down the street. "You showed much patience with Catherine."

"I wish that she'd listen. I hate this feeble man she wants to marry, and I want her to marry Jérémie. But this revolution brought things into perspective. It's more important to focus on loving and admiring her. Besides, there's nothing in the world I can do about Marcel."

"No," Xavier said with resignation. "You know she won't listen."

Michel walked tall through the streets in his military uniform despite being a marked man. People catcalled and sneered. "I don't mean to sound morbid, but anything could happen to any one of us. God forbid, someone could attack Catherine because of that salon, and I wouldn't be able to live with myself if we last parted in an argument. Furthermore, I've no idea what will happen to me. I'm no longer endeared to the monarchy, but I don't see a viable alternative."

"You're right. No one should leave in anger."

"Speaking of leaving under bad circumstances..." Michel stood erect with his hands behind his back, but his voice quivered. "I apologize for my behavior when I came to see you."

"It was nothing." Xavier started toying with the cross that hung around his neck.

Michel stopped in the street and looked down at Xavier. "I judge you too fast. We all have protected you too much. When I come to that small church, all I see is a dilapidated building and I want you to live in more luxury. I failed to account for what you need, or what you want."

"Michel, please, I understand."

"I need to say this." Michel's voice trembled, and he fought back tears. "I couldn't be prouder of you. You're worthy of sainthood." He embraced Xavier. Then he walked, ever the officer, as if trying to outpace his emotions. "You can't follow farther. It's too dangerous."

They reached the southeast corner of town, on the road to Versailles. The rioting happened there, and angry mobs marched to the palace to throw things at the king. No priest—guards or not—was safe. Xavier froze in place.

"One more thing," Michel said before he looked away. "About your relationship with Thomas. I was wrong about that, too. Do what makes you happy."

Again they hugged, a long embrace, Xavier's face pressed into the medals that dangled from his brother's chest. Finally, Michel turned to leave. He got a few paces before Xavier cried out.

When Michel turned, already composed, Xavier stammered, "I love you."

"I love you, too, Xavier."

His spirits lifted, Xavier decided to return home to talk with Jérémie about Catherine. He was happy to find Jérémie alone. Xavier poured the wine and handed it to Jérémie.

"We need to talk about Catherine," Xavier said.

"She's made her decision," Jérémie said with agitation.

"There's one thing we haven't tried. Have you considered going to her?"

"And warn her about Marcel? I thought we agreed not to."

"No, I mean to tell her how you feel."

Jérémie's gaze shot around the room as if a spy lurked. "Don't ever mention that again."

"I didn't mean to offend you. But if Catherine decided to leave him on her own, that would solve everything."

"We can't talk about this. Ever." Jérémie's voice was like iron. Hard and implacable. Jérémie slammed his glass down and stalked out of the room.

THE BASTILLE FALLS

Warmed by Marcel's medicine, Catherine headed into the streets. A headache had started an hour before, but she'd put the powder into her wine and soon all her pain vanished and she could turn her attention to her salon that operated with ease, where people discussed all sorts of matters without fighting. Lately, it was abuzz with news that Parisians assembled to demand a change.

Catherine headed east toward the Bastille. When someone had come to the salon, telling everyone what was happening, she'd donned the garb of a commoner to go see for herself. She had heard the rumors of torture and arbitrary beatings at the prison, but Michel had denounced them as false. To the citizens, however, it represented a symbol of oppression, where innocent people were sent because of poverty. *She* would rather attack les Tuileries, Louis's Parisian palace.

At the Bastille's outskirts, many people fled the scene, especially women, as the violence escalated to new heights. A huge mass of angry people, out of control, lashed out.

As the Bastille came into view and she pressed forward, the crowd rushed toward the structure, shouting as one. They stormed the Bastille, pushing past guards and slaughtering them. Catherine, like others near her, got caught in the thrust, though she did not lift a hand against anyone. Guns fired into the mob and people fell to the ground, which further enraged the rabble, causing them to shove with more determination. More and more guards fell and, before she knew it, she stood at the Bastille's entrance, watching hordes of peasants run inside with drawn weapons.

They liberated prisoners. She stood there with fascination, numb to the killing and feeling like nothing more than a distant observer. To her shock, no one paid her any attention as some man took lead of the mob and championed his cause by denouncing the monarchy.

Though it felt like it took place in the blink of an eye, the sun's position indicated that she had been there a couple of hours. After a long time, the violence subsided.

People still poured in and out of the Bastille after they freed every prisoner and murdered every guard. Catherine expected soldiers to arrive, but none did. A few regiments formed on the outskirts of the mob but retreated whenever spotted because the people attacked without provocation. Anarchy reigned.

Catherine was shocked out of her trance when the peasants dragged a recognizable face into their midst and surrounded him. They threw Jacques de Flesselles, a man Catherine knew as a rich merchant, to the ground, bleeding, in front of her. They took turns kicking and spitting on him. When the mob leaders had had enough, they charged into the center of the people surrounding him, grabbed him by the hair, and cut off his head. Catherine turned away, sick. No glorious revolution materialized before her. Something different altogether infected France.

But she stayed, despite her dread. Perhaps being a woman—an albatross for so much of her life—protected her somehow.

Next, the horde dragged the Bastille's governor, the Marquis de Launay, outside. The poor Marquis, she had entertained him when Michel had his military friends to dinner.

Whack! His head rolled into the street to cheers.

The atmosphere quieted enough that Catherine moved, still numb.

After touring the inside with everyone else, still mesmerized, Catherine exited the prison to a surprising sight. Marcel, her precious Marcel, was across the street, talking to a couple of former prisoners. He sold them something. He also looked handsome. But why was he there? He told her that he had to leave Paris. She wanted to go over to him, but thought better of it. He kept looking around like a frightened rabbit, and then, when a new mob marched down the street singing patriotic songs, he bolted the other way. She doubted she could find him in the crowds, so she spent the remainder of the afternoon watching the people. The Bastille had fallen to the commoners, and it was anyone's guess what would happen next.

She left only when the rain came. It started as a light sprinkle but then came down more in heavy sheets and people headed for cover. Catherine, drenched, started back toward the house. The one power that still had control over all—Mother Nature—ended the sightseeing at the Bastille.

She turned down one narrow alleyway, took a few steps, and realized her mistake. The residents had set up a blockade. They trapped people once they came down the street and charged a toll. They also constructed a makeshift prison and had sent certain Parisians into its exile. Catherine almost asked one of the women about their little racket when someone pulled her from behind and yanked her back around the corner.

"What are you doing here?" the man shouted.

One of the peasants, someone dirty and smelling of rot, attacked her. "Leave me alone. I'm one of you," she pleaded with fright.

"For God's sake, Catherine, it's me."

"Michel?"

"Get out of here. Stay at home. I'm in disguise and risk too much talking to you." He pushed her back into the street and pointed in the direction of their house. "Go straight down this street. Now." He shoved her and raced away. She obeyed.

Ahead of her, closer to her neighborhood, another fight broke out. Thankfully, the crowd dispersed by the time she walked two more blocks. The sight of a cowering man lying in the middle of the street appalled her. His bloodied face looked better than the broken bones that jutted from his limbs. His clothing betrayed his merchant status, another innocent victim of mob terror, in the wrong place at the wrong time.

She almost passed by, but stopped. Perhaps he was a fiend, but how could she know? She hopped off the sidewalk and hunched over the man, who was breathing but not conscious. His head bled profusely.

She had to take him to her hospital. She started to lift him, but he was very heavy, and then she noticed some women watching her.

"He's not one of us," one of the women shouted, waving a tricolored scarf. She took one of the scarves from around her neck and placed it around the man's. It seemed trivial as he lay injured, but perhaps it would give them safe passage. She tied it to him when the two women came over and hovered above her.

"We said he ain't one of us."

THOMAS'S AID

"I'm only trying to take him off the street," Catherine explained to the two glaring women as she held the beaten merchant in her arms.

One woman shook her head and laughed. "I suppose you got the colors on to try to protect yourself. You're not welcome in our parts." She shoved Catherine into the mud. Though enraged, Catherine remained calm, afraid that more barbarians might materialize to attack her.

"You're wrong," she said. "I support this revolution."

"Give us money, and we'll let you go. But you're leaving him."

Catherine seldom traveled with money and had nothing with her, but these two would never believe her and she had every intention of saving the gentleman.

"Are you deaf, bitch?" They both kicked her back into the mud and one of them stepped on her chest with a heel that dug into her bosom. Catherine heaved forward and knocked them back, but they came at her again with snarls.

"Ladies!" a male voice said. "I suggest you leave her alone."

"Who the hell are you? I see you don't wear a scarf, either. Maybe our men need to teach you the same lesson."

Catherine's eyes were covered with muck, so she only saw a dark figure.

"I think not," the man said.

He walked toward her in the street. Catherine scrambled to her feet when the women withdrew. As she stood, she heard one of them start to recite the rosary while the other ran away at full speed. She wiped the mud from her eyes in order to clear her vision.

The sight of Thomas with his fangs descended explained their fear as he picked her up. Catherine watched his fangs retract, stifling a giggle, despite her predicament.

With no effort, Thomas bent over and picked up the wounded man in his other arm. He started down the street, turned onto Rue St. Denis, and carried both of them the entire way.

Catherine marveled at the vampiric power before her. Their speed exceeded anything she'd ever witnessed, and Thomas carried both of them with no effort whatsoever. She barely saw the buildings pass. But Thomas set her down two houses before the Saint-Laurent home so no one saw her helplessness. He walked a human's pace with her to the front door, where guards ushered them inside.

"Take this man to the doctor at once," she said. Their expressions reminded her that she must look a fright, covered in mud and disheveled. She pretended that nothing was askew, trying to maintain decorum. Thomas handed the man to three attendants.

Afraid Thomas would leave to find Xavier, she hurried to change into something dry, wiped off as much mud as possible, and fixed her hair just a little before going back to the parlor.

"I'm sorry, I should have offered you dry clothing," she said.

"Nonsense."

"Well, if you want anything, let me know. It's the least I can do after you saved my life."

"I was passing and happened to see that you might need some help."

She could tell that he tried not to offend her. "I realize I've the power to get men to walk on eggshells, but you've nothing to worry about. I appreciate what you did, and it doesn't bother me in the least."

"Was I that transparent?" He smiled at her.

"I've a feeling that Xavier exaggerates my temper."

"Regardless, I'm glad I could be of service. What were you doing, anyway?"

"That poor man," Catherine answered. "He was dying. I couldn't pass without doing something. I didn't see those vultures until it was too late."

"You have the compassion of your brother," Thomas said.

"What's that supposed to mean? And why are you laughing?"

"I had no idea that it ran in the Saint-Laurent blood, this total compassion."

Catherine poured herself some wine before answering. "I don't suppose you drink anything?" She held the bottle up.

"I can but do so only for pretense."

"Good. I'm sorry I don't have any blood, but there's plenty on the streets for you."

Thomas laughed. "I've yet to find a mortal family who will stock blood for me."

"I assume you know Xavier's compassion extends to everyone, but mine is more limited. He's like an angel whereas *my* pity is more selective."

"Why do you think your actions today surprised me?"

Catherine had grown accustom to chatting with a vampire, and accepted his human emotion and longings. She nonetheless struggled with the relationship between her brother and Thomas. What did that mean for Xavier? Would he, too, become a vampire?

"Am I troubling you?" Thomas asked.

"Don't be ridiculous. It's I, Thomas, not you." She rose from her chair to sit next to him, and took his hand. Absolute impropriety, but she cared little about convention.

"I need to confess."

Thomas grabbed her other hand, now holding both tightly, and looked into her eyes.

"You know I adore you," she started. "Of course your being a vampire caught me unprepared. But I'm understanding it better. You know, too, that your sexual proclivities don't bother me. I knew about Xavier before he suspected it himself."

Thomas smiled. "What are you trying to tell me?"

"It's Xavier. If you were rich and came to steal him away to America as your slave, and he went of his own will, I wouldn't care. But I'm not sure what to feel about the fact that it entails something more."

Thomas remained quiet.

"I'd never stop Xavier from seeing you or reveal your secret. I've lived with men doing that to me my entire life. This is Xavier's decision alone and that will be hard enough."

She got up from the couch and hurried to the window, looking out at Paris. Dirty, bloody, Paris.

She did not flinch when Thomas came beside her and brushed his fingers along her cheek.

"I still want to help you with Xavier. He needs someone strong and masculine to protect him. You're perfect for that."

"I won't steal him away without your knowledge. Now, I'd like to find Xavier."

Catherine escorted Thomas to the front door. Though he chatted until she felt better, it dawned on her that he fretted the entire time about going to Xavier. Thomas worried about her brother, and she had at one time, too, but long ago, she had stopped watching over him because he led his own life. Besides, she detested people who tried to enforce their will on everyone. She gazed out the window as Thomas moved easily down the street.

XAVIER'S STRUGGLE

Xavier exited the Bastille with a horde of people, self-conscious as he walked through the streets in common garb. He'd heard the news from his guards that the Bastille had been taken over. Parisians were in full riot, and they had executed the Bastille governor. For his safety, they collected some lay clothing and demanded he wear it. Xavier hesitated before he obeyed but, once dressed, forced them to take him to the Bastille.

And so they, like hundreds of others, toured the Bastille. Xavier recognized all of it because he often administered the sacraments to prisoners. They passed the time by talking to people and exploring the empty cells until it grew dark. Xavier was weary and ready to see

Thomas. He walked out the gates and into the drenched streets, where a few remaining people still stood. He smiled as a few sprinkles hit his face. His heart fluttered when he noticed the black-clad man across the street.

"Gentlemen, I'll go with Thomas now," he told his guards.

Thomas waited as Xavier bid them adieu and promised to inform them when he returned to the church. Xavier hurried across the street, smiling, but also wondering if they suspected the nature of his evening meetings.

"Thomas," he said, a surge of pleasure racing down his spine.

Thomas met him with an icy stare. "What were you doing here?"

"I was at the church all day before the guards told me about the Bastille. I insisted that we go out. Common citizens walking in and out of cells, and no militia arrived to put them down."

Thomas stood like a statue. Xavier fumbled with the collar on his shirt and longed for the cross around his neck. "I was with my guards," Xavier continued. "They insisted I wear these clothes. I look ridiculous, I know." Xavier stopped. The cold rain irritated him, but at least it took his attention away from the disapproving figure in front of him.

Thomas turned and started down the street as Xavier followed. The mud slid around his boots as the entire scene became dank and depressing.

"What should I do?" Thomas's voice was firm, not irate, thankfully, yet not the pleasant tone that Xavier loved to hear. "They're rioting. Do you understand that many of these people hate the church and *any* representative of it? What if someone recognized you?"

They walked a couple more blocks in silence, Thomas pulling Xavier by the arm, until they reached Xavier's church. Alone in the drab space of his room, Xavier stood motionless as Thomas locked the door and then turned to him and let out a long breath of air. Xavier felt nervous and excited at the same time, his typical turmoil whenever he found himself alone with Thomas.

"If we're to be friends, or whatever you want to call us, I need to know that you're not being careless."

Xavier melted at Thomas's plea. If only he could be with Thomas all day. Being in Paris never threatened him, but Thomas, Catherine, Michel, and even his parishioners kept telling him a different story. His thoughts whirled, and then the tears came.

Thomas embraced him. "I didn't mean to hurt you." He kissed Xavier's head.

"I'm just confused. I want to be a part of this, but don't know what to do." Xavier detested sobbing. It embarrassed him and too often stifled their conversation because it made Thomas quit talking. "Do you think I'm wrong?"

"I think you have too much faith in people."

Thomas and Catherine talked as if he walked about in a daze, like a newborn puppy that trusts everyone. But Xavier disliked some people and knew of irredeemable individuals. He just allowed people to prove their worth, or lack thereof, before making a judgment. Why did that make him naïve?

"And it relates to your faith in Catholicism," Thomas continued. "You think that as a priest you have to attain an ideal in how you view people and in your own life, regardless of reality or what the people around you say to the contrary."

"I know that we live a complete contradiction." Xavier recognized that the topic switched to their relationship. "Our time together is too frequent for a common friendship. When you talk about me, and when I think about you all the time, it's with more than a passing interest."

Thomas stood and paced with the nervous energy that always consumed him. "I love you, and you deny it."

"I *never* denied it," Xavier said, agitated. "Do I need to say it over and over so that the pain increases with each day? I love you. I long for you. Is that better? Or do I need to admit the anguish I feel every night as I go to sleep and wish I were in your arms, safe from the world, away from the things that plague me?" Weeping again.

Thomas put his head in his hands and stopped in the middle of the room. He returned to Xavier's side and stared at him. Thomas's eyes were so red—from crying?—that it appeared as if blood pooled in them. "Then what keeps you from being happy with me?"

"Damnation. Because I'm afraid of going to hell," Xavier reiterated.

"Yet, you don't think any of your parishioners will? Or the nuns, who love each other?"

"No." Xavier cried even more, feeling miserable.

"But you'd go to hell for doing the same thing?"

"I don't know," he managed to shout between sobs.

Thomas's brow furrowed and his expression darkened. "You're not the only one who hurts. I know you dwell in your pity, but when you do, so do I. Your contradictions hurt more than just you. So languish in your suffering, but know that you depress others with it."

Neither spoke another word. Xavier struggled with embarrassment, anger, and mourning.

"I'm going." Thomas hugged him and kissed him on the cheek. Xavier slumped against Thomas until he was pushed away and gently laid on the bed. Thomas petted his hair a few times, then kissed him on the forehead and left.

Perhaps God had already sent Xavier to hell, and the agony was his punishment. Why would God wait until his death to discipline him for transgressions? Nothing in hell could be worse than the physical pain that ate at his heart. Purgatory confronted him. Hades engulfed him. Hellfire and damnation tortured him.

Twenty-Three: Vampires and Revolution

15 JULY 1789

Thomas left Xavier at the church without speaking to avoid bitter words designed to hurt Xavier. Anthony's admonitions for patience flooded his head through the entire conversation because he knew he crossed a line when he made Xavier cry, on purpose this time. He regretted it, though part of him thought the argument inevitable.

He needed Anthony. He stormed into Anthony's flat without knocking as blood sweat poured from his brow.

Anthony looked at him in consternation. A young soldier sat on the couch, naked, and Anthony, dressed in a robe, was fondling him. He had fed on the boy's inner thigh, but the drugged youth was oblivious to his captor's vampirism. The sight of Thomas, disheveled, enraged, and covered in blood, sent the delirious boy into hysterics. He screamed, like the howl of a dying wolf, and jumped from the couch, tripping over a rug. He landed at Thomas's feet, but crawled as fast as possible away into Anthony's arms. Incensed, Anthony bit into the first piece of flesh he could grab and drained the young man, then threw the body to the ground.

His robe had fallen open, revealing his chiseled body. Too muscular for Thomas's taste— he preferred Xavier's weaker, less defined body— but who could ignore the beauty of the blond god with his long hair, smooth chest, and rippled stomach?

"Oh, stop it," Anthony said and wrapped himself in the robe. "I suppose you've a good excuse for ruining my little game. Do you know how rare it is to find such a specimen? Someone so handsome, yet worthy of death? And have you ever heard of knocking?"

"I needed to speak with you."

Anthony rolled his eyes. "You look dreadful." He tossed the body into a trunk, then set to work discarding anything with blood on it. When he finished, he lifted the trunk without effort and set it in the hall, tidied up the room, and got dressed. "Now, let me guess. You can't control yourself. You and Xavier had another argument and I'm supposed to calm you down." Anthony threw himself across a fainting couch and ran his fingers through his hair. "Right?"

"I can't get him out of my head. There are times when keeping my patience is almost impossible. I yelled at him tonight. I intentionally made him cry."

"Charming."

"I need your help, not your wit."

"What do you expect me to say? That, of course, you'll hurt his feelings and bring him to tears, all good men do? You need to control yourself because behaving as you do is reprehensible. I don't have a magic potion to cure you."

"I found him at the Bastille, and it terrified me. He wanders around Paris with no thought to the increased danger. When I warned him about it, our conversation led to an argument about our relationship. He still refuses to accept his sexuality. You know what I'm like when my emotions take over."

"Yes, a fool."

"You're an ass."

"That wasn't wit. That was the truth. This will happen time and time again until you realize there's a natural course things take."

"What's the secret that gives you this grand forbearance?"

"You're too involved in these human affairs. I told you that. You never took the time to be objective and assess the situation. If you had taken time, perhaps you would've left Xavier alone. And the longer you withhold your true nature, the worse this'll get."

"You hid it from me."

"For a short time and then you guessed it. You two are far from dealing with it."

"I don't wish to discuss this any longer."

Without speaking and despite the tension between them, Anthony came over and hugged Thomas. "I only want to help. And you only respond to stern warnings."

Thomas smiled at the truth, but refused to admit it. "Thank you."

Anthony smacked Thomas on the side of his head. "Now, if you don't mind, I'd like to finish what I started before you rudely interrupted. I'm aching to come and have to find a new partner because I murdered that lad before he alerted the whole of Paris to our presence."

Thomas took his leave, calmed by Anthony's words, and walked through the streets, avoiding people, which became more and more difficult as a full-fledged revolution blossomed in the city. He wished he could run to Xavier to apologize. Thomas hated himself anew for pushing Xavier too far again. He even walked by the church and saw a candle in the abbé's room. But Thomas resisted his impatience and fidgeted with a number of things, masturbated twice while thinking of Xavier, and drifted to sleep in his coffin.

Part V: Stagnation

Twenty-Four: Two Years

2 JULY 1791

Xavier sat with Catherine in a back parlor of the Saint-Laurent home, enjoying a rare afternoon of calm in Paris and quiet within the walls of her salon.

"I wonder if the Americans felt this defeated after they declared independence from Great Britain?" Catherine asked. "The National Assembly produced the Declaration of the Rights of Man almost two years ago, but so little has changed in this revolution."

Xavier got up and grabbed a second bottle of wine. "Ask Thomas."

Catherine shook her head. "It's just that they had no king on their soil. We dragged Louis away from Versailles as a mob and imprisoned him in les Tuileries."

"I'd don't consider his Paris home a prison."

"We won't let him leave," Catherine pointed out.

"We do have a new Constitution," Xavier added. He started to say something else when Jérémie entered the room.

They greeted him, and then he asked Catherine if she had located some file or another, which sent her walking briskly from the room to fetch it.

"Still here," Xavier said. "Faithful Jérémie, doing the paperwork, organizing the guards for her, and pretending that all is well in the world."

"There aren't many options." Jérémie's ears burned bright red. "I'm trying to survive."

"I still think that you should talk to her."

"After all this time, how do you think she'd react? I can hear the anger, wanting to know how I could keep such a thing from her for this long. No, thank you. I accept what I created."

Xavier almost protested, but his hypocrisy hit him too hard. How could he demand something of Jérémie that he could never do for himself? Thomas had waited for him for over two years, and Xavier still felt no closer to resolving the conflicts in their relationship.

"Besides, my telling her wouldn't solve the problem about Marcel," Jérémie said.

"What about Marcel?" came Catherine's voice.

Jérémie whipped his head around in surprise, and Xavier spilled a bit of wine when they heard her voice in the hall. She entered the parlor and handed Jérémie a pile of papers.

"I was just wondering if he had returned from America," Jérémie said. "Thank you." He held up the stack she had handed him to acknowledge her, then turned on his heels and left the room before she had time to answer.

"That's a good question." Xavier wiped the red wine from the seat cushion to no avail. He hoped that Catherine hadn't noticed. "When is he returning?"

"I doubt any time soon." Catherine sat opposite him on a fainting couch and picked up her glass. "He sent another shipment of my medication this morning, enough for several months. And he increased my dosage, saying that the remedy would otherwise wear off."

"Don't you find it odd that he left two years ago, without any announcement and without even coming to see you? What kind of business in America takes two years to transact? And what kind of sickness could you have that only Marcel can remedy?"

As with Jérémie, Xavier's tone got the better of him. It frustrated him that they had at last enlisted Anne's assistance, when the fiend disappeared. Xavier wondered if that was more than coincidence.

"When did you decide to sound like Michel?" Catherine glared at him. "Would you like to assert your church's authority now, as he does with the military?"

"I'm sorry. Forgive me?" Xavier hated placating her, but she had spoken the truth. Nothing he said would change her mind.

"I can never stay angry with you. Let's change the subject."

Catherine handed him a note. Xavier read the request from Maria to take over the former servants' quarters near the cellar. "I thought you moved everyone out of there, including servants, because it was too dank and depressing?"

"I did." Catherine sipped her wine. "Maria went down there the other day because we ran out of storage for medical supplies upstairs. She asked me if I'd consider allowing her and the other nuns to convert the quarters into their new temporary nunnery."

Xavier thought about how Maria and her fellow sisters had come to the Saint-Laurent home one night, frightened and carrying everything that they could. Seeing them in the street from the patio, he had run to greet them at the door.

"We were attacked. The government shut us down, took over the nunnery, and kicked us out with nothing. We don't know what to do," Maria had explained.

Xavier had invited them inside, and ever since, they had assisted Catherine and Jérémie in the salon.

"I moved other people out of there because they hated it," Catherine continued. "I even tried to give her a different space, but they want the seclusion."

"Then give it to them." Xavier shrugged.

"Settled. I'll talk to her in the morning."

A servant entered the parlor and announced that Michel had arrived. He wanted to know if he should send their brother to them in the parlor after he freshened up in his quarters. Catherine raised her eyebrows at Xavier as she told the butler that would be fine. A short time later, Michel walked into the room.

"What happened to your commoner's garb?" Catherine asked. "Or did the king promote you, after you tried to help him escape last year?"

"One gets promoted for successful operations, not an attempted escape that failed and sent him back to prison." Michel grimaced. "Especially if you try a second time and it fails again."

"You tried again?" Xavier asked.

"A week ago. With the same result, and now the suspension of the monarchy."

"So, are you still in the military?" Catherine asked, surprised.

"I don't know. I don't know who's in charge or giving orders. But I must get going. I just stopped to say hello." Michel hugged them both goodbye and exited.

"I thought losing his authority would either devastate him or increase his attempt to control us," Catherine said when he closed the door.

"Let's change the subject."

"Agreed. How is Thomas?"

"If you can't pick on one brother, you'll go after another?"

"You mentioned him first. You keep bringing up that Marcel left all of a sudden and remind me that lovers don't do such things. Perhaps you're just worried about Thomas doing that to you."

"Your situation with Marcel has nothing to do with my *friendship* with Thomas." Xavier drank the remainder of his wine in one gulp. "We've known each other for two years, something that friends do. And I think you've had too much wine."

"Two years isn't always understood in the same way." Catherine brushed a strand of hair from her forehead. "Some may not think about the passage of time. But they won't wait forever."

Catherine got up and announced that she had to oversee the preparations for dinner. She patted him on the shoulder and then let her hand linger on his cheek as she looked down at him.

Xavier's stomach hurt again after she left. There came the churning in his stomach, the nausea, the secret and not-so-secret longings.

Over a year ago, Thomas had agreed to give Xavier time, shocking Xavier by not bringing up their relationship for several months. He still came to visit almost every night. Xavier had asked for a year, and Thomas granted it and more. Until the other day, Xavier thought that perhaps he could pretend that nothing would ever need to change.

"What would I do without you?" Xavier had slipped two nights ago and asked Thomas.

"Find a new *friend*, I should suppose," Thomas answered with a frown.

"You're more than that. I just don't know what to do."

That stung, but at least Thomas had left it at that.

•

Part VI: Into the Quagmire

Twenty-Five: The Pope's Effigy

17 JULY 1791

Xavier sat at his desk, a rare moment of solitude, when Denys Girard, the head of his parish security, burst in unannounced. "Abbé, come now to the Champ de Mars."

"The military staging ground? Why?"

"People were celebrating the one year anniversary of the Bastille's fall when rioting broke out. They're still fighting because the National Assembly sent a garrison to put the rebellion down. They declared martial law, and things only got worse."

The rioting had calmed by the time they arrived. People screamed and occasionally someone threw something at a soldier, but the combat had ceased. Xavier jumped when a small group of people started mocking the soldiers, who went after them.

Xavier looked at Denys. "It's time." The two men walked through the crowd, trying to calm people. "Please, don't risk your lives with these men. We can make our point another way!" Either Xavier's words worked or exhaustion caused people to listen and pause from the rioting.

And so it went on that day at the Champ de Mars when, out of nowhere, Maria appeared.

"Don't act so surprised." Maria laughed at Xavier's shocked expression. "Did you think I'd let you have all of the fun? Besides, I have to watch out for you. Just because the church is in disarray, you still need to be careful."

"Things are pretty calm out here for now. I'm not worried."

"Not that." Maria frowned. "Your evening meetings with an American."

"Maria, for pity's sake, I've been meeting with him for over two years."

"But you're more careless now. There was a group from your parish at the house the other night. The women were talking about their priest and his friend."

"Why does it matter? Let them gossip." Xavier sat on a stump, all at once exhausted and exasperated. He rubbed his eyes, then looked at Maria. "Why do you pry into my personal life?"

"What about the church? Why do you forsake it? You've abandoned your faith."

"The church you and I defied for all these years? The church that ignores the poor, forcing us to operate clandestine relief efforts?"

"Not the church, *your faith*," she answered and dropped to the grass before him. "You used to love serving these people first and foremost. Now, Thomas comes first."

Xavier hated how people used guilt against him, in no small part because he succumbed to it every time. "I'll watch myself," he said, in an effort to shut her up.

She scrambled off the ground and paced, her large hips swinging back and forth. Then she stopped and pointed at him. "You were arguing. They said they'd never heard you raise your voice, but you and Thomas were right there in the street shouting at each other."

Xavier remembered the quarrel, typical as it had become. Thomas loved Xavier, Xavier loved Thomas, Thomas wanted a relationship, Xavier couldn't. "I need to be more careful."

"Are you just saying that to keep me quiet?"

Xavier laughed, which even made Maria giggle. "At first, yes. I can't stop seeing him. But I'll stop the public scenes. I'm listening to you."

"Good." She sat down and patted his knee, then grinned with a mischievous gleam in her eye. "What made you angry? I've never seen you as they described."

"We disagree about our relationship."

Maria laughed. Through stifled grunts, she said, "So it surprises you that he thinks you're in some relationship, does it? What on earth do you call it?"

"Thomas started a new mantra. Well, not entirely new, but he gave it a new urgency and I've told him a million times that I won't leave Paris."

"He wanted you to leave?"

"He's terrified a mob will come after me."

"Does he still come only at night? If he's so damn worried, maybe you ought to find out where he goes through the day."

Xavier sensed another lecture coming when unexpected shouting erupted behind them from another angry mob, but it seemed the Church was the target. Xavier's heart pounded and he broke into sweat, for the first time afraid for his safety. Even Maria sat immobile. It was a small band of dirty men, perhaps twenty, who screamed at each person and demanded that everyone acknowledge their rage against the church. To wild roars of approval, one of the men lit an effigy of the pope on fire and held it high above the throng.

Mesmerized and frightened, Xavier turned to Maria, but she had disappeared. Had she fled? Or was she hidden within the crowd?

"Isn't he one of 'em?" someone shouted from within the rabble.

A man, covered in grime with but a few teeth, pointed at Xavier, who recognized him as the brother of a groom from a clandestine wedding.

"He ain't no damn priest!" An unknown woman draped herself over Xavier from behind.

"He is! Let's get him! A live bugger to burn!"

"Nah, he's my man, and no priest can do a woman like this one. I should know." She grabbed Xavier's crotch, kissing him on the neck. Bewildered, Xavier turned to see Anne Hébert's glowing brown eyes.

"He looks like the priest who married my brother and his wife," the man continued.

"I'm taking him home and stripping him down to see if he's a priest. Leave us alone."

She yanked Xavier away, clinging to his body and kissing his cheek, though some followed. His heart slowed the farther away they got, but then he halted.

"Wait. Maria's still back there." He turned to run, but Anne stopped him.

"I already took care of her. She left, probably halfway back to the house by now." She pulled him back, and they hurried through the streets. They had gotten away, but the one who recognized Xavier followed with a couple of friends in tow.

"Don't say a word," Anne said. "I don't think you can help with this. If he recognizes your voice, we're in trouble." They moved onto a busy road. "Where's that Thomas when we need him? He'd be helpful here. If only that damn sun would sink faster."

"What does the sun have to do with anything?"

Anne howled with laughter, her cackle comforting Xavier. "Forget it. More important, what were you doing with that mob? Maybe you didn't hear their opinions of the church?"

"They've never attacked me before."

"Well, that isn't true anymore, and you'd better start watching yourself better."

"Thank you for saving me," Xavier said in an understatement, despite his profound gratitude.

"You're my friend. Let's not dwell on it, and I don't want you selling me your Catholic soul. Besides, that was a nice kiss you gave me in return, and a little extra surprise—"

"Please. I've lost enough dignity. What brought you to the Champ de Mars, anyway?"

"I went there because that's where I was needed. Don't ask me how I knew. We don't agree about such things."

Xavier stopped their trek across Paris. He grabbed Anne and hugged her. His heart had stopped beating as fast, but his hands still trembled. Xavier jumped when he heard footsteps behind him, but it was only Denys.

"Abbé," he said. "They went into a church and dragged a priest into the street. When he wouldn't take their oath, they murdered him. I couldn't find you. I thought I failed."

"Anne got me away from the mob." Xavier led them to the Saint-Laurent home, where they said goodbye to Denys and waited for Catherine in the parlor.

Without warning, the door crashed open and Catherine swooped in, more frenzied than usual. "Are you hurt? Who was it? Denys told me they came after you— what happened?" She grabbed Xavier's face and checked for physical harm.

"Catherine, I'm fine. It was nothing."

"I hear that a mob attacked you and you expect me to think it's nothing?" She stared into his eyes, agitated, then clutched his face to her. He had to force her to release him.

After calming Catherine, Xavier listened to a litany of rules Anne and Catherine expected him to follow every day for his safety. He promised to do so a thousand times. The last brush with a mob had startled him enough to obey.

Strangely, the two women never mentioned the night and brushed it aside as if Xavier hadn't said anything. Of course, Thomas always protected him, but what about when he left for the night? Thomas must sleep, and what then? When he asked as much, Catherine and Anne again laughed it off. He decided to leave it alone at that point, for fear of them creating more rules.

THREE WOMEN

Xavier sat alone and exhausted at the Saint-Laurent home after a long afternoon, trying to forget that a man and his henchmen had attacked him, instead thinking about the three women in his life.

After he calmed Catherine and Anne, Maria showed up and they went through the same conversation. Remembering several afternoon appointments, Xavier tried to leave, but all three made him repeat everything. Then Catherine asked about his appointments and exploded when she heard he had a secret baptism and wedding to perform in the church.

"Absolutely not," she said with agreement from Anne and Maria.

"You can't stop me."

Maria, red with anger, began to shout when Catherine cut her off.

"You may do it on *our* terms. You'll use the chapel in this house for such occasions. It's small, so I'll transform the outer room for you. We'll say nothing else of your clandestine activities so long as they take place here and Maria helps."

Xavier left soon after with Denys and returned to the house with his entourage of parishioners seeking various rituals. He spent his afternoon administering to one person after another.

The flurry of activity and his morning adventure tired him more than usual, so Xavier slumped into a large leather chair outside the chapel to rest.

"I thought we told you not to wear that?" Catherine pointed at his clothing.

"Maria allowed it so long as I take it off before leaving," he answered.

"Well, you're done for the day. Take off those vestments."

Then she darted away. Xavier got up, locked himself in the chapel, and returned to his lay clothing. Afterward, he walked out of the chapel as Catherine buzzed toward him.

"You're safer in those clothes, even though you were made for those priestly robes and garments. But this makes me feel better. Come, sit."

Catherine sat on a leather chair, so Xavier joined her on a nearby fainting couch.

He decided to preempt her. "I'm being careful. And I'll follow all of your rules. I won't be alone unless in the church with guards outside or in this house. I'll travel with others. The only time I'll let my guard down is with Thomas, and I'll also remind him to watch out for me."

Catherine jumped up, knelt before Xavier, and gave him a gigantic hug, then kissed him on the head and left, but she turned around before she got to the door. "You reacted when we dismissed the night watch because of Thomas. Perhaps you should ask him about it."

She almost continued when Maria walked into the room.

"I just saw Michel," Maria said.

"Oh, God, is he here again to warn me about something?" Catherine asked.

"No, I was at the market and he was down a side street, involved in some quarrel."

"Can you send someone to look after him?" Xavier asked Catherine.

"He ordered us to leave him alone, and if we don't respect his wishes, how can we expect him to honor ours?"

Xavier nodded, disliking that she was correct.

"Xavier, can you come with me to purchase more bandages for our hospital?" Maria jarred him out of his contemplation with her sudden question.

"I wanted to be alone with you," Maria said outside of the house. "I was worried. We get so wrapped up in what we're doing with the church and with people. I think we need to take more time for ourselves. The girls and I are doing this already. But you and I need to do it, too."

"I'm doing well enough, given the circumstances in Paris. I hate the violence." His real anguish was with Thomas, but he did not want to bring that up with her.

As they walked through Paris, with Denys and two other guards close behind, they lamented the hostility but in general agreed they could do little but help those who crossed their path. It was like old times when they wandered around the parish on a Sunday, talking and greeting people. As they returned to the house, Xavier noticed that Maria had avoided talking much about herself.

"Are you happy living here?" he asked.

"Yes. At first, I missed the convent. And I was angry. But I'm accustomed to this and feel I'm doing good work in the hospital. Moving to our own quarters did a lot of good, too. I enjoy helping Catherine. Besides, she accepts me and my girls, no question."

"Do you possess them?"

Maria blushed. "Only when they want to be! And no more than someone possesses you!"

"That's enough." Xavier swept his hand in the air and sent a laughing Maria on her way. He started inside when a familiar form came down the street. He smiled so wide it almost hurt.

LOVE POTION

Thomas woke that evening to find a note from Anne Hébert, alerting him to an attack on Xavier she had prevented. Frantic with concern, he left his flat in a hurry and raced to Anne's place, where he knocked hard on her door until she called for him to enter.

"Why did you send me that note?"

She erupted with laughter, making him even angrier. "He's fine. No need to lose your temper. We need to discuss something, but he's safe. Were you surprised I sent you something?" she asked craftily.

"How did you discover where I sleep?"

"Because you just told me." She cackled even harder. "I only figured out how to get you a letter. I had no idea you slept there. I've my ways of acquiring such information. But, if it makes you feel better, it was very difficult to come by."

"But if you discovered it, could Marcel?"

"I hadn't thought about that. Do you sleep in the same place every night? Maybe you should move about more."

"So, he has the power to locate me?"

She smiled, a sly, protective grin. "Actually, no. It doesn't seem that he has firm control over the magic. He's an amateur. He learned from someone dumb enough to give him the black magic, but I don't think they told him all the secrets. Otherwise, things would have been much worse by now. He's haphazard. For example, he put the potion on Catherine, yet he can't control what anyone around her thinks. Do you think I'd have idiot spies running around Paris?" She slapped her knee as she laughed. "The problem for us is that he's not interested in anything good. So we must be careful, because he doesn't know how to control the black forces. And when he does, it's no doubt often by mistake."

"Is there anything else we can do for Catherine?"

"I'm trying. But I'll not do the black magic. I got Xavier and Jérémie watching her every move. His potion isn't that powerful. His teacher must have limited his powers."

"Limited?" Thomas asked.

"Yes, a mere love potion that makes people infatuated. That's why she has to take it so often. Now, about my note to you. I regret sending it. Promise you'll not come down hard on Xavier. You won't go shouting and screaming. It hurts him more than he lets on. I see it in his soul. Things bounce off you. You two argue and you forget. You return to him all fine, and he's so happy to see that you came back he pretends to be fine, too. But each time you start with him, it scars. He loves you, so treat him like you deserve it."

He scowled. "I'll keep myself under control."

"They tried getting him today. He was out, doing his preaching or whatever the hell he does, and someone recognized that he was a priest. So they came after him."

"I thought you said he was safe," Thomas snarled the words.

"He is. I was there. I got him out."

Thomas still seethed inside. He had instructed Xavier a thousand times that he endangered himself more and more as the revolution intensified and he kept performing these useless Catholic rituals. But Xavier refused to change his routine and disregarded his safety.

"I must go," Thomas said all of a sudden.

"You promised me, now."

Thomas hesitated, thinking about how Anthony told him the same things, that his temper would bring him nothing but pain. "Can't I worry about him?"

"We all do. But you're not allowed to yell at him. He was doing good for people."

"I'll follow your advice, and I'm grateful you came to me."

"I'd scold you some more, but there's a disturbance in here—" She stopped and glared at him. "I forgot again. It's *you*. That undead aspect to you." She motioned him toward the door. "You got what you want; now go to him. And remember your promise."

Thomas raced away and, despite his consternation, grinned when he saw Xavier on the porch, smiling like a damsel who just spotted her knight, charming in those peasant clothes. Thomas had intended to scold the abbé about his safety. Instead, he melted as he neared the Saint-Laurent home. Thomas blew a kiss and hurried up the steps.

CONFRONTATION

"You're here!" Xavier greeted Thomas, then blushed. "I know that I look ridiculous in these clothes."

"You need to wear them for your protection. May we speak in private?"

Xavier frowned. When Thomas used that tone of voice, it meant he wanted to remonstrate him about something. "Here or the church?"

"I'd be more comfortable at the church."

"Let's go," Xavier answered with hesitation. "I suppose you heard about this morning."

"Yes. Why are you nervous?"

"I'm embarrassed. I already promised Catherine, Maria, and Anne that I'd watch myself more carefully."

Thomas said nothing for a long moment. Then, "I know, but we still need to talk."

Xavier sighed again. He was tired and would rather stay with Thomas and talk at the house about things other than their relationship. But he accompanied him to the church anyway.

Thomas's demeanor intensified the closer they came to it. He clenched his jaw. Xavier's stomach knotted. Once inside, they went to Xavier's sparse room.

"Sit." Thomas motioned toward the bed.

Xavier fell onto it and tucked his knees under his chin.

"I don't mean to be angry," Thomas said with an edge. "But it infuriates me that you don't listen. I've begged and pleaded with you to be more serious with your safety." Thomas paced back and forth as Xavier clutched his legs even tighter. "Why do you do these stupid things?"

"Because..." Xavier hesitated, lost and trapped.

"Because you like defying death? Because you've no regard for your own life? Do you understand that you could be killed?"

"I realize there's danger. That's why I promised—"

"What good are your promises? Running out to join a riot is not careful. It's ignorant and stupid." Xavier flinched, never having seen Thomas so furious. Thomas kicked at the furniture and raised his voice. Xavier was crushed. He had pondered what almost happened, and he more and more thought about leaving the church for Thomas, but now look what he had done.

"Do you ever consider others when you do things?" Thomas demanded. "Oh, I forgot. You think about the masses all of the time. And if that hurts the people closest to you, then we all must cope with whatever happens to you. Why would we rank anywhere in your grand scheme?"

Xavier remained balled up on the bed. "You, Catherine, Michel, Anne, I can't name everyone I love. I can't believe you don't know that." Damn. The tears came again. He had fought them off and grabbed his legs with the hope to somehow capture the crying. But they came in a sudden burst, turning Xavier's words into sobs.

"Not this time," Thomas shouted. "You won't cry and make me feel bad."

"For God's sake, Thomas, I don't understand."

Thomas lunged toward him, grabbed a chair, turned it around, and sat. For a brief moment, he put his head down so that his long black hair hid his face. When he looked up, Xavier still saw the lines of anger. Thomas grimaced and snarled, then he punched the top of the chair.

"You're hiding. All this nonsense you created as important in your life, it's nothing but a ruse to keep you from giving yourself what you want because you're terrified of what other people think. So, you pour out your soul to the sorry folk in this decrepit neighborhood while those who love you—the real you—suffer."

"The people who love me know that what I do isn't a lie. Your accusations hurt. I've never denied my love for you."

Thomas shot out of the chair and threw it across the room, smashing it into pieces.

"Were I Christ, you'd be my Peter. And you know it. Don't blame me for the distance that divides us. Your stupid theology created it. What kind of god would give you these sexual feelings and then make you suffer for a lifetime without fulfilling them? What kind of god would allow people to murder each other in the streets indiscriminately? It's some sick pleasure that you get from punishing yourself and me."

Thomas pounded his chest, while Xavier withdrew further. He hated Thomas's rages, hated that he felt he could never be who Thomas wanted.

"Is that what you think of me?" Xavier whispered.

Thomas grabbed his own hair and yanked at it, some of it coming out in his hand. He paced back and forth like a caged lion ready to pounce.

Next he punched his fist through the wall, then turned his back on a motionless Xavier.

When Thomas turned back around, crying, Xavier started at the sight. The darkness cast an odd shadow that made it appear as if streams of blood ran down Thomas's face, but Thomas wiped them away before he spoke or Xavier saw them for certain.

"I'm just at wit's end. I wanted to wait, to give you time and encourage you to accept yourself and not try to please everyone else. But you're so entranced by this Catholic world that it may never happen. So I'll demand it. Come with me. Love me."

Thomas sat next to Xavier and put his arms around the priest.

Xavier's world spun in turmoil. Just as he contemplated a life with Thomas, the very man he loved threw an ultimatum at him.

"Xavier, do you hear me?" Thomas asked, stroking his head.

"Yes, of course, it's just—" Xavier cried, his entire body heaving up and down.

"We can overcome this. Whatever bothers you, we can deal with it. Whether it's theology, God, the church, whatever ails you."

"You belittled my theology, and now I'm supposed to trust that you can make it better?"

"Xavier, for the love of God, I still don't understand your problem."

"I don't, either. But you raging at me isn't going to solve anything."

"Then let yourself go." Thomas shot up and stood over Xavier.

Xavier trembled. Thomas grabbed Xavier's arms and pulled him out of his fetal position with a violent yank. He seized Xavier by the skull and jerked his head against Thomas's chest. Xavier yielded without moving, reduced to a whimpering mess. Then Thomas kissed the top of Xavier's head and moved down with deliberate slowness, his tongue lunging into Xavier's ear.

Xavier was aroused against his will. He had dreamed of such passion for so long, yet he had envisioned love, not a strained and forced interaction. Thomas bit at him, then clutched Xavier's crotch.

Distraught, Xavier sniffled out a few words. "Please, I can't."

Without warning and too quickly for a mortal man, Thomas picked Xavier up and threw him across the bed. Xavier almost hit the ceiling as he crashed down in total pain. He lay limp on the bed.

"You can't have it all your way anymore." Thomas turned to leave.

"I love you," Xavier said lamely.

"And I love you. But not enough to suffer your selfishness."

"I'm selfish?"

Xavier did not see Thomas swirl around and raise his hand, but he felt the blow all too well. Thomas backhanded him. His left eye swelled shut and blood dripped out his nose as he fell back on the mattress. Xavier lay there for a long time, his head ringing and his heart numb. He could not open one eye. He even prayed that God would take his life.

He managed to sit up after a long while, but every move ached and blood covered the room. He cried again, which made the pain worse, his swollen eye making him want to pass out. He could not even touch his face to wipe tears because it hurt too much. He dressed very slowly.

Xavier yelled into the darkness, "I love you, but this is too much. Too much."

PUNISHMENT

"I love you, but this is too much. Too much."

Thomas perched on the ledge outside Xavier's window and heard these words that cut deep inside his soul. He wished for death. For the first time, the man with all the confidence in the world, the vampire who loved life and always got what he wanted, the man who won every battle, that man despised himself. Thomas hated himself more than he had ever hated anything.

How many times had Anthony warned him? His anger. It was so tragic and yet simple. He had waited and waited for Xavier, loving him more with each passing day. He could have waited longer, but the revolution interfered when the violence exploded around them. He dreaded what they might do to his priest, which magnified his impatience. So all evening, he'd fought for control but lost the battle because of his fear.

He was a desperate animal. He was a fiend, unworthy of life, unworthy of love. Loneliness was too soft a punishment. If only Anthony would rip off his head.

When he first grabbed Xavier, he had hoped that Xavier would yield and fall into his arms. Xavier's resistance made him angrier. Again, he should have left but kept hoping that Xavier would see their love.

Instead, he'd thrown him into the air. Then he'd slapped him. A mortal blow would have wounded the delicate soul, but his vampiric strength broke bones.

So he'd fled in disarray.

He had tried to walk away, but something pulled him back, so he'd climbed the church and concealed himself in the shadows. First, he'd peeked in on Xavier, waiting for Xavier to wake up so that he could apologize a thousand times and even explain the vampirism.

But before he moved, Xavier had cast him out of his life.

It stung, but Thomas deserved it. Numb, he waited, perched outside the window because nothing else came to him. Then Xavier left the room. It took longer than usual, but Xavier limped outside and left through the gate, violating the rule that he not travel alone because everyone left the night guard to Thomas, who followed to protect him yet remained hidden.

After almost two hours, Xavier arrived at the Saint-Laurent home. He went into an alley beside the home and entered through a secret door, one Thomas had never seen. Thomas slipped in behind, using his inhuman speed to conceal himself.

Xavier limped down a dimly lit hall and into a small stairwell to the basement, full of stored goods. The cellar was dark and damp but otherwise tidy. Xavier knocked on a closed door.

When the door opened, Xavier collapsed into Maria's arms. "I can't do it anymore."

"Good heavens. What happened?"

"I—I was looking for Thomas. I wanted to leave with him, but it's all wrong."

"Did he do this to you?"

"I—" Xavier stopped, paused, and then continued. "Of course not. It was a mob. They knew I was a priest and attacked me. I was looking for Thomas, that's all. God's punished me for my sins. I must never see Thomas again, or I risk greater retribution."

He lied. Even after that experience, he protected Thomas, so Thomas cried harder, more ashamed of himself than ever before. His love cast him out, yet still sheltered him from criticism when far away from his brutality.

With Xavier safe, Thomas had to leave. The sound of his voice, so lost and distant, jabbed a stake through Thomas's heart. For the first time in his life, Thomas could not make it better. Xavier did not want to see him, and that was the end of it, so Thomas crept back into the street and wandered.

Xavier's words to Maria distressed Thomas more than ever. He had considered leaving with Thomas. But Thomas's rage spoiled everything. As Anthony and Anne had warned, he ruined his relationship.

He had to get control of his anger, loneliness, and anguish. He had the obligation to change, the rest of the world wouldn't change for him. He failed at every turn, always looking for excuses or someone else to blame. He knew that, too. So why did he continue with the behavior?

He was miserable. "Anthony...what should I do? Anthony?"

Nothing but silence.

His ire built. He stalked Paris, daring anyone to cross his path. One minute, he felt under control and wanted to change; the next, he returned to anger and hatred for the world around him.

When he passed down a narrow sidewalk, just wide enough for two people, another man enraged him by brushing against his coat. Without thinking and in one swift motion, he broke the man's neck, then, with one arm, held the man up and slurped some of the blood.

He regretted the act against an innocent man right afterward, especially because he had violated the ethic. Would the elders hunt him down? Why was he so out of control?

Running faster than ever to get away from everyone, he hurried to his flat. He locked the doors and closed the curtains, alone, still irate, but at least away from people.

Whatever punishment Anthony inflicted, he would accept it without argument. He should die. But that was too easy because life without Xavier was unthinkable. He deserved worse. He needed to suffer.

Thomas hated himself, and then he hated the church, and then he hated love, and then he hated humanity, and then he just hated.

He tried to focus his thoughts when some woman started chattering outside his window, sending him into a complete rage. She laughed and carried on, drunk, talking to every stranger that happened by. She parked herself on a nearby bench, though her volume made it seem that she sat on Thomas's couch.

"Shut up, you stupid whore," Thomas shouted out the window.

"Well, good day to you too. What's your problem?"

Thomas slammed the window and launched himself outside. "I said to shut your mouth, because that loud, annoying voice is driving me mad, you stupid bitch."

"I think you better just—" she started to say.

Thomas, in no mood for negotiation, clutched her throat to kill. As he tightened his grip, something attacked him from behind. The blow to his back was harder than anything he ever experienced. The force caused him to release the woman and fly across the street where he slammed into a brick wall. His back felt as if it broke into a thousand pieces. Thomas regained his composure and looked for his enemy, but it was not an enemy who picked the woman up.

"Leave if you know what's good for you. Run. It's the devil himself who's after you."

Anthony had her running down the street before Thomas moved. Despite his anger, Anthony's reference to Satan sent Thomas into hysterics.

Anthony turned on him, glaring. "Yes, positively hilarious. I can't think of anything funnier than your antics this evening. I saw you kill that man and stayed away because I wanted to crack your skull open. I watched to make sure you could control yourself at home, but that was too much to ask, wasn't it? What's wrong with you?"

Thomas sobered and returned to despair, following with his head down when Anthony yanked him off the ground and pulled him up the stairs into his apartment. Anthony tossed him onto the couch. He walked behind Thomas and slapped his head.

"You're a barbarian."

"Fuck you."

Another slap, harder. And, finally, Thomas reacted with sorrow instead of anger. In a matter of minutes, he retold the entire tale to Anthony. He explained how he tried to control himself, but worrying about Xavier consumed him, making them fight. Then he described in morbid detail his assault, how Xavier threw Thomas out of his life and fled to Maria.

"Lecture me all you want. Send your Council against me. Kill me, please. End my loneliness."

"Thomas, get control of yourself," Anthony said with icy calm. From complete fury a minute before, Anthony became calm and rational, a kindness Thomas did not deserve. Since Anthony refused to play executioner, Thomas would do it.

He bolted across the room, picked up a sword, and hacked off his left hand. That quickly, his hand lay on the ground, forever severed as a constant reminder of what he had done to Xavier. Crazed, the moment made him feel better as blood poured over everything.

"You idiot." Anthony sprinted over, grabbed the cut hand, took Thomas's arm, and held the unattached hand to its former location. Vampires had amazing healing powers, but Thomas stared in disbelief. With slow movement and a great deal of pain, the hand reattached to his arm. He had function and the wound closed in minutes, though still sore. He looked at his fingers, once again wiggling them, in astonishment.

"Will you please stop this insanity? Don't give up on me. Or yourself. You're not alone."

Thomas hugged Anthony with all his strength. After a long moment, he released him and returned to the couch. He put his head in his hands and whispered, "What can I do? I tried."

"Thomas, maybe now you'll listen to me. *Slow down*. Think about the implications of things before you act. Can't you see what I mean?"

Anthony made him promise that he would not approach Xavier, admit their relationship was over and no one but Xavier could rekindle it. As much as it hurt, Thomas agreed. Then he had to pledge not to interact with any humans without Anthony's approval. Again, he agreed. His abbé. Gone. That would sting for years.

"Finally," Anthony said, "you'll remain in Paris with me and watch this revolution, because it's a distraction. And you'll not go on your own until I feel you can handle it."

"That sounds wonderful," Thomas said with a dry tone.

Anthony grabbed Thomas's face and planted a kiss on the lips.

"You won't go to him? You promise? It's too dangerous."

"I promise," Thomas said.

Anthony stayed until he had to retreat from the advancing sun. They talked about a myriad of things, but staying away from topics that were too painful.

As the light came, Thomas lay in his coffin. It was strange that he felt good again. He would get through his turmoil, he promised himself. Of course, the ache in his heart remained. Xavier was still there. Thomas loved him still.

Twenty-Six: Baby Brother

19 JULY 1791

What on earth did he want, Catherine wondered. She allowed no one but Jérémie, Xavier, and Marcel to come to her unannounced. She left Michel off the list just to irritate him, but that morning, she discovered a side benefit. She had time to prepare herself before Michel strode into the room.

"Catherine, listen to me. This is no longer a little game you can play."

No greeting, no hug, just orders. "I've heard your concerns before," Catherine said as much calm as possible, "and I disagree. There's nothing we do here that challenges any government, not the National Assembly nor Louis's. It's an open forum. And security is tight."

"Damn it, I'm trying to protect you. Do you honestly believe you're insulated from the fighting? Why would you think the ragtag band of men who watch this place could ever stop an advancing mob? Catherine, listen to me."

Catherine stood behind the desk and pounded the top with her fist. "I'm not an idiot nor blind to the danger. It hangs in the air. But I won't abandon Paris. When all of the wealthy people packed up their fine china and fled, I stayed. I'm not one of them. This is my duty."

Michel turned his back and took a deep breath. She was frozen, leaning against the desk and staring at him, just as her father did to lord over people and make his point.

Michel faced her again. "You act in a rational way? You have command of yourself? Then explain Marcel." Michel frowned. "I've bitten my tongue long enough. Marcel hides in America while his fiancée stays in Paris. When he braves his home soil, he's in disguise and here to profit."

"You don't know the first thing about what he does."

"I saw the letter on your desk from him. So he wants his name on the Saint-Laurent fortune? I saw what he said about me in there, and Xavier."

"He just needs to get to know both of you better."

Michel clenched his fists. "Is that what he meant by 'getting us out of the way'?"

She had had enough. "I won't change my mind."

"Pardon my intrusion," Jérémie said and startled her as he entered the room.

"What is it?" Catherine asked.

He cast his tearing eyes to the floor, distraught. He was pale and shaking. "It's too much for me to stay around this place when you can't get along. I came to tell you my decision, Catherine, but I'm glad Michel's here. My family requested that I visit them in London, so I'm leaving this afternoon."

Jérémie smiled sheepishly and bowed before leaving the room. Catherine was stunned. She relied on Jérémie a great deal and loved him. Had she pushed him away somehow? After a long pause in which neither moved, Michel turned to her, his face bright red.

"I'll do everything in my power to block this marriage. I forbid it."

"I run this family. I control our financial empire. You're gallivanting about with that silly army, protecting a doomed king or whatever you do as you run around in peasant clothes, while I manage this house. It would crumble without me. And I comfort and protect our brother—"

She choked on the words. First, Michel had come to scold her again. She remained strong. Then Jérémie abandoned her. But she had stood tall. Thinking of Xavier, however, made her despondent. She awoke that morning to find him battered, his face a bloody pulp. Getting out of bed took a great deal of effort. He told her that he was attacked by a mob, the thing she had feared the most. How he escaped alive was beyond her. She sat on the bed for an hour, holding his hand and comforting him as he cried and cried. He'd fallen asleep at long last and she'd slipped into the hall and broken down.

She wiped away the tears, wondering how it had happened on Thomas's watch. How had a vampire lost a battle, the same man who had run through Paris carrying her and another man? Her answer came too soon, in a note:

Dear Catherine,

I apologize for Xavier's condition. I pray that he heals. You cannot know the suffering I feel at his wounds. I am responsible for it and ashamed. He could have been killed.

I will never forgive myself. I write only to tell you that because of my failure, I can no longer protect him. I cannot even see him. Please make arrangements for his nighttime safety. I am sorry to put you in the position of safeguarding him at all times, but it is necessary.

Yours affectionately, Thomas

"Catherine, what is it?" Michel asked.

"Xavier. It's Xavier."

Catherine collected herself to regain her dignity, still puzzling over what Thomas might have meant. She looked at Michel, gathering her thoughts. She loathed exhibiting weak behavior in the middle of a confrontation. At last composed, she continued.

"Xavier came to the house last night a bloody mess. His face—well, I'm sure he has broken bones in it. He was attacked in a savage manner. He says it was an anti-clerical mob. It's a miracle they didn't kill him."

Michel stared at her. "Why didn't you come to me?"

"Because, Michel, this is exactly what I was trying to tell you. *I* run this family. Xavier came to me, and by the time he arrived, there was nothing any of us could do, the damage was already done. Maria brought him to the hospital. The doctor assured me that he'll be fine."

"I'll talk to him about his safety," Michel said.

"I'm ready for you to leave. I'm sure Xavier will want to see you, but he's sleeping so you'll have to come back this afternoon."

"Catherine, I won't take orders from—"

"Out, Michel. Out." Catherine pointed toward the door. Finally, the message penetrated his thick skull and he sulked away.

Twenty-Seven: Understanding Catherine

30 AUGUST 1791

Xavier loved sitting on the balcony in the early morning, and during the late summer months even more so to bask in the last warm days of the year. The quiet of the hour also appealed to him. But many things plagued his mind. The revolution—with its violence and uncertain government. His flock was even harder to minister to now. The danger of traveling to his parish meant infrequent visits. No one allowed him to wander by himself, and despite opening the Saint-Laurent chapel to everyone, few people dared cross town to see him.

Even more than the church, his heart was broken. Xavier still had Catherine, Maria, Anne, Michel, plus the people who had always been close to him. But Thomas was gone, and no one could fill the gaping wound he felt in his stomach that forever bled and would never heal.

Yet what would he do if Thomas came? His face had healed, the bruises disappeared, and he could see out of both eyes, though his left eye was still a little blurred. The aches and pains, too, had dissipated. Only his left cheek bone ached, the one the doctor said had shattered, but it felt a little better each day. If Thomas came, could Xavier forget and forgive?

Xavier kept the assault a secret. Did he lie because the truth embarrassed him or to protect Thomas? He wished he knew. Whatever the answer, it had to do with Xavier's persistent love and longing for the man who had plunged him into constant depression and irritability.

But the quiet morning made him happy. He was so content that the sight of Michel overjoyed him, even though he too often quarreled with Catherine.

"Hello, Michel," he said with genuine affection.

"You're looking better and better. Are you staying out of trouble?"

"Of course."

"I hate to be abrupt, but I haven't much time. May I speak with you about something?" Michel fidgeted with his hat. He wore his uniform and looked very noble, very much the leader. But he also wiggled his fingers. "It's about Catherine's engagement to Marcel."

"There's nothing we can do," Xavier said to preempt his brother. "It makes her angry."

"I know, but you don't understand my responsibility." Michel sat opposite him.

Xavier thought for a moment before he answered. He did realize the responsibility Michel felt, yet he also thought much of it was invented. "I think you want to become our father because he died and you're the eldest. Do what you can, but wait until we need you. Then Catherine will listen; then she'll know you have her interests in mind."

Michel's eyes teared, which shocked Xavier, coming from such a controlled man.

"Father almost said the same thing to me as he died. But—"

Xavier hugged his brother.

"I was too young. I was supposed to serve my time in the military, then move into the family business. But he died. And there I was, with a million people telling me about the grave accountability I had to the family. I knew I had to handle you both different from what other family members and friends told me, but I worried so much about what they thought that I could never stop myself." Michel sat up straight. "And now it's too late. I don't want to upset her again."

"That's your mistake with her. You try to predict her reaction. She wants you to just speak with her. It's not about whether or not she agrees with you. She hates your attitude."

He got up but came back before leaving and hugged Xavier in a tight embrace, then released and stood over him. "Are you fine?"

Xavier detested conversation about himself. He was alone with his misery, which suited him. He paused too long, though, for his careless shrug to appease Michel.

"You haven't seen Thomas recently."

"No, he's—" Xavier wondered what to say. "—busy with things."

Michel ruffled Xavier's hair and left.

In truth, Xavier was far from fine. The pit in his stomach throbbed all the time. He wept every night before passing out. He was lonely.

Perhaps he could have handled it in a different way and Thomas would still be there, his protector. If he had quelled his own holy fear, maybe he could have led Thomas away from his inner rage.

Xavier left the porch, heading for the parlor. A few days before, by mistake, he had discovered how to make the pain go away in his first drunken stupor since Thomas had left. His head swam, things were funnier, the pain buried deeper, and he spoke his mind with more clarity. He tried it again the next night, and last night, each time with the same result.

The wine, bitter yet tasty, burned his throat as he tossed one glass back without pausing. His head floated. The world seemed to make more sense. He poured another and flung himself onto the couch, propped his head against the arm, and glanced at the ceiling. Another drink. He giggled at the thought of a priest sitting so inappropriately.

He remembered that he had appointments that afternoon for something, but what? Now he laughed that the wine caused memory lapses. He swung his leg back and forth, a million things racing through his head, and when he thought of Thomas, which happened too often, he took another gulp of wine.

Twenty-Eight: Treading Water

JANUARY 1792

Sitting alone in a corner of Anthony's flat, Thomas glanced to see if his friend watched, but he still chatted with the little beauty he'd picked up near the river. Anthony had "found" an appealing eighteen-year-old, a strapping youth who looked more in his twenties with those hard sailor's muscles. But not to kill. Anthony sought sex and the young man was ready to please, not even demanding cash.

Anthony forbade Thomas from leaving his flat alone for very long. Though he had maintained control for six months—six months since that catastrophic night—he still struggled with it. He often wanted to run back to Xavier and beg forgiveness, something Anthony outlawed, the one rule he enforced.

Thankfully, the revolution amused them. With his British bias coming out all of the time, Anthony laughed every night, snorting that the French had no idea what they did. One day, they loved Louis, and the next, they wanted to assassinate him. One day, all was calm, and the next, they rioted. And Anthony attempted to get him interested in casual sexual encounters, but none appealed to Thomas.

Thomas glanced at Anthony and his latest toy again, wanting to be alone. He hated following the ethic and giggled at how he slipped away at times, if even for a moment, from Anthony's prying eyes. He never spoke to Xavier, but Thomas saw the abbé. Thomas hurried to see Xavier from afar whenever he had a chance away from Anthony by concealing himself in the shadows. The first time, he'd spied and seen Xavier in lay clothing at the Saint-Laurent home. He returned a week later to discover the same. His spying on Xavier had become more frequent, almost every night, but he'd never approached or violated Anthony's commands because he feared Xavier's rejection, and he never stayed long, never more than a minute or two.

Next, he had sought Denys Girard and begun a clandestine payment to him and the men who protected Xavier, thus ensuring twenty-four-hour guardianship.

Thomas stepped onto the balcony and breathed in the night air, fresher than usual, as the stars twinkled above. Thomas loved the night. Unlike Anthony, who missed the sun, Thomas never regretted his reality. If darkness gave him eternal life, so be it. There was something daring, exciting even, about the vampire's mastery over darkness. They feared nothing, could see things in the pitch black, and far fewer people annoyed him. And since lanterns illuminated so much, including most of Paris, cities came to life at all hours. Thomas was so lost in thought he had not heard Anthony approach.

"Do you mind if we leave you for a while?"

"Please, I don't need to see any more of this."

Anthony smiled and spun away. Thomas, intending to behave, went to his flat without so much as a thought of seeing Xavier. He walked up the stairs and opened a window because the winter air felt good on his face. A servant's knock interrupted him.

"Sir, I apologize, but there's a lady who insists upon seeing you."

Only someone with extreme persuasion and inside knowledge could breach Thomas's first line of defense with such ease—his servants knew never to interrupt. In every city, Thomas chose a few wayward youths, just the cutest of the lot, and paid them far too much to do his bidding and therefore had their complete loyalty. Thomas smiled and pinched him one on the face, then walked to the window to look down on the carriage.

"What shall I do?" the young man asked.

"Bring her up."

Thomas recognized the Saint-Laurent carriage, guessing it was Catherine. Only she could persuade the servant to let her through. Only she was so bold. The boy ushered Catherine into the room, and Thomas smiled.

"Catherine." Thomas kissed her hand. "What a pleasure to see you."

"You've avoided me for months. I sent the first note in September, and one each week since, and the vampire I thought was my friend never answered. So I came to him instead."

Catherine, with her sly grin, was always too much.

"Have a seat. I haven't avoided you because I'm angry with you—"

She held up her hand. "Spare me, Thomas. It's not my business. I do appreciate that you continue to help in protecting Xavier. Since that mob attacked him, I worry a lot."

Thomas's stomach clenched. She thought it was a mob that attacked Xavier. "It's the least I can do. But why are you here?"

Catherine fumbled around, her usual confidence faded. "I need your help. I know you pay Denys and his men. I know you still watch after Xavier. It means you still love him." She looked into his eyes, always too perceptive. "Whatever happened, forget it."

"Impossible."

"It's worse than you can imagine. He won't talk about you or anything besides his work. But he walks around the house in a perpetual stupor and drinks all the time. Maria, Anne, myself, nothing stops him. We take the wine from him, but he finds more. I finally just gave it to him when he snuck out of the house alone to steal it."

His heart ached. "I don't want to hear any more. Nothing can heal the wounds between us. I love you too. But this is too much for me."

Catherine stood and strutted toward the door, where she turned and half-smiled. "I expected as much. I only thought—" She halted. "Never mind." Catherine offered a sad, resigned smile and took her leave.

It broke Thomas's heart. She climbed into her carriage and ordered the driver to move along. As the carriage passed, he saw Anne Hébert sitting next to her. But what followed them?

A black horse trod a few yards behind the carriage. Thomas recognized Marcel's evil designs, and he had no patience for that fool. Moody from Catherine's visit and now angry, Thomas jumped out the window and landed on the ground in front of the man, who pulled back on the reins in fright.

"Do you always follow carriages?"

"Get out of my way." He spurred the horse, but Thomas grabbed the reins and held with a tight grip. With ease, he yanked the man from his mount.

"I'll do anything," he moaned. "Please."

Thomas loved it when evil men begged, these fiends who reveled in scaring and killing others. When a regiment marched down the road, Thomas jerked the idiot into the entryway of his building. The chandelier shook when Thomas slammed the door.

"Tell me what you were doing and who sent you." Thomas's bicep bulged as he latched on to the man's throat.

"I'm following the black woman."

"For whom?" Thomas tightened his fingers as a warning.

"I don't know his name. He sent me to chase her out of Paris."

"Were you supposed to kill her?"

"Only as a last resort."

Thomas clutched harder until the man's spine snapped. With speed, he flung the fool over his shoulder, shot through Paris, and deposited him in a pile of garbage.

So Marcel watched from afar, despite his cowardice. Thomas needed to calm himself.

He went to the Saint-Laurent home and wandered through the rooms until he heard Xavier, talking to Maria. Thomas sat near the door, out of view but close enough to hear them over the crowd. Xavier slurred his words, sounding bitter, yet Thomas's heart leapt at his voice.

"Maria, stop, I didn't have much wine. There was just a bit left from communion and the good Lord won't have me wasting it. It's the blood, for heaven's sake! If I'm drunk, I'm drunk on Jesus!" Xavier snorted at his joke, a harsh, mocking laugh.

"Blasphemy!" Maria scolded. "And lower your voice. People watch you."

They scuffled as Maria removed Xavier, some of the salon visitors looking at the commotion, and without warning, she dragged Xavier through the doorway.

He stumbled, his eyes bloodshot, and laughed. "Watch out for the nun brigade!" He fell to his face laughing but with great care tilted his glass so no wine spilled. "Almost lost the good Lord on that one." When he got up, he toppled backward and landed in Thomas's lap. Thomas froze, his heart pounding.

Xavier gulped the rest of his wine while seated, then casually patted the "stranger's" knee without looking at his face. "Thanks for the seat. I had to stop to drink this last bit, so as not to spill." It took great effort for him to push off Thomas.

Maria, recognizing Thomas, hurried over and yanked Xavier away. She shoved Xavier along, and he giggled when she kicked him in the butt and moved toward the door. "You know where to go," she told Xavier. "And you—" she addressed Thomas. "Get the hell out." She scowled before following Xavier who had lurched down the hall.

Despite Xavier's condition and Maria's angry words, a sense of calm guided Thomas out of the home and into the night. He loved his abbé and held out hope that one day they would be reunited.

Part VII: The Fall

Twenty-Nine: Phase Two

25 MARCH 1792

Catherine was in no mood for more gossip about the revolution as she walked through the house. Her former excitement had dulled, yet the guard insisted he had news for her.

"If it's urgent, I'll listen. But only after I find my brother. I promised Maria I'd take charge of him every morning to give her a respite. Follow me and you can tell both of us."

"I doubt your brother cares about this anymore," the guard said with an edge of sarcasm. Xavier's constant drunkenness, bitter anger, and childish humor had alienated many people. Catherine marveled that he sobered enough every afternoon to perform church rituals. Hoping like a fool that he might snap out of it, Catherine bided her time by nurturing him.

"If you don't want to tell both of us, you may go," she said after a pause. Catherine bustled down the hall and knocked on Xavier's door.

"Who is it?" Xavier sang out.

"Open the damned door." Catherine heard stumbling, something heavy fell to the ground, and then her brother pulled the door open and bowed before her with a dramatic flourish.

"What are you doing?" Catherine laughed despite herself.

"Offering you the respect you deserve. Come, have some wine."

"I thought you agreed not to bring beverages into your room." Catherine brushed past him and grabbed the bottle.

"See, I knew you wanted some." Xavier shook his finger at her.

Staring at him, she casually opened the window and poured the rest of the wine onto the roof.

"Catherine! Why do you waste it when so many go thirsty?"

"Spare me your concern for the poor. Now, get serious. I want to talk to you."

"Wrong. Maria already told me you were coming to babysit. There's a difference between chatting and standing guard. Besides, the wine spirits uplift me."

"They descend you into a pit of idiocy. And call it what you want, you and I are stuck together and I won't watch you drink the whole time."

Xavier burst into laughter, stumbled backward, and fell onto the bed. He spoke into the pillows. "What else is there to do but drink?"

As he asked, Catherine remembered the guard. "What did you want to tell us?"

He glanced at her then at Xavier. "Did you hear about the Girondins?"

"Their revolution is no more radical than anyone else's," Catherine answered. "Who cares if they're in charge?"

"Did you know they're allowing everyone to vote? I can vote!" the guard exclaimed.

"Not everyone. *Men* may vote. There's a difference." Catherine patted him on the shoulder and grinned. He smiled, too. "Thank you, kind sir, for your news. I need to see Xavier alone now. If you would, stay outside the door."

He nodded and retreated into the hallway.

"Get up," she instructed. "You look like a fool."

"I am a fool." The comment sent Xavier into guffaws, though he did sit up to lean against the bed.

"Did you steal more communion wine?" Catherine asked.

He laughed even more, which sent her into laughter as well. "How ill I am, that I steal the communion wine for myself. But I don't spill any."

Catherine sat on the edge of a fainting couch as Xavier moved about the bed in a thousand positions every second with jerky movements, as drunk as she had ever seen. She stopped talking about the problem with him because it had no effect.

Xavier started singing some made-up silly song about Catherine and the revolution as he danced on the bed in his pajamas. Catherine racked her brain for a way to calm him.

"If you don't calm down, I'll sell you to Thomas as a slave." She regretted it once it left her mouth.

"Don't spoil my mood. I was having fun."

"Did you hear that the new government is allowing the parishes to banish priests if they defy its new laws governing the church? They can arrest them. They're going hard after the church. What if your parish becomes disgusted with your drinking? It takes but one of them to make up a story about you and away you'll go."

Xavier snapped back into his jovial mood and laughed. "Whoosh! They'll banish me to Rome where I'll have to clean the Pope's chamber pot."

Catherine had a hard time keeping up with him. One minute, he wanted to continue his clandestine engagements forever, and then he wanted to abandon the church forever. At other times, he wanted to be Catherine's secretary, or Michel's attendant, or simply float around.

"Xavier, how are you really?" Catherine asked.

"I don't have a clue."

Catherine walked to the bed and sat beside him. He held his legs to his chest, a sign since he was young that something troubled him.

"So you're confused about the church, but this doesn't bother you. I can accept that. You drink constantly. Why?" she asked, though she knew the problem: Thomas.

"I can't think of anything that would make me do this. You sound like Maria. She always wants me to talk about Thomas. Thomas, Thomas, Thomas. She hates him. She always scolded me for meeting with him, and now that he's gone, she wants to talk about him. I just don't want to hear her say she was right about him. Then she tried to sell me off onto other men—" Xavier halted his words. He had gone farther than ever before.

Catherine held her breath, then exhaled softly. "What were you saying?"

"Nothing." He studied his hands, sullen. "Look at the sun." He pointed to the window. "How marvelous. I'm getting dressed." He launched himself off the bed, talking on and on about the sun, as if he had never seen it before.

Xavier dressed in a frenzied way, disheveled with his collar turned the wrong way and his clothes wrinkled, but ran out the door nonetheless. Catherine followed down the hall and stopped him before he grabbed more liquor from the cabinet. He laughed with glee, still drunk from the wine he had consumed, and Catherine sighed, fearing she might have lost him.

Thirty: To War

20 JUNE 1792

Anthony and Thomas sat at an outside café, sipping wine on a patio under perfect weather, almost too exquisite a scene, considering France's current turmoil. They were acting human.

They had exhausted their favorite topic—the revolution, which confounded them more and more and made less sense every day. In the midst of an unstable government, with countless factions vying for control, the country had declared war and plunged into a worldwide struggle. Without surprise, the latest war went poorly for the French, with numerous defeats, economic inflation, and no one wanting to join the army, which led to rioting. The French more often than not turned to violent mobs when their plight worsened.

"Are you still monitoring Xavier?" Anthony asked.

"Yes. You gave permission to watch him from afar, and that's all I do."

Thomas thought about having seen Xavier earlier that night. Xavier was sitting on the balcony, laughing and carrying on in a loud drunken voice with anyone who would listen. It pained Thomas to see him that way. The alcohol spoke, not Xavier, and Thomas had caused the misery. Catherine sat near Xavier the whole time, protecting him and indulging him.

"How are the Saint-Laurents?" Anthony asked.

"The same. It seems Catherine's salon is doing well. I asked around the place and heard Jérémie went to London. I have my servant go in from time to time to keep me apprised about things."

Anthony ran his fingers down the stem of his wineglass. "And Marcel? Is he still there?"

"Gone, too. Apparently back to America. However, I learned that he tried to take over the salon from there, but Catherine wouldn't allow it."

"I know you still want Xavier," Anthony said. "I won't discourage it, but I'm not sure it's a good idea for you to entirely abstain from sex. It worries me."

"Sex has nothing to do with it. It doesn't mean I'm not satisfying my—" Thomas stopped himself and laughed. "What business of yours is it?"

"You're right. It's irrelevant. But what about your latest method of killing?"

"My method of killing? I comply with the ethic," Thomas said in self-defense. "What are you talking about?"

Anthony got up from the table and gestured for Thomas to follow as he sauntered down the street, ever casual. Thomas followed, bewildered, as Anthony led them away from the bars and the center of Paris. Thomas knew they were hunting, but why?

Anthony stopped when they reached a dark alley, turned to Thomas, and said, "Hunt."

"I never knew you enjoyed voyeurism."

Anthony chuckled and pointed down the alley.

A suspect appeared at once, dirty, hovering in dark corners, and scowling. He jumped out to rob Thomas. Thomas grabbed the man's throat and thrust him against the wall. His bones cracked. Thomas pushed the man to the ground and leered over him, his fangs large and his brow wrinkled. Thomas knelt and, before sinking his teeth into the skin, as one last punishment, ripped the man's testicles off. Then he enjoyed the blood. The thick syrup flowed down his throat. It burned like a good alcohol and created a sexual sensation. Not the climax, but the building tension and tingling beforehand. The task completed, he shoved the man into a corner.

Anthony was already laughing. "Still have no idea what I meant? You've become more maniacal than ever since you slapped Xavier across the room." Anthony mocked him with a snarky smile, but dread filled Thomas.

The bloodied genitals, lying five feet from the body, told him that something else propelled him. "What's going on? What have I become?"

"I'd guess you're mad about Xavier. You don't dwell on your sadness and so the tension comes out this way. It's not inappropriate, but without a doubt it's different. Better than when you were beating Xavier or attacking innocent civilians. This business with Xavier has you more emotional than ever. Maybe your love for Xavier isn't always a good thing and you need to prepare yourself for failure."

"I thought I was being patient. I've been so proud of not behaving irrationally."

"That's not my point, Thomas. You've been marvelously good. Extraordinarily so."

"I feel alone and as if no one understands."

"But I do. Love's frustration isn't yours alone. I mourned when I lost you or, should I say, when you told me about the real you. And you know about—" Anthony stopped. He never said much about his companion of many years before, though he alluded to it often. "I just mean you get into the most trouble when you try to solve things by yourself."

As dawn approached, Thomas felt better. The ache for Xavier remained because he loved him too much. But he was not alone. Whether he agreed with everything Anthony said or not, their friendship was crucial to him. They hugged goodbye, a little longer than before. Thomas fell into his sunlight-induced coma and, as always, dreamt of Xavier's arms clinging to him.

Thirty-One: Court Jester

17 JULY 1792

Michel burst into Catherine's office, with a servant close on his heels. "I hurried home to tell you something, and I don't have time to wait."

Catherine held up her hand to stop them both. "It's fine. Let him in." She almost spat something else at her brother but noticed that Michel looked troubled.

He paused until the servant left them alone. "I'm sorry." His eyes welled with tears. "I apologize for my behavior since Father died."

Catherine stood dumbfounded for a moment but then raced around her desk and embraced him. "Of course, I forgive you."

Michel nodded. "Thank you. I'm trying."

"I know. And I love you."

Michel smiled. Catherine attempted to engage him further on it, but just as fast as he entered, he withdrew. They exchanged a few more niceties and talked in general about the revolution.

More remarkable, he never mentioned Marcel. She had stopped Marcel's attempt to control the Saint-Laurent finances, but not before assuring him that he still had her utter devotion. He sent another supply of medication, which she took as instructed.

"Thank you for coming," she said to Michel as he left. "I needed our reconciliation more than ever, what with all of the energy that Xavier takes."

"He can't get over Thomas," Michel answered.

"So you know about them?"

"I'm not as dense as you think." With that, Michel ran off to his regiment, but promised to return later that evening for dinner.

Their conversation played in her head a number of times throughout the day, until she sprinted toward the kitchen to check on dinner a few hours after Michel left. It felt odd, to go about mundane tasks such as eating and organizing a family gathering amidst the revolution, but it helped to root her, and everyone in her household, to something common, without the constant sense of change swirling through the air. Seeing that dinner preparations progressed without a problem, Catherine hurried up the stairs to Xavier's room to find him, as expected, drunk and silly.

"Sissy! How splendid. I was just donning my finest attire for this formal dinner." Xavier, wearing his ceremonial robe reserved for high church affairs, danced around and curtseyed to her with a big grin. His breath smelled of liquor—not wine but whiskey.

"Xavier, you look very—what shall I say? Regal? No, you look like the pope."

"Why, thank you," he said and bowed.

"I didn't mean it as a compliment. And you aren't wearing that to dinner. Take it off. It will antagonize Maria."

Xavier became quite serious. "I love Maria. But I can't bear the scolding."

Xavier plopped himself onto a couch, slouching. Catherine pulled him up and yanked off the top garment. "Guests are waiting." Without resistance, Xavier allowed her to undress him down to his modest clerical robe that he wore about the house. Catherine hurried him toward the dining room despite his stopping to observe everything they passed.

As she feared, they arrived to see Anne, Maria, and Michel waiting, though Michel had assumed the role of host for her. Catherine orchestrated the dinner for Xavier, hoping it might shock him back to reality.

"What a surprise," Xavier cried. "All my friends are here. Welcome, I've prepared a feast. I was in the kitchen all day."

Everyone laughed, Catherine not the only one used to his drunken antics. Xavier danced about the room and kissed each of them on the cheek, except for Maria. To her, he extended his clerical ring, winked, and asked her to kiss it. She slapped his hand away, but grinned. After getting him to settle down, everyone took their seats and dinner commenced. The conversation was animated, everyone contributed, and Xavier, though drunk, appeared to have a grand time. It unburdened Catherine's heart just to see him smile.

"Oh, Catherine," Xavier called down the table. "Suppose I'm one of those peculiar correspondents from America who must interview all of France to find out how each person feels about this revolution."

"Well, Mr. American, maybe I want to hear what you think, first," Catherine said.

"I think it's a revolution and that democracy is best. Rioting is silly because it is silly," Xavier said with a strange accent, trying to sound American and not making sense.

"I'm rather numb to the whole thing," Catherine answered.

"Very well. You, of the nunnery, what do you think?"

"I won't condemn nor promote this revolution, I just do my best to help people." There were cries of "Hear, hear," from Michel and Anne. "However, there's one terrible tragedy."

"Oh, do tell," Xavier said.

"This revolution has led to a rash of drinking among the clergy," Maria said. "I don't know what it is, but those Catholic priests all took to drinking, even the communion wine."

Xavier still seemed to see humor there and laughed until tears streamed down his face. "How interesting. I think this revolution has led nuns to be irritable."

"Only because of the drunken priests," she shot back.

"Fine. We know the opinion of the nuns, but what might the military think?"

Michel frowned. "I find it confusing. Like Catherine, I'm numb."

Poor Michel, Catherine thought. *Even in the midst of play, he answered with earnest.*

"Now you, Anne, what do you think?" Xavier asked.

"It doesn't much matter to me. Won't change my life, either way."

"But does the violence lend itself to magic?"

"You're something else, Abbé. Just a fool little boy running away from the revolution."

"Hmm." Xavier put his elbow on the table and rested his head in his hand. "Let me guess. The four of you have turned this into a conspiracy against me. But I've called your bluff. *You're* the fool little beasts for thinking you could trick me." Xavier stood, pushing his chair back, and laughed. "Henceforth, you may call me the drunken abbé, who wants the entire church to drink."

"But what will the bishops say?" Catherine egged him on.

"Fie on the bishops."

"And the pope?" Maria asked.

"Bah. His edicts mean nothing to me."

"What are you going to change now that you took control?" Anne asked.

"Let me see. We'll get rid of all Catholic restrictions and laws. The only rule will be to love each other. Nothing else needed. Of course, we'll leave secular laws to the government."

"What kind of love?" Maria asked.

"Any kind. All love. Even the kind of love I have with Thomas." The moment he spoke that name, Xavier's eyes widened. Even drunk, he realized he had revealed his secret. Paralyzed, wanting to encourage him but not frighten him away, no one said a word.

Anne spoke with her blunt honesty. "Well, there's my sheepish friend letting out the skeletons because of the fire water." She laughed. "Now, Abbé, we'll ignore it for you, but I'm glad to see you're so comfortable with us."

Xavier then concluded his reform of the church, dinner ended, and everyone went their separate ways.

On her way out, however, Anne pointed to a small statue that Marcel had sent to Catherine. "Get that out of this house. It's watching you."

Catherine did not want a confrontation after the night had done so much for Xavier. She ignored the comment and thanked Anne for coming. Catherine finished the night by tucking Xavier into bed as if he were again five, when it had been her duty to act as his mother.

"You know it's not a problem, don't you?" she asked as she stroked his hair. "Loving someone, no matter what other people think is fine."

"Oh, that."

"I love Marcel though none of you approve. I go with my heart."

"But what's influencing your heart?" Xavier slurred.

She frowned. "What are you implying?"

"Nothing. You just mentioned love."

"I meant, who you love with a unique passion. You said it tonight, remember? I just want to make sure you know everyone in that room understood."

"Maybe sometime that's what I'll do. But I don't know if I can stand another beating for love."

With that, he passed out. Catherine shook him to no avail. He was sound asleep, so she kissed him on the forehead and left. What had he meant? Was his reference to a beating a metaphor? Catherine chased the thought from her mind. It was ludicrous to think that the man who loved Xavier would do such a thing to him, even if he was a vampire.

Thirty-Two: The Commune

9 AUGUST 1792

Catherine, alone in her office, gazed at the pile of paperwork in front of her and noticed a new letter with Michel's seal. She broke the seal and read the letter:

> *Catherine,*
>
> *I apologize for canceling our engagement again this evening. I know you are worried about Xavier, and I intend to come as soon as possible to assist you. But I cannot leave the edge of Paris right now as things have worsened. My regiment is still aligned too closely with Louis. Today, they imprisoned the royal family. Louis has lost all authority, and they are hunting down his regiments. I am transforming mine as we speak, to serve the people and so that my men are protected, but it will take time. I apologize again.*
>
> *Your loving brother, Michel*

Intrigued that they imprisoned the entire royal family, Catherine delayed plans to do paperwork and went to tell Xavier. She found him in the chapel with the communion wine, alone in front of the altar and praying. Catherine paused to watch. He was so complex, with his denouncing of the Catholic Church but continued identity as a priest, with his shunning of traditional religion and now constant drunkenness. But she often found him praying.

Catherine ruffled her skirt to alert him. Without leaving the altar and still kneeling, he bent backward and looked at her upside-down. He smiled and twisted back into position, gained his feet, and lurched toward her, falling on his face, laughing as he did so.

"The last time I saw you prone on a sanctuary floor, they ordained you."

"What brings you to the house of the Lord?" he asked, laughing even harder.

"This Lord's house is in my home. I came to see my brother. But I found a drunken priest instead."

Xavier laughed again. "But alas, fair lady, your brother *is* a drunken priest."

"Would he like to hear some news from Michel?"

Xavier jumped off the ground and raced to her. He hugged her and spun her around. "What? What?"

"They have imprisoned Louis."

"Michel has imprisoned Louis?"

"The Insurrectionist Commune."

"What's that?"

"The new government."

"How boring. Wine and politics just don't mix. So, where did they put Louis?"

"I'm not sure."

As they conversed, he was his usual drunken self at first, silly and laughing, which comforted Catherine in an odd way. But as his behavior persisted he reminded her why she had sent for Michel as he became morose. The alcohol depressed him and he was no longer able to keep up the charade. Two days before, she'd at last confronted him and demanded that he talk about Thomas. He had burst into tears for hours, but he still refused to say a word about it.

Thirty-Three: Drinking Away the Pain

10 AUGUST 1792

Catherine went to the library when the servants informed her that Michel had arrived.

"Michel." Catherine hugged him, holding on for a little longer than usual, as she greeted him and ushered them both to seats. He appeared tired, and his clothes were filthy.

"I came as soon as I secured my regiment. We're hiding in Paris. Only one of my men refused to abandon the monarchy, but he left without incident."

"Are you safe? You look dreadful."

"Speaking of not looking well, you look worn yourself."

"I fell asleep at my desk."

"It's because Jérémie left, isn't it?"

"Partially." She toyed with her skirts. Jérémie still wrote to her and handled their foreign affairs, but Catherine missed him something awful.

"Do you need help here?" Michel asked. 'I'm sure that Jérémie will return soon."

"I'm not so sure. His letters are distant. Besides, what would bring him back to this miserable revolution?"

Michel smiled. "He has interests here. Have you asked Xavier to help?"

Catherine roared with laughter, prompting Michel to grin.

"I know he's a drunk."

"I've grown accustomed to his being drunk all the time." Catherine cast her eyes to the ground. "But he's not happy anymore. His moods are dark, and he seldom jokes or even smiles. He sits in dim rooms, still intoxicated, and cynically condemns everything. We need to confront him. Maybe he'll listen to both of us."

Michel looked out the window, then turned to Catherine.

"I didn't tell you this, though I thought it peculiar. He came to me, on the front a few nights ago, and said he sneaked from the house. I had to prop him against the wall, he was so drunk. He was crying and talking about Thomas, but it was incoherent. Then he fell to his knees in front of me. He said he had to forget. He wanted me to take him to Rome, to flee with him to Rome, so he could serve the pope."

Catherine stared at him. "He hates the pope."

"That's what I said. He smirked and said he disliked the papacy, but that he needed punishment and he could think of nothing worse than working for his eminence. I wish I could remember more. It was confusing. I concentrated on calming him down and convinced him to allow two of my men to get him home. Xavier refuses to talk about it, but does this have anything to do with Thomas?"

"I wish I knew what kept him from acting with Thomas. He always says something about religion and obligation. Whatever it is, I need your help, I fear—" Catherine choked on the words. "I'm afraid that he'll harm himself."

Michel's eyes filled with tears.

"I watch him all the time now," Catherine continued as she wiped her own tears. "I never leave him alone. If I'm not with him, then Anne or Maria is. He stays contentedly with Anne, but he and Maria argue the entire time they're together. And she pronounces that conservative theology to anyone who'll listen. It makes things worse for Xavier. I hate to say it because I'd do anything for Xavier, but he takes so much time. What could've led him to this?"

"Let's go see him."

Michel barged into Xavier's room without knocking to find Maria reading on the bed.

She got up. "I'll be outside," she told them and closed the door.

Xavier was sitting on the ledge and staring out the window. His eyes were red, and dark circles marred his skin beneath them. He had a bottle of wine, having shunned the decorum of using a glass some time ago. He did not look at them when they entered.

"Xavier," Michel began, "Catherine and I are worried, more than ever before. This goes beyond our parental instincts." Michel walked over and forced Xavier off the sill and into a chair so that he faced them, though Xavier refused to look into their eyes.

"Yes, let us help you," Catherine said.

Xavier's eyes filled with tears, and he took another drink from the bottle. "I think that I'd like to visit New Orleans one day. To go to that part of the world would be quite an experience. Perhaps we could venture together."

"What are you talking about?" Catherine asked through a grimace. "Will you stop these games?"

"'Tis not a game. I've wanted to see New Orleans for a long time. Since I first heard about it. It sounds so different. So fascinating. I want to see plantations. I want to see the Africans. I want to judge for myself whether or not they're treated well."

"For God's sake—" Catherine stopped.

"Xavier," Michel said, "if that's what you want to talk about, fine, but why?"

"A friend." Xavier bit his lower lip and cried. It broke Catherine's heart when she realized Xavier was reaching out to them. "Thomas, of course. He's been to New Orleans and has business interests there. He promised to take me. But that would require our still being friends, so I need new companions. Because he's gone and nothing can be done. You know, you always saw me as so pure and innocent. I'm so far from that. The truth is much more complex. These robes, the church, religion, they're all full of contradictions. I love God. I want to serve Him and His people. But there are powerful personal feelings that have haunted me since he was young. I almost left the church because these urges take over, but my spiritual confusion sabotaged this impulse because I felt like a selfish traitor. I was going to New Orleans. I was going to sin because my heart longed for it. Now I'm back to the church, but the person I loved abandoned me. It's ironic, yes?" He wiped at his eyes. "I drink to forget. Which, I believe, brings me to the purpose of your visit."

Xavier lifted the bottle in the air and gulped half of it down. "I'm not prepared to give it up. Sobriety holds no allure. It threatens me with a reality that's cold and harsh. Leave me to wallow in the drink, for it comforts me with visions of what could've been. I at least have left my memory of happier times and the dreams I created and hoped would someday come true. This shouldn't affect your happiness. You both mean more to me than you can imagine. I love you, but I'm not ready to accept myself or confront my failures."

And so the solution Catherine had known all along once again haunted her. Thomas was the only answer. His passion for Xavier alone could pull her brother out of the deep funk. What had happened to these two who had always seemed happy? Did Xavier discover the vampire lurking in Thomas? Or had Thomas attacked Xavier? Or was it both? Whatever the answer, she had to find Thomas.

Thirty-Four: Death

2 SEPTEMBER 1792

Xavier stumbled on the stone street, took another swig of wine, and continued on his clandestine operation. That day, he devised a scheme that allowed him to sneak out a basement window and into the street. Maria, his guardian at the time, would not miss him until it was too late. He hurried through Paris to see the crowds and how much they hated his fellow priests who refused to support their revolution.

Some unknown man had stormed into the salon in the middle of Xavier's breakfast and announced that Catholic tyranny was about to end because the extremists intended to massacre priests. Xavier wanted to see for himself. He wondered what Thomas would think.

Thomas. Xavier stopped walking. The very name forced him to prop himself up against a wall and take another gulp of wine. The buildings around him spun even though he was stationary. He closed his eyes and dreamed of happier times, first his childhood with Michel and Catherine, the blithe innocence of youth, then about meeting Maria when he got his first parish, and later, how he accidentally fell into his relationship with Anne Hébert. But his mind played tricks on him and again he thought of Thomas, of their long walks through Paris. Then he fantasized what it would have been like to let himself go. Ah, the joy of traveling across the ocean with Thomas as his escort. As his lover.

Xavier chugged the rest of the wine and threw the bottle to the ground where it broke with a crash. He wiped the wine that spilled off his chin, then smeared it across his shirt. He tried to straighten his clothing, but it was hard to concentrate. Besides, he was on a mission.

The massacre of the priests. He headed for the prisons to see if it were true that they intended to kill priests who refused to obey the revolutionary government.

Xavier reached down to play with his cross, a very old habit, and then remembered it was no longer there. Priests *had* to wear lay clothing after the latest government outlawed clerical garments. He thought it funny for anyone to care that much about what someone wore. He laughed, and it felt good. He seldom did that anymore.

He was near the prisons when he confronted the first mob. They shouted revolutionary slogans and anti-Catholic epithets, and there was the usual burning of the pope in effigy. The crowd shoved Xavier around as it moved toward the prisons. Fearing he could not stand alone or might be trampled, Xavier worked his way into an alcove.

They had carts—jail carts—full of shackled priests, some of whom Xavier recognized, including his bishop, who had a deformed and broken pinky that clutched an iron bar. Xavier might have laughed at seeing him in prison if not for the tragedy that surrounded them. He had never gotten along with most of the priests, but it still disgusted him to see people shouting and spitting at the defenseless men.

A few men stood between the carts and the mob, protecting the priests with immense bravery. Were they soldiers? Then, as the masses became further enraged, someone joined Xavier in the alcove. Even drunk, Xavier recognized him.

"Damn scum clergy, I hate 'em all," Marcel said with a smirk. When had he returned from America? "Bet they won't get out of here alive."

Afraid, Xavier went along with the game. In his eternal drunkenness, Xavier had forgotten about his sister's wretched fiancé.

"You think they want to kill the priests?" Xavier asked.

"What else? But my mission is personal. My, but you've wine all over yourself. You damned slob." Marcel slapped Xavier on the back and continued to make fun of him. Then he looked around. "I have to take care of a problem."

Even in his fogged state, Xavier's heart was in his throat.

"And here it comes," Marcel said as he glanced away.

Xavier looked, too, at the ring of guards that surrounded the priests. Now he saw that they were soldiers, from their rigid posture and strength, though out of uniform. They pushed people away from the carts and tried to stop the assaults. The mob toyed with them and laughed.

"There he is, the scoundrel I've hunted." Marcel talked more to himself than Xavier, but Xavier listened with fear. "I sent men after him, and they failed. So it's left to me."

"What's left to you?" Xavier struggled to stand against the wall and talk at the same time.

"You drunken fool. Don't you see I'm trying to kill someone?"

Xavier jerked his head around, scanning the courtyard but saw nothing but hordes and hordes of unidentifiable people yelling at the priests.

Marcel shoved Xavier aside. Too drunk to keep his balance, Xavier thudded to the dirt and fumbled around, trying to get up. He kept falling down because the wine controlled his senses as the world spun at twice its normal rate. Xavier did see Marcel grab a bag at his side and pour a white powder into his palm, chanting a spell over it with a bird claw.

"And by the power of your suffering you shall make others suffer." Xavier grabbed at Marcel's leg as he chanted but was kicked in the face and fell back. "As you were delirious at the end of your life make this one, too, blind and confused." Xavier lurched forward, but landed several feet short of Marcel. "Finally, protect me who worships your designs on earth."

It took all the effort he could muster to pull himself up and scan the mob.

There was Marcel, with his unmistakable slouch, pushing through the crowd. Xavier started forward but stumbled back against the wall. Marcel blended into the mob, then shoved to the front and threw the powder at a guard. Michel turned just as the dust hit his coat and blew into his face. Xavier again tried to move forward, but his steps were slow and uneven.

Xavier watched helplessly as Michel staggered and looked around bewildered. He grabbed his head and then reached for his sword. His eyes were glassy, as if he could not focus on anything, and he failed to answer his men's questions. Xavier gathered himself enough to walk—at a slow stumble and by running into people—but he was in motion.

Xavier noticed the expression on everyone's face, Michel's one of pure bewilderment. First, Michel took out his sword, and then the mob attacked. They came from everywhere, ripped apart the carriages, and pulled out the priests. They threw rocks, beat on the bodies, and screamed. One by one, the masses murdered the priests and attacked anyone who defended them.

Xavier still muddled forward, but too late.

Men threw Michel against the wall. Brave, strong Michel, who under normal circumstances could have commanded the situation, could not control his muscles. Blood flowed down his head and onto his face when another stole his sword and plunged it into his chest. Then, unceremoniously, they let him fall to the ground.

Despondent, Xavier shoved himself forward to reach Michel. Without thinking, he yanked his brother off the ground and dragged him away from the angry masses, who still attacked. He managed to get a couple of blocks away before the alcohol and fatigue dulled his senses. Xavier had to stop, so he propped Michel against the wall in a quiet alley. Then he saw that in carrying Michel he had forced the sword deeper into his chest.

"Michel... dear God, Michel. Talk to me. Please."

Michel, with labored breathing, managed a slight smile at his brother. He reached up with a weak gesture and touched Xavier's head.

"My little brother," he whispered. Blood spewed out his mouth.

"We need help. I couldn't save you." Xavier started for a doctor but turned around, afraid to leave. Michel motioned for Xavier to come closer.

"Stay with me. There's nothing that can be done."

Xavier wanted to protest, but looking at the wound and the blood, he knew better, so he slumped against Michel's body and clung to it tightly.

"Xavier," Michel stuttered. "I love you. Please, you can't blame yourself or try to be responsible for everything in the world."

"I saw him do it," Xavier sobbed. "Marcel. I can never forgive myself."

Michel, who held Xavier in return, scolded him. "I don't have time for drunken games. This wasn't you. Protect Catherine. Marcel is evil. He's the culprit, not you." Michel's eyes widened in what had to be pain. He again hugged Xavier and, as the last breath escaped his body, whispered to him, "I love you. I'll always watch over you and Catherine." And Michel's body relaxed into dead weight in Xavier's arms. Xavier screamed with rage and agony.

"God, damn you! You wanted me to serve you. I gave up all my dreams for you, and *this* is how you repay me?"

Xavier had no idea how long he lay there, passed out, but he awoke when some officials came by picking up dead bodies.

"Is he dead?" they asked, pointing to Michel.

"No, no," Xavier answered. His head pounded.

He was not as drunk, which made him feel even worse. He cried the second he looked at Michel's limp body. Resolved to do something, he picked up his brother with an awkward tug, maneuvering him over his shoulders, and carried him toward the house, staggering beneath Michel's weight. He was disoriented when someone stopped him.

"Abbé?"

Xavier looked without recognition at the newcomer.

"Abbé, it's me, Denys." Denys helped set Michel down, and Xavier cried into his shoulder. "Abbé, let me help. You can't go this way."

"Isn't this the shortest way?" Xavier wept and his head hurt terribly. He needed another glass of wine. He wanted to bless a barrel of wine and then pour it all over the ground to show that God was nothing.

"You can't take this route. It passes Ata Carmelite Convent. There are no more priests or nuns there. They attacked them this afternoon. I heard that there were over one hundred fifty of them, all murdered and mutilated." Denys pulled him up. He lifted Michel onto his back and then took the priest's hand and led him along.

Denys and Xavier plodded along until they reached the Saint-Laurent house. They walked up the front stairs, and guards shouted and moved people out of the way. Without knowing how he got there, Xavier glanced around the main greeting room, where they placed Michel on the couch. Michel's blood was everywhere, covering Denys and the white couch fabric in crimson. Xavier, too, was bloody. *Oh, Michel, I have failed you.*

Xavier sat away from everyone as they looked at Michel or fussed over his body. What were they doing? Then Catherine entered the room in a rush. She stopped in the doorway and stared at Michel in shock, wavered a bit, but typical of his sister, she remained strong. She barked orders and began the funeral arrangements at once. Only Xavier recognized the fight within her to maintain control. Then her tears came.

"Xavier?" Catherine asked. "Where's Xavier?"

Denys pointed him out.

"Is he hurt? Why is he bleeding? For God's sake, call the doctor. How can you leave him?"

"Catherine," Denys answered. "He's fine. It's Michel's blood."

Catherine raced across the room and embraced Xavier. Then, without verbal instruction, she urged him to move. He followed her out of the room, and they helped each other up the stairs and into his room. Alone, they both released more of the anguish, weeping together. After what seemed hours, exhaustion clouded his mind and he drifted to sleep.

FLIGHT OF THE DRUNKEN PRIEST

Xavier awoke later that day at dusk—when Thomas used to visit, he thought—but then remembered Michel's death. Someone had tucked him in bed, no doubt Catherine, and even changed his clothes. Gone were his stained garments, replaced with clean pajamas. Xavier tilted onto the floor and looked under his bed at his precious, secret stock of wine. He grabbed a bottle and opened it while seated cross-legged on the floor. He relished the swirl in his head as intoxication took control.

He sat alone for a long time, getting very drunk as darkness took over. He did look under the door to see that they had stationed a guard as the alcohol worked its coping alchemy. Was he a prisoner because he had murdered Michel? Did they place armed soldiers at his door to arrest him? No, that was too much to hope.

He walked to the window to watch the world pass by as the wine tingled and replaced the blood in his veins with its passion. He tried not to think at all, about Thomas, Michel, or anything, but that was difficult. Indeed, he was almost positive that the black form of Thomas watched him from across the street in a shadow. The wine played tricks on him. The tall man with long black hair and a muscled body was only in Xavier's imagination. His bottle was empty too soon, so he opened another and took a drink, careful not to spill on his shirt.

But even with the wine, he wondered if he could survive. Why did he exist at all? Was it worth the pain and struggle? Just as he was spiraling into depression, he heard something. Catherine's steps. He could live for her. He loved her so much.

"Catherine, I don't know how I let it happen."

"Xavier, I don't have time for such nonsense. I've a lot to do and you need supper. It's the wine talking, nothing else, so forget about it."

Xavier had not anticipated a cold response. He wanted more hugs and mourning, to cling to each other in sorrow. However, typical of Catherine, she reacted as she did after their father died. She took control, made the arrangements, and buried herself in work. Still, it hurt that she failed to see Xavier's needs.

"I don't want to eat."

"Xavier, I'm in no mood for a three-year-old." Catherine yanked him off the floor and pushed him around the room, making him get ready to go downstairs. She was efficient, distant, and controlling, and treated him like one of the servants. Xavier reminded himself that she mourned that way—but it hurt because he needed more.

"If you don't want me around, I'll leave."

"Did you hear me? I've a brother to bury and so do you. And I'm still running this salon. So get up, stop whining, and help me. I can't attend to you every minute."

"Then I'll leave."

"Goddamn it, Xavier. You're going to keep your ass in this house and do as I say. Which begins with moving your body."

Xavier fell to the ground. The last thing he wanted was Catherine's wrath. He figured that it was God again, another punishment, for failing to save Michel and then for cursing God in public. *Damn God, too. Fuck Catherine, fuck God, fuck the entire world.*

Catherine had stopped at the door and turned around. Xavier braced himself for angry retribution and flinched when her skirt rustled toward him and she knelt down. Xavier would not look at her.

"Xavier, listen to me." She said the words almost in a whisper, and then Catherine eased herself onto the floor and touched Xavier's shoulder. "I'm sorry." She brushed his hair out of his eyes. "Forgive me. I didn't mean those things. I hurt, too."

Xavier cried.

"You're not in the way. We're all that's left, no mother or father, and now no eldest brother. I'd never contemplated children. They seemed like such a nuisance and restriction. But I think Marcel and I must have children, if anything to preserve the Saint-Laurent legacy. I'd love to raise a daughter."

Xavier felt ill at the mention of the man who, along with his failure, murdered his brother. Catherine rambled about the family and future generations, but Xavier stopped listening. Now, he indeed had nothing to say. The potion still controlled Catherine. Another of God's cruelties, that he suffered Michel's death, could have prevented it, and was watching his sister's demise as she succumbed to the same fate. God was masterful in His wicked cruelty. Or was there no God? Which was it? Maybe it was the wine, perhaps the sorrow, or Xavier might have just felt cruel. But he lashed out.

"Marcel is no Saint-Laurent and wouldn't know how to have a decent conviction if his life depended upon it."

"I refuse to have this conversation. It's not your decision, no more than it was Michel's. I was sharing my feelings with you, and this is how you repay me?"

"I just find it odd that you're hiding behind a man."

"I'm doing no such thing." Catherine sprang from the floor and hovered over him. "You won't turn into a patriarch. I forbid it."

"Oh, for the love of Heaven, Catherine, you know I'm not that way. I just hate to see you acting like a weak little woman, bowing to some fiend of a man who only cares for himself and wants to plug your hole for pleasure. I blame myself for Michel's death because Marcel did it. He killed our brother."

"You're a drunken, delusional fool right now. I told you to stop."

"And you're a blind whore courting a murderer." The wine had gone too far. He predicted without seeing it that Catherine's hand was about to smack his face. *Slap.* The sting hurt, his cheek burned, and Catherine stomped out of the room. Why did he drive those he loved to hit him?

Then he heard another familiar gait coming down the hall. Before Maria got to the door, Xavier dove under the bed and grabbed a bottle, propelled into action by some unseen force. He was rustling around when he felt her grab his legs and yank him out, which made him laugh hysterically as he gripped more wine. Maria frowned as she snatched it from him.

"You and your drinking are becoming a bigger and bigger problem. Catherine told me the cruel things you said. I don't care what we think about Marcel, now's not the time. Get control of yourself."

"But he killed Michel! How can you just take her side?"

"Shut up, Xavier. Shut up about your nonsense and the things you think you saw in some drunken stupor. Will you please snap out of this?"

"What does that mean?"

"It means your drinking, your depression, your seeing things, your acting like a child, all of this nonsensical behavior that was induced by your failed love affair with that vile man. Thomas was no better than Marcel, but you can't see it. Well, it's time that you heard the truth since you've decided to tell your version of it to everyone else."

"You don't know the first thing about Thomas." Xavier did not care to listen to Maria. Since the revelation that Maria slept with other women, and after she encouraged Xavier to do the same with priests, Xavier had a hard time understanding her. Her governing principle made no sense—you could have sex only with someone from within the church? One minute, Maria teased about her women, and the next, she made dogmatic pronouncements about her faith and God's law. Xavier lay against the bed, having been pulled back out from under it, and stared at her.

"You're in a fight for your soul. It's no coincidence this revolution happened at the same time Thomas came into your life. Xavier, come back to God. Even if we must keep it a secret, there's much work to do. Follow Him and end your misery."

"God and I don't get along."

"Such blasphemy."

His rage mounted. "I followed Him. And look what it brought. Nothing, absolutely nothing. I lost my brother. I witnessed the event and knew it was coming while I could do *nothing* about it. That's my thanks for following God. I watch people die all around me, and where is He as all of Paris turns against itself? Where is He as they burn His churches and murder masses of the men and women who swore to uphold His laws? Don't toy with me by using some trite theology when you pick and choose the parts of it that suit you while disregarding the rest. And don't talk about Thomas. You sleep with the same sex and it makes no sense that it's fine just because they're in the church. I loved him, but God told me it was wrong. So I fought my urges. I never caved in. And you see what that got me. I chased him away, though I love him. And the entire time, I told myself God needed this. Alas, all He left me was wine."

"We keep it in the church to give each other support and so we still do good works. He never forsook you. You forsook Him."

"I renounce the Church. I renounce God. Can't you understand my words? He's nothing to me. Until He shows me that He cares, that it's not all a big game so those in the church can feel powerful, I denounce Christianity and announce that none of it means anything to me."

She stared at him, horrified. "Xavier, after everything, after all that you believed, how can you feel nothing in your heart? What makes you think you could know all of the answers to the mysteries of this world? This blasphemy is unbecoming. I pray for your soul."

"You may pray to the Nothingness all you want."

Maria's voice softened, but she stood over him. "This is the test for you. Your pain."

"For God's sake, Maria. A test?" Xavier could not stop a harsh laugh.

"Abbé, you're hurting my feelings."

The giggles kept him from responding, so Maria stormed out of the room.

He settled down after she left and realized that he sat in complete darkness, with just a slight glow from the window coming into his room. He reached up and got the bottle of wine, opened it, and drank as the sadness and misery stormed back. Wonderful, Xavier told himself, you chased Thomas away, then you murdered Michel, and now you alienated Catherine and Maria. He wished Marcel had killed *him* instead. You cast God out of your life, so what remains?

Xavier picked himself off the floor and looked out his window, hoping to see Thomas's mirage again, but there was nothing but blackness, broken by little else than the fire of a lantern.

Xavier dressed in his bourgeois garb, grabbed another bottle of wine, and started to leave. No one was in the hallway. He slipped down it but remembered something. He felt naked without it, so he returned and got his cross. He dropped it under his shirt so no one could see. He returned to the hall, went down the back stairs, and snuck out a side door. He walked in the shadows for a few blocks before breaking into a run.

He had no intention of returning and getting in the way again. He loved them that much.

Thirty-Five: Crying in the Wilderness

23 SEPTEMBER 1792

Thomas woke and hurried to leave his flat. The previous two weeks had been more hell than he had ever experienced. Xavier disappeared. Gone. Without a trace. Not at the Saint-Laurent home, not at the church, or anywhere in his parish. Denys had no idea where to find him. Even Anne, busy packing because she was "closing" her business and had other things to do, had no idea.

Thomas dressed, still concerned about his appearance, and admired the black he loved to wear. Then he went to search for Xavier. All he did these days was hunt for his love.

Paris was frenzied with revolutionary talk, as usual, but Thomas cared little about the latest events. It seemed mundane to awaken two nights before to the news they had abolished the monarchy. Then they'd created a new calendar to date things according to the major events of the French Revolution, which he thought ridiculous.

The brutality that now governed the revolution startled even Thomas. As he walked, he passed another of the French symbols of their struggle. They called it a guillotine. Thomas called it hideous. An efficient machine designed to off someone's head, but it also made death a public spectacle. The victims knelt before everyone as they pleaded for forgiveness. Everyone saw the wicked death as the head dropped into a basket and the body was thrust aside. That represented French liberation? As they now arrested, attacked, and murdered anyone who even dared to disagree with the new regime? They gave up the monarchy for brutality of another kind? But for Thomas, one fear alone haunted him—that he would pass one of these baskets and see his beloved's head staring at him.

But where was Xavier? Thomas ran out of places to search and covered the same ground over and over. He obsessed about the day Xavier disappeared. Early in the evening, Thomas had had seen Xavier had been looking out his window, drinking his wine, and thought for a second that Xavier spotted him. The following night, he could not find Xavier anywhere. Odd, that he noticed patrols leaving the Saint-Laurent home on a regular basis, so he ran to the house and asked for Catherine. To Thomas's chagrin, Maria came to the door.

"Catherine's gone. Go away." She tried to slam the door in his face, but he caught it.

"Maria, I don't like you any more than you like me. Why do these patrols leave the house?"

"They're looking for Xavier." The door swung toward him again.

"What do you mean?"

"Get out of here."

Thomas smashed his fist into the door and paid no attention to how it slammed into the wall, Maria just jumping out of the way. "Where is he?"

"Would they have to search for him if we knew? Michel was murdered by a mob. Xavier saw it, he was upset, he argued with Catherine and then me. When we went to find him later, he was gone. That's all we know. Catherine is out looking and we have men searching, too. You're not welcome here, unless you know where Xavier is."

"No, I don't," Thomas said with defeat. He allowed Maria to shove him out the door and bang it behind him. He fled into the street and began his quest.

First, Thomas checked the obvious places like the church but found nothing. He even tried to remember the various secret places Xavier had revealed to him, but each of these memories brought pain.

He almost lost control and violated the ethic when he spied Marcel in his shop, mixing some concoction with three young women in the room, drugged. He hated the man.

"Where's Xavier?"

"None of my business, as you know." Marcel dropped the spoon he'd been using behind his back, as if Thomas would not see it.

"Stop toying with me. Do you know where he went?"

"No. I've upheld our bargain. And I'd get out if I were you, because this is my lair."

Thomas left when his scalp started to tingle.

He got a predictable reaction from Anthony when he spoke with him. More cautioning and admonitions that Thomas stay out of it. After

Thomas told him no one could find Xavier, Anthony allowed Thomas to search on the condition that, if he found Xavier, he had to tell Catherine without interacting with the abbé.

On that night's search, Thomas turned down a narrow street where he had seen people selling opium. Perhaps Xavier turned to something more powerful than wine as he built a resistance to alcohol. But Thomas found nothing but a couple of prostitutes and their pimp.

"Hey, mate, you look like you could use a lay," the man shouted after him.

Thomas surged ahead.

"You deaf?"

Though inaudible to humans, Thomas's keen senses heard the knife cut through the air toward his back. In one swift motion, he turned and grabbed it, making his hand bleed as he held it with a firm grip and advanced toward the man and his whores. Thomas glowered, stopped a couple of feet away, and lifted the knife before them. He cut off his finger and allowed it to heal before their eyes. One woman fainted while the other screamed in horror as the man stared in disbelief until Thomas planted the knife between the pimp's eyes down to the handle. He twisted it around, and then Anthony roared into his ear as he strangled the prostitute.

"Enough!"

"He tried to kill me. I'm sure it fits within the ethic."

Anthony glanced around and sneered at Thomas before yanking his arm. Thomas followed, despondent more than anything, thinking a berating from Anthony would at least amuse him.

Inside Anthony's flat, Thomas started the conversation. "You humor me by coming after me all the time. If I violated the code, then kill me. Otherwise, accept me for the vampire I've become. I can only obey so many edicts before my emotion governs the day. Why should vampires lose passion because we hide our identities?"

"It has nothing to do with emotion, Thomas. It's your irrational behavior."

"He was a fiend."

"I'm not defending him. I'm talking about the twisting of the knife inside his skull as some poor woman, who was terrorized by him, watched in horror."

Thomas shrugged. "I'm searching for Xavier. You'd bring your mate back from the dead if you could, right? I may have that chance. Why do you so begrudge me that?"

Anthony wiped his eyes and ran his fingers through his long blond hair before plopping into a chair and looking up at Thomas. "I'd sanction a relationship for you if it made you happy. I'm also accustomed to your anger. For better or worse, you've a flair for the theatrical."

"Then why do you stop me all the time?"

"Because I love you." Anthony got up and paced, scratching his chin with his elegant fingers. He moved toward the window and spoke with his back to Thomas. "I know you think some vampire coven watches everything that all vampires do and then administers punishments for those who fail to obey our laws. I'm sworn to secrecy about the exact nature of this group, but you needn't worry about anyone swooping in and condemning you. It'd have to be quite an egregious offense and risk the safety of more than just yourself before this force is mobilized, and I'd alert you well in advance. Though you're loath to admit it, my concern is for you and your well-being when you're alone."

Anthony turned from the window and looked at Thomas. A lamp gave him a halo, like an angel sent from heaven.

"You're young, Thomas, regardless of how you feel so in command and all-knowing. You can't understand the stamina it takes to live for centuries. Your impatience is a problem. You can hardly wait for an hour, let alone a decade, or perhaps much, much longer, before you find a mate. I had one and have looked for centuries to replace him and have yet to do it. You can't jump into bed with the first beauty you meet if he's not amenable to the situation."

Anthony grabbed Thomas's hand, moved them to the couch, and sat, putting his arm around Thomas and squeezed. "You're ruthless on a good day, let alone when something angers you. You insist Xavier's the one, but he hasn't even accepted his attraction to other men. How will someone with such a deep Christian faith ever deal with vampirism? All I want is for you to be happy. You may fail, and I don't want it to devastate you. When I see you terrorize people and stalk the streets like a madman, I worry. What happens if you find Xavier dead? What if you find him and he casts you out? Can you handle that brutal honesty? Xavier is lost. He's gone. This isn't the character of someone who can handle the life we lead. How could he feed himself when all he wants is to save people? I think you're on a hopeless mission."

He finally said it. The brutal truth. Thomas was not angry. On the contrary. He had to hear the words. Thomas hugged Anthony. "You're wrong about him, and I intend to find him. I'll keep you informed."

Thirty-Six: Death to Tyrants

21 JANUARY 1793

Catherine headed toward the Saint-Laurent home, numb as usual, because much troubled her about the government, the revolution, and all that happened around her. But her heart's sorrow dwarfed those concerns. Losing two brothers in one year had deflated her. She'd wandered into the street earlier that day only after her friend burst into her office and insisted that she come outside. She followed, though not surprised by the news and reluctant to witness whatever demonic plans the fiends had concocted for Louis. But she followed nonetheless.

The latest government had trumped up charges against Louis. Of all things, they accused the monarch of treason against his own country. Catherine thought it ludicrous. You could call him neglectful, aloof, stubborn, aristocratic, or absorbed in his power and blinded by his alleged divine calling. But Louis was not a traitor to France. Yet Paris buzzed with excitement because treason was a capital offense—they had to execute Louis.

The crowd propelled her toward the scene.

Louis stepped down from his carriage and shook off the guards as they attempted to remove his clothing, which he did himself. First the greatcoat and then his hat, shirt, and collar. He recoiled when the guards went to bind his hands, but finally acquiesced. He yielded his hands and took on the appearance of a commoner about to suffer public execution. There was a dignity, however, to the way Louis carried himself.

Louis stood beside the scaffolding, a crude construction built to hold the guillotine, upright and rigid as if at Versailles with a foreign diplomat. He fought to maintain decorum, even to the bitter end acting as king. Perhaps there was a bit of honor in the odd little man after all. Catherine remembered seeing him at official palace functions, long before the revolution, which she attended as her father's escort. He had been haughty yet overwhelmed with the attention, and Catherine was struck more by his short, pudgy build than his rank. Today, after all the stress and turmoil, he overcame that awkwardness.

Even the boisterous crowd quieted at the event's awe. Everyone gave full attention as Louis ascended the stairs toward death. The drums tapped for effect, beating the heartbeat of Paris as it pumped out a diseased political system.

When Louis reached the guillotine, he signaled for the drummers to stop, who obeyed, and he spoke to the crowd in a loud voice: "I forgive those who are guilty of my death, and I pray to God the blood you are about to shed may never be required of France. I only sanctioned upon compulsion the Civil Constitution of the Clergy—"

An officer broke in and ordered the drummers to continue, cutting Louis short. Catherine jumped when the bang of wooden drumsticks met canvas drumheads.

The men positioned Louis on the guillotine and let the blade fall, but it failed to sever his head. Perhaps because of his fat or a defect in the wicked machine, they had to lift the thing and do it again. It took a great effort to again slam the blade into his neck before the king's head fell before the crowd. A hush fell over the throng as a young guard hoisted the head before them. There was a moment of silence before shouts of "*Vive la Nation*" and "*Vive la République*" filled the air. People ran forward with handkerchiefs and scarves in an attempt to get a drop of the royal blood as it dripped from the severed neck onto the crowd.

That was enough madness for Catherine. She shoved her way through the people. With effort, she got through the crowd and headed home.

But her true despondency came from her personal plight. She had lost two brothers to the madness. Two. Catherine had lived for her family, and now it was gone.

Her mind drifted each day to the cemetery a few months before when she buried her older brother. It was a bitter day, standing before the coffin as it disappeared into the ground. And, though she wept often for Michel, her tears that day and most others were for Xavier.

In a nefarious mood, Catherine had rebuked Xavier and his drinking, causing him to disappear into Paris's darkness. Why had she lashed out at the one man who needed sensitivity more than any other in France? She chastised herself again and again for driving him away. And so the funeral had become a punishment she suffered alone.

For five months, she had searched for Xavier, had organized patrols, and marshaled everything at her command to find him. Some days, she found her confidence, but other days brought horrific images of Xavier, drowned in a river or murdered for spite.

After telling Maria what she witnessed at the king's execution, Catherine felt compelled to spill her latest thoughts to the nun. "I provoked Xavier. He lashed out at me and said things I never expected to hear from him. Can you believe he criticized Marcel? He even accused Marcel of murdering Michel."

Maria backed away and straightened her skirt. "Maybe he had good reason."

"What do you mean?"

"It's not my place. I'm sorry."

"Maria, what is it? All of you avoid me whenever I mention the man I intend to marry. This will never do. Why do you recoil? Why does everyone shy away?"

"Catherine, forgive me, but did you ever suspect he had ulterior motives? We think—some think—or at least I suspect...that...this medicine he gives you has ill effects. I think that you love him because he's so forceful toward you."

"Maria, I don't mean to laugh, but what you think is insane."

Maria smiled weakly. "Silly balderdash, I suppose." She left the room. Catherine worried she'd offended her, but then she was the one who should be offended. A potion, indeed. Was everyone going mad? She pushed herself out of the chair and bustled to her office, where the paperwork had piled up over the last few months. Hoping to clear her head, she dove into the latest batch of mail.

The first letter, however, brought back the sadness. She ripped it open:

Dear Catherine,

Just a quick note to tell you that the provisions you requested should arrive within the month. In London, we hear much news about the revolution, but it is hard to know what is truth. I rely on your letters to tell me what occurs. They think the French will execute Louis! I hope that you have found Xavier by now. I, of course, watch for him to arrive in London, but doubt I will see him here. I must tell you, Catherine, that I miss all of you. I think of Michel often. It is difficult to believe that I will never again speak with him, who was a brother to me, too. As for returning to Paris, I appreciate your request and only wish I could. There are reasons that keep me away that have nothing to do with the revolution. Perhaps someday, I will have the bravery to convey to you all that I feel. Until then, know that you, too, are in my thoughts each day, more than Michel or Xavier, I miss you.

Yours faithfully, Jérémie

Catherine dropped the letter to her desk. She missed Jérémie as much as he missed her. She longed for Xavier, her rock, and Marcel, whom she believed to be her shield from the world, but Jérémie had always been a true and loyal friend. She had urged him in every letter to return to Paris, but he always declined. He had some personal problem that kept him away and refused to tell her about it. How strange.

PLEA FOR HELP

As she sat at her desk, Catherine reread Jérémie's letter. She was about to throw it in a drawer when someone knocked on the door.

"Who is it?" she asked, but before the man answered, she saw the black cape swish through the door. Thomas entered with a smile and his arms extended. They hugged, though Catherine detected a slight slump in Thomas's normal erect posture. His presence conflicted her, too. She had believed that a mob attacked Xavier when she went pleading with Thomas for help a year ago. His rebuke and Xavier's comments since then had given her other ideas about what might have happened to her brother. Catherine withdrew and managed a smile.

"I'm sorry for the way I treated you," he began without preamble. "I know that you came to me for help and I rebuffed you. There were reasons, not the best, that made me cold to you. I was wrong and come for your forgiveness. And perhaps your help."

"I imagine based on Xavier's mood after you stopped seeing each other that it had something to do with your relationship." She eased into the real conversation she needed to have with him. "I'm glad that you returned. Xavier's gone and I can't find him."

Thomas hung his head and shook it, as if failing to guard himself from the grief. When he looked at her, she saw his tears, like streaks of blood on his cheeks. "I've looked throughout Paris for him to no avail. I'm not sure what brought me here tonight. Perhaps it was the hope that together we could locate him." Thomas had already controlled the tears. Much like herself.

"I see you got over your failed courtship of him," Catherine tested.

He stood up and paced frantically, and again his eyes turned red. He made no attempt to hide his tears, and his body language answered Catherine's inquiry. He was still in love.

"I never stopped loving your brother. Suffice it to say that I didn't follow your advice enough. I pushed him too much."

"I wanted to know your intentions."

"My intentions haven't changed." Thomas returned to her and knelt, taking her hand and holding it firm in his cool grip. She resisted pulling it away. "I love him more than you can imagine, and I need your help. Are you hiding him from me? Where is he?"

"I wish I knew. I told you everything." Catherine looked away, about to cry. "I have already looked," she whispered. "And, of course, we can combine our efforts, but I'm afraid—" She couldn't finish the thought.

"He's somewhere in Paris. We'll find him together."

While she sat in misery, Thomas became energized and paced about the room. He asked her a thousand questions about Xavier's habits, going clear back to childhood. He kept striding back and forth as he quizzed her until he found a new subject.

"He told me he always fled to the church when distraught, from a young early age. As a priest, he still hid from the world in his religion."

Catherine nodded. "As a youth, he went to Notre Dame or the chapel here. But we looked there. Besides, he hated Notre Dame after he entered the clergy. And we watch his old church until a mob burned it to the ground."

"Anne, then," Thomas shouted. "All of this time, we ignored Anne."

"I looked for her, and she's as scarce as Xavier. Do you think I'm dense? Xavier had few friends, and she's the sole one missing. I found her after he disappeared, and she wasn't interested in talking. It was as if she stopped caring about him altogether," Catherine replied, her voice quivering.

"How could I have missed this?" Thomas said. "I went to see her, too, and she rushed around her flat, closing the business and fleeing. She hardly batted an eye when I asked about Xavier. Oh, how could I have been so blind?"

"You sound delusional," Catherine said with alarm. Had Thomas lost his mind, too?

"It's the one logical possibility left. When something distresses Xavier, he flees to religion, not the church. He was searching for answers to life and happened to go to Catholic institutions because that's what he knew. But when he began questioning the theology they forced on him, he talked to Anne. She wanted to protect Xavier and, I would guess, kept it secret at his request."

Catherine nodded. "But it gets us no closer to finding either one of them."

"She gives us a different focus. Anne isn't from the world in which you, Xavier, or I exist. She's from a people who can disappear into the shadows and live secret lives in the midst of public ones. She knows an underworld we can't fathom, and her religion, those charms and spells, strengthen her abilities tenfold."

Catherine was convinced. Maybe Xavier *was* alive. Before returning to practical matters, however, she had to know the truth about what happened between Xavier and Thomas.

"Thomas, just one thing. Sit down, please."

"Yes?" Thomas took a seat opposite her.

"Should we find Xavier, should he see you? Or should you remain hidden?"

Thomas looked bewildered. "Is this about my vampirism?"

"No. I've danced around it for fear of offending you. I want to know what happened between you two. Long before he ran away, you stopped calling on him. He was devastated and missed you. He never spoke ill of you, and yet he refused to talk about you. He insisted he was attacked in the streets, but well, I've wondered of late if it wasn't you who attacked my brother." With it in the open, her blood boiled and she prepared the speech she wanted to give the man since her suspicions began.

Thomas looked at her without saying a word. The sadness returned. Gone was the excitement of looking for Xavier. "Did he say something to you?"

"Never. I happened to hear a whisper of something as he fell asleep one night talking to himself."

"I don't expect forgiveness, from you or him. It sounds trite to explain that I had no idea what my strength might do or that I was lost in the moment, a moment of passionate anger, because none of that undoes the harm."

Catherine could feel her face redden as he spoke.

Thomas ran his hand across a table. "We were arguing. That wasn't uncommon in those last few nights as I pressed him to embrace his true feelings and come to me. Mind you, I never said a word about vampirism, only that I loved him, that he loved me, and that we should stay together."

Thomas stared at the floor. "The Church had a stranglehold on Xavier. He could forgive anyone else any transgression and even condemned the church when it outcast others, but he placed the highest standards on himself. Our relationship caused him to doubt that for the first time. He was moving away from it, but my anger—" Thomas rubbed his face and ran his hand through his hair. He looked into Catherine's eyes through his crimson tears. "He was afraid of eternal damnation. I know he was frightened, but I couldn't contain my anger anymore. The teasing, the innuendo, the pretend relationship disguised as friendship. I pleaded with him, but he wouldn't give in to our relationship, and then we fought and I hit him. I have told no one but my mentor, Anthony, and in these long months, I came to pretend I could redeem all I'd wrought if I found him. You've pointed out the obvious, that it's much more complicated."

Catherine stood and stomped to where Thomas sat, hovering inches above him. "I've lost everything. A woman with nothing to live for is a dangerous thing. I know where you live. I know more about you than you ever intended for me to learn. If I find out that you did anything else, or if we find him and you ever harm him again, I'll do everything in my power against you. If we get so lucky as to see him again, he will be all I live for. That slight hope is the one thing that has kept me going. Make no mistake, Thomas, you may mess with the rest of the world and use it as your toy. But I will destroy you."

Thomas nodded his head without flinching or apparent anger. "I deserve far worse."

Strange, that Catherine did not despise him for hurting Xavier. She believed Thomas. His admission came with love. And she had made her point. Perhaps he suspected that Marcel gave her the secret to getting rid of him: fire. The only thing that kept her from doing it already was the knowledge that Xavier would never allow it.

"Thank you," Catherine said in a hushed tone. "I don't pretend to understand how you could harm him. I suppose I'm too worried about him to be angry right now. So please, help me find him."

Thirty-Seven: Searching

26 MARCH 1793

Yet another evening of gathering at the Saint-Laurent home, a routine Thomas established with Catherine in order to search for the still-missing Xavier. Thomas vacillated between despair and hope, sometimes daily, sometimes every hour.

The salon guard escorted Thomas and Anthony into Catherine's office and went off to get her. Anthony joined the search often since Catherine and Thomas's reunion in January. Thomas first believed that Anthony had agreed to assist them to watch over Thomas, but he came to know that Anthony stayed in Paris to help Thomas because he loved him. Catherine expressed her surprise that Thomas never mentioned a mentor and held her distance from Anthony for the first month.

"How many vampires can I handle at once?" she had asked as they walked through Paris one night.

"You need one to search for your brother, and one to control the other," Anthony had answered, half kidding. From that moment, Catherine had taken to Anthony.

Thomas now searched for Xavier and did little else, vowing not to stop until they found him. He fed when necessary, forsaking his vampiric hunger because a holy quest consumed him.

When Catherine turned the corner, Thomas noted that she had lost the spring in her step. She limped behind her desk without a greeting, then looked through darkened eyes at Thomas.

"Six months. He's been gone for six months."

"I know," was all Thomas could think to say.

"You've never lost two brothers. You can't understand. Michel was furious with me about Marcel when he died, and Xavier said awful things too."

"So brooding will help?"

He picked up Catherine's coat and pushed her toward the door. The cold March air made it hard to move through Paris, but Thomas and Anthony always assisted her. He wrapped the garment around her without a protest. She had done the same act before. She would enter the room in despair but would work her way out of it as they searched. Anthony took control, too, and grabbed Catherine's hand and pulled her outside.

As they exited, Maria burst from around the corner. She scowled at Thomas as she fell in line. She was like a wildcat, the way she waited for them in the hallway and pounced upon them. No one ever invited her. Neither Anthony nor Thomas wanted anything to do with her, and Catherine left Maria out because of the tension. Yet Thomas reminded himself of how much the woman meant to Xavier, and her devotion to him matched the will of the others.

Thomas reacted to each evening's search in complete contrast to Catherine. Where she began morose and in despair but gained steam through the night, he became more and more pessimistic and depressed, wondering if perhaps Xavier was gone forever. When the night ended again with no sign of him, Thomas wept himself to sleep for the millionth time.

Part VIII: Resurrection

Thirty-Eight: The Sighting

8 JUNE 1793

Catherine walked out the door with Anthony and Thomas, embarrassed that she did it again. The vampires had arrived at dusk to search Paris, Thomas with exciting news that he'd located Denys Girard by passing him in the street. He enlisted Denys in their hunt. But despite Thomas's enthusiasm, Catherine greeted his zeal with pessimism.

He ignored her, ushered her out the door, and she regained hope after a couple hours. Thus the embarrassment. She put her two friends—about the only two she had left in Paris—through these awkward scenes.

As Catherine became more vigilant, Thomas became angrier. That pattern, too, occurred every night, but of late, his mood darkened and he threatened people for minor offenses. Catherine witnessed Thomas's anger for the first time that month. It made him volatile, with an air of menace toward even the most innocent passersby. It made her think of how he slapped Xavier, though his own actions and Anthony's reassurances helped her trust his reform in that regard. Last of all, she had confidence that with Marcel's help she could dispatch if needed.

They plodded along in silence, near an open market where people still sold their goods, the hour being dark enough to awaken Thomas and Anthony but bright enough to continue trading.

A few feet ahead, Thomas turned down a narrow alley. Catherine jumped with alarm when she and Anthony followed Thomas around the corner. She glimpsed it for but a second before Anthony shot in front of her and blocked her view. Thomas had some old man by the neck, suspending him three feet in the air. Catherine heard Anthony scold Thomas as the vampire released the man and tossed him toward Catherine. She helped him to his feet, his eyes wild with fear, and he tripped again trying to flee.

"The Devil, Madame, in Paris. You should run." He tried to yank Catherine along but abandoned her when she resisted.

Anthony yelled at Thomas. "Because he thought you foolish for looking for a voodoo witch and a priest? What did you expect? Have you gone mad?"

"We're running out of solutions," Thomas answered.

Anthony started to shout but caught himself, pulled at his hair, walked in a circle, and returned to Thomas. "You knew this was a possibility. You may never find him." These words stung even Catherine, who let out a slight cry. Anthony grabbed Thomas's hand. "Both of you want Xavier, but you can't get angry about it. Strangling old men solves nothing."

Anthony pulled Thomas toward him by the shoulder, then took hold of Catherine.

"It frustrates me," Thomas whispered. "How can I control my emotions? I wasn't going to kill him."

"This search is impossible," Catherine said to change the subject.

"Madame, Madame!" someone interrupted her. The man was red and out of breath when he got to them and bent over.

When he looked up, Catherine recognized Denys, with a wild expression in his eyes. "May I speak with you?" He looked over her shoulder at the vampires.

"Gentlemen, will you excuse us?" she asked.

"Of course," Anthony said. But Anthony had to use force to guide Thomas toward the Saint-Laurent home. Thomas glanced behind them a number of times the entire way. Catherine maintained composure as Denys watched until the two men were out of sight.

"It's Xavier," Denys said without emotion. "I think it best that you see for yourself."

With that, Denys pulled her toward the river, walking fast and in silence. Catherine wanted to run, but that would call too much attention to them. She chafed at their progress, thinking she also wanted to slap Denys for the mystery.

LAZARUS RISEN

Denys slowed as they neared the Seine, almost on the outskirts of Paris. He glanced around every second with his knife drawn in these unfriendly parts. The night darkened away from the city, and the path muddied. They picked their way around garbage, passing a few dirty creatures, in an area even the authorities feared to venture, where anarchy ruled. Denys held the criminals at bay with his imposing figure. Then, as if someone had drawn a warning line in the dirt that no one dared cross, all signs of life ceased near a bridge, underneath which burned a bright fire. Goose bumps spread across Catherine's arms as she searched the shadows. She squealed and jumped when some man shouted at them.

"I wouldn't be going there if I was you," he said. "That there knife won't stop her."

Denys scowled and kept going.

"She'll get you. That one comes from the devil," the man shouted after them.

Denys moved forward on high alert. Closer to the bridge, Catherine noticed two people hovering over the fire and talking, laughing even. Then Denys stopped.

"You'd best go alone."

Catherine, her self-assurance waning, hesitated after a couple steps and looked back at Denys, who still protected her though he went no farther. She turned back toward the bridge, going at a slow pace, a bit fearful, attempting to convince herself to disregard the warnings from a deranged tramp, but the blackness surrounding her tricked her. Every crunch of a branch and squish of the mud seemed ominous as she moved along toward the fire.

Closer to the bridge, it became apparent the two figures were cooking something. The contented scene relaxed her enough to recognize their mannerisms. She involuntarily cried out and lurched into a run.

"I warned you, I even showed you my powers, and still one of you dares—"

Anne stopped midsentence and stood still. In a split second, Xavier wrapped Catherine in his arms as she wept, unable to control the emotion. Her body convulsed. She could not hold him tightly enough, afraid he might disappear if she let go.

"Xavier," she said, "Xavier...Xavier."

He, too, held her against himself in a tight hold, then patted her head in comfort. Overwrought, Catherine leaned against him when he moved them toward a log to sit.

Catherine noticed Anne and Xavier had decorated the walls under the bridge and created furniture out of rocks and logs. The large fire illuminated the area with safety and warmth. When Catherine at last pulled away from Xavier, he offered a shy grin.

Anne giggled from the other side of the fire. "We've been expecting one of you."

"I've been looking everywhere."

"I'm sorry for not coming to you. I needed to be away for a while. And I needed you to discover me instead of my begging to come back." He sounded like the old Xavier, soothing, taking control of the emotion and placating her anxiety. He was also sober.

"You've been here all along?" Catherine asked.

"No," Xavier answered. "We've been throughout Paris, here, there, everywhere, and even into the countryside and to the coast. The night I left, I went to Anne. She was leaving Paris, ready to meander and tired of the laundress façade, so she allowed me to come along. She saved me."

Anne laughed again. "My little abbé saved himself. I just prodded him along."

"What have you been doing?" Xavier asked.

Catherine managed a laugh of her own. "Looking for you." Catherine put her hand up. "Don't feel bad. The salon runs because Jérémie helps me out with bookkeeping as much as possible from London, and Maria manages daily affairs. I helped when necessary, but otherwise, I looked for you."

Xavier shook his head, and their tears stopped, to be replaced by enormous grins on each of their faces.

"So, you fled to Anne. Thomas predicted as much." Catherine flinched at his mention.

"It's all right," Xavier said. "I should've guessed."

"We were talking about how you used to hide in the church, and then we realized that you took your theological quandaries to Anne, and—" Catherine stopped again.

Anne chortled. "Such a predictable one, our abbé."

"It's true," Xavier said. "In a drunken stupor, I told her of my lifelong struggle to find meaning and of my fight with the feelings I tried to keep locked deep inside. Anne allowed me to rant and drink for as long as I needed. She hardly said a word, never scolded, but just let me talk. Mind you, I'm speaking about months. Months of my drinking and blabbering.

Anne dragged me all over Paris to a million hiding places. She made me help earn money. I had to set up the tables when the aristocracy paid her to contact dead relatives. She took me throughout France, but it was time to return to this bridge and wait for you to find us."

Catherine's cheeks hurt from smiling. "What changed? Was it my fault?" She choked on her words and started crying again. "I was wrong, after Michel died."

Xavier hugged her. "It wasn't you, or anyone. Let me tell you what happened. I was in a drunken daze. The revolution, the destruction of my church, the changes in my life, and then Michel's death."

At least he did not repeat his accusation against Marcel.

"When you and Maria came to me that night, I felt like a failure and burden, so I fled to relieve you of the responsibility. It was me, not you. My world was in turmoil. So I sought Anne."

Anne laughed and winked at Xavier.

"In May, I decided the wine failed me. I stopped drinking, almost overnight, and then Anne and I started *really* talking. I didn't change my outlook on life. Anne just helped me focus. She took my previous ideas that relied on Catholicism and showed me how they applied whether or not guided by some grand theological scheme. Does this make sense?"

Catherine nodded. Then Xavier addressed her one doubt without prompting, though he spoke in a softer voice and held her hand.

"I know nothing will make you feel better about my disappearance. I thought I was protecting you, as strange as it sounds. I was afraid to come back."

"Afraid of what?" Catherine asked.

"I was afraid you'd be angry."

"No, Xavier. I love you. You did what you needed to." Catherine cupped Xavier's cheeks. "I don't understand all of it. But I hope you'll return, because I do love you."

Xavier smiled and jumped up, grabbed two glasses, and then a bottle of wine. He poured each of them a glass and then laughed. "Get that frightened look off your face. 'Tis merely a toast, and I didn't stop drinking altogether, I only stopped drinking into oblivion."

Catherine laughed too. Her face had betrayed her, so she lifted her glass to Xavier's. They each drank, and Anne smiled in agreement, but Catherine wanted to know more and urged Xavier on.

He sighed. "I'm still bitter about Michel. I should have saved him. There are things you can't know about that day. I'm still angry with the church and with myself for believing that its theology could change the world. I hate that I hid from my true feelings for so long. I still hope and love people. I still think that religion, even Catholicism, must play a role. But I'm not convinced that any one religion has it right or wrong. This new idea, being talked about in Paris, about a Supreme Being or some such thing. Why, it's as valid as Christianity."

The old Xavier had returned, but Catherine detected a new maturity. His tone rang the familiar song of wanting to do good, yet he sounded more cautious and confident, not looking for outside answers from false authorities. His theology was more sophisticated.

Catherine then caught him up on her life. She avoided, however, mentioning the person who had become more important to her than any other, fearful of Xavier's reaction.

Thankfully, during a lull, Anne came over and sat between them, laughing as usual.

"There's my abbé again. He left out one detail. We snapped him out of his drunkenness, we got him thinking right about that Catholic Church, and we even managed to save his faith in humanity. But there's one other thing, isn't there, Abbé?"

Xavier smiled in his sheepish way, then played with the buttons on his shirt. "Anne, please."

"Well, go on, you find out which of us is right. Remember the pact we made? You said yourself not to let you get scared, and so I promised you I'd be telling others if you failed to."

"Maybe we should wait."

"Catherine, part of Xavier's journey, part of what he needs to do, is accept *all* the feelings inside. He loved another man and wants to pursue it. I told him you already knew, but he's afraid you'll be upset."

Anne got it into the open. But, just as relief spread through her, Catherine tensed at the thought of the quagmire Thomas's and Xavier's love would yet create. Could she trust Thomas again? And how had Xavier dealt with that awful event?

PRIVATE CONVERSATION

"This is embarrassing," Xavier said as he squirmed on the log. Catherine warmed her hands by the fire and glanced up at the unused bridge under which they sat.

After Xavier admitted what Anne said, and after Catherine comforted him and revealed that she, indeed, always suspected, the conversation drifted away because neither felt comfortable with it—Catherine because it had to lead to Thomas.

"Shall we invite our guest to a meager dinner?" Anne asked Xavier. "Not much, but we spice it up a little with some remedies from New Orleans. Now, go fetch the meat."

"If you'd rather not eat here—" Xavier motioned to the dirt and stones around them. "—you won't offend us."

"I'd love to join you."

Anne pushed him away. "Always making airs about you. Now get the meat. We keep it a ways out, in the river, so as not to let it spoil. I suppose you've noticed no one else comes into these parts."

"It sounds like you scared them away," Catherine offered.

"I did." Anne watched Xavier walk away and turned to Catherine. "I'm glad you came at last. He's been waiting for you, afraid you were angry. He's ready, I think. He told you the truth. But you and I have one other thing dwelling."

"I was afraid to mention Thomas. I've seen him."

"You need to know *he* don't know about him." Anne pointed toward Xavier. "Through all this, he's still the innocent one. Thomas doesn't act any more human than that toad over there, but Xavier hasn't a notion about it. And I didn't tell him. To tell him the man of his dreams walks around dead, well, you can imagine that conversation would've sent him right back to the wine."

"I know. Thomas searched for Xavier, too. He's still in love. You're certain, though, that he understands his attraction to men?"

Anne howled with delight. "Since he sobered up, it's all he talks about. He'd kill me for telling this, but one of the things that brought him out of the wine was that very topic. Here we were, over on the coast, near Belle Isle. Xavier was still drunk as could be, and he goes wandering around and ends up chatting with a bunch of sailors. I went to retrieve him and he's having a grand time. Well, it doesn't take me long to realize that one of them likes our Xavier. So I let him go on. This one was tall and well-built with curly blond hair. They started something. Xavier even moved into a room with him for a bit."

"He was in a relationship?" Catherine stared, astonished.

"I suppose you could call it that. Didn't last more than a couple weeks. And, poor sailor, he helped sober up the abbé, but that made Xavier deal with Thomas. So, he comes to me and realizes that he doesn't love the sailor. He just likes the protection and being in the arms of another man. So he leaves the poor gent, who was devastated, and we had to leave the isle. And from that point on, Xavier either talks about his changed theology or Thomas.

"So, like you, I think, oh my goodness, he's in love with a corpse." Anne burst into laughter. "So, I start steering the conversation to talking about souls and evil, getting Xavier to shun those Catholic condemnations, trying to get him just to accept things. Did I succeed?" Anne shrugged. "I think he agrees that evil is what a person does, not what makes him up. Now, mind you, this was never in the context of vampires." She sighed.

"Perhaps, if he overcame demanding such rigid ideals of himself, he can also allow for Thomas to be something that we otherwise can't explain."

"I'm hoping that too. He's just got to focus on the loving."

"Did he tell you everything about Thomas?" Catherine asked.

Anne nodded her head and grimaced a bit. "Yeah. I worried when he blamed himself at first, but he explained it well. He wants to talk to Thomas about that, too, and he'll not allow it to happen again. Nor will I. I know how to handle that one."

"I've been with Thomas all this time, looking for Xavier. I see a real change. He still gets angry, but not in the same way. It's not as volatile. He hates himself for what he did to Xavier."

"Good. Xavier deserves a kind, loving relationship."

"I see that you took the opportunity of my leaving to gossip," Xavier said, making both women jump.

"I've been telling her all your secrets," Anne said.

The laughter halted when Anne held up her hand and looked around. Catherine saw nothing. Anne turned her head and watched, like a tiger waiting for prey, until, with great caution, she let her guard down.

"Must have been the wind," she said without convincing anyone, including herself, and peered into the darkness as if something stared back.

SPYING

It pained him beyond belief to go with Anthony when he knew that Denys had news about Xavier. "Can you believe it?" Thomas asked. "We found him. They're on their way. Let's follow."

"No spying."

"There's no harm in my seeing him. I promise not to let them know I'm watching."

Anthony raised his arms in the air in exasperation. "When Catherine or Xavier decides that it's time, Catherine knows where to find you. Leave it to her."

"I will, I will." Thomas stopped and tried to pull Anthony the other way.

"Hold on. *Catherine* accepted you, not Xavier. Did you ever think he'll resent the man who almost whacked his head off? *Leave it alone.*"

Thomas grabbed Anthony's shoulders as an involuntary smile illuminated his face. "I love him. I must see him." He kissed Anthony on the cheek, and Anthony reciprocated without a word. Then Thomas slapped Anthony on the back and skipped away.

Breezing past everyone too fast for the human eye to see, Thomas caught up with Catherine and Denys. They walked for some time along the river until all traces of humanity stopped.

To avoid detection, Thomas followed far behind in the darkness. He made his move when Anne and Xavier saw Catherine and the two embraced. The distraction allowed him to move to the other side of the bridge and perch on the stone arch. The shadows hid him, as did the inaccessibility of his position. Once concealed, Thomas took in the scene. There was his abbé! Catherine clung to her brother and lost control, and so, too, did Thomas, who sobbed.

The minutes flew by as Thomas heard that Xavier had stopped drinking, and he rejoiced to learn about Xavier leaving behind his strict Catholicism. Not to mention the illusions Xavier had about loving men, or perhaps a specific man. He could only hope.

When Xavier walked toward the river, the lay clothes revealed the lean muscles he'd always hidden underneath his robes, and the familiar gait sent shivers through him.

Then, without warning, the happiness evaporated. Thomas gripped the stone hard enough that it crumbled as Anne told Catherine about Xavier's transformation. Thomas thought he misheard at first. But no, he was correct. How could they be so nonchalant? What did that news mean?

A sailor? A dirty, whore sailor?

Thomas fought for control as the anger built. Xavier was his! *Thomas* was supposed to bring Xavier into that life, not some filthy wretch who lived among the rats.

Thomas held on to the bridge in an attempt to stabilize his emotions. His anger was wrong. He could hear Anthony admonish him, yet it mounted out of control. Was he angry with Xavier? No. The sailor deserved punishment. The sailor must suffer.

He sat for a long time as Catherine, Anne, and Xavier, *his* Xavier, conversed. But the words filtered into the air without Thomas hearing. He struggled but lost the battle against anger. He became so angry that he lost himself and allowed Anne to sense his presence. Thomas slipped off the other side of the arch and flipped onto the bridge above. Within seconds, he was down the road and far enough away from Anne's intuition.

Still he raved.

Using vampiric speed, Thomas reached Brittany Province moments later. Anne had given a good description, and the little she said about where Xavier met the swine told Thomas enough.

Thomas's body moved involuntarily through the throngs of men, some gambling, some drinking, some negotiating with a prostitute. It was never difficult, either, to find the male whores in the dark corners, most of them disrobed.

Thomas passed an officer who offered to pay Thomas for a good suck. Thomas, too angry for offense, glared the man away. Then he found someone who might help.

"You a regular here?" he asked the thirty-something man.

"You paying?" the guy asked.

Thomas whipped out a large sum of money, so the man pulled out his penis.

"Put that away. I need information. Is there a sailor who lives here? He likes the boys, but he brings them into his home."

"There's more than one in these parts. Who you looking for?"

"I don't know his name. But he knows a friend of mine by the name of Xavier."

"The abbé who lived with Christophe for a time. He's still heartbroken—"

"Where is he?"

The man moved into the street and led Thomas to a small stone house. Thomas peered through the window to discover a fire burning and two men inside. Without speaking, Thomas handed his guide double the sum he had shown him and ordered him away.

His prey at last within reach, Thomas crashed into the room. Christophe and his latest toy jumped with fright, and Christophe grabbed a knife and aimed it at Thomas without a word. Thomas grabbed the knife by the blade in midair and laughed like a crazed fool. He threw a shirt at the young man and instructed him to get out, which he did, leaving Christophe and Thomas alone.

Christophe shook with fear. He appeared pleasant enough, with the muscles of a sailor, piercing green eyes, and curly blond hair. And he had a quaint little home. Perhaps he had a genuine love for the abbé, but someone must suffer for his transgressions. At first, Thomas wanted to torture him, to make him feel the same anguish and torment that surged through Thomas at the thought of Xavier having been with another man. Yet Christophe appeared guiltless. He at least deserved a swift death.

Thomas reached out to break the man's neck when he saw one of Xavier's crucifixes on the mantel, evident from the Saint-Laurent crest emblazoned on the bottom. He paused. Was his action that of a vampire reformed? Did it accomplish anything toward getting his anger under control?

He released the man and staggered out of the home, afraid of himself.

Thomas headed back to Paris, with angst in his heart. The sailor seemed sincere, not the fiend who Thomas envisioned. At any rate, he felt better but guilt-ridden at the same time. He had stopped himself, but the anger had begun without his knowing it.

Anthony waited in his flat. "You killed someone, didn't you?"

"I'm a vampire."

"Enough games, Thomas. What happened?"

Thomas told him the entire tale. "So, despite my anger, I didn't kill anyone."

"You won't say a word, and you'll listen." Anthony sat Thomas down and held him there. "I'm leaving. I'll no longer be party to your fits of rage. You didn't kill this sailor. How noble. You love Xavier. How wonderful. But what kind of vicious love are you offering? You're attempting to control a situation that's not yours to govern. I won't stay and watch you destroy yourself."

Anthony waited until the sun began to sear Thomas's skin to release him, just in time to flee to the casket. Losing Anthony made Thomas more determined than ever to get control of himself and win back Xavier at the same time.

SEEK HIM

It was very late, almost midnight, and Catherine and Xavier had talked for a long time with Anne before leaving her under the bridge because she had no desire to return to Paris. They had invited Anne to move into their home, but the trappings of wealth held no allure for her.

As Catherine walked toward Denys, who would escort them home, Xavier drew back alone with Anne. "Thank you again, for everything. You saved me."

"It's what friends do. You help me too. Now go on with your life."

"I may have been a drunk, but I remember your promise—that if I sobered you'd help with Catherine, regardless of the consequences or black magic."

"And I keep my promises. Give me time. I need something I can't get here, from the New World."

Xavier nodded and then hugged Anne goodbye. Perhaps he could never seek justice against Marcel for what he had done to their brother, but he would do everything he could to get him away from Catherine and trusted Anne to do the job. He caught up with Catherine and Denys on the edge of Anne's territory. Xavier had a short reunion with his old friend before they returned to the house and Denys went home.

Despite the hour, neither Catherine nor Xavier could sleep. Too much excitement pumped through Xavier at having taken the step to return home. He had to tell people he had left the church, and some people would learn about his secret desires.

Despite everything, Xavier loved Thomas with the same passion and missed him with aching desperation. Whether they could renew even a friendship, Xavier had no idea, but at some point, he had to see him. But not yet. He wasn't ready.

He and Catherine settled into her office and opened another bottle of wine as they caught each other up on the smaller details of their lives. When the slight intoxication loosened Xavier's tongue, he stopped drinking for the night. It was like old times—nothing could have felt better.

The evening's conversation got to what Xavier wanted to know. "Catherine, where's Jérémie?"

She looked away. "His last dispatch was still from London. He and his family hid there, and I believe remain there. He still assists me from afar and we correspond as much as possible, and I miss him."

"And Marcel?" he asked despite some hesitation.

"Still frightened of Paris. Isn't that ridiculous? We gave up on the wedding date because he can't be sure when it'll be safe to return!" Catherine giggled like a nonsensical teen, her eyes glassed over. So Marcel still pretended to be in America. "Which is fine, that I'm not dealing with a husband yet."

"If you feel that way, maybe you don't have the right man."

Catherine just frowned at him, which ended the discussion. Marcel still had her under his spell. Xavier's one hope was that Anne could come through with a solution. Thankfully, Catherine changed the subject when a couple of guards strode by.

"Every time I see a uniform, I remember Michel."

They fell silent as the pain flooded back. Xavier admired Catherine's resilience, that she maintained her salon even after Michel's death and his own disappearance. She brushed it aside, crediting Jérémie and Maria, but Xavier knew that it had been all Catherine.

Catherine sighed. "I'd rather save that misery for another day. I'm more interested in having you back."

Xavier smiled and wiped away a tear.

"You can't imagine how much I went over this moment in my head. It took all of my willpower not to give you up for dead. Why, Thomas—" Catherine stopped midsentence. The awkward moment became worse because Xavier was at a loss. Why had she not continued with her thought? Should he admit his love for Thomas? "Thomas was just as earnest in looking," she finished. "There's one thing I know Anne and you never broached," Catherine continued. "Since you were born and until you left, you lived this idealistic life as a model citizen and trusting priest."

"We were all raised that way."

"Yes, but Michel and I didn't take it to heart. I'm not criticizing you. Father, Michel, and I sheltered you too much. You heard the lessons about helping everyone, but we refused to let you know about the more troubling aspects of this world. We all wanted to protect you. So you had farther to fall when you discovered reality."

Catherine came across the room and held Xavier's hand. She brushed Xavier's hair out of his eyes. He found himself fidgeting with the buttons on his shirt and felt the cross underneath. He had no idea what to say.

"Being a woman has always grounded me in reality. Father raised me as a boy, but the rest of the world only sees my breasts."

Xavier chuckled.

"It's true. And Michel, he felt so much pressure after Father died. Even before, he saw things in the military that balanced his perceptions. You were a free spirit. You loved with such intensity. And we sheltered you, fearing that the corrupted world would ruin our little angel."

Even that evening, Xavier fretted about telling Catherine he was leaving the church despite knowing it would make her happy. And a million times, they mentioned he had no sexual attraction to women, and yet they still never spoke with such direct words about it. Not because of her, because of him.

"You're right," Xavier said after a long pause. "I struggle with my identity."

"So change. Be the person *you* want to be. You can still help people as you indulge in your passions."

"Anne and I talked about it. In my mind, all this makes sense and I want to do it. But I can't change in one night. It's easy for you. You've always balanced obligation and personal desire. I end up feeling guilty. I'll embarrass myself."

"Will you at least try to be comfortable saying it to me? You love other men. How does it embarrass you to say it to me? It makes no difference. Even Michel told you to follow your dreams. Say it, Xavier, admit it to me."

The room fell silent. "I've come to terms with it," he said after a long moment.

"Then talk about it."

"You know that idea you detest, that, because you're a woman, you should marry and hide behind a protector the rest of your life? It sounds spectacular to me. I can't think of anything better than the thought of lying in another man's arms and having him protect me. When I was with Thomas, I pretended we had such a relationship. He nurtured my dreams and indulged my every whim. It was wonderful, but something didn't allow me to take the next step. The thought of kissing him or a simple touch, it was magnificent and terrible at the same time. I wish I could recapture the moment and respond with a different reaction."

"Thomas told me everything. If your heart tells you that you can forgive him, maybe you should. He'd protect you, despite what happened. He loves you."

Xavier smiled. Of course Thomas had confessed. It was so Thomas to purge the guilt. "Give me some time. Let me be at home a while before I take this step. We better get to sleep."

The emotion had drained them, and Xavier could not wait to fall into a real bed for the first time in months. They had reached the stairs when Catherine paused. She turned to stare at him.

"About Thomas. Can you accept things that you never dreamed existed?"

"What are you talking about?" Xavier asked.

"Nothing. Never mind. Just be open." And with that, she headed to her room, leaving him to puzzle after her.

Thirty-Nine: Potion

9 JUNE 1793

Catherine rushed to get ready after realizing she was supposed to meet Anne. She had received a note that morning, requesting a meeting away from the house and in public, Catherine assumed about Xavier. Catherine arrived at a small café in her carriage, where Anne waited.

Anne nodded toward a bench without greeting her. "If you don't mind, could we just sit over there? This won't take long."

The women made their way to a nearby bench.

"I didn't thank you for taking care of my brother."

"You don't have to mention that. He's a close friend, and he helps me as much as I help him, even if he doesn't admit it. It was the least I could do."

Anne stood up, looked down at Catherine, then sat back down and stared at her, as if peering into Catherine's soul. "I didn't ask to meet because of your brother."

"What is it?" Catherine asked, feeling a strange nervousness creep into her bones.

"There isn't a way of making this easy. You can hate me if you want."

"Anne, please. Out with it."

"Marcel. That man—I know you think you love him. But he's not everything that you think. He's got you under a spell. He's manipulating you."

Catherine laughed at the utter lunacy. She'd accepted a vampire and knew Anne had magical powers, but the thought of Marcel, a common merchant, seducing her was absurd.

"I won't engage in this foolery. I'm busy." She got up and headed toward the carriage, but Anne followed.

"He's here, in Paris, you know. I've been watching him, seduce girls, steal from the poor, work his magic all around."

"You sound more and more unstable with every word."

"How else do you explain the sexual longing you don't have for any other man?"

Catherine turned, anger welling within her. "I won't discuss that."

"Catherine, listen to me. There's evil afoot, and it wasn't brought by the vampire. There's pure evil, and it's after you. I can help protect you, but you have to let me in."

"Anne, I have made myself clear."

"Will you at least take and keep this?" She held out a purple velvet pouch, a bit heavy and full of some powder and who knows what. Catherine started to take it to appease the woman but thought better of it.

"I appreciate your concern, but I don't need this."

Anne took it back. "I meant no harm. Just to tell you what I know."

"What you *think* you know," Catherine corrected. With that, Anne walked down the street. Catherine entered her carriage and ordered the driver home.

THOMAS SWOONS

Thomas woke determined, exhilarated that Xavier had returned the previous night but embarrassed with himself for going after the innocent sailor. The self-revelation of the night before had changed everything.

So, too, had seeing Xavier. If Thomas wanted Xavier to end his loneliness, he had to fix himself first. He had to end the cycle of violent despair, he had to embrace the emotion and humiliation of his past so he could reform himself. Thomas smiled, calm and in control, just as Anthony wanted. Waiting for Xavier to make the first move would be the first sign he had conquered his demons.

Thomas went to glance at Xavier just one time, so he hid in shadow as the priest talked to Catherine. When it got darker and Catherine left, Thomas moved from his hiding spot as Xavier walked to his bedroom, and then Thomas moved onto the roof and peered into the room to see his love one more time.

Xavier was talking to himself, something Thomas had noticed a number of times, especially when he worked through difficult problems, but what he heard stopped his heart.

"Catherine's right, of course. I've got to overcome my fear." Xavier was undressing, so Thomas glanced at the slim body, firing his passion anew.

"Why didn't I tell her I almost went to find Thomas today, but was too scared?" Xavier crawled into bed and chuckled. "I just delayed because it's the next big step that Anne talked about. I'm just frightened. I'll mark my calendar and promise that if I don't go to him by the end of the month, I'll have Catherine do it for me." Xavier extinguished the candle, rolled over, and hugged a pillow, looking happy, determined, and proud.

Thomas crept off the roof, full of hope. Xavier wanted to come to him!

Forty: The Prodigal Returns

10 JUNE 1793

Catherine had grown accustom to having Xavier around again when more shocking news came. Jérémie was in Paris. He sent word he would come to the Saint-Laurent salon at noon, so Catherine ordered a private lunch, per his request.

Hearing Jérémie in the hall, Catherine went to greet him. What she saw startled her. Jérémie stood with his charming smile but also a more mature stature, as if the trip abroad had transformed him, much like Xavier's absence changed her brother. Catherine admired his musculature and captivating presence, as well as his soft demeanor. He came down the hall, kissed her cheek, and gave her a warm hug.

"Catherine, I'm glad to see you."

"You look wonderful. I arranged for lunch in my study." Catherine ushered Jérémie into the room and sat across from him.

"I hope my return hasn't shocked you."

"Not at all. I'm happy you're here. Is your family safe?"

"Yes, hiding in Rome now. They tired of London. Painfully aristocratic, but I expected as much. They were incensed when I told them I was returning to Paris, but I was worried about you and the salon. Besides, I was ready to be back. I wish Michel were here."

"His death has been hard on all of us."

"Despite it all, you look beautiful," Jérémie said out of the blue.

"Thank you." Catherine was surprised. "But things have been difficult around here. I'm exhausted. I lost two brothers in a short period of time, then regained one, which was just as fatiguing. It wasn't until you were gone a while that I realized how much I missed you."

Jérémie fumbled with his tricolored hat. His face was bright red.

"I hardly meant to embarrass you."

"No, I felt the same way. Please, continue."

"Well, I told you that Xavier has returned from the dead. He's very much himself, full of life and love. However, he's struggling with a lot. You realize he struggles with sex?" Catherine laughed again at how Jérémie squirmed. "He doesn't like women. He likes men. Thomas is no help because he needs Xavier to come first to him, which compounds the issue because I think he's the man in their relationship."

"Catherine! You sound like a common sailor," he said, horrified.

"Then get a drink and we'll toast," she shot back. "Regardless, things are more complicated because of Maria's drivel. She's always talking about Catholicism, warning Xavier and making him question things all over again. It drives me quite mad, because that woman romps around with all sorts of her own kind but tells Xavier it's different because they all serve the church." She shook her head, disgusted. "Rubbish."

Jérémie smiled. After a pause, he asked, "What about you?"

"Everything else runs as usual."

"I meant to ask about *you*."

She brushed him off. "I'm fine. Now that Xavier has returned, I'm fine."

"Are you still engaged to Marcel?"

"I don't need anyone to take Michel's place."

"Catherine," Jérémie said in a stern tone she had never heard from him, "this isn't about Michel. *I* asked and would appreciate an answer. I bit my tongue with you too much in the past. Marcel is a fiend. He's using you." Jérémie sweated.

"Marcel and I are fine," Catherine said. "How dare you insult my fiancé?"

"Can't someone disagree with you?" Jérémie retorted.

"I don't see why all of you dwell on it."

"You're blind."

"This is about that ridiculous idea of a spell, isn't it?"

"You know about it?" Jérémie stared at her.

"I know that Anne has a crazy idea that Marcel has me under some love potion." Catherine stood up, and Jérémie followed. "Stay out of my life. I was happy to see you again, but if this is our new relationship, I think it best if you leave."

Catherine planted herself in front of him. He grew quiet, and the meek Jérémie returned.

"Forgive me, I just wanted to suggest that there may be others who love you, too, and deserve a chance. I at least deserve the right to be heard if I'm to respect your wishes in return."

Catherine touched Jérémie's arm as a sign of peace. She had not meant to be that harsh.

"We're still friends?" she asked.

"Of course," Jérémie said.

Forty-One: Bewitched

20 JUNE 1793

Thomas awoke with a giddy euphoria every night, even more excited about life than when Anthony first embraced him with that fatal kiss. He rushed to take care of a few business matters, donned his black cloak, and headed out. His patience had not wavered, his anger had been in check, and he had controlled himself since his transformation.

As usual, he first went to see Xavier from afar and smiled at the beautiful night. The stars shone and the moon illuminated even the darkest allies. He had almost turned down Rue St. Denis when a familiar voice echoed down a passageway. A stone arch blackened the scene, but Thomas heard Marcel. The fiend.

Thomas slid along the stone, not making a sound. Candlelight shone from around a corner, so Thomas peeked.

Marcel sat there, picking through the pockets of several jackets while laughing. The sight disgusted even Thomas. Marcel piled a stack of dead, naked, and rotting bodies in the corner to scavenge. Marcel got up, so Thomas jumped to the ceiling and clung to the stones as Marcel hurried away. As he turned the corner, Thomas saw that he carried a small, green velvet bag.

Thomas followed.

Marcel stalked through Paris, clutching the bag as if someone might steal it. To hide himself, Thomas swung onto a nearby roof and watched from above by jumping from roof to roof.

After a few blocks, Marcel stopped and watched a man who was down a small street, peeing on the side of a building. Marcel glanced around and reached into his bag. He looked at a couple of vials of powder, selected one, and slunk toward the unsuspecting victim. Marcel startled the poor man, who jerked around to face Marcel.

"Sorry to alarm you," Marcel said with a jovial inflection. At the same time, he took a pinch of his powder and flicked it at the man. Under his breath, he whispered, "Signpost."

"I—what…oh my," the man said.

When Marcel approached, the man stopped peeing but could not lift his trousers. He fumbled for them, but whatever Marcel had cast at him aroused the poor gent, who fondled himself. Acting as if alone, he dropped his pants, hugged an apothecary's signpost, and gyrated against it.

Thomas shadowed Marcel a few more blocks and watched him infect two other people with different mixes. A woman became enraged and screamed at everyone, while a second man wet himself and cried with fear, screaming that a huge rat chased him.

Marcel next approached a young child crying in the street, alone and afraid. He reached into his bag and knelt before the little boy, saying something soothing. When he rubbed an ointment in the child's hair, another figure approached. As the intruder got closer, the child fell into odd laughter and batted at imagined bugs flying through the air. Marcel got up to see who drew near and then ducked.

Thomas recognized Xavier at once. He picked the child up, held him close to his chest, and muttered about irresponsible adults when he saw Marcel in the dark. Then, the priest, perplexed, noticed that the boy failed to respond to him.

"What did you do to him?" Xavier asked Marcel.

The boy giggled but never acknowledged Xavier, so Xavier put him down, prompting him to chase more imaginary bugs. Xavier glared at Marcel, then his eyes grew wide with fright. He backed up slowly, ignoring the child and trembling. Thomas clutched the ledge of a roof until the bricks crumbled in his hands.

Then, without another word, Xavier ran. He snatched up the boy and raced as fast as he could away from Marcel. Marcel followed and closed the distance between them, Xavier at a disadvantage because of the child in his arms. Marcel fumbled in his bag for something as Thomas hurried behind them from above.

For better or worse, Thomas leaped off the building and landed in Marcel's path. Marcel dropped the bag and halted in shock. He snatched it up and scowled.

"You wretched beast, always taking back our deal," Thomas said.

"He got in my way this time. I didn't seek him."

Thomas raised his hand to strike Marcel and send him against the wall, but Marcel threw something in his face. The powder stung. Thomas closed his eyes and wiped at them as blood tears ran down his cheeks. His body healed fast, but Marcel had disappeared.

Fearing the worst, Thomas raced toward Xavier and found him a few blocks away, giving the child water with Marcel nowhere in sight. Thomas sucked in a few deep breaths as Xavier cared for the child. When the boy came to his senses, he cried all the harder and pleaded to go home. The boy explained that he lived in an orphanage but that many of the priests and nuns had gone, so the boys went out to explore all the time. He wandered away from the older boys and got lost. Xavier comforted him and guided him back to a dwelling, where a kind old man scolded him but in a kind voice and took him inside.

Thomas followed Xavier until he returned home, where Catherine waited on the steps.

"Did you go to him?" she asked.

Xavier slapped his sister lightly on the arm and laughed. "People might hear you."

Thomas smiled. Xavier and Catherine's love calmed all of the nerves Marcel had tweaked. He walked away contented, thrilled because he had passed the first test of his new patience. He had stayed in the background until necessary, and still he had not interfered with the abbé.

Which reminded Thomas, he had a letter to write, so he ran to his flat and picked up his quill. He wrote with furious intent, a long and impassioned letter, telling Anthony everything that had happened since he had stormed away. Only then did he notice his fatigue, brought on by failing to feed in several days. He searched Paris and found another worthy victim before returning to his quarters for sleep.

Forty-Two: Revelations

28 JUNE 1793

Xavier was ready, at long last. So the previous night, he left a note on Catherine's door, asking if they could dine the following day. Being an early riser, Catherine raced to Xavier's room and barged in as the sun began to rise.

"Let's do breakfast instead of dinner," she said and tugged at his covers.

Xavier rolled over and pretended to fall back asleep, so Catherine tickled him without mercy until he promised to join her. She left, and he dressed in a hurry and went downstairs, where Catherine paced the room.

"You won't get a bite to eat until you explain this note." She waved it in his face.

"It's time, that's all. I want to take the next step."

Catherine squealed and jumped up to hug Xavier. "I've been waiting to hear that."

"But I've no idea where to find him."

"I think I know," Catherine said but hesitated. "What about the church? Does this mean you're leaving the priesthood?"

Xavier nodded solemnly. To follow his dreams meant defying the church. He could not lead a double life. He was leaving the priesthood forever. "Yes, I'm leaving."

"You'll be much happier out of it." Catherine's eyes filled with tears without warning. "Michel would be so happy for you. He worried as much as I did about you in that church and how it stifled you. I wish he could see you today."

Xavier cried, too, though with more anguish than Catherine, knowing that Michel's killer still lurked in their lives.

After breakfast, Xavier kissed Catherine on the cheek and said he had other people to tell. She, too, ran off to begin her day, so Xavier went into the sitting room to meet Denys, who sat amidst a sea of papers as part of his new duties: salon accountant. The man who always wore the clothes of a worker sat in formal attire.

"I'll never get used to seeing you as a gentleman."

"Abbé," Denys said, "and you in citizen's clothing."

"I have something to tell you," Xavier said as they took seats opposite one another. Xavier fumbled with his shirt buttons, searching for his cross, and then ran his fingers through his hair. "I'm leaving the priesthood."

"Nothing will change how I feel about you. We're friends."

The two men hugged, said goodbye, and Xavier started down the hall.

"So, you abandon everything that was important and forsake God—the one thing should cling to." There stood Maria, behind the door, eavesdropping.

"I was coming to find you next."

Maria grunted and pushed past him.

"Wait." Xavier tugged her arm.

She whipped around in a rage. "You abandon your vows and expect understanding? We've an obligation to these people. How can you cast God aside?"

"I haven't changed what I believe. But I can do that and take care of myself at the same time. There's nothing wrong with that."

"I suppose this means that you intend to disappear with that heathen Thomas."

Unable to keep his frustration inside, Xavier yanked her into a nearby parlor and slammed the door. "How dare you? How dare you question my commitment to helping people?"

"We made promises to each other, and to everyone. We made vows. There are rules to follow. You can't just throw them out the window on a whim."

"For the love of God, listen to yourself. You run around with a pack of nuns as lovers. How is that different? And don't preach to me about it being different because you keep it in the church."

Maria turned bright red, but whether out of anger or embarrassment, he didn't know.

"And don't tell me about my responsibility to that dying church. Why do you cling to something so many people question? As the Catholic Church collapses in its blind hierarchy, why do you still hide behind it?"

"You're such an elitist," she snapped. "Of course, you can't understand, with all of your wealth and manhood to protect you. I don't have the resources to just take up whatever fancies me at a particular moment. And did you forget that we're single women? What, pray tell, did you think our options were if we left the nunnery? Marriage to a man? Spinsterhood? Think about it. This was the one option that offered some independence. We did it because it was safe."

"Why does that condemn me for leaving?" Xavier asked, baffled.

"Because—oh, forget it and go lead your selfish life and leave me alone."

The two fell silent.

"Maria," Xavier whispered and walked toward her.

"No. You can't choose to have everything as you want it," she said and left the room.

Part IX: I Know the One My Heart Loves

Forty-Three: Ringing of the Bells

29 July 1793

At long last, the screaming mobs stopped startling Xavier. He sat in complete darkness on the porch, watching the occasional passerby and wondering when the rioting would stop. He had tried to search for Thomas the previous night, but the uprisings made it too dangerous, so he waited on the porch, hoping Thomas might chance by. But another name plagued Xavier's mind.

Maximillan Robespierre. Two days before, the man had taken control of the Committee on Public Safety and transformed it into a private police force, intent on initiating a reign of terror. He had further attacked the church, and any peasant or citizen who dared question him found themselves on the guillotine. In the fashion of the day, when people had enough of him, they rioted in protest.

Xavier sat in shadows when a small group of about ten people approached the door. The guards blocked their way because Catherine and Jérémie ordered tighter security until the rioting subsided, but they explained their purpose in defiance of one guard's orders to leave.

"Please, sir," an elderly woman begged, "we must see our abbé."

Xavier could not resist the soft pleading of the woman who had supported him in his old parish. He walked to the ledge and looked down.

"Good evening." Each of their faces lit up at his voice.

"Abbé, we've a request of you," the elderly woman began.

A well-respected carpenter in his late fifties continued. "They burned our church to the ground. All the priests refuse to come to our neighborhood. But, Abbé, can you do one thing for us? We just—well, we need someone to ring the bells."

The group fell silent and cast their eyes to the ground, as if they knew they implored him to do something he disdained. The peasants believed that ringing church bells warded off evil spirits. When Xavier first arrived in his parish, they'd instructed that all previous priests rang the bells once a week and expected him to do the same, but he had shunned the practice. Though some feared he was wrong, they acquiesced, and that was the last he'd heard of it until tonight.

"You know how I feel about this."

"Abbé, look what's occurred since we stopped."

"God doesn't work that way."

The elderly woman started weeping.

"I'll do it."

As they all smiled with delight, the elderly woman recited the rosary and cried out with joy. Xavier hurried to join them after grabbing his cloak. "Where will we go?"

"A chapel near the edge of town is abandoned. Come," the carpenter said.

Xavier followed as the throng moved into the street and hurried along, a couple of times changing directions to avoid angry mobs that blockaded the streets, and wound their way through Paris. They arrived together at a small, abandoned church unknown to Xavier at the edge of Paris, away from residences and near a row of workshops. The darkened, broken windows gave it a foreboding feel, but they pushed forward and soon stood inside the sanctuary.

Its inside mirrored the outside: black, dirty, and desolate. Xavier took a tentative step and started up the bell tower alone, hearing each step creak, his own breathing sounding louder than usual. His flock stayed behind, reciting the rosary. Xavier would ring these bells but a few times and run back home. That night was hardly one on which to assert the Catholic Church's authority.

Near the top, Xavier almost toppled backward when cobwebs hit his face. He rushed into action and grappled for the rope, not able to see much because just a glint of moonlight came from small openings just big enough to release the bell sounds.

Dong. Dong. Dong.

The chiming filled the quiet night. Xavier rang them for but a minute and then descended the stairs, frightened out of his mind. He neared the bottom but stopped when he heard cries of pain and the pounding of fists. Xavier ran back up the narrow passage, but not before seeing five or six men beating even the poor old woman.

"There he is!" Two men came after Xavier. "You a priest? You're in violation of the laws of Robespierre."

They blocked his only exit. He thought of jumping, but the windows were too small and his pursuers too close behind, so he tried to run around the large bell toward the stairs, but the two men had each gone a different direction. Instead of fighting, Xavier prayed and halted in fear.

Yet something miraculous answered Xavier's prayer. Just before one of the thugs hit Xavier over the head with a board, the roof caved in and some force threw the man across the room. As he thudded against the wall, his savior, a man, snapped the neck of the other assailant. The new man returned to the first attacker as he regained his senses and smashed his skull on the bell. Xavier winced as his brains splattered about.

Before Xavier could worry about the sounds of other men charging up the stairs, his savior grabbed him by the waist, leaped onto the roof, and then onto the next nearest building. They sped through Paris in an instant, away from the danger and far away from humanity.

Xavier buried his head in the chest of the man and clung with a fierce hold, too afraid to look, relieved at being saved and terrified at the stranger's strength and quickness. Xavier fought to rationalize, but it was extraordinary, not possible for a human. How could someone crash through a roof four stories high? How could one man fend off those muscular attackers?

After they arrived at some unknown building and entered a room unfamiliar to Xavier, the man gently laid him on a bed. Xavier glanced up and burst into tears.

He had wondered before about Thomas's nature, the first time when Thomas fended off the would-be robber in the garden. Why else had his love only come at night? Why else the mystery about his life? And there was the night he had assaulted Xavier. The emotional pain blinded Xavier to the reality of broken bones in his face from the mere slap of his hand, with no more effort than it took to swat a fly.

With desperation, Xavier had wanted to find Thomas, and here was the man of his dreams— protecting and nurturing him as he desired. Yet he drew his knees to his chin and hugged them for protection and stared at Thomas with exhilaration and fear.

"Xavier, I never meant for you to find out like this. I was waiting for you—"

Tears rolled down Xavier's face as he searched for a reaction.

First Kiss

Thomas wanted to smother Xavier in a protective hug, dreading what almost happened to him in that bell tower. He almost always rose and went at once to spy on Xavier, but an urgent financial matter had demanded his attention, and a messenger had waited to take a packet to a departing ship. So, Thomas had left late and arrived just as Xavier led a small contingent away, otherwise Thomas might have visited and already been gone for the night. Instead, he'd followed.

Thomas had to act when that motley gang came after Xavier.

Running through Paris as Xavier clung to him had been exhilarating. To touch him, to smell his soft hair, it was everything Thomas wanted. He feared the aftermath once they were arrived safe and sound in his rooms, knowing his actions had revealed his vampirism.

"Xavier, I never meant for you to find out like this. I was waiting for you, but they attacked. I had to get you out of there. I won't harm you."

Xavier's crying pained Thomas. Was he miserable, happy, or just confused?

"I've wanted to tell you since we met, but I was always afraid that you'd hate me. I'm lost."

Xavier chuckled, though he still clutched his knees. "You never did know how to handle delicate moments." Xavier wiped away his tears while Thomas waited, then he released his legs, sat up, and moved closer to Thomas, looking at him with a hint of their former love. "What are you?"

"There are unexplained things in this world that people won't accept as possibilities. I don't have all of the answers. But I can never die. Fire and the sun alone can doom me, but otherwise, I'll walk the earth forever."

"A vampire?" Xavier's eyes widened. "But that's impossible."

"There's nothing evil about it. I'm still the man you fell in love with."

Xavier moved back and leaned against the wall, drawing his feet up again and hugging himself. "I love you. After I left with Anne, I knew I'd never be able to return to the church because I'd fallen in love, like a swooning madman. I came back to Paris for you. I wanted your protection and to shower you with the love I'd always been afraid to reveal."

Thomas had waited for too long to hear these words. "The irony was that the more I got to know you and the deeper that my love became, the more I tried to hide my nature, the more I dreaded your finding out. I know I was wrong to keep it from you. I'm ashamed, but because of the time I—"

"No, don't mention it. We'll discuss it, but not yet."

"I punish myself every day for what I did."

"I just need to know that you won't do it again."

"Of course, I won't, but how can you ever believe me?"

Xavier smiled and seized Thomas's arm. He moved closer again, no longer huddled in a ball. Xavier held tightly to Thomas.

"I wanted to go away with you." Xavier cried harder now. "I left the church. I told Catherine and everyone. I accept who I am." He paused, staring hard at Thomas. "Are you a monster?"

"No."

"Then why did you lie? Why not tell me?"

"I was afraid to tell you because I feared rejection. I hide my nature from everyone because the world would assassinate me. We're in constant danger of exposure, you know what the Church alone would do."

Xavier nodded. With his free hand, he traced Thomas's finger.

"I'm the same man you wanted to run away with. I never lied about my beliefs or attitudes. I was honest with you about everything else. You've only learned the last part about my life."

"But you're not alive?" Xavier asked.

"I'm dead, in a physical, human sense, but I walk around and have the same emotions. So, is that death? I know that I love you and want to take care of you forever."

The two fell silent. Then, without hesitation, Thomas reached over and turned Xavier's shoulders so they faced one another. Xavier complied, even when Thomas grasped his head and pulled him forward. He closed his eyes as Thomas pressed their lips together. Thomas kept his eyes open as Xavier gave in to the kiss and his entire body relaxed, leaning into Thomas. Thomas held him close and stroked his hair as the embrace lingered. Xavier opened his mouth first, and a fire lurched through Thomas's body as their tongues touched, lasting for several minutes before Thomas pushed them apart and gazed into Xavier's eyes.

"Xavier, I love you."

Then Xavier cried and spun off the bed, running his hands through his hair. He walked toward the door, looking at Thomas as if he might attack. Thomas predicted what happened next, though it stung nonetheless. Xavier grabbed the doorknob without turning away and talked with great effort through the tears.

"I love you too. But after everything, after all that I went through, I can't believe you hid this from me. I just can't—"

Xavier raced out the door. The final test of his patience had come, and Thomas passed with flying colors when he simply walked to the window as his beloved ran. Perhaps he had lost his quest. Maybe Xavier would come back. Thomas had no idea. At least there were no more secrets, nothing else to hinder the final decision that was Xavier's alone.

Forty-Four: Lashing Out

30 July 1793

Xavier startled Catherine when he barged into her office. Her door swung open and hit the wall with a crash, sending an entire row of books onto the floor. Xavier stood there, breathing heavily and sweating, and glared at her, tears coursing down his cheeks.

Catherine rushed to her brother. She took him by the arm and brought him into the room before closing the door and setting him into a chair. She sat opposite him. Without a word, he got up, strode to the bar, and poured himself a glass of calvados. He sucked it down in one gulp before refilling and returning to the seat.

"I suppose you haven't any idea what might have gotten into me," he said with a dripping sarcasm.

"If you want to tell me something, then let me know, but this has got to stop." Catherine snatched the glass from him and smashed it against the bookcase.

Xavier smirked, shook his head, got a second glass, and filled it. "I won't yell at you, but I need the alcohol." He took a swig. "You knew, didn't you? All along, you knew."

"Knew what?" Catherine racked her brain for answers but figured it out at the same time he said it.

"He isn't human. You hid it from me. Me! I trusted you." Xavier finished the calvados and poured even more. He already staggered as he walked back. "And you never thought I might be interested in that little tidbit of information?" Xavier was drunk enough to giggle.

"Why should I have told you when you didn't even acknowledge feelings for him? You would've run in fear. Until you came to terms with what you wanted, I saw no reason to drive a bigger wedge between you two. Besides, it was his secret to tell you, not mine."

Xavier laughed with derision. "We're not talking about some minor secret. The man is dead. And he could've killed me."

"For heaven's sake, he worships the ground you walk on. Here you made a grand announcement about leaving the church, and at the first sign of a challenge, you revert to an archaic view of the world, good versus evil. Can't you stop for one second and think of other possibilities? There is nothing to fear from Thomas except utter devotion to a fool priest."

Xavier drank more as she scolded him. He put his empty glass down. "I still don't see how you could encourage me to be with someone who doesn't live."

"I saw you happy for the first time since childhood. I saw the same Xavier who wandered around this house in love with life. I saw that adulthood and the Catholic Church had taken those things away from me and I hoped against hope that Thomas could restore them."

Xavier leaned toward her. "He *kills* to survive. And that never bothered you?"

"Did you ask him about it? I asked him. Because he explained everything and it makes more sense than castigating something you don't understand." Catherine crossed the space between them and knelt before her brother. "You left the church. You don't have to believe in a black-and-white world anymore. Imagine shades of gray. Maybe you should see if you two can work things out. I can't answer that for you. But maybe you should try."

"*You* sound mad. You sit there and with complete sincerity hand me over to a vampire. A creature that feeds off humans. Do you honestly believe I could lead such a life?"

His thought had given her pause a number of times. Though she trusted Thomas's explanation and never feared him, she often wondered if he intended to bring Xavier into that existence as well, which Catherine thought doomed to failure. Regardless of their love, Thomas viewed the world as did she: a cruel and random place where people injured one another without cause. For a vampire to live in the midst of that reality and yet adhere to principles higher than most people underscored her acceptance of his varied nature. But Xavier was different. He could not harm another person, let alone live off blood.

"Why do you have to take things that far?" she asked.

Xavier hesitated, then started to reply but withdrew before saying, "I don't know."

"Then don't condemn him like those bishops always condemned you. Take things one step at a time. Allow him to explain and make your own judgments after giving it some thought."

Xavier sat up in the chair and fumbled with his hands. Catherine worried anew about him. The drinking, the lost expression, and the condemnation of Thomas concerned her.

Xavier sat and sobbed. Then, without a word, he left the room. Catherine followed, and when he closed the door to his room, she instructed a guard not to let him leave the house. Maybe he needed to sleep, or perhaps the morning would bring him to his senses. To calm her nerves, Catherine hurried to her quarters, plopped Marcel's medication into her wine, and watched the soothing fizzle before drinking it all in one swallow.

Forty-Five: The Zealot

1 AUGUST 1793

After almost being killed by an angry group mob, then rescued by a vampire, Thomas no less, Xavier stayed in his room the entire next day. It took all of his energy just to eat. He ordered some wine and drank by himself, hoping that the spinning of the room would provide answers.

He loved Thomas, of that he was sure. His heart ached too much for it not to be genuine. But vampirism? He first hoped it was a bad dream, but somehow it was true.

At least the wine numbed him, so he drank more. The notion was so beyond comprehension the wine became a necessity. Thomas, a vampire, and Catherine loved a killer, too.

The thought rocked Xavier out of bed and propelled him to dress. He straightened his hair and headed down the hall. Before, Xavier's wrestling with theology offered solace in troubled times. Had he been wrong to give up on his faith?

Maria sat in the hospital, working with the patients at a furious pace. Xavier stood in the doorway until she finished and then moved so she would see him.

"What do you want?"

Xavier had forgotten their fight. "Can we talk?"

"I suppose," she said and led them down the hall into a small room of medical supplies.

He took a deep breath. "I know you're angry, but I need your advice."

Maria plopped down on a wooden chair and commanded him to sit.

Xavier launched into his tale, from the moment he left the house, through the ringing of the bells, to Thomas saving him, and to the fact that Thomas lived beyond the grave. He poured out his heart, cried as if the tears would never end, and described how lost he felt.

"This is what I tried to warn you about," Maria answered in all her terse glory. "Maybe you should leave again. We can't risk him finding you. You can't have any contact with him. With one bite, he could bring you to Satanism forever."

"Where would I go? I left the church to go with Thomas, remember?"

"God will take you back. We can work together again."

"It's not that simple for me. I left for many reasons. It wasn't all about Thomas. The church won't do what I need it to do for me any longer."

"Think about those innocent souls murdered in that church yesterday because they wanted to ring the bells. Maybe if you'd stayed in the church, they would've believed your theology and not tried to ward off spirits like that." Xavier bit his tongue and ignored Maria's warped views as she continued. "You were under Satan's evil influence. You were under the tutelage of Beelzebub. He sent Thomas to you. How else can you explain it? But you can conquer him." With that, Maria bustled back to the patients, leaving Xavier bewildered.

Her theology pestered him. He had never accepted that Satan lurked around and caused evil. Humans did so on their own. Xavier wondered if Satan even existed. Which brought him to Thomas. Had he condemned Thomas too quickly, as Maria did, because of his own fear? Should he return to a life of serving others, without concern for his own desires? Or did that mere thought, yet again, betray himself?

Forty-Six: Terror

12 AUGUST 1793

Catherine had first heard it a week before, dismissing it as a gross exaggeration, but that day's events proved it. Someone described Robespierre's rule as a reign of terror. On her way to see Thomas, Catherine tried to forget politics by listening to the horses' hooves on the cobbled streets. Since Xavier had fled Thomas once again, no one had heard from Thomas, so Catherine went to check on him.

Her visit to Robespierre earlier that afternoon had shaken and convinced her that it *was* terror. He and his armies used the guillotine quite often and otherwise imprisoned vast numbers of people, especially if they resisted conscription into his army. His government had also banned Roman Catholicism in France. When peasants who otherwise cared little about the revolution protested the closing of their churches, he arrested them and often killed to make his point. Recalcitrant priests were hunted and murdered. So it did not surprise Catherine when she received notice to appear before him on that day on charges that she operated a counterrevolutionary salon.

Catherine had gone to him to fulfill her duty, surprised to find the man himself presiding over his kangaroo court. Catherine hated the treatment afforded women, but on that occasion, she used flirting to her advantage. She took a double dose of Marcel's medicine to arouse her into seduction. She was deferential toward Robespierre, smiled a lot, and giggled at everything. Within seconds, she'd won the beast over and he dismissed the case.

As the horses rounded a corner too fast, her latest letter from Marcel dropped out of her bag. She snatched it off the carriage floor and read again his request for funds and control over the Saint-Laurent American interests. He promised to make them thousands. But she could not accomplish such a major transaction without Xavier's signature, and he still refused.

"Marcel is dangerous," Xavier had told her again that morning.

Thomas greeted her at his flat, explaining that he sent the help home as a reward for diligent service. He kissed her cheek and ushered her inside.

"I suppose you came because of your brother?" Thomas asked.

"Perhaps. I worried about you, too, though. I came—" She paused before continuing. "Xavier was planning to find you for weeks, since he returned to Paris he talked about nothing else. But the vampirism, as we predicted, frightened him to death. He's no idea what to make of it. But I don't think all is lost between you and my brother."

Thomas cocked his head and smiled. "I didn't come to the house at first because Xavier needed time to adjust, and then after he found out about me, I did not want to intrude. Xavier has to make his own decisions about us."

"But you're doing well?" Catherine asked.

"I accepted that it's out of my hands, which was difficult. I miss him."

"He'll come to you. I believe it."

Catherine left, feeling better about Thomas than she had since confirming his attack on Xavier. His actions demonstrated a new demeanor and patience.

Forty-Seven: Calming Effect

25 AUGUST 1793

The note awaited Thomas when he woke:

Against my better judgment, I have returned to this vile city. All for you, of course. I will come this evening. Anthony.

Thomas's heart leapt for joy. Anthony liked to enter with great drama instead of knocking. Thomas watched the Seine out his window when someone dropped from the roof, burst through his open window, and tackled Thomas to the floor, where he pinned him to the ground. Thomas shoved Anthony off as he got a mouth full of blond hair.

"You can't surprise someone if you warn them in advance with a note."

"How else could I have entered? It's the only way I can wrap my arms around you." Anthony stood up. "I know how hard you've worked. I still need more time before believing that you changed for good, but since the episode with the sailor, I see a changed vampire."

Thomas grinned, then jumped off the floor to stand before Anthony. "I don't blame you."

Anthony nodded and played with the curtain sash. "What else?"

"Xavier stays in the house all day and has yet to come to me. He talks too much to that rat of a nun, Maria, and they work together, but Catherine says he cries a lot when alone. He's conflicted, which is to be expected."

"And what about you?" Anthony asked.

For the first time in days, tears returned to release the pain. Anthony moved behind and hugged him, then pulled him by the hand and sat on the couch as Thomas cried.

Thomas regained his composure. "I love him from afar, but I don't threaten your sacred ethic. I'm not interfering."

Anthony smiled. "I still worry that you're too insistent Xavier become your mate. Humanity can't consume you like this if you want to survive throughout the ages."

"That's not what you did with me."

"I admit I should not have come to you that way. I was mesmerized by your beauty and charm. I wanted you as my companion because you were warm, funny, and full of energy. I made the mistake of not watching you first. I'd have seen that vampirism would present no obstacle and that you'd embrace it. But I also would've noticed your...tendencies, shall we say. I'd have seen that you like to dominate, whether a five-minute conversation or a lifetime friendship. This isn't to say that I regret bringing you over. But I'm not convinced that Xavier has stamina to be a vampire. He's delicate, nurturing, and sensitive. It's easy to see why you fell in love, but it's also easy to see there was no easy way for him to accept vampirism."

"I understand." Thomas nodded and put his hands together. "But you, and most others, miss what's underneath Xavier. There's a rougher side to him and a callused soul that's been hurt and doesn't trust people as much as the outer person would have you believe. He understands this world on a complex level. Even you, who's lived for hundreds of years, can't approach his quick insight. I'm not only in love with the soft, meek Xavier everyone sees. I'm also in love with the man's contradictions. That's why I know he can do this, even the vampirism and killing."

"Is this the truth or blind love?" Anthony asked.

"Both. And that's why I love him so much."

"Fine, but allow me a test before I respond further," Anthony answered. He stood and yanked Thomas out of the chair. They soon stood outside the Saint-Laurent home.

"How do you feel about the Catholic Church?" Anthony asked.

Thomas launched into a diatribe about how many people the church injured, about how it blinded Xavier or at least fed on his guilt, and called it a group of power-hungry men who lorded over people with their alleged superiority. Thomas was beginning to attack the pope when Xavier appeared at the window, looking into the darkness.

Thomas hushed and stared at Xavier, his beautiful eyes gleaming in the candlelight and his hand moving the curtain. He stayed but a second, yet heartened Thomas, who forgot what Anthony and he had been discussing.

"Where were we?" Thomas asked.

"Going to a seedier establishment to watch the clientele," Anthony answered. "*You* may devote all of your sexual energy to Xavier, but I have needs. Come on."

Thomas laughed and they raced through Paris. When they arrived at another nameless brothel, they took a seat in the corner as Anthony observed the men around them. He pointed out a young man who sat alone, watching the room in awe.

"Can you imagine going to bed with him?" Anthony asked.

"No," Thomas answered. "Will you explain what mission we went on?"

"It was a test. I wanted to see something for myself. Xavier has a calming effect on you. I had you angry about the Catholic Church, and then I wanted you to see him. There you were, in the midst of a most hilarious and scathing attack on the pope, when you fell silent and looked at Xavier with total adoration until he left." Anthony looked away when his prey went back to the bar. Anthony stared at the young man, then spoke. "It's simple. Underneath your gruff exterior, you're quite sensitive, which is what draws you to Xavier." Anthony smiled at the young man across the room, making him blush. He returned the grin before staring into his beer.

"You can go to him in a minute," Thomas said, rolling his eyes.

"I'm leaving Paris and not returning, at least not for a very long time. They have gone too far, more so this time than ever before. And that's saying something. I'm not leaving because of you." Anthony paused when his prey switched tables, moving closer to the vampires. Anthony sent a beer to the young man via a barmaid. "You won't need me again. You love Xavier and he could become a wonderful mate for you. I'll condone whatever happens. But never do anything against his will." Anthony looked at Thomas. "I'll even sanction your changing him into a vampire, so long as it's *his* choice. Do you hear me?"

"You have my word."

"Then you have my blessing."

With that, Anthony kissed Thomas on the lips and held his head. "Go to him. And, if you'll be so kind, leave this establishment so that I may get on with the night's business."

Forty-Eight: Hiding Pirate

2 SEPTEMBER 1793

Catherine's eyes deceived her. Marcel's letter from just the day before described him still in America. Yet she was sure that Marcel stood down that alley, selling Indian remedies. She ordered the driver to halt and jumped out before he opened the door.

"It *is* you," she said, staring at him.

"Catherine," Marcel mumbled. "What brings—"

She stormed back and hopped into the coach, which lurched away as Marcel ran to the window and begged for Catherine to listen. She ignored him, but he jumped onto the runner and clung to the exterior as the horses clopped through Paris. Something about his charming persistence kept her from pushing him off, so he stayed until they got to the house. She headed inside to an empty parlor, hoping he would follow.

Catherine's head spun with rage one minute and sympathy the next. When Marcel appeared in the doorway, she broke into a big smile despite her anger. "America?"

"Can I offer you some wine?" Marcel's soothing voice controlled her rage, but he would not easily woo her, she told herself, without a complete explanation. "I arrived today, and of course, I was going to come see you, but some of my clients insisted I first come to them. Will you forgive me? I was in America but weeks ago and dispatched a letter to you. I'd no idea business would necessitate my return this soon."

Marcel handed her a glass of red wine, which bubbled, though Catherine assumed she was seeing things, so she took a big swig and a feeling of numbness and peace swept through her.

"It was my fault," Marcel said as he eased over and stroked Catherine's hair. "I should have come to you sooner. Perhaps I've neglected you too long."

Marcel handed Catherine another glass of wine, which she drank. Her glass also fizzled, but it came from the same bottle so Catherine figured it was a trait of the wine. A tingling sensation swept through her, more powerful than from the first glass; and her private parts throbbed and moistened. She snuggled up to Marcel.

"I wish you'd tell that awful friend of your brother's not to interfere in your family. Thomas is a liar and troublemaker."

"What did Thomas do? He just wants to bed my brother."

"He's more evil than that." Marcel's tone alarmed her. "Thomas threatened my life if I continue to see you. He demanded that I never come here again."

Catherine's head whirled. She sat up, uncomfortable with her swooning, and fought to control her senses. She corrected her posture but allowed Marcel to hold her hand.

"Besides, two *men* can't court."

Catherine patted his hand. "Leave them alone."

"You're not drinking your wine."

"I've had enough. Will you please forget Thomas? I want to talk about us."

Marcel hesitated. His face convulsed with anger and reddened, but he softened.

"Just promise you'll be careful around Thomas. I'm sorry to say I'll soon sail again for the New World, New Orleans, but I want you to go with me."

"What would you think of my sailing just before winter?" she asked. "I can't go right now. If you give me a couple of months, I can finish some work here and join you later, and maybe Xavier will come."

Marcel winced. He stood and pulled Catherine out of her chair, grabbed her from behind, and yanked her toward him, smashing their bodies together, their faces just inches apart. He kissed her with force and sent electricity through her body.

"Come to me in New Orleans as soon as you can," he said. "Promise you'll hurry. Maybe Thomas will have taken Xavier away by then and we can be alone."

He kissed her again and was about to leave when he turned around. "I almost forgot. How are your nerves?"

"The same."

Marcel reached into his bag and handed her more headache elixir. He left with another kiss and sweet grin.

Catherine closed the door and fell onto a fainting couch, exhausted. Contradictions and confusion spun through her head as she tried to convince herself she had made the correct decisions. When she at last saw straight, Catherine started with surprise when a man entered the room. Her heart calmed when she saw Jérémie, though he looked menacing.

"Jérémie," she acknowledged.

"Can't you see what that man is doing to you? Do you think all these medicines are for your headaches?"

"You were spying on us?"

"Only for your protection."

"Michel did enough to try to control my relationships and died knowing that he was wrong. There's no need for someone to take his place. You'll have to accept my decisions, or you can leave." Catherine stood her ground and watched Jérémie turn from a defiant giant who surprised her into a little puppy, rebuffed and retreating with his tail between its legs.

Forty-Nine: Xavier's Struggle

8 SEPTEMBER 1793

An empty pit still sat in Xavier's stomach since he'd learned of Thomas's vampirism. His journey back to serving people and working with Maria failed to fulfill him. Nothing soothed his pain, his head spun, and his heart ached. He still pined for Thomas.

Yet why had Thomas hid it for so long from him? And he had killed those men who'd attacked Xavier without remorse. One person could help Xavier, and it was not Maria. And so he found himself outside Thomas's door, nervous. He leaned against the wall to find the courage just to knock.

Xavier took in Thomas's luxurious life, even by Saint-Laurent standards, as he delayed the inevitable. His flat was decorated to make even a king jealous and located among Paris's former nobility. Xavier had always suspected Thomas's wealth based on his clothing, yet Thomas's rare mention of his past indicated he'd come from the lower sorts. The vampirism explained the discrepancy. He stared at the gold-encrusted nameplate when he heard someone coming from down the street.

"You can't be here," a lad of about sixteen ordered. "Mr. Lord refuses guests unless invited." He was courteous but betrayed his alarm.

"I came to see Mr. Lord," Xavier said. "Can you tell him I'm here?"

The servant sighed. "Perhaps I can give him your name, but that's all."

"Xavier Saint-Laurent."

The lad's eyes lit with recognition and he hesitated. "If you'll wait a moment, Abbé," he said as he took out a key and entered the flat.

How did he know Xavier? Xavier's heart sank as each second ticked by, sure Thomas would turn him away or, worse, be angry. Then he heard rustling and Thomas yanked the door open.

"Xavier!" Thomas grabbed Xavier's hand and pulled him inside. The interior was just as lavish, though darker. "Please, sit. Can I get you anything? Some wine?"

Xavier wanted the wine to calm his nerves but thought better of it. "No, thank you," he answered.

Thomas sat across from him and waited, but Xavier panicked inside. Thomas got up and came to Xavier on the couch, put his arm around him, and held his hand. "What is it?"

"I wanted to see you because—" Nothing sounded right.

Thomas touched Xavier's hair and looked into his eyes, his brown eyes piercing Xavier's soul in return. But the soft expression gave him courage.

"I left you that night because I was so confused. I should not have behaved that way. And I trust you won't hurt me again."

Thomas shook his head.

"I just wanted you to know." Now, Xavier grabbed Thomas's hand with both of his for courage and stability. "I came because I don't know how to feel or what to do. I still love you." Xavier's heart pounded through his chest as Thomas hugged him closer.

"I love you too. You'll always be my little abbé."

"I tried to go back to serving people," Xavier continued. "But I don't trust humanity as I used to. But I can't give it up, either. I'm lost. In the past, I always fled to the church, not because it answered any of my questions, but because I could hide. But Maria's didactic pronouncements run cold in me. I suppose you know she despises you. She thinks you're the devil."

Thomas smirked and nodded.

"Sometimes, Maria is insightful and loving, but other times, she becomes a frightened child. I can't live in the world again." Xavier paused to catch his breath. The more words that came out, the better he felt. "I mean, what is religion? Why do humans crave it and talk about loving each other while making more rules and condemning? Religion either functions as the most profound statement of our love or the ugliest tool for oppressing I've ever seen. And then there's you. You confuse me even more. Are you a monster?"

"Not to my knowledge."

"Then what are you?" Xavier asked.

"That is far more difficult to answer." Thomas held Xavier's hand as if afraid to ever let go, nothing but devotion and love emanated from his eyes. "I've no idea what created me. I know as much as you, which is nothing. My emotions are the same as when I was human. There's nothing evil about what I think or do most of the time, and it's never outside of what is typical human behavior. The vampires I've met act like any group of people. Some are good and some quite vile. So I don't know where vampires came from or why we're here. The difference is just in our strength and ability to defy aging and death. We die only in sunlight or fire. I'm not sure if that helps you. I know you want more."

Xavier believed him, not because he analyzed every sentence or because Thomas manifested some rational explanation, but because his instincts told him the truth. Xavier leaned his head into Thomas for comfort, and his hard chest strengthened Xavier's conviction and pulled him toward the vampire.

Thomas kissed Xavier's head. "Maybe the world is simpler than you imagine. Maybe you should allow things to exist without judgment, even upon yourself."

"I'm frightened of this final leap. What happens if I transform?"

"No transformation would affect how you see things. My passion for life intensified in death because I lost the fear of mortality. You'll still be yourself if you transform, but more protected from dying. You could even continue to help people." Thomas hugged him. "Besides all that, I want you to join me. I want you by my side forever."

Hearing that Thomas wanted him to become a vampire sent chills through his bones. Was he ready for that step? "I'm scared."

"I know." Thomas hugged Xavier tighter. "I am, too. I'm afraid of losing you. I would do anything to take care of you forever and ever."

Xavier tried to lose himself in the moment but doubt plagued him. "Does this mean it all means nothing? Is everything arbitrary? I spent my entire life trying to live up to the angelic status bestowed upon me by my father, Catherine, and Michel. I thought it must be true if they always expected it of me. I thought that God would give me a vision so I could understand the lofty position they put me on, but that never worked. Do I sound mad?"

Thomas again kissed Xavier's head. "None of us chooses a destiny. It's impossible. You were placed in a loving family that perhaps cared too much, but now you need to release yourself of that burden so you can experience life. Your childhood, and everyone's, is not your own doing. Adulthood is much different. You're free to choose a path that befits the man you've grown into."

Xavier wanted to follow his advice and believed it deep in his heart. But what if Thomas left him? Were there any guarantees?

Thomas kissed his head again, then kissed Xavier's cheek. Xavier fell limp in his arms, and when he whispered into his ear, shivers of passion coursed through his body.

"I love you, Xavier. That's the one thing I can guarantee. My heart belongs to you."

THE FIRST TIME

Sitting in his parlor, Thomas kissed Xavier's ear again. The smell of Xavier's perfumed body intoxicated him. He picked Xavier up and carried him into the bedroom, placed him on a pillow, and stretched out next to him, then caressed Xavier's cheeks and looked down at his yielding body.

Xavier wrapped his arms around Thomas. "Do you mind if I ask you something else?"

"Of course not."

"What made you?"

"Anthony made me by having me drink his blood. That's all I know."

"Were you his lover?" Xavier questioned with a worried expression.

"That's even more complicated. For a time, perhaps, but not anymore, so don't worry. We were incompatible as lovers." Thomas wanted to tell Xavier the entire story of his making and life in America, but now hardly seemed the time.

Xavier kissed Thomas on the cheek. "And you can die only from the sun?"

"Or fire. We'd burn to ash."

"If I join you, then, you'll make me one? A vampire?"

"If you wish." Thomas's heart soared with hope.

"And you wouldn't leave me afterward?"

Thomas embraced Xavier, trying to force the fear out of him. "Never."

"Tell me more about this life." Xavier played with Thomas's hair.

"Let's see." Thomas ran his finger along Xavier's face. He leaned in so their bodies touched. "You'll have the same body as you do now, which is perfect." Where Thomas had the muscles of a Greek statue, Xavier was leaner. He had no fat and some definition to his torso, but for the most part, he had the boyish appearance that Thomas adored: an attractive, feminine face, soft skin, and a hint of muscles all around. "You'll never worry about money, you'll have powers of persuasion beyond belief, and little can harm you."

"But the killing."

"It's not arbitrary. There's an ethic vampires follow that Anthony taught me. We never kill the innocent. It's to be done to feed ourselves, and then it must be someone worthy of death who harms others."

Xavier fell silent as he twirled more hair in his hands. "I hope I can do this," he whispered.

"Take things slowly. We'll make sure that you're convinced before we do it."

The ultimate sacrifice arrived, that Thomas refused to take Xavier despite his obvious vulnerability, and demonstrated to Thomas his most profound love for the man.

Xavier's eyes filled with tears as he clung to Thomas. "Are you sure you don't want someone with fewer problems?"

Thomas held Xavier even harder, again hoping to squeeze out the pain. "You're the one I love. My longing and love for you are so overwhelming I know this is right."

Xavier smiled and wrapped both arms around Thomas, who watched as he fell toward Xavier, but his abbé gave no sign of discomfort and instead closed his eyes and yielded.

"Be mine, Xavier."

"I already am."

Thomas kissed Xavier, who opened his mouth, their tongues intertwined with passion. Thomas removed his coat, then Xavier's and stripped them of all their clothes. He kissed every inch of Xavier's body, followed by Xavier exploring every inch of Thomas in return.

Being cautious about his strength, Thomas braced his hands on either side of Xavier's shoulders and hovered above. Just his head bent so they could kiss. Without prompting or force, Xavier lifted his legs and Thomas held them up as he sank closer to Xavier, who accepted all of Thomas. His body writhed with pleasure. As he moved in and out of

Xavier, he groped Xavier to help him climax at the same time that Thomas erupted inside Xavier.

Thomas then lay next to Xavier and cuddled. They lay that way for over an hour, neither saying a thing, neither wanting the moment to end. When they moved, however, Thomas sensed something was wrong.

Xavier sat up, stretched, and put his clothes on while Thomas remained naked on the bed. Neither said a word, but the predictable tears in Xavier's eyes did not surprise him, though they tugged at his heart.

"It's not you," Xavier said.

"I know," Thomas answered.

"I just can't—"

"You don't need to explain anything. I'll be here when you need me."

Xavier cried as he returned to the bed, sat down, and grabbed Thomas's hand. "I know you're not a monster." He played with Thomas's finger. "I'm not even worried about God or sin. But the killing. I can't—"

Streams of tears ran down his face. Thomas felt awful and helpless as he tried to comfort Xavier by holding him and letting the abbé rest his head on his shoulder.

"I don't think I can kill," Xavier said. "You deserve someone without these issues."

"If you think I can leave now and forget everything I feel, then you're more blind than I realized."

The pain on Xavier's face showed that the words cut him to the core.

"I'm sorry," Thomas said. "I didn't mean that."

"Wouldn't you rather have someone longing for eternal life?"

"No. I love you." Thomas cried, too, which he hated because his tears stained his face red.

"I'm not ready to give up on people. And I can't kill, even the most degenerate of them."

"Try as you might, you won't convince me to go away. So you have to realize that what happens between us, you must initiate." He pulled Xavier closer. "I love you."

"And I love you."

"Then leave it at that. There's no reason to worry about your inability to become a vampire. Can't we just embrace the fact that we're together again?"

Xavier nodded. Drained of all emotion, they agreed to return Xavier to the Saint-Laurent home. They walked in silence, holding hands in the deserted streets until reaching the doors. Thomas escorted Xavier to his room and kissed him goodbye, which started them both crying again.

Thomas cried most of his way home. At least Xavier got to fall asleep and forget some of his misery. Thomas had the rest of the night to think about it. Through all the agony, Thomas always focused on Xavier's trying to accept his true feelings and assumed that their relationship could begin once that happened. How had he ignored the even larger problem? Xavier was too innocent to fall into a life of killing for survival. Anthony had been right again.

Fifty: Jérémie's Sign

11 SEPTEMBER 1793

Since they'd made love, the nights passed more strangely than Thomas would ever have predicted. Xavier and he resumed their routine meetings and even had sex, yet neither mentioned the vampirism. That night, Xavier greeted him at the door and explained that a former parishioner had come to him for a baptism, so, despite having left the church, Xavier was doing the service in the chapel. To occupy his time while waiting, Thomas joined Catherine in the parlor.

She and Jérémie sat discussing what to do next with the salon, since so many avoided it for fear that Robespierre's thugs would appear. The hospital, too, had become less important because most people were murdered now. Not caring about the revolution, which bored him, Thomas instead observed Jérémie and Catherine. He could not believe she had no idea about Jérémie's utter and transparent devotion. Thomas was about to excuse himself when Jérémie shouted at Catherine without warning.

"You're still taking that?" He pointed to a small vial.

"It's not your concern," Catherine answered.

"For the love of God, your independence becomes insane blindness. Why would all of us lie about it? Wait here," Jérémie commanded and stormed out.

To Thomas's surprise, Catherine obeyed. Neither said a word, Catherine because she was as angry as her bright red face indicated and Thomas because it would be too awkward to do so.

"I won't stop," Catherine said to no one. "This talk about magic and potions is ridiculous."

Thomas remained silent, obeying Anthony's rule not to interfere. It had become difficult to remain true to the ethic after Xavier revealed that Marcel murdered Michel.

"What do you think?" Catherine startled Thomas by asking.

Thomas still fumbled for an appropriate answer when Jérémie came back with Anne, letting him off the hook.

"You brought your ally, but she knows I don't believe it and I doubt there's much either of you can say to change my mind about Marcel."

"I'm not here to interfere with your love life. I see the potion has hold of you and know there isn't much I can do if you refuse to see it."

"Then why are you here?" Catherine asked.

"Catherine, at least listen to her," Jérémie said.

"Make it quick."

"You're the feistiest one I ever met."

"I told you that I wasn't interested in hearing about witches and warlocks."

"And so you won't. Hear me out, though."

"I'm listening."

"If it's the headache medicine as you suggest, and not a spell, then will you do Jérémie a favor because he cares for you? You don't have to agree with it. You can think he's all wrong, but it'd make him feel better. What if I gave you a small amount of a counter-potion I made, nothing that'll harm and nothing that would reverse the effects of a headache medicine. But, if we're right, it'll combat the spell. Will you do that for Jérémie?"

Though Anne struck Thomas as blunt, she acted as a politician quite well. He wondered if it was in preparation for the item she had promised Xavier was on its way from America.

"Ridiculous."

"For Jérémie. It could prove you right, after all. What's the harm in that?"

Catherine glared from Anne to Jérémie, then shrugged. "I suppose." Catherine took a pouch from Anne and listened to her instructions for taking one scoop of the powder with wine once a day.

"Do it for a couple of weeks," Anne said. "Then we can talk. If nothing changes by that time, I'll apologize and take it back. It may take some time. He's a tricky one, that Marcel. You do this a couple weeks and we'll see how you're feeling."

Catherine shook her head, her expression full of suspicion. "It won't change a thing," she said.

"Then there's no harm in doing a favor for a friend, is there?"

Catherine rolled her eyes and sighed. "Very well. But only because Jérémie has been a very good friend for a long time."

With that, Jérémie withdrew from the room with Anne.

"Will you take the potion?" Thomas asked Catherine. "I mean, do it and not pretend?"

"Yes," Catherine answered. "To prove that nothing will change. I don't want to risk their finding out that I did nothing and then hearing again and again about some stupid spell."

Thomas changed the subject to avoid the topic and move on to his personal interests. "I don't suppose Xavier talked to you?"

"No. He came back the night you told him about the undead thing, or whatever you call it, irate that I knew about you and hid it from him. I fretted that he was going back to some dogmatic religion, and for a time, it seemed he tried. Now, he walks about as if nothing has changed in all these years since he met you. He acts as if you're just dear friends who spend time together. Don't be embarrassed, but he did share that you had intercourse. Is that what you call it with two men? At any rate, I know the depth of intimacy you share, but beyond that, I've no idea about his intentions. He loves you. That much is painfully obvious, but he says nothing else."

Catherine said her thoughts all in one breath, thus returning to her usual self. Thomas chatted with her a while longer but learned nothing new about Xavier. He bid her good night and went to find his abbé.

Part X: Conversion

Fifty-One: Mayhem

16 OCTOBER 1793

As with the revolution outside that spiraled out of control, Xavier's confusion had continued to rage within himself over the past month. His desperate heart desired to run away with Thomas and learn to kill evil people, while his mind instructed him that he could never bring himself to murder.

Of course, Xavier cherished that Thomas came each night, and the fact of Thomas's vampirism no longer bothered him. And the sex was wonderful. Xavier never imagined such utter bliss and wondered how he ever thought the celibate life of a priest could hold him forever.

To get his mind off it, Catherine, Maria, and he headed out to see Paris. While it distracted him from Thomas, it disgusted him to see what France had become. Fear governed Paris. One after another, they passed the guillotines, thankfully silent but present nonetheless. The public nature of the executions bothered Xavier even more. They became events, not deaths, and people lined up to witness the latest head come flying off a body. Xavier almost vomited the day he saw citizens picnicking in front of the guillotines. Hawkers plied their wares near the scaffolding, selling wine and biscuits to the throngs who gathered for a little "thrill." Others placed bets on the order of execution.

They strode through the streets in silence until someone told them that Marie Antoinette had been executed.

"Good Lord," Maria gasped and crossed herself. "They're mad."

"Stop talking about this in public," Xavier admonished, but too late.

"Mademoiselle Saint-Laurent, yes?" a uniformed officer asked.

"Yes," Catherine said.

He tipped his hat to thank her without saying a word.

Catherine rolled her eyes and remained calm, which steadied Xavier's nerves. Though she still insisted that Anne's counter-potion did nothing, she had agreed to continue with it for another month, and in the last few days, Xavier had noticed a change. Nothing dramatic, but she seemed less interested in Marcel, less enthralled with mention of his name.

As Catherine launched ahead, Xavier fell back with Maria.

Maria sighed. "Thomas is Satan. I'm glad you work for God again."

"I told you, and I know you don't want to hear this, but I'm not returning to the Church."

She grunted and trudged ahead, but it irritated Xavier more than usual so he stopped. "What is it? Why stay in the church?"

"I stay because I made a pledge I intend to keep."

"To whom? You hate the Roman authorities as much as I do."

Maria stalked back to Xavier. "We all need something to guide us, and I don't understand why you insist on denigrating what is important to me. Can we leave it at that?"

Her comments befuddled Xavier. He agreed, on one condition, just to make peace. "I'll agree if you stop berating Thomas."

She shook her head, her face red, but he had her trapped.

The sight of another guillotine took his attention elsewhere. Xavier questioned all he believed about humankind. What if wickedness was just as common as purity? These decapitations proved something evil lingered in the people of Paris who watched the beheadings as a sport.

Unable to cope, Xavier waved to Maria and ran through Paris, bumping into people and almost sick, not stopping until he reached home where he threw himself on his bed. Once again, his world spiraled out of control. He escaped into sleep, and though early in the day, he drifted off to dream of better things.

Fifty-Two: Murder

18 OCTOBER 1793

Xavier continued to ponder his dilemma, no closer to a solution, when he heard screams and shouts at the door. With Catherine and Jérémie gone for the day, Xavier ran down the stairs in time to see four thugs, dressed in uniforms, smash clubs over the heads of two guards and storm into the foyer.

"We hear this house don't support our government," one said.

"And we hear that nuns are harbored here," another shouted.

"I don't know what you mean," Xavier lied.

"Out of the way." With that, he shoved Xavier to the ground and the four rampaged through the first and second floor, destroying artwork, overturning tables, and assaulting anyone who got in their way. Xavier followed them, but they continued to shove him aside, the officer who had asked Catherine her name the other day among them. Fearing they meant to harm the nuns, Xavier slunk toward the basement and into the dank cellar.

Too late, he realized his mistake, for one of them spied Xavier leaving and was close behind. Xavier stopped in the wine room and turned to go back upstairs.

"Who is it?" Maria called from behind him.

The fiend grinned, strode toward Xavier and, before Xavier could do anything, smashed his fist into Xavier's face, causing Xavier to crash into a wine rack and crumple to the ground.

Xavier had no idea how long he'd lain there, but he awoke in a pool of blood, his head aching. He checked to see that the bleeding had stopped as he got up with great care. It took a few moments to gain his senses, to recognize the wine cellar, and to recall what happened. He looked around at the overturned racks and smashed bottles. One of the fiends lay in a corner with a piece of glass sticking out of his head. He still breathed.

Then Xavier panicked. When the room stopped spinning, Xavier went toward the hallway that led to Maria's rooms. He stopped, bent over, and vomited.

There was a nun's dismembered body, naked and torn limb from limb, her head smashed against the wall. Xavier cautiously continued down the hall but heard nothing as he stepped around the flesh and blood splattered everywhere. His heart pounded.

In the first room, he discovered another nun, tied naked to a bed, her body intact but her head hanging to the side at a grotesque angle. She, too, was dead. Again, he vomited as he progressed and found one after another of the nuns, naked and bloody, raped and murdered.

Now, he cried, his head whirled, and then he thought again of Maria. Where was Maria?

As he walked back toward the cellar, rage infused his soul. Tears streamed down his face and mixed with the dried blood as he seethed, letting his fury take control in the wine cellar. Without hesitating, he picked up a sharp piece of glass, lunged at the bloodied man in the corner and stabbed him over and over in the chest until his breathing stopped. Dead. Killed. Murdered.

For the first time, Xavier understood justice, which his theology had lacked with its sense that God punished those who sinned. He spit in the man's face.

His body ached as he climbed the steps, noticing a trail of blood, a continuous stream two feet wide and thick. Xavier stopped, toppled over, and heaved again. He knew whose blood covered the floor before he reached the upper hallway and found Maria lying facedown, unable to move farther.

"No, no, no." He knelt beside her still-breathing body, lifted her head onto his lap, and cradled it in his arms. His body convulsed into sobs as he held her. She bled a lot between her legs and her head was black-and-blue, and yet slowly she opened her eyes. At first, she recoiled until she recognized Xavier, then rested her head back on his legs.

"I tried to stop them." Now, she coughed up blood. "I got one of them in the cellar."

"Shh, Maria, shh. I'll get a doctor."

"No," she said with conviction despite laboring to breathe. "Stay with me."

He obeyed.

"I thought they had killed you, too, when I went by your body. They raped us."

"Shh, save your strength. Please don't die. I know what they did. We'll catch them."

"I don't want to live."

"Shh, you'll heal. I need you. I already lost Michel. I can't lose you too."

She shook her head and called him closer. "Abbé, listen to me. I hope you know that I always loved you. You were my best friend."

"I know. I love you too. Now please be quiet." Xavier wanted to deny her next words.

"I can't live with this humiliation. Don't call the doctor, Xavier. Please take me away."

"What about your faith? You can't give up on your faith now. Suicide is forbidden."

"That's why you need to do it, and give my final rites." More blood came from her mouth. Maria closed her eyes as if to gather strength, her voice serious but not angry. "I wasn't always right. I tried to do the right thing, but it didn't always happen how it should. Please don't hold that against me. I just need to know I'm going to a better place."

"Of course, you are, of course."

"God gave me a message." Maria paused, breathing with tremendous effort. "First, He said that you'd live. I told Him I saw you lying in blood, but He said you'd live to preserve goodness through eternal life. Go to Thomas. Continue our work."

Xavier cried a violent grief. He did not want to hear what she said. Not another dead beloved, not now.

"I can't ki—" He started to say it. But he realized that he *had* killed. A moment ago, he murdered the one monster left inside.

"Be merciful," Maria pleaded. "It hurts. Help me now by ending this and in doing so find the strength to go to Thomas. Continue our mission."

Maria gasped out the last words. Her chest heaved and blood dripped from her lips. But she was alive and might survive for some time, perhaps until others arrived, and then the shame that she so feared would begin.

Do it for her. Swiftly, he got out from underneath her, hurried to his father's den, took down a sword, and clutched the handle. He ran back and stood over her, before leaning over and caressing her head.

He kissed her forehead, and said, "I love you." Then he stood upright, lifted the sword over his head, and whacked it down, slicing her throat open.

WAR AND PEACE

The front doors to the Saint-Laurent home stood wide open with no guards, and a loud cry of anguish reverberated from within. Catherine ran down the street, climbed the stairs, and hurried inside.

Maria lay on the marble floor, naked, bloodied, and with her neck sliced wide open. Xavier wavered above Maria with a sword. The guards lay nearby, both dead. Catherine fought her panic and controlled herself, telling herself that Xavier could explain the scene.

"What are you doing?" she asked in an even voice.

Xavier hesitated, swayed, and dropped the sword before standing immobile. She went to him and pulled him away.

Hearing people walk by outside, Catherine made sure to bolt the doors shut, then she ran through the house, pulled the curtains, and locked every door from inside. Xavier had disappeared by the time she returned to the foyer, but she found him in the living room, closing the drapes, helping her conceal the attack.

"What happened?" she asked, hoping he'd answer.

"We don't have time. You're still in danger. Come on." Xavier tugged her along. "There are bodies everywhere."

They hurried to the servants' quarters and gathered cleaning supplies, an unspoken communication telling them to clean the house and bury the evidence.

Catherine took control. They first explored the second floor but found nothing but destroyed furniture and possessions. Then they went to the first floor and dragged the bodies to the wine cellar. They returned upstairs and cleaned everything, scrubbed the walls, the floor, discarded broken furniture and did their best to make it look as if nothing happened. Halfway through, she ordered Xavier to take a bath and get rid of his clothes, though his black-and-blue face would still give away an attack. She was appalled to find a glass shard sticking out of his head and marveled that he had survived at all.

Finished up there, they turned to the gruesome basement. Thankfully, the family crypt lay deep in the ground, deeper even than the wine cellar and nuns' quarters. One by one, they moved the bodies, cleaned the stone, and repaired the damage. Again, they worked until finished, amazing Catherine at how they masked the crime. It took hours, and the sun was setting as they finished.

Once finished and safe, she grabbed Xavier's hand, forced him to lock the tomb, and headed upstairs. She needed three things: wine, to hear Xavier's story, and Thomas.

She poured two glasses of wine, reopened a curtain to watch the sun set, and sat down. Xavier shook but otherwise controlled himself. Without prompting, Xavier launched into his tale and told her everything. He explained hideous details, his response, and every emotion.

"How are you? You look composed, but is that possible?" she asked.

"I can't explain it to you," Xavier said in a flat tone but without his usual hint of total shock or despair. He got up and slumped next to her, sipping his wine and holding her hand. "This was predictable. The more this revolution persists, the more I lose faith in humanity. I've awakened more than ever to human evil."

"And Maria?"

Xavier's eyes filled with tears. "Her humiliation, fear, and pleading for death will haunt me forever. I was there to put an end to it. I killed two people. I acted the part of God and became executioner to an enemy and a friend." He looked out the window and paused. "But I have to continue with life. That's what she wanted and that's what I'll do."

It almost sounded too simple, but its very simplicity convinced her of its truth. Catherine had braced since childhood for the moment when Xavier would confront a harsh reality that collapsed his world.

Catherine ran her finger around the rim of her glass. "You're right. This was predictable, in a strange way. And we can't tell anyone. Of course, we'll tell Thomas, but otherwise, it's our secret. Yet another irony—that this heinous crime turns *us* into the criminals when the government did it."

"They'd frame us," Xavier added.

"At least in destroying the salon and turning this into a mere home again, we no longer threaten them. Besides, one of them died and that will only make them quieter."

Xavier nodded and fell quiet. "Do you believe me?" he asked after a long moment.

"I believe every word." Catherine hugged him.

Xavier got up in silence, paced the room, and then knelt before Catherine. He choked on the words, unable to speak, so Catherine said it for him.

"You'll go to him. Whatever that means. He may whisk you away and demand that you not return. I've no idea. But don't hesitate because of me. Even if I lose you, I'll be happy to see you liberated. Knowing you're with Thomas is all the comfort I need." Catherine, too, wept.

"I don't want to abandon you. I won't leave without saying goodbye. I promise."

Without responding, Catherine led Xavier to the hall and hugged him before opening the door for Thomas, confident that he alone could take care of her youngest brother.

CONVERSION

Xavier stood in the Saint-Laurent foyer, now scrubbed clean, and stared at Thomas, whose expression was one of horror when he saw Xavier's face. He glanced at Catherine, asking what happened without saying a word.

Catherine kissed Thomas's cheek. "Forgive me. I must attend to other matters."

"What are these bruises all over Xavier?" Thomas asked, as if he were not standing in front of Xavier.

"I have to go. Ask him. Come for dinner tomorrow. I'll talk then." Catherine hurried down the hall and slammed the door to her office.

Thomas stared at Xavier, searching for an answer. He seized Xavier and ran his fingers across his scalp as well as the wound that still throbbed, then carried Xavier into the parlor. Xavier yielded to him. Thomas placed Xavier in a chair and examined his wound again.

"No, Thomas, listen—"

"I don't know how you'll respond to this, but I insist." Thomas turned Xavier around and groped through his hair. A few seconds elapsed before Thomas ran his fingers across the cut, applying something wet and warm. When he finished, Xavier's head no longer hurt. He turned to face Thomas and discovered a cut on Thomas's arm as it healed itself before him.

They sat quietly before Xavier collapsed into Thomas, hugged him and cried.

Xavier purged himself of guilt by telling Thomas the entire story, remembering the horror. Xavier feared Thomas would think him evil and so elaborated every detail until Thomas stopped him with an embrace and assured him he believed every word. Then Thomas asked to take Xavier somewhere private.

Before leaving, Thomas further checked the house and surrounding area, and called for more guards via a passing boy whose eyes lit up when Thomas showed him ten golden coins. Thomas gave him directions to Xavier's parish and described the man he wanted the boy to get. Thomas waited for Denys and a couple of men to arrive to protect Catherine, paid the boy another handsome sum, and then instructed Denys to secure the house. Xavier allowed Thomas to take the lead.

Outside, Thomas lifted Xavier and away they went. Xavier could not tell if they literally flew above the ground or if Thomas just ran that fast because of the velocity and grace with which they arrived in the countryside and at an abandoned barn. Xavier shivered in the cool night before Thomas wrapped his coat around him and sat him in the loft, on top of hay and near a window. The wheat in the moonlit field in front of them swayed in the wind, the quietest, most peaceful scene Xavier had witnessed in forever. Thomas sat behind him with his legs around Xavier, then pulled Xavier back to rest against his chest.

"Could a vampire have stopped what happened today?" Xavier asked.

Thomas hesitated. "Not in the daylight."

"I killed today," Xavier said matter-of-factly.

"You told me about Maria. That wasn't murder."

"Don't forget the thug I stabbed. He was unconscious but alive, and I executed him."

"You did the right thing," Thomas said. "I would have protected you if I could have—"

"That's not what I meant," Xavier interrupted. "I'm trying to tell you that I'm not deranged, despite what you might think. I killed him and Maria, something I never expected I could do, but I know it was right." Xavier stopped. "This is all wrong."

Xavier pulled away and walked farther into the barn. All his words sounded contrived. Xavier covered his face and cried. Thomas retrieved him, guided him back into the hay, and engulfed Xavier in an enormous hug. He kissed the top of his head before they turned to face one another.

"Just tell me what you want to say," Thomas pled.

"I don't know what you call it, but I want to be with you. Will you take me?"

Thomas hugged Xavier tighter. "Of course, if that's what you want. Soon, I promise. But first I need to teach you."

"Does this mean you might not do it?"

"You know my heart won't change. But have you thought about the ethic and all that it implies? For example, you can't interfere with humanity. You can see people and interact with them. You can even save the innocent. But you can't get so involved with people that you knew in life."

"Should I follow the edict as well as you have with my sister and me?" Xavier grinned. Thomas grabbed and tickled him.

"I can explain where I went wrong later. We need to deal with you at the moment. Vampires have to conceal our supernatural abilities and hide our immortality. So you can't remain with those you love once I take you. It's too dangerous."

"I don't understand."

"Here's an example. I know more about Marcel than I've told you. I know he uses black magic. I know he tried to manipulate your family from America and returned to Paris long before he went to see Catherine. I've had many chances to kill him, but never did because it would interfere too much with your family, though I love Catherine. I've allowed it to develop without interference as much as possible. I acted to protect you."

Xavier nodded. "You won't let me see Catherine ever again?"

"Maybe. Can you do that?"

"*You* disobeyed. Why can't we ignore that part and beg forgiveness later? We could kill Marcel and protect Catherine, *then* worry about the ethic. He murdered my brother."

"I'm not a model vampire. But it's dangerous. I can't risk their wrath against you if you do something. I've fought too hard to win you to let them take you away."

"Who is this mysterious 'them'?"

"I don't know. Anthony and others who govern the vampires and ensure that we obey the ethic. They call themselves the Vampire Council. They have great power and act together. I want your assurance you'll at least consult with me before you do anything."

"Of course, you have my word. But there's one more thing."

"What?"

"It will be very hard for me not to protect Catherine. If I trust that we'll be open and you'll assist me, then I need to know how you transformed without emotional suffering. Weren't there people you left behind? Thomas, where do you come from?"

THOMAS LORD

Thomas played with Xavier's fingers but fell silent as he thought about the question.

"I didn't mean to pry." Xavier pulled away, but Thomas pulled him back with a gentle tug.

"I've never told anyone the entire story. Not even Anthony." Thomas ran his hand down Xavier's arm. "Where to begin? I'm American."

Xavier giggled, which relaxed Thomas.

"My father was born in the colonies, the son of a British official. But I never knew my grandfather or any of my father's relatives because he was banished for marrying my mother. She was an Indian, and she, too, was banished from her tribe. They met when my father went on a military expedition to explore the western territories of Massachusetts. I just remember that they were affectionate. They cultivated some land on the frontier, between her homeland and my father's but as far away from people as possible.

"My father's farm did pretty well, but he earned most of his income by trading. It was a precarious business. Some of the Indians didn't like that he took one of their own, and the Americans were wary. Yet plenty of people wanted to profit and my father's knowledge of both cultures was invaluable. We didn't live as Americans or as Indians. We just did things our own way. I was raised in an atmosphere that was both wonderful and alienating. I learned about both cultures, and my parents insisted that we not judge others for their choices. I was free to play with

Indians or white children. I liked running through the woods with Indian boys as they taught me about the land and how to hunt. Yet there weren't many people who visited us. Most of the time it was traders. My parents loved me, though their discipline could be harsh."

Thomas pondered how to continue. "Anthony says I always portray too happy a picture of my growing up. But there were bad times. And a lot of isolation. White people despised me for my 'savage' blood, and the Indians cast me aside because of my white father. So, while I could traverse either world, I belonged to neither. People made fun of me, and threatened me, too. It took a long time for me to understand, after too many mistakes, that this loneliness intensified my longing for a mate. It made me angry." Thomas hated saying these words out loud. It embarrassed him, but he had to say them to Xavier. "It made me violent."

"Shh. Stop. I have forgiven you." Xavier pushed himself up, grabbed Thomas's head, and pulled him into a kiss. "What else about your childhood?"

"There's nothing else. That was my entire life until I was twenty-six. I got a solid education from my father and mother, both practical and book learning. As I grew, I helped with the trading and became a very good interpreter, even better than my father. I stayed near my home and did my part as a dutiful son."

"You expect me to believe that you sat around the farm and obeyed all of their wishes?"

Thomas laughed. "I had a tendency to roam. I wanted to know what lay beyond the limits of our small world, so I traveled with Indians into western Massachusetts and with Americans to the east, often Boston. Though often alone or mocked when I went with people, I wanted to see other things. I never left the New England area, but at the time, it seemed so far away from home. Each time, my father reprimanded me, beat me for insubordination, and my mother used guilt. So I'd stay until called away again."

Thomas cringed at the next memory. "Then my world exploded. First, the war with France erupted. We lived between the Indians, French, and English, and none of us cared about their stupid war. But everyone tried to force us to choose sides. Our farm was raided and we were in constant danger. My mother and father pleaded with me to leave so I wouldn't be killed, but I had to protect them. I wandered the countryside, protecting my family and others caught between the factions, too many times it was unsuspecting Indians. In the middle of this, a friend who owned a small pub in a nearby village asked me to come see a new arrival who concerned him. He said the gentleman was British, but came around in the evening and refused to tell anyone his business."

"Anthony?" Xavier asked.

"Yes. I later learned that he came to watch the war. He was excited to observe how Indians fought. So, there he sat in the pub when I walked in. I was stunned by his beauty. I had always been comfortable with my attraction to men because my mother's brother had the same inclinations. I had always done sexual things with boys. It didn't take much for me to seduce Anthony. He relied on me to teach him about the war and Indians, and all the while, I was learning that there was something different about him. Long before he told me, I knew that he was a vampire."

"Didn't that frighten you?"

"No, I wanted him to convert me. So, I seduced him into making me a vampire. We were in love, though I deceived Anthony from the beginning."

"How?"

"I knew Anthony wanted to dominate in sex. So I played along."

"You? In the passive role?"

Thomas laughed, too, mostly because Xavier laughed so hard.

"I disdained it, but knew Anthony wanted it. This was my hope of becoming a vampire. So, I played the perfect lover, just like the little man in my arms tonight."

Xavier smacked Thomas on the shoulder.

"I fooled him until he admitted he was a vampire and transformed me. Then, over the next couple of weeks, I admitted what I had done."

"Wasn't he furious?"

"No. He was more disappointed than angry. Sad. We tried to be partners, but it was impossible, so we ended our sexual attachment. But he's my dearest friend. He taught me about the ethic and guided me through the transition as if we were still lovers and never held a grudge about what I had done. I still feel guilty about tricking him, because I really did like him."

"So you just left your parents forever?" Xavier asked.

"Yes. I often wonder what happened to them. But I made my decision and never looked back. We were a close family, but nothing compared to you, Michel, and Catherine. They never suspected I was leaving. To this day, I've no idea what they think. They loved me and taught me well, but their suspicion of others' motives kept them distant. Sometimes from themselves and often from me. So, to answer your question, when Anthony agreed to transform me, I left them. I thought of plotting some ruse to see them one more time or of saying goodbye, but my mother would have known I'd changed. It would have killed her." Thomas cuddled Xavier closer, kissed his ear, and whispered. "You're not like me, Xavier. I could abandon my former life and never miss it, but I don't expect you to feel the same way."

"Then what did you do?"

"Anthony and I wandered the globe and fell into a favorite pastime: watching humanity. It was intriguing to watch the American Revolution. I came to Paris when the vaguest rumors started that such a thing might happen here, but he hates the French and stayed behind."

"My God. You're almost sixty-five," Xavier said, stunned.

"Not so old for a vampire."

"But you look like me. I've always assumed, even after I knew, that you were my age. You could be my father."

"That's disgusting." Thomas tickled Xavier again until he begged him to stop.

Thomas rolled Xavier onto his back and pinned him in the hay. Xavier smiled, happier than Thomas had ever seen him. His eyes sparkled, his teeth gleamed, and he relaxed.

"So, that's it. I got to France, and then to Paris on a day I'll never forget, when I saw the most beautiful angel helping a lost child. I fell in love at once."

They made more passionate love than ever, then lay naked in the hay. Xavier fidgeted with Thomas's hair, and Thomas watched the clouds drift by, marveling that the little corner of France was so calm with the rest of it in complete upheaval. Xavier fell asleep after a while, using Thomas and their clothes as blankets, and Thomas watched him slumber in peace.

After a few hours, Thomas nudged his love awake.

"Shall we return you to Paris before the sun rises?" Thomas asked as dawn approached.

"Wait," Xavier said after they had dressed and Thomas started to whisk them away. "Will you make me a vampire?"

Thomas smothered Xavier in another hug. "You know I will. But do me one last favor. Wait one more day. Promise that you'll stay indoors away from danger, and I'll come for you first thing tomorrow evening. Then, if you still feel this way, I'll bring you to me forever."

Fifty-Three: Transformation

19 OCTOBER 1793

Thomas woke, anxious to take Xavier, but he had one item that could not wait. To calm his fears, Thomas raced through Paris even before the sun disappeared and hid outside the Saint-Laurent home. There Xavier sat at the window, waiting and safe. So, Thomas went to address a fear that engulfed him that morning as he drifted to sleep. Those fiends who had attacked the Saint-Laurent home remained at large.

With preternatural speed, Thomas combed Paris, listening to conversations and lurking in shadows. His journey took him to Robespierre's headquarters where he slipped in and pretended to be a soldier. Thomas passed among the guards, asking simple questions that might reveal who had ransacked the Saint-Laurent mansion. Then, spotting three brutes hovering together, one with a fresh scab across his face, Thomas knew he'd found them.

"We seek whores," one stated.

"Better be more careful than you were with them nuns," another responded.

"Never you mind that. We gave them nuns the thrill of their lives," someone else said.

"Yes," another sneered. "And that's why four of you left and three returned."

Thomas hurried outside to hide in the shadows, excitement coursing through his veins as he planned his torment. The idiots were lucky. Had Xavier died, Thomas would have tortured them alive for years. When they approached in drunken stupors, he stepped out of the darkness, picked all of them up, and leaped onto the roof of the nearest building, several stories up.

Each shook with complete terror, staring in horror at Thomas. He tied two together with their own clothes and attached them to a nearby post. They struggled to no avail. The other ran around the roof, screaming and searching for escape, and eventually jumped across an alley and onto another dwelling, but Thomas caught him with ease and dragged him back to the others.

"Do you remember those nuns? You will suffer for what you did." He broke both legs of the one who tried to run away. Then Thomas untied the second and cut out his entrails with his own knife. He, too, lived but could do nothing to save himself.

"Please, I didn't do it. They made me," the one still tied up lied. His earlier demeanor had betrayed him, however, as the leader of the gang.

"Die with dignity. That's more than you offered the nuns."

Thomas returned to the man with broken legs and lifted him off the ground. With his fingernails, he slit long cuts in the man's wrists, enough to bleed to death but small enough to allow him to witness more torture before he died. Thomas next jabbed into the exposed guts of the man who sat motionless and in shock. He screamed with each jab but hadn't the power to escape. When the first died, Thomas ripped out his organs.

"Do you see what it's like to torture the helpless?" Thomas asked their leader, who remained tied up. "Is it still so funny to think of those nuns?" Thomas clutched his throat.

"But I can change. Please don't kill me."

"Take off your clothes," Thomas said with a deliberate calm. "If you want to live. Hurry."

The man removed everything but his underwear until Thomas instructed him to get rid of those too. Thomas could not help but laugh that the man was aroused.

"When I'm done with you, you can leave. I'll make sure you won't die."

"I'll do anything."

As the man stood shivering, Thomas walked around him, glaring, and pricked his arm with a fingernail to get a taste of his blood. The man had no remorse, only self-pity. Tiring of the game and wanting to see Xavier, he reached around and ripped off the man's testicles, then applied some of his own blood to the wound to stop the bleeding and pain.

"Now you may live." Thomas patted him on the shoulder.

But the vampire was not surprised as the fiend bumbled to the edge of the building, peered to the street, and launched himself four stories to the ground and impalement on a light post. Pleased, Thomas left the bodies and hurried back to the Saint-Laurent house.

"Thomas!" Xavier exclaimed. "I worried you'd changed your mind."

"Never." Thomas hugged Xavier. "A matter demanded my attention."

"I'm ready. What do I need to do? Where will we go? Should I talk to Catherine?"

"Slow down. You'll see Catherine again. Why don't we walk to my flat?"

Xavier talked nervously the entire time and stayed close to Thomas until they arrived and hurried up the stairs.

"—so I avoided her all day because I couldn't hide my nervousness, but didn't want to anger you or betray some ethic I didn't understand—"

Thomas grabbed Xavier by the shoulders and stared into his eyes. "You may tell Catherine when you wish, and I'll protect you from making any errors that might endanger you. Calm yourself, or you'll have a heart attack before I can transform you." Thomas cupped Xavier's head and pulled him close. "I had to take care of the fiends who attacked you. I couldn't allow them to live."

Thomas held Xavier again, then guided him into the bedroom, picked him up, and placed him on the silky sheets.

Thomas lowered himself onto Xavier and kissed his forehead, cheeks, and last of all his lips. He undressed them, first Xavier and then himself, their kisses more impassioned than ever, their bodies stiff and yearning. Xavier spread his legs as Thomas gently inserted himself, and then his body went limp with pleasure as Thomas moved in and out while he grabbed Xavier and masturbated him. As they reached climax together, Thomas leaned over and sank his teeth into Xavier's neck.

Xavier's body collapsed as Thomas drank the blood and saw Xavier's life pass before him, with all the visions he anticipated: the loving, trusting abbé; the loyal brother; the affectionate soul; Xavier's vulnerability and need for reassurance; the utter devotion to their relationship. Thomas winced when he saw Xavier crying, both as a child and as an adult when tragedy struck. And his anger boiled anew when he saw what those bastards did to Maria.

Too quickly, the sweet taste of Xavier's blood stopped flowing down his throat. Thomas at once lifted the abbé's head, ripped at his own throat with his nails, and pressed Xavier against him to drink. The blood trickled into his mouth, Xavier taking his time before he sucked volumes into himself.

And so Xavier awoke from the dead, gone for but a second, and now lay with his vampiric eyes staring with Thomas, who admired his companion, brushed along his chest, and kissed him.

"My little abbé," he whispered in Xavier's ear. "Stand up."

Xavier obeyed. "I'm stronger," he exclaimed, wonderment in his eyes.

"Infinitely so. And you can move faster through the night."

Then Thomas grabbed Xavier and threw him back on the bed. Xavier yielded as they had sex, more passionate than before now that Thomas did not worry about injuring him.

At last satisfied, Thomas led Xavier into the street to teach him about his nature. They practiced moving with sudden speed, seeing through vampiric eyes, and watching crowds for danger. Then they hunted. Thomas explained the ethic once more and told Xavier how to pick a worthy victim. He watched his abbé kill to make sure he did not put himself in danger, but Xavier lured his prey with a unique grace, choosing a hardened murderer. Of course, he sought the worst of humanity. Then the angst came, as Thomas knew it would, so he helped his love through that, too. Xavier shuddered a bit but reminded himself over and over about the awful images he had seen in the victim's blood.

Thomas had never felt better than when they lay that morning in his coffin. Xavier's contented face grinned at Thomas, and he drifted away first, his vampiric blood not yet as strong as Thomas's. Thomas drifted to sleep, happier than ever before.

Fifty-Four: Delusions

21 OCTOBER 1793

Catherine sat alone in her office after waking on the sofa. She'd locked herself in the office to find a solution to what to do without her salon, to no avail before she passed out. Vying to regain control after she awoke, Catherine exited the office, walked through the library, and went to the parlor.

Wine and Marcel's potion brought her to her senses, and she regained confidence. Then, quite suddenly, she panicked at not having seen Xavier all night. Catherine's heart skipped, so she hurried down the hall to his room and found it empty. Next she ran to her room: vacant. She almost lost hope when she walked by her office door and saw a note attached in Xavier's handwriting.

> *Catherine,*
>
> *I am going with Thomas to England to see Anthony. Rest assured that all is well and we will come to you as soon as we return to France. Catherine, I have never been more in love!*
>
> *Xavier*

Happy for him, she hurried to her room to change her rumpled clothes and thought about Jérémie's return to live with her as she redid her hair. Other than Xavier, she was most comfortable with her longtime friend. Yet he brought a dimension of late that Catherine disliked in his penchant for championing Michel's causes, especially when it came to Marcel. Yet she was glad to have him living back at the house, since she realized Xavier would not be returning to it.

When Catherine heard a key in the front door, she went to greet Jérémie.

"My trunks will follow," he said. "Are you alone?"

"For now, which is why it's nice to have you here."

"Where's Xavier?"

"It's a rather long story. Suffice it to say he went to London."

Catherine ushered Jérémie into the parlor and poured him a glass of sherry, his favorite drink. Then she got herself some wine and tried to conceal Marcel's headache medicine.

"Do you still take that stuff? What about Anne's remedy?"

"Oh, don't fuss. I take that stuff that Anne gave me, too, but it has no effect whatsoever. It gives me more of a headache."

"Remember you agreed that I could bring Anne to the house today. I had planned—"

To Catherine's chagrin, someone at the door interrupted Jérémie, and then she sighed at seeing Anne.

"So, you're still convinced that the man has honest aims?" Anne asked with a blunt force.

Catherine almost lashed out, but stopped herself from such cruelty toward the woman who had saved Xavier.

"Catherine, please listen to Anne," Jérémie said.

"I respect your opinions and took your counter-potion as instructed, but it gave me a headache, a fierce one, and instead of reversing anything, it required more—" Catherine halted. For the first time, she questioned what Marcel gave her. She felt vapid. Why had she never questioned it? Why *did* she trust Marcel at all, let alone with her entire being? "I'll make you both happy, but just to prove my point," Catherine lied. "I'll return to my former doses of Marcel's medicine and take this 'potion' for another week. Then we can discuss it again. Agreed?"

Jérémie smiled, but said nothing while Anne howled with laughter.

"That's my girl, defiant to the end! We can talk in a week. Now, if you'll pardon me."

Catherine and Jérémie escorted Anne to the door and said goodbye. Something in Anne's stare startled Catherine. How much did the woman know? If she were correct about a spell, did she also sense Catherine's doubt? After all, why did Catherine cling to Marcel with such vehemence? *Was* it a potion?

Fifty-Five: London

30 OCTOBER 1793

Thomas still had a hard time believing that Xavier crossed over as they lay together in a coffin before sundown in England. The fledgling vampire lay next to him as Thomas caressed his soft cheeks and held the thin body tightly.

Thomas slid out from under Xavier, still in a sound sleep. Thomas had always awakened after the sun set before its light entirely disappeared. His ability to move about so early surprised even Anthony, who had taken years to leave the coffin before total darkness.

Since his conversion, Thomas took Xavier out each night to teach him about the ethic and to survive, disguise himself, and find appropriate victims. It continued to astonish Thomas that Xavier relished the new game, despite occasional bouts of doubt about killing. On the second night, Thomas forced Xavier to hunt alone to see that he could do it. Though Xavier obeyed, he did so as fast as possible and came back within minutes.

And tonight, they would go to Anthony. But first, Xavier needed one more lesson, one he'd avoided every night since his transformation. Thomas had no choice but to impose it upon Xavier, however, because the ethic demanded it. Yet even Thomas disdained killing a child. Xavier protested that it was unnecessary. He asked what child could threaten humanity.

Thomas knew better. Children, in fact, might pose a greater risk because mothers and fathers often believed their offspring, no matter how strange the accusation. One child, one sinister child, could play on society's weaknesses to create a witch-hunt for vampires.

As he paced the room, Thomas sensed Xavier's approach before his lover put his arms around his waist and hugged him.

"Hello, angel. Are you ready to see Anthony?"

"Of course." Xavier paused. "Now?"

"You know we can't."

"If the need arose, I'd protect myself, but to insist upon this makes no sense. It feels like torture. I'd snap a child in half if I saw it harming another."

Xavier's pleading eyes gave him a new conviction. He had defied the ethic countless times, and so he would again. If Anthony thought it so crucial, then he could do it himself.

"I won't make you."

"Thank you." Xavier buried his head against Thomas's chest.

They soon arrived at Anthony's and Thomas greeted the latest butler. For centuries, Anthony had maintained a palatial estate outside the city. He'd hired dependable staff that he kept for five- to ten-year stints because of good treatment and all too generous salaries. They seldom questioned his nocturnal habits, and Anthony disguised his eternal youth by sometimes leaving the country for a number of years and returning as the son of the man who'd left. Despite being new, the butler recognized Thomas.

"Mr. Lord, I'll inform Master Yates that you've come."

As the young man trotted off, Xavier leaned into Thomas. "Rather formal, isn't it?"

Thomas grinned and grabbed Xavier's chin before pecking him on the forehead. "Anthony likes to indulge in the opulent life of a British nobleman."

"It happened!" Anthony whisked around the corner, grinning from ear to ear. "All he's talked about since he first laid eyes on this handsome priest was making him a lifemate. He had profound lapses of judgment, and yet here the two of you stand, and *you*...one of the most attractive vampires I've seen," Anthony said as he looked Xavier up and down.

"You can stop the theatrics," Thomas said. "Xavier is your guest."

Anthony erupted with laughter. "Xavier, if I ever make you uncomfortable, tell me. Thomas and I have a strange relationship. I'd never mean to use you as a pawn in our little game. Welcome to our legion, and I mean this with all sincerity. You make a fine addition."

Anthony moved them down the hall and into a grand dining room before entering a smaller study in which they all sat in fine silk chairs.

"I heard before you arrived in London that Thomas transformed you."

"He has spies all over the world," Thomas broke in, more caustic than intended, but he despised the mysterious council's secrecy. "He learns too much about all of us. The Vampire Council, and all that."

"That's unfair. I don't watch your every move. Something of this magnitude came to my attention and I've nothing but approval. I need to remind Xavier to be careful in your interactions with humans. I know you'll see Catherine, which is fine, but avoid seeing the other people you knew in life."

"We'll obey the ethic," Thomas said.

"As you always do?" Anthony raised his eyebrow.

"You know I try."

"I'm not always convinced. I already trust Xavier more than you."

Thankfully, the conversation turned toward life in London and the mundane, yet with enthusiasm enough that in the blink of an eye, the three men spent an entire night together.

"Thank you for this evening. We need to go. Xavier's ability to resist the sun isn't as strong as ours. Any chance you'll join us in Paris?" Thomas asked Anthony.

"Not for a long time. I mean no offense, but I detest the French and this revolution."

"As if the English had nothing to be ashamed of." Thomas was glad to hear Xavier tease in return.

"We've our troubles, most of all with those damnable Americans."

"And so we depart his royal highness." Thomas bowed in mock deference. "I'll write soon, and no doubt your little spies will keep you informed of our whereabouts."

"I don't spy on you."

Thomas had never believed that assertion, but they departed with a hug.

"Hurry," Thomas told Xavier as the sun approached, although it was not yet visible. Xavier seemed tired and weak as his eyes drifted shut. Thomas cuddled Xavier, lifted him up, and ran toward their flat. As Xavier leaned his head on Thomas's chest, already asleep, Thomas used his cloak to shield Xavier lest the sun appear sooner than anticipated. Once home, he placed Xavier in the coffin but, before joining him, took a moment to watch his abbé sleeping like a peaceful child. He cherished the minutes before he fell asleep when he could gaze at his sleeping lover and hold him.

Part XI: The Stone Removed

Fifty-Six: Melisent Returned

1 NOVEMBER 1793

The weeks since Thomas had converted Xavier went quickly. And all the while Xavier and Thomas fell more in love. They talked a lot and lay in each other's arms for hours.

Yet on that night, Xavier alone wandered Paris for the first time since his transformation. Thomas had business, which bored Xavier, so he explored the city alone, no longer afraid because his vampirism protected him.

So much of him embraced his vampiric nature and relished the role as society's protector. The blood visions from the people he'd killed always assuaged any guilt. Thomas had given him strength whenever he faltered at his murdering, never belittling him and the more time that passed since his transformation, the more he accepted his acts of murder.

He had meandered for an hour before stumbling into his former parish. He almost did not recognize it, filthy with dirt and vagrants, decorated by the nearby guillotine. This scene forced Xavier to acknowledge the pit in his stomach. But why? Released from the church and his angelic image, with his sister safe and his love at his side, he expected tranquility, but instead found discomfort. And then it came to him.

He had lost all trust in humanity. He clung to protecting the guiltless, but with a cynicism that the world was doomed nonetheless. Xavier, the loving, trusting abbé, had lost his faith. That thought enveloped him when the perfect symbol came into view ahead: the ruins of his church, burned to the ground. Xavier approached and scooped ashes into his hand, letting them cascade like snow back to the earth.

"Sad, isn't it?" A woman's voice startled Xavier from behind.

"I didn't mean to frighten you," she said. "I'm just sad that they burned the church."

A beautiful woman stood before him, dressed in common clothes and holding a toddler's hand. The woman stared hard at the ground, a tear trickling down her cheek.

"I'm sorry, Mademoiselle. But no one cares about this place anymore."

Then she looked him in the eye, took a deep breath, and spoke in a quiet voice but with conviction. "I still care about this place and what it meant for me. Some of us still care, Abbé."

No one but Thomas had called him that in months.

"Don't you remember me? It's Melisent. And this is my son, Pierre," she said and instructed him to say hello, which he did with his head downcast and in a whisper.

At last, Xavier recognized her, the dancing, innocent eyes jarring his memory. She had grown into a woman since Maria and he had helped her flee Paris. Xavier recalled telling Thomas her story, about her rape by the man for whom she worked, her pregnancy, and getting her to safety with the story that she was a widow of the revolution. Xavier smiled and hugged her.

"Melisent, it's good to see you. I'm sorry about what I said, it's just—"

"I understand. I returned to Paris to introduce my son to my parents, but I also came to thank you for saving me. You're the most unselfish man I know. I'll always cherish you and the Church, no matter what the revolution brings. In my heart, I know that you did God's work."

"It was just my duty," Xavier said. "How did you return? What did you tell your family?"

"I told them the truth, and I told my husband." Melisent patted Xavier's arm and smiled. "It sounds mad, I know. I vowed that I couldn't live a lie with the man I married. So, after he'd courted me for some time, I took a great risk and the possibility of public humiliation and told him. I trusted him and knew that he loved me. How many young men in a village would court a widow with a child? No one else there gave me even a thought. They were all very kind and gentle. I was accepted but had no hope of marriage. Until André. And that night he asked me to marry him. We can't tell the other villagers, of course. We made this trip to Paris at my request and I told my parents everything."

"And their reaction?" Xavier asked.

"They were stunned to see me, even more so with a child and husband. But they accepted both Pierre and André." Melisent played with her son's hair before returning her gaze to Xavier. "We leave soon. André thinks Paris is too dangerous. He grew up in the country and has lived there his whole life. But I said I had to find you first for I owed you everything. I wasn't surprised to find the church gone, just sad, but God acted again in bringing you here tonight."

Xavier stood lost when a strapping man with blond hair and a farmer's hands ran around the corner.

"Melisent, there you are—I've been worried."

"André," she said, "I'd like you to meet Abbé Saint-Laurent." Melisent beamed with pride.

"Abbé, I've heard wonderful things about you. It's a pleasure," the young man said as he wrapped his arm around his wife. "I'd like to talk more, but we must go."

"Please, don't let me keep you," Xavier said.

André picked up the boy and started away, but Melisent waited. Her eyes welled with tears but a smile spread across her face.

"I doubt I'll ever see you again, Abbé. May I kiss you?"

Xavier stifled his tears and nodded. With that, Melisent pecked him on the cheek before returning to her husband, who took her hand and led them away. Alone in the blackened rubble, his tears burst from within.

Xavier prayed for the first time in months. He crawled to the altar's remnants and bowed his head.

"God, I don't pretend to understand. Your mystery confounds me. Yet you guide us. Even in my death, you watch over me. I won't forget again. I'll live a good life and protect people. You've called me back to your service, and I'm ready."

Xavier finished and wept in a huddled mass.

"Xavier, what happened?" Thomas sounded panicked.

Xavier wiped away the blood tears, grabbed Thomas's arm, and pulled him down, where the remaining brick walls and piles of charred wood concealed them.

Xavier reminded Thomas of Melisent's story, explained that she came to thank him, and told him about her. Then he told Thomas how it reminded him of his calling. "And that's why I'm crying."

Thomas seized Xavier's face in his hands. "I love *you*. Be yourself." Thomas stared into his eyes. "Be yourself. I'm happy for you." Thomas kissed Xavier.

They sat for a moment before Xavier felt Thomas giggling.

"What's so funny?"

"I've enough cynicism for a legion of vampires. We need you to balance us."

"Amen."

Fifty-Seven: Counterspell

6 NOVEMBER 1793

One of Thomas's servants told him upon waking that the government had executed Phillippe Egalité, the Duc D'Orleans. Thomas scoffed. The revolution bored him except that it upset Xavier, who worried that it more and more endangered Catherine. Thomas worked on some business while Xavier read in the other room until he heard a servant announce a visitor. He went to the study, where Xavier stood greeting Anne.

Thomas shot Xavier a look because of his clenched his jaw. "What's wrong?"

"I came about Catherine." Anne held up a bulging black velvet bag she had carried in with her. "I got something that might solve the problem."

"Now, after all these years, you decided to help?" Thomas spat.

Xavier put his hand on Thomas's knee, as he often did to calm him. "Let her explain. It took some time to get the last—what would you call it? Ingredient. I told you about this."

"Listen, don't think I came upon this action on a whim." Anne set the bag down. "I told you both a million times I don't do black magic. I tried simpler things, but it don't work. Catherine's too strong, and Marcel's potion even stronger. So I got this from America." She pointed at the bag. "Sent for it when you all found Xavier again and I realized that spell was still on Catherine. My friends there don't do black magic any more than I do. I convinced them of the urgency."

"What's in that bag?" Thomas asked.

"You don't want to know. I best be getting to my bridge. Hurry and bring her."

Terrified, Xavier begged Thomas for help. They headed out at once.

"How are you?" Thomas asked Xavier, who walked with silent determination toward the Saint-Laurent home.

"I'm afraid."

"Don't shut me out."

"I'm sorry," Xavier whispered. "Just nervous. You know how she'll react."

The rest of the way, Xavier said that he would get to the point before his courage left him but not before they arrived. And that he did, for they walked through the door and into the parlor when Xavier spoke to Catherine.

"Thomas and I came for a specific reason. I haven't been the best brother because I treaded lightly for fear of angering you. Forgive me, I love you. And please don't dismiss my comments as an attempt to control you. But you need to stop taking this potion and get away from Marcel. He's dangerous."

Catherine stared daggers back at him, like a trapped animal. She poured wine into the glass, opened a canister, and spooned in a heap of grayish-blue powder. Then she gulped it down.

Catherine backed away. Then, without a word, Xavier moved into action. In seconds, Xavier swept across the room, captured his sister, and escaped into the Paris night. Catherine screamed in protest as they raced through the streets too fast for anyone to see. Thomas followed until they came to the underneath of Anne's bridge. There sat Anne next to a roaring fire with Jérémie.

Xavier forced Catherine to sit near the fire and covered her with his coat. He brushed some hair out of her eyes as the cackling Anne approached.

"This is too much. Jérémie's sure to find out now, because no human can come swooping in like the gods carrying a woman on their back. My how far you've fallen, Abbé. Right into the darkness of the night." Anne roared with laughter. "Now, I have two of you demons running around bothering me."

Catherine jumped off her log and moved toward them. "Leave me alone."

"You're looking mighty mean this evening. Are you still taking the medicine I gave you?"

"No," Catherine said in defiance. "I stopped again. The headaches were unbearable. You two—" Catherine pointed toward Anne and Jérémie. "—almost had me convinced. And I see you poisoned my brother's mind."

"That's unfair. We all came to our own conclusions," Jérémie stated. "We're trying to save you."

Catherine barked out a crazed and bitter laugh.

"She's taken too much," Anne said. "It's the demon controlling her. Poor thing, she fought it a long time, but you can't win against these things if you don't admit they're there."

Anne instructed them without further pause. She had them hold Catherine to the ground, which took all three men as Catherine thrashed about and tried to bite them. While they struggled with Catherine, Anne hurried to the far end of the bridge and opened a couple of crates, preparing something. Then she grabbed the black velvet bag and yanked out a skull.

"Is it human?" Xavier exclaimed, losing his grip on Catherine. Thomas's hold proved more secure and held until Xavier regained his control.

Anne wiped the top of it off. "Yes, it's human. It's the skull of a powerful witch. We need her spirit. Only she can save Catherine now."

Once they had Catherine pinned to the ground despite her squirming, Anne rushed over and smeared a pasty white substance over Catherine's face. It smelled like vile sewage. Catherine lashed about with more violence and in the lowest of tones, Anne mumbled words in a language even Thomas, in all of his travels, did not recognize. Anne swayed back and forth, closed her eyes, and continued a mantra that mesmerized him with its steady rhythm. Then Anne burst into angry denunciations, switching to French, before taking out charms and a small leather pouch of silver dust and sprinkling it over Catherine.

As Catherine calmed, Anne reached over and picked up the skull. She talked to it in the same mysterious language from before. Then the most frightening thing Thomas had ever seen happened before his eyes. The skull talked back. It chanted and sang, and Anne joined its mantra. Forces swirled about Catherine, changing colors and moving more and more rapidly until they flew through the air and right into the skull's mouth. When the last spirit entered it, the skull exploded into a thousand pieces and sent Anne flying backward into the stones of the bridge.

Within seconds, the world quieted around them. Catherine lay fast asleep. Anne got up and arched her back before joining everyone around Catherine.

Anne removed the horrid white paste from Catherine's face. She had Xavier apply damp towels to her head as Jérémie watched in utter confusion. Thomas knelt beside Catherine in case she woke and struggled, but instead, she opened her eyes and looked around as if lost. She first saw Xavier.

"How did I get here? What's going on?" she asked.

Anne answered, "We don't have much time and these three gentlemen are worried about you. How is your head? Is your thinking clear?"

"Yes, of course. What's this about?"

"The spell I've been trying to tell you about. I used a powerful counter-measure, but it doesn't last forever and I have to have your cooperation if this is to work."

The three men stepped aside and allowed Anne total control. Catherine looked bewildered, but there was no defiance as Anne leaned over and stared at her, then walked around her, mumbling in a mystical language until she at last sat Catherine up and seated herself opposite.

"I got the demons away. It's temporary because you have to want to continue it. Those headaches will come back if you won't take this last bit of medicine, and then you have to stay away from the potion he gave you. Stay away from him because these are powerful demons."

Catherine just nodded and drank an elixir Anne had brewed over the fire. She wrinkled her face at the taste. "My God, what have I done? What did he do to me?"

"He put a spell on you, but nothing else and you're safe now."

"I lost all my dignity." Catherine gained her feet. "Can you forgive me?"

"We all forgive you." Xavier reached over to hold her. She collapsed into his arms in convulsions of sorrow.

"Dear God." Catherine pulled away from Xavier and looked at each of them. "You told me that he killed Michel. Is that true?" Xavier stood frozen in place and shot a glance at Thomas. Catherine spun to look at him. With but a slight nod, he told Catherine what he imagined she never wanted to learn. She fell back into her brother's arms and wept, whispering over and over that she had killed her brother.

Xavier still often told Thomas that he blamed himself for allowing Marcel to murder Michel, and now Catherine's words took the burden on as well. Despite the sorrow, a beautiful family love showed through, something Thomas thought Michel would be proud of.

Xavier and Catherine cried themselves into exhaustion, with Jérémie joining them.

"I suppose this makes it even harder for you to forgive me," Catherine said to Xavier.

"You've done nothing wrong. No transgressions need forgiving."

Catherine began acting more like herself. She straightened her posture and regained her air of authority.

"Transgressions." Catherine smiled at Xavier and wiped away the last tear. "A vampiric priest." Everyone laughed except Jérémie. "I don't deserve exoneration. My God, I thought I loved that scoundrel." Her voice dropped lower. "That murderer."

"Just promise you won't do this again," Xavier said.

Thomas nodded agreement, but Catherine turned her attention elsewhere, her eyes wide but not afraid, as if she had a profound revelation. Xavier noticed, too, for he stopped talking and looked to see what she watched. Then it came to Thomas, for Catherine glanced at Jérémie before looking away.

"I'm awfully tired," Catherine said. "Anne, thank you. I'm sorry to go, but I need to sleep."

"You take care of yourself, and we'll be seeing each other soon."

Then Catherine strode to Jérémie. "I owe you just as much for saving me." Jérémie's face turned red as Catherine grabbed his hand. "Join me for dinner tomorrow night, please."

"Of course," he answered.

Catherine issued more orders. "And you two—" She pointed at Xavier and Thomas. "—will escort me home at once."

When they returned to the road, Xavier asked if she wanted them to take her at vampiric speed.

"I prefer a slow speed to that of your inhuman quickness. It unsettles my stomach. Besides, you've kept a secret long enough and I need confirmation regardless of what promises you made to others. This is a bond between sister and brother, so no priestly protesting."

"What is it?" Xavier asked.

"Michel began this little charade, no doubt at the behest of the one he represented. But why not come to me? Why not tell me the truth? Did anyone consider that a woman could help in these matters, instead of having men blunder about in secrecy, one of them quite miserable, and now I know why. And two of the principle players must be the meekest men I know, and yes, Xavier, you're one of them."

"How did you find out? Do you really know?" Xavier asked.

"The question isn't how I found out but why it took me this long. The spell had to have kept me from knowing. It's Jérémie."

Xavier smiled at Thomas, sending the vampire into laughter as the three walked back to Paris.

Fifty-Eight: Engagement II

7 NOVEMBER 1793

Catherine rectified her tragic mistake with Marcel the very next morning after Anne had saved her. She first wrote a note of apology to Thomas and Xavier, reiterating what she said the night before. Then Catherine unpacked. She had spent an entire week collecting things in secret to take to New Orleans, and now sneaking around to unload her trunks embarrassed her even more.

That task completed, she drafted a curt, one line letter to Marcel, in which she terminated their engagement. She signed off with a hope that he suffer. Next she dashed off a note to Jérémie. It, too, was succinct, reminding him of their dinner appointment.

After she sent someone to deliver the letters, she gathered her small staff and explained her dinner plans. She outlined the menu and requested that they prepare the dining room as if for a formal party.

It seemed like months passed before the butler came into the dining room and announced her guest.

"Jérémie," she greeted with her heart melting at his presence.

"Catherine," he responded in a rigid voice, his face full of anxiety. "Are we dining alone?"

"Yes. I need to discuss something with you. You look like you're going to faint."

He was stiff throughout dinner. They talked as usual, but his language was reserved. Worse, his wide eyes gave away a certain trepidation, which heightened her anxiety and caused her to talk even faster, covering the awkward periods of silence with the most trivial of matters as he sat like a statue. With dinner completed, Catherine pulled him into her study and closed the door. Jérémie sat at the edge of the couch and scooted away when Catherine sat next to him.

"Afraid of me?"

"Catherine, really," he half scolded.

"I brought you here alone for a reason. I thanked Xavier and Thomas last night," she began, but he interrupted.

"What's going on with those two, anyway?"

She rolled her eyes. "I'll explain that later, but for now I need your attention. I wanted to thank you for worrying about me while I pursued Marcel like a deranged fool. It took a strong person to stand up to me, and you saved my life. You're my dearest friend."

"Thank you," he said, relieved. "I feel the same. There was no need to prepare this special meal and get us alone to thank me."

"Come now, Jérémie. We've always been honest with each other. I think you've been hiding something from me for far too long."

Jérémie paled, then lurched off the couch, red with anger. "You've had your fun and it's been pure torture. Isn't it enough that I've wasted my life on it already? If you'll excuse me."

Catherine chased him as he headed toward the door, grabbed his arm, swung him around, and held him tightly in her grasp. "I wasn't ridiculing you." She took a huge breath and yanked Jérémie back into the room. "I was blind. I never knew it until last night. I'd no idea that you were Michel's suitor." Now his eyes filled with tears, as did hers. She smiled. "I was so petrified Michel had picked some domineering man that it blinded me."

"May I please go?" Jérémie asked.

Catherine shook her head. "You still don't see it, do you? After all of this, after I planned this dinner, I've so hurt you that you can't see what I want to say."

He looked at her with a blank expression.

"Jérémie, I love you."

"You mean—" He hesitated. "What *does* this mean?"

Catherine grabbed both of his hands. "Will you marry me?"

Catherine's boldness stunned even her. After a moment of silence, a grin spread across his face. Then he laughed. "Yes. Yes, Catherine, I'll marry you."

Catherine flung herself at him and the two clung to each other.

"Does this mean you forgive me?" she asked.

They pulled apart and sat side by side on the couch.

"I'm speechless," he said. "All this time I thought you avoided talking about it because you didn't feel the same way. And how appropriate that you acted the part of a man in asking for *my* hand in marriage." He chuckled.

Fifty-Nine: Adieu

10 November 1793

Though Xavier grew accustomed to his vampire life, his heart reminded him that in the process he lost dear things from his human life. He ignored close friendships that had to end because it hurt too much to say goodbye. Now, he had no choice.

So he sat near a fire, next to one of his dearest friends, talking about life and faith as they had so often. Xavier delayed saying goodbye to Anne for too long because the emotional scar might never heal. When she first saw him, she told him that she knew he came to say goodbye. But she never mentioned it again, and now the sun neared and forced the inevitable.

"I waited far too long to say this," he said.

Anne's smile disappeared as she shook her head and waved her hand at him. "You don't need to say anything. I already know."

"Anne, I need to. You saved my sister. I dragged you into that underworld with Marcel, and you did it for me. You even accepted a vampire. In all my time with the Catholic Church, you're the one person I've ever met who's worthy of sainthood. And you *literally* saved my life. Even Thomas didn't know what to do to help me. There's no way I can ever repay you." Blood tears clouded his eyes so he stopped. At least he had said it.

"Oh, 'twas only human, just helping someone that needed what little I could give. But you got one thing wrong." Anne stoked the fire before sitting next to him. "You gave me as much as I ever gave you. It's a harsh world in which I live, a black woman in a white world. I do my best with the gifts my people gave me in New Orleans. I think it's all my ancestors would want. But it isn't easy, this life.

"Did you ever notice, you and your family were the only people who entered my place through the front door? Did you ever see that I went nowhere but to your place outside of my neighborhood?" Anne fell silent and patted his hand. "So," she continued, "that's that. I'm going to cry myself to sleep tonight but I see the sun on the horizon. We've done a lot for each other and let's leave it at that."

"So this is it?" he asked.

"Afraid so. You take care of yourself."

Impulsively and with desperation, Xavier grasped for one more thing. "Come with us. I know how to do it. You deserve everything that I have."

Anne bent over, laughing. "Are you asking me to become a vampire? Oh, Abbé Saint-Laurent, you've lost your mind this time. Besides, I think you knew my answer before you asked."

Xavier guessed that she would shun the very notion, no matter how much she accepted Thomas and Xavier, Anne was too strong to need eternity. Xavier hugged her goodbye. "Yes, I knew. I'll find you when I visit Paris."

Anne's sad smile broke Xavier's heart. Both seemed to recognize the lie.

The sun weakened him though its rays just started to light the horizon. Xavier hugged Anne and turned to leave. Then, just before he climbed back to the road, she stopped him.

"You know, Abbé, this may be goodbye. But in my faith, people with a connection tend to keep that connection, even when separated. We may meet again. When one of us needs it. You may repay me some day for the things I did. You never know how the spirits work."

Xavier's eyes blurred with tears as he stumbled toward the road. He hurried toward Paris and, though weakened, would make it to their flat without question.

Yet there Thomas came, hurrying down the road and without a word, he picked Xavier up and bore him across the city. As he went, he scolded Xavier for remaining out so long but kissed his forehead and hugged him.

Sixty: Farewell

11 NOVEMBER 1793

"Catherine?" Xavier asked. "Are you even listening? I've never seen you so distracted. I asked if you were still leaving tomorrow."

"Oh, of course. Jérémie and I wanted to get married first, but it's rather difficult to find a priest around here. Most of them don't have heads or became vampires. So we're off to join his family. He's already arranged a small ceremony."

Xavier looked at the floor.

"Jérémie and I understand that you can't be there. Besides, it's too late to change it now. We've already killed you and had a burial."

Catherine laughed, bringing Xavier out of his gloom. Morbid as it seemed, they waited until after another Parisian battle and had Xavier pretend to die during the mob violence. The authorities informed Catherine, so she, Jérémie, and Thomas retrieved the body, and the following day Jérémie and she orchestrated a funeral and buried a coffin full of rocks in the family vault. They enacted the charade so Catherine and Jérémie, who now knew everything, could control the Saint-Laurent fortune.

"This transition is more difficult than I expected," Xavier said. "I thought it'd be easy once Thomas convinced Anthony that I could still see you without threatening any vampiric secrets, but I'm used to seeing you every day. That'll never be the same again."

"Except when you ran away to seminary or into the wilderness with Anne, remember? We've survived separation before. Why don't you visit Jérémie and me in three months? That gives you ample time in America and isn't too long apart," Catherine suggested.

"That sounds quite good." Xavier stopped fumbling with the cross he still wore under his shirt and his shoulders relaxed, his smile lighting up his face. "Where will we meet?"

"I'll write through Thomas's agent and tell you closer to the time. Things are still unstable here and I doubt Jérémie and I will return until this damnable revolution ends, which may take years. Though, have you heard about Napoleon? That he wins battle after battle? The news couldn't be better, I think."

"Oh, yes. He served with Michel."

"Actually, Michel served under him, long before he became a general. I hear that troops are quite taken with him and that he may return to lead France."

"I'm glad to see you so happy," Xavier said. "I noticed how perfect Jérémie was for you by the way he followed your orders for packing."

"Don't patronize me." Catherine punched Xavier in the arm. "Isn't it time for you to leave on some boat?"

They fell silent, a signal Xavier had something to tell her, and after a few agonizing moments, he looked at her, a drop of blood in the corner of his eye. "So, I haven't disappointed you?"

"What are you talking about?"

"You've said a million times that you want me to be myself. I'm trying, and I succeed more often than not. But have I fallen too far?"

Catherine hugged him closely. He articulated his eternal struggle and she doubted he would ever overcome it.

"You haven't fallen at all. Be happy with Thomas and don't worry so much about what the rest of the world thinks. I love you."

"I've always worried that I wasn't as good or pure as you and Michel believed."

"You *are* that wonderful. But there's nothing to live up to. Just be yourself and this goodness pours out. Now stop being so hard on yourself. You've an eternity of living with it."

"I have to go," Xavier said. "You promise to write soon?"

"Xavier, relax." Catherine grabbed his hand. "I love you. Now, go. Thomas was anxious for you to depart to America." Catherine escorted Xavier to the door and they hugged goodbye.

DECEPTION

Xavier's heart ached at leaving Catherine, so he went to the bank to see the man who managed Thomas's French affairs and whom Thomas promised could help Xavier with his strange request.

After exchanging pleasantries, the banker raised his eyebrow as he sat behind a desk and put his feet up. Xavier slid into a chair opposite with his vampiric grace.

"I don't have to tell you this is most unusual." The man tapped his fingers together. "If you weren't an associate of Mr. Lord's, I'd have dismissed you at once."

"I appreciate your efforts," Xavier said, grateful but irritated at the lecture.

"I apologize, Abbé," the man said. "As I said, your association with Mr. Lord is recommendation enough. I've just never heard of a secret arrangement that everyone forgot to record, not with matters of this importance. How he was a member of your family and yet didn't know it until recently baffles me."

"As I explained, the family prefers to keep the embarrassing matter private," Xavier lied.

"Your sister—you claim that she forgot where the actual papers are?"

"Typical. She can be a little haphazard."

"I was under the impression that Mademoiselle Saint-Laurent managed finances quite well."

Xavier sighed. "I don't mean to be rude, but I must be off. Is everything arranged?" The banker nodded as Xavier stood and shook his hand. "You're sure?"

"Yes, sir," he said and plopped his feet onto the ground. "I altered Marcel André's finances to reflect that he is a member of the Saint-Laurent family. Your sister controls all his money and property, and will own it upon his death."

"Thank you." Xavier bowed and left before the man annoyed him further or detected his nervousness. He was unsure why he had done it in the first place. Catherine did not need the money. It was a game, part of the new Xavier who played with life and wanted total vindication from the fiend who killed Michel and tried to ruin his family.

Sixty-One: Sweet Revenge

24 December 1793

Thomas relished the smell and atmosphere of his beloved America. Despite New Orleans not being his home region, its atmosphere reflected the New World's liberating feel and defiance of European convention, where anyone could blend into the people, merchants, traders, sailors, and prostitutes. Plus, the city was a paradise for thieves, rapists, and all the degenerates vampires hunted.

New Orleans also assisted him with Xavier. His abbé learned everything he needed to know about vampirism, and their life together exceeded Thomas's dreams. Thomas loved their contrasting styles. Killing empowered him and he enjoyed inflicting terror upon the fearless and torturing them to death, while Xavier focused on ridding the world of people who hurt others, more altruistic than Thomas's narcissism.

Xavier at first saw the killing as too much of a duty, but Thomas encouraged him to fulfill the duty with more pleasure. Xavier laughed the first time Thomas suggested it, calling Thomas a pure demon. Here in New Orleans, Xavier still despised cruelty, but he embraced the idea of a game for Thomas. Tonight, without prompting, Xavier had done so and then laughed when finished.

Xavier had led Thomas to the waterfront and started kissing him in the shadows. The tree cover enveloped them in darkness but a bright moon reflected light through the leaves. Then Xavier smiled and instructed Thomas to kiss him again. In but a minute, two sailors sneaked up, scoffed at their buggery, and demanded their money. Xavier and Thomas feigned fear, but Xavier's next move surprised even Thomas. He cried out as a woman in distress, prompting the sailors to threaten him more if he did not shut up. Then, when one went to whack him over the head, Xavier grabbed his knife, crushed his hand, and threw him to the ground. Thomas, not wanting to miss the show, just snapped the other sailor's neck and let him drop. Xavier had ripped off the man's pants accidentally as he squirmed away and now plunged his fangs into the man's ass. Then he bit into his thigh and drained his blood.

Thomas bent over laughing and looked up to see his abbé, the innocent, pure angel, in tears of laughter. They giggled even more as they sauntered toward the city, holding hands and leaning against one another.

They continued until they passed a small lodge on the outskirts of town. Kissing Xavier agitated his sexual desire, so Thomas dragged Xavier into the lodge, rented a room, and whisked him upstairs onto a bed where they made love. Then, satisfied, Thomas asked Xavier if he wanted to hunt some more.

"I was wondering if tonight could be the night." A huge smile spread across Xavier's face. "I think you'll find this more enjoyable than how we killed those sailors."

Thomas grinned. "Then we're off."

"Wait." Xavier pulled Thomas back. "I need to do this alone."

"I do insist on watching. This man has frightening powers that can even incapacitate a vampire, but it's your show."

Thomas and Xavier headed to the pier and scouted the territory where Marcel docked his ship, which had no sign of life on board. In advanced spying that week, they learned that Marcel's sailors slept in town with prostitutes and Marcel remained alone on the ship. With no sign of Marcel, Xavier strode aboard and concealed himself behind some crates while Thomas climbed up the mast and hid inside the sail.

They sat for over an hour, Xavier carving things into the deck with a knife and Thomas watching his lover. Not until that moment did Thomas realize that Xavier wore his clerical garb. He asked Xavier why he lugged a bag around with them that night, but Xavier refused to tell him. He had his robe with him and switched into it when he ducked behind a crate earlier.

The silence had almost become deafening when Thomas heard steps on the gangplank. Xavier winked before putting the knife away. He leaned against a huge crate, Thomas watching with special care.

Xavier said hello when Marcel had almost entered his cabin, causing Marcel to stumble backward and draw a dagger from the sheath at his belt. He squinted into the darkness before Xavier stepped out of the shadow.

"Abbé?" Marcel stammered.

"I'm pleased you remember."

"I thought you were a burglar. Someone stole all my money. I have nothing left and I'm hunting for the crook. They claim I don't even own this boat anymore. *My* boat." Marcel broke into a sweat. "And your sister rebuffed me. If you've come to plead forgiveness for your part in it or because she wants me back, you can tell her I'm no longer interested in her whorish ways."

Xavier walked toward Marcel, giving no sign of his vampirism, the clerical robe making him look as he had when Thomas first spotted him in Paris. "I know the harm you did to my family and I want you to pay for your crimes."

"I'm warning you. It's been a bad month. I'll rob you just to feel better."

"You killed Michel," Xavier said.

Marcel lunged at Xavier, aiming for his heart. Xavier, however, stepped aside and grabbed the knife. He also shoved Marcel against the crates, causing them to crack open as Marcel groaned in pain, but at the sight of Xavier standing over him, he drew himself up. "So, your bugger friend brought you over. No doubt so he could use you as his woman."

"No, you misunderstand. I'm your executioner." Xavier walked slowly toward him while Marcel laughed in his face. Marcel grabbed a leather pouch and thrust his hand into it. Xavier saw the movement and, before Marcel removed his hand, Xavier seized his shoulder and ripped Marcel's entire arm from its socket. Blood gushed everywhere as Xavier threw the limb overboard and tossed the pouch aside. He stood over Marcel, who was moaning and cowering in pain.

"Did you think another one of your potions would conquer me?" Xavier was angrier than Thomas had ever seen him. "You've wreaked enough havoc on this world."

Then Xavier lifted Marcel off the ground, snatched the dagger, and stabbed it through his remaining hand into the crate. Marcel howled. Xavier moved fast to apply his own blood to Marcel's shoulder to stop the bleeding and avoid too quick a death, talking the entire time to Marcel, about how much he hated him, about his anger at what he had done to Catherine, and about the fact that Xavier was the one who stole his money and took control of his empire. He even chuckled when he saw Marcel's horrified reaction to the fact that Catherine now owned all his possessions and left him for dead here in New Orleans. Marcel trembled and gasped for breath, still alive and hearing every word.

Xavier next tore off Marcel's pants, grabbed his genitals, and ripped them off. Marcel screamed. Again, Xavier staunched the bleeding to keep him alive, to torture him. For the first time, Xavier seemed to understand deep in his soul what Thomas meant about the joy of the game in killing these evil people. Marcel continued to cry, for several hours in extreme anguish, until at last he fell into a soft whimpering. A few times he almost passed out, so Xavier wounded him anew and spoke to him of revenge. Only the approaching sunrise forced Xavier to gash Marcel across the throat so the he could bleed to death from his wounds. Xavier watched Marcel the entire time until he died, even after Thomas came down and held him in a suffocating embrace.

"I'm not sure he suffered enough," Xavier said. "I hope Michel saw the way I defended myself and his honor like a soldier in battle."

Thomas burst out laughing, and though Xavier tried not to, he, too, laughed. Thomas grabbed Xavier and spun him in a circle before kissing him firmly on the lips.

"That was evil."

"I learned from the best," Xavier answered and flung his arms around Thomas's shoulders.

About the Author

Damian Serbu lives in the Chicago area with his husband and two dogs, Akasha and Chewbacca. The dogs control his life, tell him what to write, and threaten to eat him in the middle of the night if he disobeys. He has published *The Vampire's Angel* and *The Vampire's Protégé* with NineStar Press.

Email: DamianSerbu@aol.com

Facebook: www.facebook.com/DamianSerbu

Twitter: @DamianSerbu

Website: www.DamianSerbu.com

Other books by this author

The Vampire's Protégé

Also Available from NineStar Press

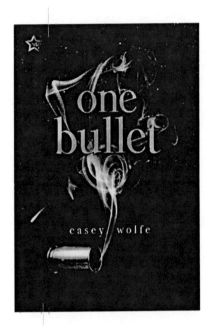
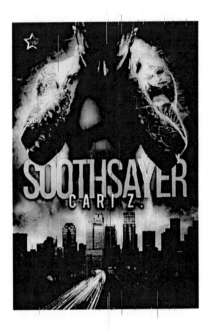

Connect with NineStar Press

www.ninestarpress.com

www.facebook.com/ninestarpress

www.facebook.com/groups/NineStarNiche

www.twitter.com/ninestarpress

www.tumblr.com/blog/ninestarpress

CPSIA information can be obtained
at www.ICGtesting.com
Printed in the USA
FFOW03n0524310318
46065030-46999FF